LIVING IN CLEVELAND WITH THE GHOST OF JOSEPH STALIN

LIVING IN CLEVELAND WITH THE GHOST OF JOSEPH STALIN

MARC SERCOMB

Blue Dog Press

Dedication

For my wonderful family, thank you for all
of your kind support and encouragement.

First Printing, 2021 Blue Dog Press, Los Angeles

This is a work of fiction. The characters, names, incidents, places,
and dialogue are products of the author's imagination, and are not to
be construed as real.

Chapter 1

So, my name is Calvin Jefferson Coolidge, and I started seeing dead people when I was thirteen years old. I'm not talking about bodies – corpses – here. I'm talking about the real deal. You know, *spirits*, the essence of the living far removed from this corporeal plane. But I'll get to that a little later.

First, the name. Whenever I tell people, they always laugh and say, "C'mon, kid. Stop pulling my leg. What's your *real* name?" Or, "Say, what's a white kid doing with a name like *that*?" But the real punchline is, I don't even know my real name. So I guess Calvin Jefferson Coolidge has done by me just fine.

I'm not an orphan, as has often been misstated by the willfully uninformed. I have a mother and a father, both living. I just don't know where they are at the moment. Basically, you see, from the age of 12 or so, I pretty much raised myself.

I was born in 1940 in San Diego, I think. I guess that's as good a place as any. Anyway, it sure looks beautiful in the pictures in magazines, and I'd sure like to get back there someday and see it again. Or, for the first time. After Pearl Harbor, my Old Man joined the Navy but got thrown into the brig a few months later for gambling. Rather harsh punishment for gambling, don't you think? But you see, he'd been cheating at cards and ripped off an ensign for forty bucks. That ensign testified against him at the court-martial, and the United States

Navy, in the middle of a pretty intense shooting war with the Empire of Japan, kicked him out for "wanton and criminal immorality." My Old Man always got a good chuckle out of that line.

After that, my Mom made him promise to go straight, and to give him credit, he gave it his best shot. He got a job fixing tires and pumping ethyl at a gas station, but after a few months he was back to his old ways. He didn't tell her he got fired. Instead, he'd get up, put on his greasy gas station overalls, and go to "work." What he was really doing was gambling in an alley behind a seedy bar for chump change. You know the score – dice, cards, the horses – whatever would bring in a few easy bucks. He was able to carry on this ruse for about six months before Mom caught on.

My mother, Amelia, was no saint. She was not easy to live with. In fact, most people called her nuts. You know, as in "cuckoo." In those days, people didn't beat around the bush with nicey-nice euphemisms for mental illness. They called it like it was, and my Mom was a real whack-job.

Depression, mostly – and booze. Lots of booze. When she was down, it was best to leave her to her bottle and stay outside and play. I learned that the hard way at a very young age. I wouldn't say she was exactly *abusive,* per se. More like distant, unavailable. When she was like that, the Old Man had to step in and clean up the place, do the dishes, make my meals. And I got real good at taking care of myself, too. But it wasn't like that all the time. The darkness came and went in cycles. When she was "normal," we really had a good time. It's just that she was like two different people or something. Yeah, between her and the Old Man, it was a real roller coaster ride around my place.

I think I read somewhere it was the Ancient Greeks who invented tragedy, but when I was a kid I was pretty sure it must have been my parents.

A couple of years later, all hell broke loose when we got evicted from our ramshackle cottage – a sort of shotgun shack near skid row – and Mom took off to Florida to live with an old boyfriend who, ha-ha, happened to be a male nurse in a Pensacola psychiatric ward. Even if she couldn't find him, the war was over and Florida must have been absolutely crawling with eligible young men to latch onto.

We lived on the streets for a couple of days, then the Old Man got in a fight cheating at pool and was thrown in the slammer. They say there's a real fine line between tragedy and comedy, between laughter and tears. I guess that's basically the story of my life.

Social Services put me in a foster home with a Baptist minister and his wife. They were swell people and all, but kinda creepy. Reverend Welles was a towering cadaverous man dressed all in black, and his wife was kind but very mousy and quiet.

They lived in a big, dark, empty house with closed curtains and didn't even have a radio or television set. They never had company over or held cocktail or dinner parties like the people I had read about in magazines.

"Why don't you have a TV set, like regular people do?" I innocently asked. The Reverend fixed me with a cold stare.

"Idleness. Sloth. Covetousness. Intemperance. These are the Devil's hand-tools, son!"

Every night the three of us sat around the dining room table reading the Bible. It was kinda interesting, hearing all of those amazing stories about Daniel in the lion's den and Cain killing his brother Abel and Noah building that huge boat and all those people getting wiped out by a flood and the plagues on Egypt and the parting of the Red Sea and Moses coming down from Mount Sinai with the Ten Commandments, and all.

It got to where I really enjoyed reading the Bible and hearing all those stories. But my many questions seemed to annoy

Reverend Welles, who took a rather black and white view of things.

One evening we read in the book of Genesis about Adam and Eve, the first couple. Apparently, they weren't too educated, being the first people and all. They just walked around in the Garden of Eden without any clothes on and they didn't even know they were naked. God told them they could eat the fruit from all of the trees in the garden except for one: the Tree of the Knowledge of Good and Evil. He told them that if they ate fruit from that tree, they would surely die.

But the serpent came along and tricked Eve into eating that fruit, and she even gave some to Adam to eat. That's when all the trouble started. Then they knew they were naked and hid themselves in the bushes. When God came along in the cool of the day, He found them hiding and it didn't take Him long to figure out exactly what had happened. Their punishment for eating the fruit was pretty strict: they got evicted from the Garden of Eden and Adam had to work hard to grow his own food and Eve had to suffer a lot of pain whenever she had a baby. The snake didn't get off the hook, either. God said he would have to slither on his belly and eat dust the rest of his days, and people would always be trying to step on his head.

But that wasn't the end of the story. Even though it was painful, Eve did give birth to two boys: Cain and Abel. When they grew up, Cain worked in the fields while Abel tended the flocks. Each one brought a nice offering to God, but God accepted Abel's offering and disregarded Cain's offering.

Well, that made Cain mighty sore, and one day he went and killed his brother Abel right there in the field. So God put a mark on Cain and sent him wandering for the rest of his life. He really sent him to the Land of Nod, but Reverend Welles said "the Land of Nod" means "the Land of Wandering." Well, there in Nod it wasn't all bad, because Cain soon found himself a wife and they had a little boy.

"Wait a minute," I interrupted. "If Adam and Eve were the only people, and Cain and Abel were their only children, who did Cain marry in the Land of Nod?"

Reverend Welles looked slightly perturbed. "Son, you're missing the whole point of the story."

"But where did the people in Nod come from, for Cain to find a wife?"

"Don't be obstinate, son." He looked rather annoyed at this point.

"Were there people there before Adam and Eve?"

"We just read about that, son," he sighed heavily. "The Lord made Adam, the first man, out of the dust of the earth. Then He made Eve from one of Adam's ribs. Weren't you paying attention?"

"But where did Cain's wife come from?"

The Reverend stopped short and fixed me with a steely stare. "Adam and Eve must have had *other* children besides Cain and Abel."

"You mean, Cain married his own *sister?*" I said in disgust.

"In those days, it wasn't a sin," Reverend Welles said, his patience wearing thin. "The Good Lord saw fit to just look the other way..."

That story about Adam and Eve sure made you think, though. Was it better to be innocent and stupid, or smart and guilty? I guess a lot of people have a hard time with that one.

Another evening we read about a righteous man named Abraham, who had a son named Isaac. Now, Abraham really loved Isaac, but one day he took him up on a mountain, tied him to an altar, and started to sacrifice him.

"But, why would he kill his own son?" I blurted, without thinking.

The Reverend glared at me a long time with impatient eyes. "Because, God *told* him to!" he finally blared, and I buttoned it up for the rest of the reading. Turns out, it was just a test, and Abraham didn't have to kill his own son after all. *Whew*!

Reverend Welles was a fire and brimstone preacher, and he didn't skimp on the fire or the brimstone in his sermons. A change seemed to come over him whenever he stepped into the pulpit. His voice became dark and gravelly, and his face turned beet-red. His eyes bulged and veins popped on his sweaty forehead. His white hair seemed to stand up on end. I really didn't know what he was getting so worked up about. But I dared not ask him, for fear his wrath would be turned on me.

One time, in the middle of a sermon, my mind was wandering and without warning, he suddenly reached out and snatched me from the pew and plunged me into a tank of pea-green water. He held me down for a long time while he sent a prayer up to heaven, but I couldn't hear the words under water. Finally, he pulled me out of the water and slapped me on the back hard with his huge, meaty hand while I sputtered and gulped air.

"Why – why did you try to *drown* me?" I gasped.

"I wasn't trying to drown you, son!" he shouted joyfully. "You needed to be baptized to be saved from hell! You're born again now! A completely new creature!"

"But I don't feel any different," I said. "Just wet."

"Now don't you grieve the Spirit!" the Reverend roared. "You've been washed in the blood, son! Washed in the *blood*!"

Sometimes, the old reverend really gave me the willies.

Later that day at lunch, Reverend Welles started in on me again. "Sin is the enemy, son. You've got to sweep it out of your heart!"

"I don't get it," I admitted.

"You're not listening to me, son," he blared. "You've got to sweep the sin out of your heart! Look what happened to Sodom and Gomorrah."

"Who are they?"

"Sodom and Gomorrah weren't people," he replied. "They were cities. So wicked and sinful that the Lord decided to destroy them and kill everyone with fire and brimstone from the sky. There was only one righteous man – Lot. So the Lord told Lot to take his family and flee – and to never look back."

"Did they escape in time?"

"Yes, but Lot's wife looked back, so God turned her into a pillar of salt."

"Why'd he do that?"

The Reverend shook his head impatiently. "What's wrong with you, son? Aren't you listening?"

"I'm listening," I said.

"God turned her into a pillar of salt because she disobeyed His command! The lesson here is, if God tells you to do something, you better do it!"

Reverend Welles picked up a salt shaker and began to sprinkle some on his mashed potatoes.

"Reverend, STOP!" I cried, without thinking.

The Reverend startled. "What is it?"

"That might be Lot's wife!"

The Reverend gave me a slow burn, then continued to sprinkle salt on his potatoes.

A few weeks later, the Reverend invited a faith healer to come lay hands on anyone in the congregation who needed healing. Many people went forward, and the faith healer laid hands on them and spoke in a language I did not understand. After he was finished laying hands on them, they all looked happy and said "Hallelujah!" But they didn't look much different to me.

Then the faith healer looked right at me and asked, "And what's *your* name, son?"

"Calvin Jefferson Coolidge, sir," I replied, terrified at what might be coming next.

"What kind of a name is *that*?" he asked, laughing. "Never mind. Come here, son. I gotta healing for you."

"But I'm not sick," I told him.

"The Lord told me all about your malady," he insisted firmly. "Come here, son."

Obediently, I stood and walked to the front on shaky legs. The faith healer laid hands on me and prayed in his strange language. Then he stopped and said, "Oh, yes Lord! I see it clear as day, Lord! I see it clear as day!" And then to me, "Do you like baseball, son?"

"Yes," I lied. I'd never played a day of baseball in my life.

Then he grabbed my right arm and held it up for everyone to see. "You see this arm? The Lord has done a miracle! He has healed this boy's withered arm! Look at it – as good as new!" Then to me: "The Lord showed me, son. Your dream is going to come true. When you grow up, you are going to be a pitcher for the Brooklyn Dodgers!"

There were shouts of "Hallelujah!" and "Praise the Lord!" from the congregation. The faith healer looked down at me and smiled. That's how much he knew. When I grew up, the Dodgers wouldn't even be in Brooklyn anymore.

Another time, when I was alone with Mrs. Welles, she told me a story that made my blood curdle. "Do you know how I got the Holy Spirit?" she asked quietly.

"No, Ma'am."

"Well, it was when the Reverend and I were first married. I wanted to be a Godly wife and to please him in every way, but I knew that I didn't have the Holy Spirit and I could never be a Godly wife to him without it. So I prayed and prayed for the Holy Spirit, but I didn't get it. I felt like a failure. Then God told me, 'If you don't get the Holy Spirit soon, I'm going to kill you so the Reverend can marry a Godly woman who has it.' Yes, that's exactly what God told me. So I told God, 'But sir, I've been praying and praying to get it, but it never comes.' And do you know what God told me then?"

"No, Ma'am."

"'Pray *harder!*' So I did, and I got the Holy Spirit. Now I am fit to be a true Prophet's wife."

I'm not making this stuff up. It actually happened.

You can take it to the bank.

* * *

One day, the Reverend's wife asked me when my birthday was. Now, while most kids would know the answer to that, I wasn't most kids. See, my mother never told me what my birthday was. And the Old Man didn't have a clue. So my mother would just choose a random day about every year or so and call it my birthday.

But for the Welles', I knew this wouldn't do. So, in a panic, I blurted out the first date that popped into my head: "June 19th." I had no idea it was the day the Rosenbergs were going to be executed.

The Rosenbergs. A nice Jewish couple from New York City, convicted of espionage against the United States of America and sentenced to death in Sing Sing prison. They were charged with passing on top secret information about jet engines and the atom bomb to the Russians, charges they denied all the way up to the end.

Julius Rosenberg, an Army engineer, allegedly joined the Communist Party and sold delicate information about jet airplanes and guided missiles to the Russians. Ethel, his wife, was convicted of convincing her brother, who worked on the top secret Manhattan Project, to hand over plans for the atom bomb to the Russians. Julius also recruited others in the government to steal sensitive secrets and pass them along to their superiors in Moscow. This went on for about ten years, until the spy ring collapsed and the FBI arrested them all in 1950.

The alert reader may ask, what's all this boring stuff about the Rosenbergs got to do with the story? Oh, you'll find out later on. Just wait.

Anyway, everybody was talking about them, but being a kid, I didn't pay much attention to all the hub-bub at the time. I didn't get it, but to grownups, I guess it was kind of a big deal.

So on June 19th, my "birthday," Mrs. Welles made me a big chocolate cake with vanilla frosting and my name and (approximate) age written on it in pretty cursive letters. It looked really great, and she planned a nice little party for me with all the boys and girls from the church who brought me neat presents like socks and clip-on neckties and yo-yo's and a real-life pocket knife with a pop bottle opener and a picture of the Lone Ranger and Tonto and their horses on it. To tell you the truth, I didn't care much for the socks and clip-on neckties, but I sure thought the pocket knife was neat.

It was a real nice party until Reverend Welles borrowed a neighbor's TV set to watch the news coverage of the Rosenberg execution. Then it turned a little sad. It was the only time he ever allowed a television set in the house, and it happened to be during my birthday party.

Mrs. Welles was just cutting the cake and handing out slices to all the excited kids when a terrible thing happened on TV. Reverend Welles had it tuned to the news and there were crowds of people demonstrating in the streets of New York City. Some of them were carrying signs that said "Free the Rosenbergs!" and "The Rosenbergs are Innocent!" Other people carried signs like "Fry the Red Jews!" and "Kill the Commie Kikes!" Then the two sides started yelling at each other and calling each other terrible names and stuff. Then a fist fight broke out between the two sides, and there was more yelling and kicking and screaming, right there on the streets of New York City!

A little girl sat her uneaten cake on the table and started to cry. "Dear, I wish you would move that television set into another room," Mrs. Welles said. "It's upsetting the party guests."

"I'm not moving it into another room," the Reverend grumbled.

"I just don't think the children should be exposed to such violence," Mrs. Welles persisted.

"Violence?" Reverend Welles exclaimed. "This is *history*!" Then he went back to watching the fracas on the black and white screen.

Eventually, the police came in and tried to separate the two sides, but the protestors started hitting the policemen with their signs, and it turned into a real mess.

"Oh, no," Mrs. Welles fretted. "Children, cover your eyes — you shouldn't see such anti-social behavior!"

"This is *exactly* what they should see," the Reverend argued. "They need to know what kind of a world they're growing up in!"

Then it got worse. Police trucks arrived on the scene and the policemen started herding protestors into them, kicking and screaming. The protestors were calling the policemen terrible names on live TV.

"Children, cover your ears!" Mrs. Welles was going from child to child, putting their hands over their ears. "If you're not going to move the television set to another room, at least tune it to another channel!" she pleaded with her husband.

"Oh, all right," Reverend Welles said, getting up out of his chair to turn the channel. Now it was a man in a dark suit giving a speech in a big room filled with other men in dark suits. The words "Senator Joseph McCarthy" appeared in white letters at the bottom of the screen.

"Ha! Now we're finally going to hear some sense!" the Reverend huffed, sitting back down in his chair. "Listen to *this*, kids!"

The man seemed very angry, and he was telling the other men in the big room that communists were everywhere, even in Congress.

"You bet they are!" Reverend Welles shouted at the TV screen.

"Now, Dear...you'll frighten the children," Mrs. Welles cautioned.

The man on the TV kept talking. He said the communists were in the Army and in our schools and colleges and even in our churches.

"Not in my church, by God!" the Reverend roared. Two more children started to cry.

The man on the TV kept talking. He said the communists were in the FBI, and they were working very hard to bring down our country. Then he said the communists were going to use the atom bomb secrets they got from the Rosenbergs to blow up every school and city in our country.

"I want to go home now," a red-haired girl said to Mrs. Welles.

The man on the TV kept talking. He said your neighbors could be communists and you wouldn't even know it, because they look just like everybody else and they know how to blend in so well. He said communists never tell you who they really are because they want to fool you into trusting them so they can brainwash you with their evil ideas. It was part of their training and part of their plan to take over the world. He said millions of people were being brainwashed by these communists and didn't even know it. Their messages were in popular books and songs on the radio and movies and even in TV advertisements. He said America was too big and powerful to be conquered from the outside, but we could rot from the inside by listening to traitors and communist propaganda. He said that's how they're going to do it – from the *inside!*

"That's right!" Reverend Welles agreed loudly. I'd only seen him this wound up when he was in the pulpit preaching a sermon. "If this country doesn't listen to this man, we're all doomed!"

The man on the TV kept talking. He said everybody had to be on the alert. Everyone had to watch his neighbor, watch his friends – even his own family members – and report anything suspicious to the FBI. Turn them in right away, before they hurt our country. It was every patriotic citizen's duty, he said. Some of the men in the big room clapped their hands and cheered. The others stood up and made booing sounds. Then, they started calling each other names, just like the demonstrators on the street did on the other channel.

Now, I had no idea what communists were, but I thought they must have been pretty bad people to make everybody on television so upset.

"It's a fight for this country's soul, I tell you," The Reverend blared. "It's very soul!" He was getting worked up again. Reverend Welles was an old-time communist fighter.

But to me there was something wrong with the man on the TV's logic. "How can people turn them in to the FBI if the communists are already *in* the FBI?" I asked.

"You turn them in to FBI agents you can *trust*," Reverend Welles replied.

"But how do you know which agents you can trust if you can't tell which ones are communists?"

The Reverend's face turned progressively deeper shades of crimson as he tried to come up with an answer. "You're grieving my patience again, son!"

For her part, Mrs. Welles had finally had enough. She quietly ushered all the children outside into the backyard.

"Calvin, bring the cake."

Outside, we all sat down at a wooden picnic table in the sunshine. It was a clear, bright spring day, and the thought of communists and atom bombs and demonstrations seemed suddenly preposterous in all this beauty. I looked at the other kids, who still looked traumatized and confused. Nobody said a word. Finally, Mrs. Welles sighed, smoothed out her pretty flower apron, and asked cheerfully, "Now then: who's up for a nice game of pin the tail on the donkey?"

Chapter 2

One day in the summer of 1953, the Old Man "sprung" me from foster care. I was playing in the front yard by myself when he showed up in a big shiny car.

"Where did you get this?" I asked.

"Never mind. Get in."

"Wait – I need to get something." I ran into the dining room and grabbed the Bible from the table. Then I ran back outside and got in the car.

"Is that all you're bringing?" the Old Man asked.

"Mrs. Welles is praying upstairs. I can't get my suitcase without her seeing me."

"Don't worry, kid. I'll buy you a new suitcase."

We pulled away from the Welles' house and left town. The Old Man saw the Bible in my lap.

"What's that?" he asked.

"This...is the Word of God," I said reverently.

"Oh, brother..." the Old Man shook his head. He wasn't really that old. He was only in his early thirties, and still looked pretty good. But to me, he's always been the Old Man.

We drove up to Los Angeles. On the way, I told the Old Man about the Bible stories I'd been learning. I told him how Joseph's brothers sold him into slavery in Egypt because they were jealous that their Old Man liked him best. Then I told him how Joseph won Pharaoh's favor by interpreting a dream for him, and how Pharaoh was so grateful that he put him second in command of all of Egypt, and how Joseph ended up saving Egypt from famine. Then I told him about Salome's dance that got King Herod all worked up and how she asked Herod for the head of John the Baptist, which was brought to her on a platter.

The Old Man listened intently for mile after mile.

When I was finished, he looked over at me and said, "You know, Sport, those are just stories – like fables, or myths."

"What does that mean?"

"Fake. They didn't really happen. That book's nothing but a bunch of fairy tales."

"But Reverend Welles said they're true. Reverend Welles said that God wrote this book Himself."

"Yeah, well he would, wouldn't he? That's why I came and got you, before he had time to really mess you up."

"But, I like these stories."

"You just listen to your Old Man on this one: you can read that book for entertainment, as long as you remember it's about as real as Peter Pan."

I let the Old Man have the last word, but I still couldn't help thinking that somehow, my time with the Welleses wasn't just a mistake or accident. It was my first inkling that there might be a divine providence woven into the inscrutable tapestry of the universe. Or something like that.

You can take it to the bank.

In Los Angeles, the Old Man drove to Santa Monica and we parked by the beach. We walked on the pier and I took a ride on the big Ferris wheel. Then he bought me an ice cream cone and we looked at the ocean. Its vastness gave me a weird feeling, like I was only temporary, and very, very small.

After that, we drove down Hollywood Boulevard and stopped and saw Douglas Fairbanks, Jr. and Charlie Chaplin's stars on the Walk of Fame. *From Here to Eternity* was playing at Grauman's Chinese Theatre, and *Roman Holiday* was playing down the street at the Egyptian. Then we drove down to Sunset and stopped in at Schwab's Drugstore for a milkshake. We were on the lookout for stars, but didn't see any. The closest I got to seeing any stars in Hollywood that day was spotting a guy who kinda looked like Peter Lorre loading an old station wagon with boxes near Sunset and Vine.

Then the Old Man found a dice game behind Canter's Deli and pocketed a few extra bucks before leaving town.

From L.A., we took Route 66 east.

"Where are we going?" I asked.

"Nowhere," the Old Man answered. "And everywhere."

We drove across the Mojave Desert that night. The moon was bright and the details on the stark, craggy mountains were in high relief. We didn't talk. Old timey band music – Tommy Dorsey or something from the War years – played softly on the radio. I felt a lightness – an anticipatory sense of freedom that I'd never felt before. We were embarking upon a great adventure, like Christopher Columbus – only our sea was an endless expanse of continent that stretched before us like a great lost dream, an impossibly unconquerable Promised Land.

It was just like the Children of Israel leaving Egypt and finding themselves lost in a hostile but alluring wilderness. Just as my eyes were closing for the night, I was convinced that we, too, would wander aimlessly for forty years in our own vast and seductive wilderness – America.

Life on the road was exhilarating – just me and the Old Man and the open road ahead. I was experiencing total freedom for the first time in my life. Route 66 in 1953 was nothing short of a Wonderland, a veritable cornucopia of thrills, flavorfully exotic foods, colorful characters, cheap mementos, and memorable sights. Time stopped in a world populated by truck drivers, vacationing families loaded into shiny chrome travel trailers, Indian trading posts selling "genuine" Navajo blankets, and an endless supply of those wonderfully sticky, gooey pecan logs from Stuckey's travel stops.

We slept in the car and washed up in gas station washrooms. We lived off of hamburgers, French fries, and chocolate milk-shakes. The Old Man knew how to sniff out the gambling action whenever we hit a new town: you find the crummiest, most dangerous-looking dive bar on skid row and slip the bartender a five-spot. "It never fails," the Old Man said.

In Flagstaff, we hit pay dirt. He parked the car in front of a crumbling beer joint in the seediest part of town. The sun was just going down.

"You stay here until I get back. And keep the doors locked." He cracked the windows for air, and then disappeared inside the bar. I thought about listening to the radio, but didn't want to risk running the battery down. So I opened Reverend Welles's big Bible and started reading. It opened to the story of Naboth's vineyard.

It was your standard property dispute that got out of hand when some dusty old king named Ahab and his wife Jezebel schemed to have Naboth killed so they could turn his vineyard into a vegetable garden. But that ticked God off so much that God sent Elijah, a pretty heavy-weight prophet, down to chew Ahab out but good. He pretty much told Ahab he and his children were finished, and that the dogs that licked up Naboth's blood in the streets of Jezreel would be licking up Ahab's own blood pretty soon.

So, Ahab heard this and got really scared. He tore his fancy king clothes and went around in sackcloth and wouldn't eat anything, for fear God would take his vengeance. Then God saw Ahab like this and decided maybe he'd been a little hard on the guy after all, and told Elijah he was gonna spare Ahab for now but take it out double on his sons later on.

Gee whiz. All this bearing false witness and murder conspiracies and angst and gnashing of teeth, all over a little patch of ground. It kinda makes you think.

It must have been one pretty spot, though.

I was snapped back to reality by the Old Man getting into the car. I guess it had been about an hour, but the time passed by pretty fast with that story about Naboth and Ahab and all.

The Old Man was in a good mood. He showed me a handful of cash. There must've been at least eight dollars and some change in his hand.

"Where'd that come from?" I asked.

"Three Card Monte," he grinned back.

"Huh?"

"It's a card game," he said, taking a deck of cards out of his pocket. He pulled three cards from the deck. "You start with two black jacks and a red queen." He showed me the cards then placed them face-down on the seat between us. "Now, say you're the mark. I show you the red queen, like this. Then I turn it over and shuffle the cards around like this. Try to keep your eye on that queen. Now you bet two bits or a buck if you're feeling lucky, and pick the red queen. Go ahead, point to it."

I pointed. He turned over a jack.

"Go ahead, pick another."

I did. He turned over a jack.

"One more time, Sport."

I did. This time, he turned over another jack.

"But, they're all jacks," I said. "Where's the queen?"

The Old Man reached up his sleeve and pulled out the queen.

"You cheated," I said.

The Old Man shook his head. "It's not cheating. It's the oldest game in the world. It's a form of entertainment. It's like magic, Sport. Sleight of hand. Or the movies. People *expect* the wool to be pulled over their eyes. People *want* to be tricked. It's just a show."

"But you took their money."

"And they were entertained and dazzled for an hour. That's the price of admission. There's always some old-timer who thinks he can beat me. But I'm too fast. Now he's trying to fig-ure out how I did it, and he'll be thinking about it all night. Keeps him busy, gives him something to do while he's drinking. I think that's worth a buck, don't you?"

"I still think you cheated."

"Think what you will, but who's making sure we got gas in the tank? Who's paying for those pecan logs you love so much?"

He had me there. But I still wasn't comfortable with the cheating.

In Winslow, Arizona, we stopped at an Indian trading post and the Old Man bought me a straw cowboy hat with a red and white braided drawstring, just like the Lone Ranger's. I wore the hat proudly while I browsed the aisles of cheap trinkets, fake turquoise jewelry, and smooth polished stones they had for sale, while the Old Man bought a tank of gas.

I noticed an old Indian sitting in a rocking chair in the cor-ner. He had a Navajo blanket wrapped around his shoulders, and he was smoking a hand-rolled cigarette. He was the oldest man I'd ever seen – he must have been about 107 or so. His face was stony and craggy, like the side of a badly-eroded mountain, and his eyes were dark, impenetrable slits behind the white smoke curling up from his cigarette.

He was my first Indian.

He saw me and made a gun with his hand. He "shot" me with it. I made a gun with my hand, and "shot" him back. He clutched his chest, and pretended to slump over dead. Then he raised his head and motioned for me to come closer.

I stepped forward, and he said, "My people were not from this land. We had a beautiful, forested, green land in the east, full of many animals good for hunting. There were many lakes and rivers full of fish for us to catch and eat. My people lived on that land since the Great Spirit made everything. Then the army came and made us move. I was small, like you. The army made us march many days, carrying everything on our backs. Many of the people died, but the army would not let us stop to bury them. They took us to a place we did not know. It was a place of flat lands and no trees, just tall grass. There were few animals to hunt, and few rivers to find fish. It was strange, we did not fit that land, but the soldiers said 'This is your land now, you will get used to it.' But the people did not like that land, and they did not get used to it. That land was not part of their spirit. The ancestors were back in the old land. The people were not connected with their ancestors anymore. The people felt lost.

"After a few years, the soldiers came back and said, 'We have a new land for you. You will be happier on this new land.' But the elders told the soldiers 'No, we will not go to this new land. We will stay here, because the new land might be worse.' The soldiers said, 'You must go,' so the people packed their things and we marched many, many days carrying everything on our backs, with the soldiers in front of us and behind us. Many of the people died, but the soldiers would not let us stop and bury them. They took us to a place we did not know. It was a place of no trees and no grass, no lakes and no rivers. No animals to hunt and no fish to catch. Only hot, hot sun and rocks. It was *this* place. It was strange, the people did not fit this land, but the soldiers said, 'This is your land now, you will get used to it.'

"But the ancestors were far away, and the people did not get used to it. 'There are no animals to hunt and no fish to catch,' the elders told the soldiers. But the soldiers said, 'Don't worry,

we will take care of you.' That did not sound good to the people. We like to hunt, we like to fish. The people always took
care of themselves, with their ancestors close by. This place
was not good.

"But I married a lusty woman who gave me many children.
Too many to count. The children grew up, but I could not teach
them the ways of the people because there were no animals
to hunt or fish to catch. There was not much for them to do.
Some of them stayed with the people. But most of them moved
away and took up the white man's ways. I never heard from
them again. But it is all right. I hope they had a good life.

"My woman's dead now. All of my children are dead. My
grandchildren and great-grandchildren live in the white man's
world. They don't want to know an old man who is still of the
people. It is said of the ancestors back in the old land that
they knew the time of their own death. I know that I will die
tonight."

Then he stopped talking, and reached into his pocket and
pulled out an old Buffalo nickel. He gave it to me and said,
"Here, take this. It is my lucky nickel. It will bring you much
luck. I don't need it anymore."

I put the nickel in my pocket and walked slowly away. The
old Indian just kept smoking his hand-rolled cigarette in the
corner.

To this day, I'm pretty sure my "first Indian" story is better
than most people's.

* * *

By Albuquerque, we were low on cash again, and the Old
Man pulled a classic bait-and-switch routine. We pulled up in
front of a downtown drugstore and he craned his neck to see
inside. There was a pretty girl behind the counter. She looked
about high school age.

"This is perfect," the Old Man beamed. "Come on inside
with me." We got out of the car and walked into the drugstore.

"Now watch this and learn, Sport," he said to me as we saun-
tered inside. We looked around the place. There were no cus-
tomers. The Old Man went into action. He walked up to the
counter and smiled at the girl.

"Hi there," he said in a very friendly voice. "That's a very
pretty face you've got there. Now if I just had a name to go
along with it, I'd be all set." I thought he was laying it on a bit
thick. The girl blushed immediately.

"Betty," she said shyly.

"Well, Betty, I'm wondering if you could do us a favor today.
I need some change for a kid's birthday card."

Betty instinctively glanced at me.

"Oh, no, not for Sparky here," the Old Man chuckled. "For
his sister, Joanie." He pulled a twenty out of his pocket. "Could
you give me two tens for a twenty?"

"Sure," Betty said, taking the twenty. She opened the cash
drawer and handed him two tens.

"Thanks a lot." The Old Man smiled and turned to leave.
Then he snapped his fingers and turned back around. "Oh, I
just thought of something. I'm gonna need some fives as well.
I'll give you back a ten for two fives, okay?" He gave her a ten,
and she gave him two fives.

"Thanks. Say, I don't want to embarrass you or anything,
but...haven't I seen you on TV?"

"TV? Why, no sir..." Betty was blushing again.

"Are you sure? I'm from L.A. and I work in the entertainment industry, and I could swear I've seen you on TV."

"No, sir..." She was really blushing now.

"You know what? I'm just not thinking straight today," the
Old Man said. "I don't need change at all. I need large bills.
There's a pretty dress that's just her size in a shop window
down the street, and I forgot all about it. Give me back the
twenty I gave you, and I'll give you back a ten and a five."

Betty opened the cash drawer and pulled the twenty out. As she handed it to him, he said suddenly, "Are you sure I haven't seen you on TV? A chewing gum advertisement, maybe?"

"No, sir." She was really crimson now.

"Oh, my mistake I guess. Sorry. You look so doggone familiar. Oh well. Here's the ten and the five back."

The girl looked at the bills in confusion. "But this is only fifteen dollars."

"That's right," the Old Man said cheerfully.

"But I gave you back a twenty."

"No, honey. *I* gave *you* the twenty. Then I asked for it back. And gave you the ten and the five that you gave me."

"But...but shouldn't you give me back the twenty dollars in change that I gave you in the first place?"

"No, see: one ten and two fives *is* twenty dollars."

"But you only gave me one ten and one five back," Betty said, holding the bills up.

"Yeah, see, the other five," he held it up, "was from when I asked you for two fives for a ten. But I gave you the *ten* back because I remembered that I really didn't need two fives after all. See, you've got the ten I gave you back right there in your hand."

"But...but, what about the *other* five?" she stammered.

"It's right there in your hand, sweetheart!"

The girl's face was redder than ever, and she looked completely lost. She kept looking at the bills in her hand, trying to figure it out.

Then the Old Man snapped his fingers again. "Say, I've got it! You're a *singer*, right?"

"Well, I sing a little..."

"I knew it! On the radio, right? I'd know your voice anywhere!"

"I, umm, I don't sing on the radio," she said, distracted. "Look, mister, something's not right with these bills..."

Just then, the manager came out from a back room. He was a middle-aged guy wearing a white apron and a bow tie. "Is everything all right, Betty?"

I felt like bolting. I looked at the Old Man, who was as cool as a cucumber.

"Well, this gentleman asked for some change, but something's not right with these bills..."

"No, no – everything's fine now," the Old Man piped up confidently. "You've got the ten and two fives, and I've got my twenty. We're square now, honey."

"But...I've only got a ten and a five now."

"Yeah, because *this* five," he held up the five, "was from when I asked you for two fives for a ten. But I gave you the ten back because I really didn't need the fives after all. Remember?"

"But you have the five *and* the twenty now." I could see the dizzy girl's head swimming.

"This is the original twenty you gave me back when I gave you the tens back, remember?"

Betty looked at the bills in her hand, hopelessly lost. The Old Man turned to the manager.

"Kids today, with their heads in the clouds," he said conversationally. "She started talking about being a singer on the radio and somehow got all mixed up. Trust me, I was a math major in college and now I'm a CPA in Hollywood. I do Bing Crosby and Bill Holden's taxes every year. When you close your register and count everything up tonight, I guarantee you, you'll see we're square."

The manager sighed. "Well, this isn't the first time she's gotten confused giving change, I guess."

"But Mr. Dell, I..." Betty burst into tears.

"There, there – don't be too hard on the girl now," The Old Man advised sagely. "She's awfully young for this kind of responsibility, you know."

"Tell me about it," the manager opined. "But my regular cashier called in sick today. What am I gonna do?"

"We all do what we can, Mack" the Old Man commiserated. "We all do what we can..."

When we got back in the car, the Old Man proudly put the bills back into his wallet. "Did you see what I did there? Were you able to follow my moves?"

"That was a lot of work for five dollars," I observed.

"Look, don't try to make me feel bad, because it won't work," he said. "It wasn't that girl's money. Do you know how much that place must pull in every week? Five bucks is nothing to them. But it sure means a lot to *us* right now."

He didn't say anything else for forty miles. You had to hand it to him: the Old Man was a master. My pride at his actually being so good at something was immediately tempered with my disgust that it was something so *bad*.

Chapter 3

In Tulsa, it was the old Western Union routine. We drove through town until we found a Western Union office and parked in front of it. The Old Man studied the shops up and down the street, and I could see the wheels turning as he put the scam together.

"Now watch carefully, Sport. The trick is to pick just the right mark. See that woman over there? We don't want her."

"Why not?" I asked.

"Her dress is frayed along the bottom hem. And see how worn her heels are? She's too poor. We need someone with some real dough, who wants to make *more* dough. This gag plays on their greed, see?"

"What about that guy?" I asked, indicating a man in an expensive suit.

The Old Man wasn't impressed. "Nah, he looks like a banker. They never want to let go of their money."

An older man in a Cadillac pulled up and parked up the street from us. He got out and started walking toward the Western Union office. The Old Man sat up straight.

"Now see that? There's our man. White hair, he's in good shape, casual but expensive golf shirt, nice car. He's probably retired and likes to play the stock market, maybe bets on a horse or two every now and then. Yep, he's our guy. Now remember to look sick."

The Old Man got out of the car and stood in front of the Western Union office, waiting for the mark to pass by.

"Say, Pal. You gotta second?"

The mark stopped.

"Hey, yeah, listen, I got this problem, and I figure you might be able to help me out here."

"What is your problem, young man?" the mark asked warily.

"Well, I'm just passing through town, see, but I'm stuck here waiting for a hundred dollars to be wired to me right here in this office."

The mark's eyebrows raised a bit at the mention of the money. "That doesn't sound like much of a problem to me."

"But see, it's not supposed to be here for another hour, and I got a sick kid in the car over there burning up with fever."

The mark looked over at me in the car. I did my best to look sick.

"And I gotta get him some medicine," the Old Man continued. "But that pharmacy across the street closes in fifteen minutes."

"How much does the medicine cost?" the mark asked.

"Twenty bucks."

"*Twenty bucks*?" the mark exclaimed. "That's some expensive medicine."

"Well, he's real sick, see. The doctor said it's gotta be this new medicine. But the pharmacist won't give it to me until I have the money, and the money isn't here yet."

"And you don't have twenty dollars on you now?"

"I'm tapped out. Road trip, motels, gas. You know."

The mark looked at the Old Man, over at me, at the pharmacy, then back at the Old Man, weighing everything.

"Sorry, I can't help you, young man."

"Wait a minute, Mack." The Old Man was smooth. "I'm not asking you to spot me twenty bucks with nothing in it for you."

"You're not?"

"No, sirree. Look, I told you I got a hundred bucks coming in an hour. Here's what I'm thinking: you spot me the twenty now, I get the kid his medicine so the wife doesn't kill me when I bring home an even *sicker* kid. Then, when the hundred dollars gets here, I'll give you back your twenty and I'll give you an extra *fifty* bucks for helping me out. How does *that* sound?"

"Fifty bucks?" the mark asked. "On top of my twenty?"

"That's what I'm saying. But we gotta do this quick, before little Sparky gets worse."

The mark rubbed his chin, thinking. "I dunno..."

"C'mon. It's the easiest fifty you'll *ever* make!"

"But I have an important appointment right now," the mark said. "I can't wait around an hour for the money to get here."

"I see the problem," the Old Man sympathized, pretending to be deep in thought. "Hey, I got it. You spot me the twenty now, and go to your appointment. I'll get the kid his medicine and meet you right back here after your appointment, to give you your twenty back plus the fifty I promised. What do you say?"

"I...I'm not sure, young man..." the mark hemmed, but I knew the Old Man wasn't about to let him go.

"I know, you don't know me from Adam. I could just skip out with your twenty, right? So how about this: I give you my grandfather's watch to take to your appointment – you know, as security. Then when I give you the money, I get the watch back." He took the watch off his wrist, ready to hand it over to the mark.

"Your grandfather's watch, you say?"

"That's right. See right here? Read that inscription."

"I don't have my reading glasses."

"I'll read it for you, then: '*To Duffy*' – that was his nickname – '*from all the guys down at the lodge. Happy retirement, see you on the links.*' My grandfather, God rest his soul, was a well-liked man. I cherish this watch."

The mark cleared his throat. "How much – how much is it worth?"

"Watch like this? Seventy, eighty bucks, easy," the Old Man said. "Look at that gold plating."

The mark was very quiet, thinking hard. "Okay, if I give you the twenty, you'll be here when I get back from my appointment?"

"That's right, sir."

"Right *here*, in front of this Western Union office? With my money?"

"I swear on my dear grandfather's grave."

"Well, I guess everything's on the up-and-up," the mark said, taking out his wallet and handing the Old Man a crisp twenty-dollar bill.

"And here is the watch," the Old Man said, handing it to the mark. "Please be careful with it. It sure means a lot to me."

"I will. Don't you worry, young man."

"I'm going right over to the pharmacy now and get that medicine before it closes," the Old Man promised. "And I'll see you right back here after your appointment."

"And you'll have my money?"

"I promise I'll have your money."

"All right then, see you in about an hour."

The Old Man crossed the street like he was heading for the pharmacy, while the mark walked away to his appointment. When he was out of view, the Old Man rushed back across the street and hopped into the car.

"And there you have it: twenty beautiful bucks!" He held it up for me to see. "We eat tonight, Sport!"

"But what about your grandfather's watch?" I naively asked.

The Old Man reached over and opened the glovebox. It was full of gold-plated watches.

"It's a fake," he said proudly. "The old guy can keep it – it's only worth two dollars."

"I don't like tricking people. It isn't nice."

"You like to eat, I notice. Besides, *I'm* the one taking all the risks."

But that wouldn't turn out to be entirely true. There was one scam where he needed my help: The Good Samaritan. In Joplin, Missouri, he found the next mark: an elderly woman sitting on a bench waiting for a bus.

"Now look, this is the easiest gag yet," he told me. "All you gotta do is run up and grab that lady's purse, and keep running down the street. I'll be coming the other way and stop you. We'll have a tussle, then you break away and run off, leaving the purse with me. I return her purse, while you wait on the next block for me to pick you up in the car. That's it. Got it?"

I nodded. I didn't want to do it, but I knew the Old Man wouldn't have any of it. At the time, I thought it best to just get it over with.

I went up around the block and came from the west. I waited until no one else was around, then I started walking toward the lady on the bench. It was warm; she was wearing a faded, threadbare house dress and therapeutic shoes. Her purse sat on her lap.

When I got up to her, she looked at me, and I froze. *I can't do this,* I thought. Then I saw the Old Man sitting in the car a dozen or so yards up the street. He just nodded at me. The look on his face said I'd better do it.

"Are you lost, sonny?" the lady asked. I nearly jumped out of my shoes. Steeling myself, I took a deep breath and grabbed her purse right off her lap. Then I just started running up the street, in the direction of the Old Man's car. I could hear the lady screaming "Stop! Thief!" behind me.

It was perfect. The Old Man got out of the car and blocked the sidewalk ahead of me.

"Stop that boy!" I heard the lady call. "He stole my purse!"

I ran right into him, and we "tussled" over the purse. While we "tussled," I could see him reach his hand inside the purse, rifle through the lady's wallet, and pull out a handful of cash. Then he put the empty wallet back into the purse, and I let go of it and ran away.

When I rounded a corner, I peeked back around the fence and saw the Old Man returning the purse to the very relieved lady. "Oh, thank you so much, young man! That was very brave of you!"

"I'm sorry the brat got away," I heard the Old Man apologize.

"Oh, that's alright! At least I got my purse back. That's all that matters right now!"

"You'd better check to make sure everything's there."

She opened her purse and pulled the wallet out. "Yes, my wallet's still here, young man. Safe and sound." Somehow, he knew she wouldn't look inside the wallet.

"Well, you hold onto that purse good and tight from now on," he told her, turning to go.

"You can bet I will," she said with a big smile. "Here, why don't you let me give you a little something for your trouble." She started to open her wallet, but the Old Man reached out and covered it with his hand.

"Oh, no! I wouldn't hear of it! You keep your money now. I'm just happy you got your purse back. Really, I won't take a dime!"

She relented, and slipped the wallet back into the purse. "Well, I just don't know how I can ever thank you, young man..."

"Nonsense...my pleasure. You have a good day now." And he turned and walked back to the car, just as cool as you please. He started the car, pulled around the block, and found me near the corner. I got in the car, shaking.

"You were great, Sport! I'm real proud of you."

"I will never do that again!"

"But we got seventeen dollars and some change."

I didn't care. I was good and sore at him, and didn't care to talk at the moment.

"Let's find something good on the radio," he said, trying to make amends. "It'll make you feel better." He turned the radio on, but I wasn't interested in feeling better. I stuck my fingers in my ears until he gave up and turned the radio off.

"Have it your way!" he huffed.

The only thing I felt like doing was reading. I grabbed the Bible from the back seat and turned my body away from the Old Man so he couldn't see what I was reading. Man, I was really steamed!

The well-used Bible fell open to the story of Jacob and Esau. How fitting. I started reading and was sucked into the story immediately.

From the very beginning, there was trouble between Jacob and Esau. They even fought inside Rebekah's womb. It was so bad, she went to tell God what was going on and He told her, "Look, there are two nations fighting a war inside you." That's just what you want to hear when you're pregnant, isn't it? When they were born, the first one, Esau, came out all red and hairy. Jacob came out more normal, but holding onto his brother's heel as if he were trying to slow him down or something.

When the brothers grew up, Esau was a big strong outdoorsman, while Jacob preferred staying indoors where it was safe and comfortable. Isaac, their father, loved Esau because Esau brought all sorts of tasty things to eat from the forest. Jacob was a mama's boy. But Jacob was more clever than Esau, see. One day while his brother was out in the fields, Jacob made a tasty stew. When Esau came back, he was starving to death, but Jacob wouldn't give him any stew unless Esau promised to sell him his birthright.

Now, no one would sell their birthright for a little bit of bean stew, right? But Esau said he was dying, and it seemed worth it to him, so he gave his birthright to Jacob. Back in those days, being the first born was super important, and that's probably why Jacob was holding onto Esau's heel when they were born, trying to pull him back inside so *he* could be first. Well, he ended up figuring out another way to get that birthright, and old Esau was none too happy about that.

Then one day when Isaac was just about to kick the bucket, he called Esau in and asked him to go out hunting and cook him one last savory meal, and he would get his father's blessing. Well, while he was out hunting, see, Rebekah came up with a plan to steal Esau's blessing. She told Jacob to bring in a couple of goats and she would prepare a savory meal for old Isaac. Then she dressed Jacob up like Esau to fool old Isaac into giving his blessing to Jacob. She dressed Jacob up in Esau's clothes and put animal skins on his arms and neck to make him feel all hairy like Esau.

When Jacob took the savory meal to his father, blind old Isaac bid him come closer so he could feel and smell him. He touched Jacob's arms covered with animal furs, and smelled his clothes which were Esau's. Then, convinced it was really Esau, Isaac ate the savory meal and gave Jacob his blessing.

When Esau came back from the forest and found out that his father had blessed Jacob by mistake, things started to get dicey. First, Esau asked why Isaac had only one blessing to give, but Isaac told him trick or not, the damage was done, and now Jacob was Esau's master. Well, the red hairy man blew a gasket and told everybody that when Isaac finally kicked the bucket, he was going to kill Jacob and get his birthright back.

Rebekah heard about this and sent Jacob to live with her brother Laban until Esau cooled off. But before he left, old blind Isaac told Jacob never to marry a girl from Canaan because they didn't have a very good reputation, if you get my drift, and his mother wouldn't want to go on living if he ever did such a thing. So, instead, Isaac told him to go to Laban and marry one of his cousins, because in those days it was okay to marry cousins and sometimes even brothers and sisters if the Lord said to.

So on the way to his uncle's place, Jacob got tired and laid down with his head on a rock for a pillow. He fell asleep and had a dream about a ladder going up to heaven, with angels walking up and down the ladder. Then he got up and said, "Hey, why are all you angels going up and down that ladder?" But God was at the top of the ladder, and promised to give Jacob and all his descendants this land. Then Jacob used the rock his head was on to make an altar, and promised God that all He gave him, he would always give back a tenth.

When Jacob made it to his uncle's flocks, he took one look at his cousin Rachel, who apparently was a real looker, and felt like showing off a little, so he rolled a huge stone away from the mouth of the well so that Rachel's sheep and all his uncle's flocks could drink from the cool waters. Then Jacob grabbed Rachel and planted a big wet one right on her mouth and started crying like a baby. So romantic...

So then Jacob bee-lined it right to his uncle Laban and offered to work for him for seven years to win the hand of Rachel in marriage. He could have cut a deal for three and a half years, and Laban probably would have snatched it up, but he landed on the number seven for some reason, so Laban agreed. At the end of seven years, Jacob went to Laban and said, "Here I am, ready to marry Rachel as we agreed."

But Laban switched daughters, and put the near-sighted Leah in Jacob's tent instead of Rachel. And instead of checking out the merchandise first, Jacob was in such a hurry that he didn't even realize it wasn't really Rachel until the next morning. When he confronted his uncle about this deception, Laban said he could keep Leah but he'd have to work another seven years to get Rachel.

Jacob had met his match.

So he worked another seven years and was finally able to marry Rachel. Now, if my math is correct, that's fourteen years of hard labor to get this girl. But she was worth it, and Jacob loved her well.

But not so fast, Jacob. The Lord saw that Rachel was loved and Leah was unloved, so he opened Leah's womb and made Rachel barren. Leah bore Jacob four sons. Not to be outdone, Rachel gave Jacob her maid Bilhah and she bore Jacob more sons. When Leah got wind of this, she sent her maid Zilpah in to Jacob and Zilpah bore Jacob more sons. Then God remembered Rachel and opened her womb, and she bore Jacob sons. Then Leah's womb opened again and bore Jacob more sons.

Soon, Jacob was swimming in so many sons, he asked his uncle to release him so he could go back to his own country and live in peace. But Jacob had one last parting shot at his uncle before he left: to let him take all the striped, speckled and spotted sheep with him. So he set up striped, speckled, and spotted rods around the watering holes where the sheep mated, so that the offspring would have those patterns. But when the feeble sheep were mating, he would take away the rods so that Laban would get the feeble sheep. In this way, Jacob became exceedingly prosperous with virile sheep while Laban faltered with weak, substandard livestock.

And that's how Jacob got the upper hand over Laban for tricking him into working fourteen years to marry Rachel. After that, everybody pretty much knew that you don't mess with Jacob.

* * *

The Old Man scored big in a card game in Kansas City. It was an exclusive high stakes game, and he had to shell out twenty bucks – just about all we had – to sit in. We parked the car outside the shabby pool hall where the game was taking place. He left the motor running.

"You wait in the car and keep the motor running."

"Why?"

"Don't argue, just do what I say." His voice sounded tight, tense. Then he eased up a bit and tried to smile. "Look, Sport, just wait here. If the engine stalls, start it up again and keep an eye out for me."

"Okay."

He got out of the car and disappeared into the pool hall. It was about 8:30 p.m. Twenty minutes passed. The engine idled smoothly. My eyelids started to get heavy. I shook myself awake and pinched my arm. That bought me another fifteen minutes or so. My eyelids started to droop again. It was no use, I must have dozed off for I don't know how long.

I woke up to the Old Man frantically banging on the driver's side window. "Open up!" he was shouting. "Unlock the door!" It took me a moment to remember where I was. I fumbled with the door lock and managed to pull it up. The door flung open and the Old Man scooted onto the seat like his life depended on it. He threw the car into gear and screeched away from the pool hall like a banshee.

I turned around and looked out the back window. I saw four big guys with pool cues spilling out of the pool hall and standing in the middle of the street. They were shouting and cursing and waving the pool cues in the air. Then we turned a corner and were out of view. The Old Man hit Route 66 and headed east out of town.

"Damn. That was, that was really...stupid!" Then he started laughing. "But I got us a boatload of dough!" He reached into his pocket and pulled out a handful of cash. He sprinkled in onto the seat between us.

"You mean, you cheated?" I asked.

"Well, yeah..." he was at a loss for words. "Technically. But we needed the dough..."

"You could've gotten killed!"

"Now, Sport, let's not over-react here," the Old Man sputtered. "Those gentlemen were definitely upset, but I don't think they would've actually *killed* me..."

The farther we got from Kansas City, the lighter the Old Man's mood grew. He turned on the radio and found some boisterous swing music to take our minds off our troubles for a while.

"You know what we're gonna do, Sport?" he asked cheerfully. "When we get far enough away, we're gonna stop and get us a room. Yes sir, a real motel room – with hot water, and a shower, and soft beds, and maybe even a TV set. Then we're going to get cleaned up and go out for a real hot meal – no hamburgers, I'm talkin' pork chops, steak – whatever you want. And you can have all you can eat! How's that sound, eh, Sport?"

I stared at him in disbelief. I'd never seen the Old Man so happy.

We drove all night and part of the next day. We found a nice-looking motel outside of St. Louis. The room seemed like a palace after living out of the car for weeks. We took showers, then laid on the twin beds and watched TV for a while, feeling like princes.

"Well, Sport. How about that dinner I promised you? You hungry yet?"

"I'm starved," I said, jumping up and pulling my shoes on. The Old Man got up and combed his hair in front of the mirror, and we were off. It was just starting to get dark.

"It's a nice evening," the Old Man observed. "What say we take a little walk?"

We left the car at the motel and walked to a steakhouse a few blocks away. I ordered pork chops and the Old Man had a beer and T-bone steak. He was absolutely carefree. We ate and joked and talked about where we'd head next. I ordered a big slice of banana cream pie for dessert.

We walked back to the motel in high spirits, ready for some more TV and a good night's sleep. The Old Man checked his watch. "I think we can still catch most of *Amos and Andy* if we're lucky," he said, opening the door. We walked inside and turned on the light.

The four big guys from the pool hall were waiting for us. One of them had a long scar down the right side of his face. Another one wore a pair of brass knuckles. The other two held baseball bats. The Old Man went white as a sheet.

"Look, I realize you fellas might be a little steamed, but –"

"Where's the money?" the one with the scar croaked.

"Well, I can explain all of that if you just give me a chance."

Two of the gorillas grabbed the Old Man and slammed him up against the wall. Plaster cracked and sprinkled down to the worn carpet. A cheap watercolor of a ship slid down to the floor. They rifled through his pockets and pulled out all the money we had left.

"Is that all of it?" Scarface asked.

"Well –well, there was the motel room, and some gas, and we just had a very modest dinner..."

"That's all right. You'll pay for the missing amount – one way or another."

"Not to mention our trouble having to drive all the way up here," the one with the brass knuckles said.

"Take the kid outside," Scarface said. One of the guys leaned his baseball bat against the wall and took me by the arm. He gently led me outside and closed the door. "What – what are they gonna do to him?" I choked out. My throat was constricted with fear.

"It's all right, kid. They're just gonna teach your Old Man a lesson."

We stood in the parking lot while the three of them worked the Old Man over.

I was shaking. The guy from Kansas City caught it. He pulled a stick of gum from his pocket and handed it to me. I took it, unwrapped it, and popped it into my mouth. Beech-Nut. It was good. My mouth was dry. The guy from Kansas City smiled down at me, then looked away.

We could both hear the sounds of the beating going on inside. We pretended not to notice. A few minutes later, it got quiet, and the three guys came outside and closed the motel room door after them. The guy who gave me the gum ruffled my hair affectionately. The other goons stared at him strangely.

"What? He's really a nice kid," he told his friends.

"I know," said Scarface, shaking his head. "It's really a shame..." He knelt down to my level and took both my shoulders in his hands. "I want you to look at me so I know you're listening," he said. I did. He looked me square in the eye. "What your Old Man did was not only stupid, but morally wrong. There's such a thing as right and wrong in this world. You're old enough to know that. When somebody does something wrong, there have to be consequences, or the whole universe gets out of whack, you get me? It's nothing personal. Business is business. Understand?"

I nodded.

"Good. Now, shake hands and go inside and take care of your pop, all right?"

I nodded again. I shook his hand.

"Good boy." He patted me on the shoulders and stood up. I watched the guys from Kansas City walk to their car and pile inside. The car started, and drove slowly out of the motel parking lot.

I went into the motel room feeling numb. The Old Man was sitting up against the wall on the floor. He was semi-conscious, breathing heavily. One eye was already swollen shut, and blood streamed down his face and onto his shirt. I helped him up and sat him on the bed, and he started to come to. He looked at me through the streams of blood and lowered his head.

"Oh, Sport. I'm so sorry...I'm so sorry..."

"It's all right, Pop."

"No, it's not all right. I let you down. No one should ever have to see his Old Man like this..."

I got a towel, wet it at the sink, and brought it to him. He held it to his forehead to try to stop the bleeding.

"What else do you want me to do?" I asked helplessly.

"Nothing. Just let me lie here a while. I think they broke one of my ribs..."

I helped him lay back on the bed, and propped his head up with the pillows.

"I'll be okay, Sport. Why don't you just watch TV or something."

"I don't feel like watching TV right now," I said. I sat on my twin bed and picked up my stolen Bible. I opened it at random and just started reading. It was the book of Exodus, the part where the Children of Israel were wandering in the desert and griping about leaving Egypt and having to eat manna and so they made a golden calf and started worshipping it. Like that was going to solve all their problems. When their leader, Moses, saw the golden calf, he just about had a cow himself and smashed the precious stone tablets to pieces. These were the tablets written by the very finger of God. Now, that being the case, you would think that God would be a little bit upset with Moses, but He wasn't mad at all. He just told old Moses to cut out two more stone tablets and He would re-write them with the same words that were on the tablets Moses shattered.

I thought about this story all night. In other parts of the Bible God always seemed a bit touchy. But here he was, saying "Oh, so you say you shattered the first tablets I wrote with the

Divine Finger? No problem, Moses. Bring me a couple of blank tablets, and I'll just do all that work over again." Amazing.

Being God must be the most demanding job in the world. You've got millions of people praying to you all the time, and I'd bet at least half of those prayers are totally unnecessary, selfish prayers about finding a better-paying job or finding your lost glasses or getting the right sports car that your neighbors will envy or finding that coupon in your kitchen drawer that will save you ten cents on a can of spring peas or something.

Yes, God must be very busy, running the world and all. Anybody would be angry having to do the same work over again. I bet if you said to your boss, "Say, you know that report you spent a week working on? Well, on the way to the post office I got distracted by a billboard about a new movie I've been wanting to see and that made me remember I was hungry so I stopped into a newsstand for a Mars bar and that made me thirsty so I went to a coffee shop across the street for a cup of coffee, and on the way back to work I realized I must have left the report in the coffee shop, so you'll just have to do it over again," he wouldn't be very happy. I bet you'd get fired.

And it wasn't just some crummy business report. This was the *Ten Commandments* we're talking about. It wasn't some shopping list or an advertisement for a new electric can opener or anything. I bet God put a lot of thought into the Ten Commandments. I mean, "Thou shalt not murder," all by itself, is a real day's work, I'll bet.

But God didn't fire Moses. Why didn't God fire Moses? Nothing was going right. He didn't want to take the job in the first place. He wasn't a very inspiring speaker. He couldn't keep the Children of Israel in line. He had a devil of a time controlling his temper, and smashed those blasted tablets to pieces.

Why didn't God fire Moses?

By this time, I'd forgotten all about my Old Man and was slipping into the sweet unconscious state of light stage sleep. A moment later, I was completely out until morning.

Chapter 4

We met the girl at a roadside burger joint outside Poca-hontas, Illinois, a few days later. She was about seventeen or eighteen years old, dressed neatly in capri slacks and a brown Eisenhower jacket over a pink tight-waisted blouse. She had clean, bobbed hair and looked like she should have been at her high school sock-hop instead of a greasy spoon diner some-where on Route 66. She wore wayfarer sunglasses and carried an expensive-looking suitcase.

She walked right up to the counter and asked for a glass of water. It was a hot summer day. We watched as she drank the whole glass down in three big gulps. Then she set the glass down on the counter and looked around the place. There was an old farmer and fat truck driver sitting at the lunch counter. Then she spotted us and walked over to our booth.

"Good afternoon, gentlemen. Mind if I join you?"

She certainly wasn't shy. The Old Man motioned for her to sit down. She sat her suitcase on the floor and slid into the seat beside me. "I don't want you to get the wrong idea. I'm not usually this straight-forward. It's just that I've been on the road a long time, and some of the truck drivers I've thumbed a ride with haven't been the greatest conversationalists, if you get my drift."

She looked really thin. She took off her sunglasses and rubbed her tired eyes.

"When was the last time you've eaten?" the Old Man asked.

"What day is it?" she asked, sweeping a strand of auburn hair out of her eyes.

We bought her a burger and a milkshake. She ate like she hadn't seen food in days. Then she started talking.

"My name's Darleen Fontaine. Well, that's not my real name. That's my stage name."

"Oh. Are you in show business?" asked the Old Man.

"Yes. Well, I'm *going* to be. Very soon. I've been on the road quite a while. I was headed to L.A. to get into the movies. I had a contact at Warner Brothers who was holding a job for me. It was all set up: I had a nice little one-bedroom apartment lined up in Carey Grant's publicity man's sister-in-law's basement in Silver Lake. But then I found out it was all off on account of some producer's wife's second cousin twice removed who got the job instead of me. So now I'm heading to New York City to break into television."

"Television?" I asked, suddenly perking up.

"That's right," she said between bites. Then she swallowed, cleared her throat, and said, as if reciting from an employment agency newsletter, "Television is an up-and-coming multi-million dollar industry and to get in on the action, ground zero is the Big Apple."

"Sounds exciting," the Old Man observed.

"I'm what you call multi-talented," she explained enthusiastically. "I can sing and dance and tell jokes, so I'm sure I can land a spot on the *Colgate Comedy Hour* or the *Milton Berle Show*, easy. Until then, I could be one of those girls in a short skirt who holds up the cards on the game shows. I *know* I could do that. Easy-peasy! Or, I can do advertisements." Here she picked up a French fry and smoked it like a cigarette. "'Anytime of the year, choose Pall Mall for that smooth, rich, satisfying flavor!' Pretty good huh?"

"You just made me wanna go out and buy a pack of Pall Mall's," the Old Man said.

"See what I mean? Like I said, I've already got a name for myself – Darleen *Fontaine*. Isn't it divine? You gotta have a flashy name to break into television in New York City."

"Hey sister, we're headed east," the Old Man said, paying the bill. "You can ride with us, if you want."

"You mean it? Oh, that would be simply *divine*..."

In the car, she started talking and *never* stopped. "Hey, this is a straight-up car, mister. I like it. Did you get this car in L.A.? It looks like an L.A. car to me. I'm going to get a car like this when I get to New York City and land a job in television. Only, see, in New York City, you don't really need a car, 'cause they got the subway and all kinds of neat public transportation. In New York City, it's almost easier *not* to have car, but I'll probably get one anyway and hire a chauffeur to drive me around because when you make the kind of money they pay in television, you'll want to have all kinds of tax write-offs and stuff so you don't get taken to the cleaners by the Internal Revenue Service and stuff. But before I move into a Manhattan highrise, I'm going to find an apartment in Greenwich Village because the rent's a lot cheaper there. Yeah, I've got all this stuff figured out ahead of time so I don't make the mistakes most people make when they go to New York City and land a high-paying job in television..."

For the rest of that afternoon and evening, she told us of her deprivation as a child, how she started out as an orphan when her parents were killed in a plane crash in the Andes Mountains in Peru and she was raised in a series of harsh orphanages on starvation rations and little medical care. Despite this, she was able to overcome her circumstances and win a full scholarship to Kansas State University, where she excelled as a cheerleader and starred in several college productions of Shakespeare and Tennessee Williams plays before winning the Miss Topeka Kansas Beauty pageant in which her talent was baton twirling and astrological forecasting.

"Yeah, some people call it *'psychic ability,'* but whatever you call it, I got it in spades! Wouldn't that make a great television show? Me, with a crystal ball, telling people's fortunes? But not just *anybody's* fortunes – *celebrities*. That's the ticket! You could call it *'Celebrity Crystal Ball.'* I could have Lana Turner on and tell her fortune, and the next week have Marlon Brando on! See, I'm always thinking of ideas. You gotta do that to break into television in New York City!"

Then Darleen asked the Old Man to turn on the radio, but every station was wrong. "I don't want music. Find some advertisements. I need to brush up on my skills."

The Old Man told me to do it while he drove. I pushed buttons on the console randomly until I found an ad for orange juice: "Unparalleled flavor from the sunny state of Florida!" Darleen mimicked the ad perfectly. The next ad was for canned spinach, and she nailed that one. Then a car ad: "The luxuriously smooth ride of Studebaker – it takes you where you want to go!" She was pretty good!

She did the ads all night. The Old Man kept driving. When the sun started to rise, he finally pulled over and found a travel stop outside Lillyville, Illinois. While the Old Man caught some Z's in the car, Darleen took me into the diner and we sat down at a soda counter. There was a pimply-faced high school kid behind the counter, and I could see that Darleen caught his eye right away. Darleen ordered two chocolate sodas for us for breakfast. Then she started in on the soda jerk kid.

"We're headed for New York City," she told him matter-of-factly. "I've got a job waiting for me in television."

The soda jerk looked at me.

"That's my kid brother, Carl," she told him. "We're gonna live in Greenwich Village and feed the ducks in Central Park." Even at my tender age, I noticed how easily the lies seemed to roll off her tongue.

As I greedily slurped my chocolate soda, Darleen asked the kid how much we owed him.

"Two chocolate sodas, let's see, that's, umm, twenty cents."

She opened her wallet and pulled out a twenty-dollar bill. I immediately realized she had taken us for that burger and milkshake the day before, but stayed quiet.

"Oh, all I've got's a twenty," she said with mock dismay. "Can you change that?"

The soda jerk looked at the twenty-dollar bill and his Adam's apple bobbed up and down. "Umm, yeah – I guess so..."

I slurped up the rest of my soda and watched, transfixed, as Darleen executed as good a "change for a twenty routine" as I'd ever seen. She had that poor kid right in the palm of her hand. In all honesty, the Old Man would have been envious.

When all was said and done, Darleen walked away from that soda counter eight dollars and some change in the black. She was smooth.

But before we got to the door, she suddenly stopped and turned around slightly. I looked at the door and saw a couple of scruffy beatnik types – chin beards, sunglasses, long, un-washed hair. They were just entering and scoping the place out. Darleen put on her sunglasses and pulled her bangs down over her forehead. Then she put me in front of her and walked me toward the door.

"Darleen? Is that you?" One of the beatniks scowled. Dar-leen stopped walking, but stayed quiet.

"We've been looking for you," the other beatnik said. "Hey, that was a heavy deal you laid on us back in St. Louis, baby."

They walked over to us and looked me up and down. "Who's the ankle-biter, Darleen? Is he part of your latest gimmick, or what?"

"He's my kid brother," Darleen said quietly.

The beatniks looked at each other and laughed. "Yeah, right, babe. Hey, I was wondering. Just when were you planning on returning all that dough you stole from us back at that coffee house in Missouri?"

Darleen grabbed me by the wrist and tried to walk around them. They moved in front of us.

"We want the bread back. *Now.*" One of them grabbed for her wallet. She didn't let go. "Come on, baby – let's do this nice and easy, so things don't get messy..."

I grabbed his hand to pull it away from Darleen. The other beatnik grabbed my arm and jerked me away. It hurt bad.

The first beatnik had her wallet open and was pulling bills out. "Help!" Darleen called. "Someone help!" The other beatnik held onto my arm tight.

Then, the Old Man was there. "Let go of my son."

The beatniks turned around to face him. "Oh, who's this, Darleen? Your new sugar daddy?"

"I said, let go of my son."

The beatnik holding my arm let go. "It's all cool, Daddy-O. No problem here."

"Now give the young lady her wallet back."

The beatnik holding her wallet spoke up. "See, we can't do that, Daddy-O, because she rolled us back in St. Louis. This is *our* money..."

The Old Man threw a pretty convincing right hook and smashed the beatnik in the nose.

"Now, why'd you have to go and do a thing like that, Daddy-O?" the beatnik said, letting go of Darleen's wallet and holding his nose. The other beatnik moved towards the Old Man, but the Old Man feigned a punch at him and the beatnik shrunk away.

"Let's get out of here, Chas," he said to his friend, who was still holding his busted nose. "It ain't worth it!"

The beatniks backed off, and we walked out to the car.

"I wouldn't blame you if you didn't want to..." Darleen said to the Old Man.

"It's all right. Get in."

We all got in the car and drove away. Darleen was relieved but unusually quiet. The Old Man was quiet, too, which meant he was thinking. I could tell he was putting two and two together about Darleen. One con man could always smell another one a mile away. But I could tell he wasn't mad.

No, he was hatching a new scam.

When we got to the next decent-sized town, he drove down the main street and parked in front of a pawn shop. "I'll be right back," he said, and left the car.

"Hey kid – what's up with your Old Man, anyway?" Darleen asked.

"He probably wants your help with something," I predicted. I opened the Bible and read to myself for a while.

"What's with the Bible?" she asked.

"I find it very interesting," I said, and kept reading.

"Yeah? Like what? I mean, tell me something interesting about the Bible."

"Well, like this part I'm reading now," I said calmly. "Abram and his wife Sarai left the land of Canaan because of this terrible famine, and they went down to the land of Egypt. In those times, Egypt was ruled by a king called a pharaoh, and pharaohs were famous for always having a lot of pretty women around so Abram told Sarai to say that she was his sister because she was so beautiful and he knew the moment old pharaoh laid eyes on her he'd have Abram put to death and take her for his wife. So when they got way down into Egypt, it didn't take long for old pharaoh to hear about Sarai and he took her into his palace as his wife."

"But, wasn't she already married to that other guy?" Darleen asked in astonishment.

"Yeah, but pharaoh didn't know that on account of they called Sarai his sister."

"And this Abram – he just let the king take his own wife?"

"That's what it says."

"Why didn't he do anything about it?"

"Because Sarai pleased pharaoh so much that he gave Abram all sorts of neat stuff."

"Like what?"

"Like sheep and oxen and donkeys and male and female servants and female donkeys and camels."

"He traded his own wife for a bunch of animals? What kind of a clown was this guy?"

"In those times, animals were as valuable as gold. Pharaoh made Abram very rich."

"Still, something doesn't seem right about this guy..."

"Then God got sore at pharaoh and sent great plagues to torment Egypt," I continued. "Then pharaoh got sore at Abram and said, 'Why didn't you *tell* me she was your wife?' So to stop the plagues, pharaoh gave Sarai back to Abram and sent them out of Egypt."

"What about all the sheep and oxen and donkeys and camels and stuff?"

"Abram got to take it all with him. He was loaded from that day on."

Darleen's eyes were open very wide. I could see the wheels turning in her mind.

"That's gotta be the greatest con in history, kid," she marveled. "That's a pretty neat book, after all..."

The Old Man came out of the pawn shop with an old violin case, tossed it in the backseat, and got behind the wheel.

"What's that?" I asked.

"Our next routine," he replied, starting the car. He drove around town a little bit, then picked out a greasy spoon diner and pulled into the parking lot. He parked way in the back.

"Why'd you park so far away?" I asked.

"Just listen, and stay quiet," he said, lost in thought. He looked at Darleen. "Okay, this is our new gag, and you're gonna be in it. All you gotta do is go inside with this violin and sit at the counter. Order whatever you like. While you're eating, we'll come inside and sit down, but you don't know us, see? When you finish eating, you tell the guy you left your wallet back at the motel and you'll be back in a jiffy with the dough. Let him keep the violin as security. He'll do it, because even this cheap violin is worth more than a hamburger, right? Then you leave and stay outside until you see us come out and get in the car. Then you go inside, pay your bill, and get your violin. Only, after I'm through with him, see, he's gonna offer you a hundred bucks for the violin. Take the money, only not too fast, or it'll make him suspicious – this violin has sentimental value for you, it belonged to your grandfather and he taught you how to play it. But in the end, you take the dough and meet us outside."

Darleen looked confused. "I – I don't get it."

"Don't worry about it, doll. Just do exactly what I told you."

She took the old violin from the backseat and walked into the diner. We watched her as she sat down at the counter and ordered. She sat the violin on the stool next to her. It was an older guy behind the counter – probably the owner. When he brought her the burger, the Old Man and I got out of the car and walked into the diner.

We sat down at the counter, a few stools away from Darleen, and pretended not to know her.

"What'll it be?" the old guy asked us.

"Bowl of tomato soup for me and a grilled cheese sandwich for the kid," the Old Man said.

"Coming right up."

Darleen ate quietly while our food was being prepared. She finished up right when our food arrived. Out of the corner of my eye, I could see her going through her pockets as if looking for her wallet. "Why, that's strange," she said.

"Something wrong, miss?" the owner asked.

"I – I thought I brought my wallet with me, but I must have left it at the motel."

"How far is your motel?" the owner asked suspiciously.

"Not too far," she charmed him with her smile. "I'll just run along and get it and be back here with the money in a jiffy."

"Well, I dunno miss..."

"Why don't you keep my grandfather's violin until I get back? It'll just take me a minute, and I sure want to pay for my dinner."

"Well, I guess that'd be all right," the owner said. She handed him the violin.

"Just, please, be careful with it. I don't really know how much it's worth, but it was my dear old grandfather's and it sure means a lot to me."

"Oh, I will, miss. I'll be real careful with it, I promise."

Darleen walked out and disappeared around the corner. We finished up our meal and stood up.

"How much do we owe you?"

"Umm, let's see...that'll be sixty-five cents," the owner replied, still thinking about the violin. The Old Man paid him.

"Say, you mind if I have a look at that old violin?" he asked the owner.

"Well, it belongs to the young lady..."

"I'll be careful with it, I promise."

"Well, I guess so." He carefully handed the instrument to the Old Man. The Old Man opened the case and gingerly took the violin out. He held it up and looked it all over.

"Oh, yes – she's a real beaut, isn't she?"

"I wouldn't know," the old guy admitted. "I don't know any-thing about music."

The Old Man held it up to the light and peered inside the f-hole. "A *Monte Verde*. Very nice...very nice indeed..."

"You a musician?" the owner asked.

"Me? No, I don't play myself. I'm an instrument broker in Chicago. I deal in all kinds of rare vintage instruments. This one, for instance, the *Monte Verde*. Made in Spain by a craftsman in the tiny village of *Monte Verde* in the Castillian Mountains."

"You don't say!" the owner exclaimed.

"Yes, a very interesting piece. See this wood? Pure, aged Spanish spruce from the forests around the village of *Monte Verde*. Very rare wood. And see this varnish? It's made with honey from the hives of the very rare Iberian honey bee. These bees are found in only one place in the world – the Castillian Mountains of Spain. Gives it that satiny-goldish glow, don't you think?"

"You don't say!" the owner repeated.

"I could sell this instrument in Chicago in about thirty minutes," the Old Man said, placing the violin back in its case. "One of a kind, really."

"What's it worth?"

"Oh, I don't know. If I found the right buyer, I could probably get five hundred – no, six hundred dollars for this instrument. Easy."

"You don't say!" the owner's eyes got real wide.

"Say, I'll tell you what, my good man," the Old Man said, reaching into his shirt pocket. "Let me leave you my card. It's got my number in Chicago on it. If that young lady doesn't come back, you give me a call and I'll have a buyer for that violin before you can say Jack Robinson. I'll cut you in for a 20% finder's fee."

"You don't say!" the owner said, taking the card. "Well, I'll be!"

We left the diner and got into the car. We waited. A minute later, Darleen came from around the corner and walked into the diner. She paid for her burger, picked up the violin case, and started to go. The old guy stopped her. They talked a while. We could see her shaking her head – *No, no, it was my grandfather's violin.*

"She's playing it just right," the Old Man said with approval.

They talked some more. We could see the owner throwing out some numbers – forty dollars, fifty dollars, seventy-five dollars. When he got to a hundred dollars, Darleen nodded – sadly. He went to the back room and came back with a handful of cash. He counted it out to her and tucked the violin under his arm proudly.

Before walking out, Darleen touched the violin case one last time, longingly, then turned and left.

"Nice touch!" The Old Man was impressed.

Darleen got into the front seat and counted out fifty bucks. She handed it to the Old Man.

"What about the other fifty?" he asked, astonished.

"I keep it."

"But it was *my* gag!"

"I did half the work. I get half the money."

She had him good. There was nothing he could do. "All right. Fifty-fifty," he said, stuffing the bills into his pocket.

"But what about the card?" I asked.

"Do you think I'd actually give him a *real* number?" the Old Man asked. "He'll probably get some Chinese laundry in Detroit when he tries to call it!" He started the car and pulled out of the parking lot.

Chapter 5

And it went like that, day after day. Every time we hit a town, the Old Man would find a pawn shop and buy a two-dollar violin. Then he and Darleen would work their magic. Sometimes, for old time's sake, they'd pull a Western Union gag, using a cheap violin as security instead of a cheap watch.

In a week, we were rolling in cash. The Old Man was happy, carefree. We even started staying in motels – me and the Old Man in one room, and Darleen in an adjoining room. Things seemed to be working out fine, all around. Until we got to Indianapolis.

That evening I was hanging out in Darleen's room – you know, just watching TV and goofing around and stuff. She was telling me all about how television works.

"You see, the shows are recorded live in front of an audience, on videotape," she explained, like an expert. "That means, if somebody makes a mistake, you just keep going and try to pretend it was supposed to be like that. You can't stop and do another take like the movies, because it's going out live all over the country. That's called *improvisation*. You've got to be good at improvisation to work in television, and that just happens to be one of my strongest talents – covering up mistakes."

She got up and went into the bathroom, leaving the door partly open. I heard the shower come on, and saw her starting to undress through the crack in the door. Surprised, I looked away and kept my eyes fixed on Howdy Doody on TV. When the shower turned off, I dared a peek through the crack in the door and saw her standing in front of the mirror, wrapped in a white towel. She brushed her hair and primped in the mirror, seemingly oblivious to my presence in the other room. I looked away again and kept watching TV.

She came out of the bathroom and sat down on the corner of the bed I was reclining on, still wrapped in the towel. She was all wet, and she was looking at me funny. I started to feel kind of funny, too, and wanted to leave, but I didn't move. We were both quiet for a long time.

"You know, you've got your Old Man's looks," she finally said. I didn't look at her. "Have you ever kissed a girl before?"

"No." I felt my face getting flush. She scooted a little closer to me. She put her hand on my thigh. I was starting to feel a little nauseous and a little excited all at the same time.

"How old are you, kid?" That was it. I could tell she was getting ideas.

"Thirteen."

"Thirteen, huh?" she asked, still eyeing me. I could see the wheels turning behind those sleepy bedroom eyes. "Well, I suppose that's a little young, isn't it?" She got up and walked back to the bathroom, but stopped and turned around in the doorway.

"Someday you're gonna get real lucky. But not tonight, kid..." Then she turned and went into the bathroom, and that was that.

I think I kinda understood what she meant. I also realized that all of a sudden she seemed kinda lonely.

The next morning we were sitting in a coffee shop having breakfast, just like nothing had ever happened. We were eating fine these days. The Old Man had eggs and bacon. I had waffles. Darleen, always watching her figure, picked at a grapefruit and a bowl of Post Toasties.

I was reading the Bible. The waitress came to pour more coffee for the Old Man. "Oh, how sweet!" the waitress said. "What a good little man, reading the Lord's Good Book!"

"Just trying to raise the boy right," the Old Man gloated.

"Well, that book is full of such wisdom!" the waitress beamed.

"Yes, it certainly is *full* of it!" The Old Man couldn't help himself. The waitress floated to another table.

"Why do you have to be so mean?" Darleen asked.

"It was just a joke," the Old Man said, slurping coffee.

"Well, maybe God doesn't like jokes," she countered.

"Why not? Don't you think He has a sense of humor?"

"I wouldn't think so."

The Old Man looked at me. "How about it, Sport? Are there funny things in that book, or what?"

"Sometimes," I said.

"See? The kid's an expert, and he says God has a sense of humor."

"Maybe not in the way you think," Darleen shot back. Then she looked at me. "So, whatever happened to that couple who went to Egypt – oh, you know – Adam and Sally?"

I couldn't help laughing. "Abram and Sarai," I corrected her.

"Oh, you know what I mean."

I filled her in. "Well, first God changed their names to Abraham and Sarah."

"Why'd He do that?" Darleen asked.

"It sounds better. Then, Abraham kept passing her off as his sister for a while, and it caused a lot of folks in the land of Canaan to be confused. But every time he did it, it made Abraham richer than before."

The Old Man really pricked up his ears at this part.

"So they pulled the same old scam again, huh?" Darleen asked.

"Yeah, this time it was Abimelech, a rich King. But when he found out about it, he gave Abraham even *more* loot. Then Sarah, who wasn't supposed to have children, got pregnant because God opened up her womb when she was ninety years old. They had a baby boy named Isaac. Only on account of God's command, Abraham had to cut his foreskin off when he was only eight days old."

I saw the Old Man wince.

"It's okay," Darleen said. "Baby boys don't feel that sort of thing."

"How do *you* know?" the Old Man responded.

"Come on, what else?" Darleen asked me, really interested.

"Well, Isaac didn't get to be raised with his brother, Ishmael, who was born back when Sarah thought she couldn't have babies so she made Abraham lie with her maid Hagar."

"Do you even know what 'lie with' means?" asked Darleen.

"I kind of have an idea. But after Ishmael was born, Hagar lorded it all over Sarah that she had a baby and Sarah didn't, and that made Sarah kinda sore. Then, after Isaac was born, Ishmael mocked him and that was it for Sarah. She made Abraham send Hagar and Ishmael out into the desert alone."

"What happened to them?" Darleen wanted to know.

"God gave them food and water, and Ishmael grew up in the wilderness and became an archer, and Hagar picked out a fine Egyptian woman for him to marry. In those times, parents picked husbands and wives for their children. And the Angel of the Lord told Hagar that Ishmael would be the father of a great nation."

"Wow," Darleen said. "That's juicier than a TV soap opera!"

Right about then, we heard a loud rumble and looked out the diner's wide front window. A motorcycle gang was pulling into the parking lot. They were the real deal – black leather jackets and greasy, slicked-back hair.

"Uh-oh," Darleen murmured, sliding down low in her seat. She put on her sunglasses and tried to hide behind a menu as the gang parked their bikes and headed for the front door.

"Who are they?" the Old Man asked.

"That's Mitch's gang," Darleen said, peering out from behind the menu.

"Mitch?"

"Yeah, he's the leader," she said. "He – ha ha – he thinks we're having a – you know – relationship. Guy just can't take no for an answer."

"Is Mitch the big guy in front, with the chains on his jacket?" the Old Man asked.

"Yeah, that's him."

The bikers walked in and looked around, but didn't notice Darleen.

"We gotta get outta here!" she said, trying to sound calm.

"Okay, look, stay calm," the Old Man advised. He pulled the car keys out of his pocket and handed them to me. "Sport, go out to the car and start it up. Pull it up slowly around to the back of the diner."

"But I don't know how to drive!" I reminded him.

"It's easy. You've seen me do it a million times. You'll figure it out. Just put it in Drive and meet us around back."

"Okay." I took the keys and the Bible and stood up. I could see the Old Man leaving money on the table to cover the tab.

"It's okay, Sport. They're not looking for a boy. Just walk right past them."

I started walking. The bikers were looking for a booth big enough for all of them. They didn't even notice me. Other patrons were staring at them and moving out of their way.

I got outside and found the car. I had to sit on the Bible to be able to see over the steering wheel. I tried desperately to remember what the Old Man did. I closed my eyes and visualized it.

I slid the key into the ignition and turned it clockwise. The engine started up. So far, so good. Then I put my foot on the middle pedal and put the car into Drive. Fortunately, the Old Man had backed into the parking spot – an old habit of his, for quick getaways and such. I lifted my foot off the middle pedal, but it wouldn't go forward. Then I remembered, and reached down to release the emergency brake. Now the car would go.

I idled the car as slow as it would go. I steered it back behind the diner and found the back door. Then I put my foot on the middle pedal and stopped it. And waited.

I didn't have to wait long. Darleen and the Old Man came out the back door in a real hurry, followed by Mitch and the other bikers. I got out of the way as the Old Man slid behind the wheel and Darleen got in on the passenger side. The bikers were right on their tail. The Old Man peeled out and the car lurched forward, several bikers holding onto the rear bumper.

The Old Man fish-tailed it, trying to shake them off, but they held on. I have to give it to them: they held on a good hundred yards before, one by one, they finally lost their grips and tumbled away behind us.

Then the Old Man turned around and headed back to the diner.

"What are you *doing?*" Darleen screamed.

"You'll see."

Back in the parking lot, he side-swiped the first motorcycle, causing the whole row to go down like dominoes. They were now one twisted, intertwined mass.

"It'll take them a few minutes to untangle that mess!" the Old Man exclaimed. Then he found the highway, got back on it, and headed east out of town.

Darleen admitted that the biker gang had been after her since she tried to hustle them in a pool game back in Missouri. When the hustle fell flat, the leader, Mitch, took a liking to her anyway and wanted to make her his Old Lady. She was able to ditch them sometime before hooking up with us, and had been on the lookout for them ever since.

"I'm sorry," she said. "I never meant to drag you guys into the middle of this."

The Old Man didn't say anything, but I could tell he was probably wondering what was going to come next with her.

We drove all day. That evening we stopped for the night at a roadside motor lodge and had dinner in its coffee shop. Darleen was still a little quiet – for her. Then we went to our respective rooms and watched TV for a while.

"Why don't you go check on Darleen," the Old Man suggested. "Just make sure she's all right." I guess he'd noticed how quiet she'd been at dinner.

To tell you the truth, after what had happened the night before, I was a bit hesitant. But when the Old Man asked me to do something, it usually wasn't optional.

I got up and went over to her room next door. I knocked and she said, "Come in." I walked inside, steeling myself for the worst, but was relieved to see she wasn't in the shower or wrapped in a motel towel or anything. She was just lying on the bed watching TV and looking at a magazine.

"Hi, kid."

"Hi," I said. "You okay?"

"Why wouldn't I be?"

"The Old Man thought you might be lonely or something."

"I'm *never* lonely," she said. "Hey, I'm glad you came over. Let's go grab some ice cream or something."

"Okay."

We went outside and started walking. There was a drugstore with a soda fountain down the road. There were a few other people at the counter, but it wasn't crowded at all. We ordered ice cream cones. I got a double, but Darleen only wanted a single.

"So, how come you don't have any brothers or sisters?" she asked.

"I don't know," I replied.

"Where's your mother?"

"Florida."

"What's she doing in Florida?"

"She ran off."

"Why?"

"I think she got fed up with the Old Man," I said.

"On account of the gambling and grifting?"

"Uh-huh."

"I can see that," Darleen said, licking her cone. "When I settle down, I'm leaving this life behind me. Besides, I'll have my own television show by then. I told myself, I'm not getting married until I have my own television show, like Lucille Ball. Now she's got it made. A handsome celebrity husband. Her own show where nobody tells her what to do and she gets to do anything she wants. She's even allowed to have a kid, because she's such a big star that nobody can tell her not to. Yeah, that's the kind of life *I'm* looking for, kid."

"Uh-huh."

"Do you think your mom will ever come back?"

"I guess so," I said. "But I'm not sure she loves me."

"All mothers love their kids," Darleen said knowingly. "If your Old Man straightens himself out, she'll be back."

"Well, she's not like other moms," I said.

"What do you mean?"

"Well, sometimes she's normal but other times she's real sad and sleeps a lot. She drinks a lot of booze but it doesn't really make her feel better."

"Oh, I see," Darleen said. "It sounds like *depression*."

"Uh-huh."

"Depressed people can't help it," Darleen said. "They don't mean to be that way. It's a disease. Only I don't think there's a cure for it."

"She never went to a doctor," I said.

"Depressed people never go voluntarily," Darleen explained. "It always takes somebody forcing them to go. Like your Old Man. Why didn't *he* force her to go to a doctor?"

"Guess he never thought of it."

"Do you think he wants her back?"

"I guess so," I replied. "I do. I'd sure like to be a family again."

"Aw, poor kid," she ruffled my hair in a big sister way. "I hope she comes back someday."

"Me, too."

"So, you think you and your Old Man will take me all the way to New York City?" she asked.

"I guess so."

"Oh, you just wait, kid," she beamed, her old self again. "You'll just love the Big Apple. There's nothing else like it. The buildings are so tall, you can't even see the tops of them. There's so many cars in the streets that they can't even move sometimes. There's so many people on the sidewalks that it's hard to get anywhere. They call them *pedestrians*. And they have a subway train that goes under the city and the Empire State Building and Broadway and Central Park and the Statue of Liberty. All the most famous landmarks are in New York City. I can't wait to show you around when we get there!"

"Me, too."

We were finished with our ice cream, so we got up and left the drugstore. We walked back to the motor lodge and went to her room. We watched TV and she showed me how to play Gin Rummy. She won every hand, but it didn't matter because we were only hanging out and goofing off and having a lot of fun anyway.

She told me more about New York City and her plans for when she got her own television show. I got the feeling she'd been thinking about it a lot, on account of she already knew what restaurants she was going to eat in and what she was going to order and what stores she was going to shop in and what kinds of clothes and dresses and shoes and hats and jewelry she was going to buy.

She even knew what kind of apartment building she wanted to live in and what kind of neighbors she wanted to live on her floor. She told me she wanted a Broadway producer to live next door so she could keep up on the latest parts opening in big shows and could get tickets to all the big shows for half-price. She said it was important to show up and be seen at all the big premieres and shows if you wanted to break into the entertainment business in New York City. She called it *networking*.

Across the hall would live an editor for *Vogue* magazine, so Darleen could keep up on all the latest fashion trends and get tickets to attend runway fashion shows and meet all the top designers. She said all the top designers lived in either Paris or New York.

Two doors down would live a top talent agent so she could hob-nob with all his famous clients and get solid representation for herself. Also on her floor, there should be a TV director, a newspaper columnist, and someone in the publicity business, just to round things out and cover all the bases. Darleen said you could *never* get too much publicity.

"Yessiree, kid," she told me enthusiastically. "That would be the Dream Floor to live on if you wanted to break into television in New York City."

Boy, Darleen was sure smart. I'd never met anyone who knew so much about breaking into television in New York City. She could have written a book about it. To hear her talk, it seemed like a sure bet she was going to end up a big success.

"It sure is easy to talk to you, kid," she said. "I wish I had a younger brother just like you. Hey, I know: when I make it big in New York City, you can come visit me and I'll take you to Central Park and the Statue of Liberty and even to a Yankees game and buy you a hot dog and soda pop and peanuts and cotton candy and everything. How does that sound?"

"Pretty neat, I guess." It was nice talking to her like this. All the awkwardness of the previous night was gone now, and we were just like good friends again. We were having such a good time and talked so late that I don't remember exactly but I must have passed out on the other bed in her room because that's where I woke up the next morning. I hadn't even changed into my pajamas or anything.

Chapter 6

The next day we hit the road again and the Old Man found a little diner he thought would be perfect for the violin gag. He and Darleen had pulled that job so many times that they knew their parts by heart and worked it like a well-oiled machine. This set-up seemed perfect: a small greasy spoon with a lunch counter and a couple of worn booths. The proprietor was a middle-aged guy with an uncooperative toupee that curled up at the edges and a grease-stained apron.

We parked way in the back of the lot and Darleen entered and ordered her usual hamburger and vanilla shake. It was her good luck order. The Old Man and I entered and sat at the counter just as she was finishing up. The Old Man ordered a bowl of chili and I ordered a cheesesteak sandwich.

"Oh, my – I seem to have left my wallet back at the motel," Darleen said, checking her pockets. The owner seemed very cooperative when she suggested leaving the violin as security while she went to get her wallet. She walked out of the establishment and the Old Man immediately went into his spiel.

"Say, mind if I take a look at that violin?" he asked the owner.

"Not at all, mister," the owner said as if on cue. "Do you play?"

"Me? No," the Old Man said, taking the violin out of its case and examining it carefully. "I'm an instrument broker out of

Chicago. I deal in all kinds of rare musical instruments. You'd be surprised what I find out here on the road."

"Yeah?"

"That's right, Mack. Sometimes people have no idea how valuable their instrument is. No idea."

"Is that so?" the owner said skeptically. "I suppose you're going to tell me that one there is very valuable, aren't you?" He had a funny look on his face.

"As a matter of fact, you don't find many of these around at all," the Old Man said. "This is a *Ternini*, made by fine craftsmen in the Tuscany region of Italy."

"Is that so?" the owner said. "I suppose you're going to tell me that it's worth five or six hundred dollars, aren't you?"

Something was wrong. This guy seemed to know the Old Man's script, almost word for word.

"Something like that," the Old Man said, catching on. "On the other hand, it may not be that rare, after all."

"That's a great story, mister," the owner said. "You know, about the fine craftsmen in Italy and all. But I got an interesting story, too. See, my brother owns a diner in Plainfield, and he told me about a girl just like that young lady who was here earlier and how she said she left her wallet at her motel and had to go get it to pay for her hamburger. She left an old violin as security, too. Then my brother said a dark-haired man in his thirties – oh, about your height and build – and a boy came in and the man said he was a rare instrument dealer from Chicago, just like you. He told my brother that the violin was worth six hundred dollars and gave him a card. He said he'd cut my brother in for a nice piece of the deal if the young lady didn't come back for her violin. So my brother, not being the sharpest tool in the shed, paid the girl a hundred bucks for the violin, only when he called the number on the card all he got was someone speaking Chinese. So he took the violin to have it appraised, and you know how much it was worth?"

"No," the Old Man said.

"Zilch," the owner said. "It was worthless. So my brother was out a hundred bucks and got stuck with a worthless piece of firewood. You like that story, mister?"

"That's an amazing story," the Old Man said. I'd never seen him so deflated. "Look, why don't you tell us what we owe you for the food and we'll just settle up and be on our way."

"Don't worry about the food," the owner said, pulling a shotgun out from under the counter. "It's on the house."

"Say, brother, I don't know what you're doing with that gun," the Old Man said. "But we don't want any trouble here."

"Oh, there won't be any trouble," the man said, pointing the gun at us. "I just want to tell you that I have another brother, see, and this one's the county sheriff. I think he'd have a lot he'd like to say to you. It seems like your luck just ran out, fella."

"I'm – I'm sure we can find a way to work this out," the Old Man said. "You know, without involving the law."

"We'll work everything out when my brother the sheriff gets here," the owner said. "Now you two just take a seat at the counter while I give him a call." Keeping the shotgun trained on us, he picked up a phone and dialed a number. "Earl, I've got the violin guy here. Come on over as quick as you can." Then he hung up and stared at us.

"I wish there was another way we could do this," the Old Man said.

"Oh, no. I'm sure this is the best way to handle it. You'll like Earl when you meet him. He'll be right over." Then he looked at me. "Want a bottle of pop or something while we're waiting, kid?"

"No thank you," I replied.

"Polite boy," the owner said, lighting a cigarette. We waited in silence for a long time. Of course, Darleen never came back – she had to have known something was up when we didn't come out. I hoped she was high-tailing it as far away as she could get.

Finally, a patrol car pulled up outside the diner and Sheriff Earl got out and came inside.

"Well lookie what we got here," Earl said, eyeing us up and down. "Believe it or not, I've heard quite a bit about you two. Yessiree, the traveling instrument broker and his boy. Where's the girl?"

"She never came back," his brother told him.

"Well, at least we got these two," Earl said, putting the violin back in its case and latching it up. Earl was tall and range-y. He had a big belly and an over-sized belt buckle with a bucking bronco engraved on it. He wore a star on his chest and a Western-style sheriff's hat. "You boys are coming with me."

He picked up the violin case and herded us outside to his car. I looked around the lot and didn't see the Old Man's car where we left it parked. He noticed, too, and our eyes met: *she got away.*

Earl put us in the back of his car and got in the front. He started it up and drove away from the diner in silence. We drove for several minutes, and I noticed we seemed to be driving away from the town rather than towards it.

"Where are you taking us?" the Old Man finally asked.

"Patience is a virtue to be nurtured and cultivated, just like a fine garden," Earl replied.

The Old Man stayed quiet. Earl seemed to be driving us out into the countryside, where there was nothing but fields and wide-open farmland and livestock. I looked at the Old Man for reassurance. He reached over and squeezed my hand.

"Have you boys been about the Devil's handy-work?" Earl asked.

"Excuse me?" the Old Man asked.

"Don't lie to me, young man," the sheriff warned. "How long have you been on the Devil's payroll?"

"A long time, sir."

"I thought as much," Earl said, nodding his head in satisfaction. "You've been toiling long and hard in the Devil's orchard, earning the wages of sin."

"Yes, sir."

"Do you know what the wages of sin are, young man?"

"No, sir."

"Death," Earl said flatly. "Death of the conscience. Death of the soul. Death of the body. *Death*."

"Yes, sir."

"You would have done better to put your youth and energy into keeping the Lord's commandments instead of punching the Devil's time clock the way you've been."

"Now I see the error of my ways, sir," the Old Man assured him.

"Do you?" Earl asked. "You're bringing up this fine boy in the ways of darkness. You should be laboring in the fields of righteousness, reaping the Lord's bountiful harvest."

"I'm ashamed of myself for not being a better father, sir."

"It's not too late, young man," Earl said. "The Lord's mercy cannot be exhausted by all the sinners in the world nor contained in all its oceans."

"That's good to know, sir."

We drove along in silence for a while. We were on a dirt road now, way out in the boonies. Earl stopped the car and told us to get out.

We did. He got out and came around to the back of the car. He pulled his revolver out of his holster and told us to walk out into the middle of a field.

"Sir, I don't think you need to do this," the Old Man said in a shaky voice.

"Be quiet, young man," Earl said. In the center of the field he told us to stop. There was no one else around. There was no use in running. "Now get on your knees. Both of you."

We got on our knees. "Are you a praying man?" he asked.

"Not really," the Old Man answered.

"Do you read the Good Book?"

"The boy does."

"Why don't *you*?"

"I don't – I don't really believe in it."

"Have you been washed in the blood?"

"I have," I blurted out, remembering Reverend Welles's words.

"So you've been baptized?" the sheriff asked.

"Reverend Welles dunked me but good," I said.

"Then your name's already written in the Lamb's Book of Life," Earl said, pleased. "But *your* name's not yet written there," he told the Old Man. "You're still under contract to Lucifer. Do you know how to get your name written in the Lamb's Book of Life, son?"

"No."

"Then repeat after me."

Then, at gunpoint, Sheriff Earl led the Old Man in his own stylized version of the sinner's prayer.

"Lord, I'm sorry I hired myself out to the Devil and have collected his wages all these years." Then he stopped while the Old Man repeated it. "I promise to leave the Devil's wicked orchard and toil in the fields of righteousness from now on." The Old Man repeated it word for word. "Please help me be fruitful and set a good example for my boy, so he may be brought up in the right ways of the Lord. Amen." The Old Man finished up reverently.

"Thank you, sir. I feel so much better already."

"But you ain't been washed in the blood yet."

"Sir?"

"You still need the *dunking*," Earl explained. "Your boy here knows what I'm talking about. You don't get your name written in the Lamb's Book of Life without the *dunking*."

"No, sir."

"So here's what I'm going to do," Earl went on. "I'm going to let you fellas go so long as you promise to go to the first preacher you can find and get yourself dunked. You understand? Don't wait – you got to strike while the iron's hot."

"Yes, sir."

"And son, you make sure your Old Man here follows through with it, you got it? Don't you let him off the hook, now."

I nodded.

"Good boy," Earl said, holstering his gun. "You two can go now. You walk right along this road and it'll take you right into the next county. I don't want to see ya'll back in these parts again, you hear? Now get walking."

We started walking back to the road.

"Don't forget to get dunked, and I mean all the way under, now," he called after us. "And no more of this violin nonsense, you hear?"

We got to the little dirt road and started walking east. Earl got back into his car, turned around, and drove back the other way.

As we walked, I could tell the Old Man was relieved. No jail time, no standing up in front of some strict country judge and getting the book thrown at him. I mean, Sheriff Earl was pretty nutty and all, but he turned out to be harmless in the end. On the other hand, we were stuck out in the middle of nowhere with no car and only the few dollars the Old Man had in his pocket. There was no telling where Darleen was, or if we'd ever see her again.

We walked and walked and walked along fields of corn and wheat and green beans and cabbage. Finally, a farmer came along and gave us a ride in the back of his old truck. When we got to the main highway, he pulled into a gas station and told us it was the end of the line because he was just going to head back the way he'd come after filling up.

The Old Man thanked him and went inside the gas station to buy us two bottles of cold pop because we were so thirsty from walking. We sat in the shade under the overhang of the front of the station and drank them down very quickly. It was as refreshing as heaven, even with the fizzy carbonation tickling our noses.

"We gotta get you dunked," I reminded him.

"I don't see any churches around here," the Old Man replied. I knew it would be a real fight holding him to it, but I promised Earl that I would try, so try I would.

We spent most of the rest of the day trying to thumb a ride along the highway. The only takers we got were a pair of sisters – Patty and Lizzie – who said they were on their way to visit a sick aunt in Muncie. They were probably in their late twenties and Patty was pretty normal looking but Lizzie was tall and probably weighed close to three hundred pounds. They were really nice but Lizzie kept turning around in her seat and looking at me and messing up my hair and pinching me on the cheek and stuff. As we drove on she got even more "handsy" with me, and I felt like telling her to knock it off and keep her hands to herself but I didn't want to be rude on account of them giving us a ride and all.

"So what are two boys doing hitchhiking along the highway like that?" Patty, who was doing the driving, asked in a pleasant voice. She was kinda the pretty one, and kept eyeing the Old Man in the rearview mirror.

"Oh, you know, just out seeing the country," the Old Man said.

"Headed anywhere special?" Patty asked. She licked her lips and winked at him in the rearview mirror.

"Not really," the Old Man said. "Just leaving that part up to fate, I guess."

They both seemed very happy and merry and conversational and laughing and having a good time. Patty was really laying it on thick with the Old Man, laughing and smiling and flirting with him every chance she got, even though he didn't do anything to encourage her. The other one, Lizzie, kept looking at me and smiling with her big, thick, lipstick-covered lips.

"I've got a nice plump little brother just like you back home," Lizzie said, reaching around and tickling my waist inappropriately. "And I just want to squeeze him so tight and pop him just like a tick!"

Yeah, everybody seemed in a good mood, but I remember thinking there was something really *off* about the whole thing, too.

Anyway, at one point, Patty pulled the car off the main highway and drove a couple of hundred yards down a side road. She found a secluded place hidden by a grove of trees and stopped.

"What are we doing here?" the Old Man asked.

"I don't know," Patty replied. "What *are* we doing here?"

"I don't get you," the Old Man said.

"I don't get *you*," Patty said. The sisters laughed simultaneously. I started getting a real creepy feeling.

"Uh, girls, I'm not sure what's going on here," the Old Man said.

"He's not sure what's going on here," Patty said strangely to Lizzie. Lizzie looked at the Old Man and said, "We just want to have a little fun, Pops. You like to have a little bit of fun sometimes, don't you?"

"Okay, thanks for the ride," the Old Man said. "We can walk back to the highway on our own." He started to open the door but Lizzie reached into the glove compartment and pulled out a revolver. She aimed it right at the Old Man and he stopped.

"What are you doing?" he asked.

"Oh, honey — I told you: we're just going to have a little bit of fun here, that's all."

"Yeah – you know, some good, clean *fun*," Patty said, smiling.

"Not with the boy here," the Old Man said.

"Come on, it's just a little harmless fun," Lizzie said. "I mean, nobody's gonna get *hurt* or anything..."

They made the Old Man strip down to his t-shirt and boxers. Patty kept reaching back and snapping the waistband of his shorts. "What you got in there? Huh? What you got in there?" she asked in a psycho-playful voice.

Then Patty carefully tied his hands behind his back with a nylon pantyhose while the other one held the gun on him and giggled maniacally. Patty went to work on the Old Man while Lizzie scanned the radio for a pop Hit Parade station. Patty applied red lipstick and eyeliner on the Old Man, purposefully smearing it in a creepy, clownish way. Then she pulled out a woman's wig and put it on his head, slightly askew.

Patty pulled a cigarette out of her purse and lit it. Only it didn't look like any of the cigarettes I'd ever seen. It was kind of funny-shaped and smelled real bitter. Patty took a long drag on it and reached over to let her sister take a puff. Both of them giggled in an odd way as they exhaled the heavy, bitter smoke. Lizzie reached under the seat and pulled out a fifth of bourbon. She knocked it back and took a long slug, then handed the bottle to Patty.

Patty climbed into the backseat and sat on the Old Man's lap. She took a drink of bourbon, then put the funny cigarette up to the Old Man's lips.

"No," he said, turning his head away.

"Aw now, you're no fun at all," Patty said, forcing his head back around and putting the cigarette between his lips. He took a small puff.

"Come on, Pops – it doesn't do any good unless you *inhale*," Patty said. Then she held the bottle up to his lips and made him drink.

I must have looked traumatized, because Lizzie said, "Relax, kid. This is just how girls unwind these days. We're just having a good time, you know? Here, give the kid a little puff of the magic stuff, Patty."

"No!" the Old Man said. His eyes looked a little unfocused and red. "Leave the kid alone!"

"Aw, it won't hurt him," Patty said, holding the funny cigarette up to my mouth.

"I don't want to," I said.

"You guys are no fun at all," Lizzie, the big one, said. I could tell she was just about to force it into my mouth when somebody reached through her open window and smashed her in the back of the head with a big rock. Lizzie's eyes rolled up into her head and she went down, slumped over the bench seat. An arm reached in and grabbed the gun out of her slack hand.

Then I could see: it was *Darleen*, and she was pointing the gun at Patty.

"Get off of him!" Darleen said. Patty got off the Old Man's lap and crawled back into the front seat.

"Who the hell are *you*?" Patty asked Darleen. Darleen grabbed the cigarette out of Patty's hand and threw it out the window.

"Kid, are you all right?" Darleen asked me.

"Yeah."

"Untie your Old Man," she said.

"Hey, what is this?" Patty demanded. The cigarette she'd been smoking seemed to make her slow and groggy. "We were only trying to have a little fun..."

I got the Old Man untied and found a rag for him to wipe off the lipstick with. Then he got dressed and we got out of the sisters' car. Darleen told us to stand away from the car while she shot out all four tires. Then she threw the gun into some bushes. I saw the Old man's car parked a couple of yards away.

"Key's in the ignition," Darleen said. "Let's go."

We piled into the Old Man's car – him and me in front, and Darleen in her customary place in the backseat. The Old Man started it up and drove us back up the road to the main highway.

"Where did you learn to shoot a gun like that?" the Old Man asked.

"Cop shows on television," Darleen answered without missing a beat. The Old Man got on the highway and headed east. Boy, was I glad to see good old Darleen again.

"I knew something was wrong when you never came out of the diner," Darleen said. "So I hopped in the car and took off before the police showed up. I've been driving up and down this stretch of highway ever since, looking for you guys."

She could've just taken off with the car and most of the money. She didn't have to come back for us. Darleen was a real stand-up girl, after all.

A couple hours later, it happened. The Old Man and I were listening to the radio. Darleen was in the backseat, casually thumbing through a *Life* magazine. The state trooper came out of nowhere, suddenly behind us with his lights flashing and siren blaring.

"What the..?" the Old Man looked rattled. He slowed down and pulled over onto the shoulder of the highway. Darleen put her sunglasses on and slunk down in the seat. A moment later, the trooper was at the window.

"What's the problem, officer?" the Old Man asked.

"License and registration," the trooper said.

The Old Man handed them over. "Was I speeding? Because if I was speeding, it's not really my fault, see, because the speedometer's broken and I was going to get it fixed in the next town."

The trooper looked over the documents and handed them back to the Old Man. He didn't say a word. He just looked at me and looked at Darleen in the backseat. Darleen didn't say anything. She looked kinda spooked.

The trooper motioned someone else forward. A man in a suit and nice fedora walked up and looked inside the car. He looked at Darleen.

"Can you take the sunglasses off, miss?" he asked. Darleen complied. He looked at her again, comparing her to a picture he was holding in his hand. Then he nodded at the trooper.

"Hello Becky Sue Petersen," he said to Darleen.

"Step out of the car, miss," the trooper ordered Darleen.

"What's this about, officer?" the Old Man asked.

The trooper ignored him. "Step out of the car, miss," he repeated in a serious tone. Darleen opened the back door and got out. The man in the fedora led her to the patrol car and put her in the backseat. The Old Man got out and started talking to the trooper and the man with the fedora at the back of our car. I could just make out what they were saying.

Turns out, Darleen's real name was Becky Sue Petersen. She was a rich girl who ran away from home several months before. Her old man owned a car dealership in Kansas. The man with the fedora was a private dick her old man hired to track her down and bring her home.

The Old Man swore he had no idea. He told them she was just some hitchhiker we were giving a ride to – just some girl wanting to break into television in New York City. He left out the part about the violins.

They bought it. They apologized for the inconvenience and thanked him for his cooperation. Then the Old Man opened the trunk and pulled her suitcase out. The private dick took it and put it in the trunk of the patrol car.

And that was that. We watched the patrol car pull away and head back to Indianapolis, with Darleen – Becky Sue Petersen – in the back.

We sat there thinking about what had just happened for a while. The backseat seemed emptier and the car seemed a lot quieter without her. He would never have admitted it, but I actually think the Old Man felt a little lost.

Until he checked the glove compartment.

"Where's the envelope?" he asked, in a panic.

"What envelope?"

"The envelope – the one with all our cash in it – did you take it?"

"No."

"There was over three hundred dollars in there!"

He stopped and thought a moment. "That little..."

I was about to say we should go find the state trooper and get the money back, but I realized we couldn't do that. Then he'd find out about the violins and we'd all be in the hoosegow.

The Old Man was quiet. I think his pride was hurt the most – being had by a *girl*. Anyway, he just wasn't the same for the next few days. All we had left was whatever he had in his pockets – about thirty-eight dollars and some change. Oh well – there went the nice motels and fancy breakfasts every morning. Back to eating hamburgers and sleeping in the car, I guess. When the money started to dwindle, the Old Man went back to scrounging up dice games and hustling pool for a few lousy bucks.

After a few days, the Old Man's anger began to wear off and he started acting like himself again. It was a lot quieter without Darleen's constant chatter, but we both sort of missed her, too.

Then, in Dayton, we stopped at a drive-in diner and ordered the usual burgers and milkshakes. But instead of the carhop, it was good old Darleen who brought our orders to our car.

"Hi, boys. Miss me?" She hooked the tray to my window and beamed us a big smile. There was a fat envelope on the tray with our food. "The meal's on me. Oh, and here's your three hundred dollars back, with interest. Thanks for the loan. It was seed money for a little hustle I pulled in Indianapolis. I made enough to get me all the way to New York City in style. So I bought a ticket to travel the rest of the way by bus."

"But, how did you get away from the State Police?" the Old Man asked.

"I pulled the old bathroom stop routine, then climbed out the bathroom window. Works every time."

She hopped in the backseat and chatted while we ate our burgers. "Well, guess I gotta be going now. Don't want to miss my bus." She looked around the inside of the car. "Gee, I'm really gonna miss this old car!"

Then she reached over and tousled my hair. "See ya later, kid! Look me up if you ever get to the Big Apple!"

And she was gone.

Chapter 7

Needless to say, I was having the time of my life – until we hit Cleveland.

We drove around town aimlessly for a while. I thought the Old Man was just looking for his next game, but then he pulled up in front of a big old house. It was painted a faded peeling yellow, with white trim and eaves, and dormer windows. It was going for cheery, but somehow missed by a mile or two. It had a sign out front that read "*Madame Adrienne, Psychic, Divination, Palm Reader.*" Definitely not your typical gambling den.

"What are we doing here?" I asked suspiciously.

"This is my older sister Evelyn's house."

"You have a sister?"

"Look, Sport, the last few weeks have been a real blast, but I need to leave you here for a while."

"Leave me *here?*"

"Yeah, just for a while. I gotta swing down to Florida and find your mother. When I find her, I promise we'll come back and get you. Then we'll be a real family again."

"Take me with you!" I begged.

"Sport, I can't. I gotta do this alone. I'll be back, I promise..."

"What if she won't come back with you?"

"She will. I gotta plan for that. Don't you worry."

I took another look at the house, and that creepy sign. "I don't wanna stay here! I wanna go to Florida with you!"

The Old Man didn't say anything, just looked straight ahead through the windshield. I got the message. I got my cowboy hat and new suitcase and the Bible, and got out of the car.

"Look, I'll see ya in a few weeks, Sport."

"You're not coming in?"

"No, I better not. We don't...we never got along very well. She's expecting you, though. I called from Dayton. Go on in now."

He waited at the curb while I slouched up the front walk and rang the doorbell. I had to ring it three times. When the door finally opened, I saw the car slink slowly away out of the corner of my eye.

A woman answered the door and stared down at me blankly for a few seconds. She was tall, a little on the heavy side, wearing a pair of white capri pants and a yellow blouse with the sleeves rolled up, exposing her plump white arms. She wore cat-rimmed eyeglasses and had a large red mole on her upper lip. Her bleach-blonde hair was tied up in a red-checkered scarf. I thought she looked a bit like Rosie the Riveter, only older.

Finally, she spoke. "Oh, you must be the kid."

"Calvin."

"Whatever. Come in and sit down and be quiet. I'm in the middle of a session right now."

I hauled my suitcase inside and set it down in the foyer. She pointed at a chair opposite the door, and I sat down as she walked back into the front parlor. By leaning forward slightly, I could just see another woman, this one a few years older than Aunt Evelyn, sitting at a card table near the fireplace. This woman was better dressed, in a very neat blue housedress and pearls, and wearing nice shoes.

Aunt Evelyn sat down opposite the woman, who got right down to business.

"I want to contact my dead husband."

"I don't do séances," Aunt Evelyn said curtly.

"But I have something very urgent to tell him!"

"Look," Aunt Evelyn said bluntly. "I read Tarot Cards and tea leaves. I'll tell your fortune and do your astrological forecast. I'll even read the lines in your palms. But for the last time – I don't do séances!"

The woman pulled a crumpled-up shirt out of her handbag. "Look at this!"

"What is it?" Aunt Evelyn asked.

"It's his favorite golf shirt."

"I don't understand," Aunt Evelyn said. "Does he need it? I mean, where he is now?"

"Of course not. About a month before he died, this shirt went missing. He accused *me* of throwing it away. 'You always hated that shirt,' he said. Then he died. Well, last week I found his shirt. And do you know where I found it?"

"The suspense is killing me," Aunt Evelyn dead-panned, lighting a Lucky Strike.

"In his *golf bag*. I didn't throw it away! He left it in his golf bag, and forgot all about it! Don't you see? He owes me an apology! I want you to find him, tell him where I found the shirt, and get him to *apologize* for all the mental pain he's caused me since his death!"

Aunt Evelyn took a long drag on her cigarette and exhaled loudly. "Mrs. Waggoner. As I said before, I can advise you about whether or not to go into business with a stranger, make a large investment, or purchase a major appliance. I can tell you to be wary about family members you haven't seen in years and people from your distant past. I can tell you who you can trust and who to avoid at all costs. I can tell you whether your daughter should marry that foreign man she met in the produce section last week, or whether your brother should quit his job as a stockbroker and move to Costa Rica to take up basket weaving. I can tell you not to ride the bus on Mondays or wear black on Fridays. I can even tell you whether you're about to come into a large sum of money or get audited by the IRS. But I'm going to say this for the last time, and I hope you understand me clearly – *I don't contact dead people.*"

"Well, I suppose I shouldn't waste any more of your time, then," Mrs. Waggoner said, stuffing her husband's shirt back into her purse and standing to go. "I'll just have to find another medium with better contacts on the other side."

"Good luck with that," Aunt Evelyn smiled insincerely. "I'll see you out now."

When Mrs. Waggoner was gone, Aunt Evelyn closed the front door and said, "God, I need a drink..." She went into the kitchen and poured herself a glass of Johnny Walker, then came back out to the foyer. I was still sitting in the chair.

"Look, kid, I don't cook, so you'll have to fend for yourself. Just take whatever you want in the kitchen, and try not to make too much of a mess." She walked into the parlor, plopped herself down on the couch, and began thumbing through a *Look* magazine.

"Where – umm, where should I put my suitcase?" I asked.

"There's a couple of spare bedrooms upstairs," she replied distractedly. "Knock yourself out."

I stood up and picked up my suitcase. To my right there was a den with a television set. *Bingo!*

"Does that TV set work?" I asked.

"How should I know?" she asked, fully engrossed in an article on the French Riviera. She paused long enough to light up another Lucky Strike, then continued reading.

I took my suitcase upstairs and found a bedroom with a pink bedspread and frilly curtains. That certainly wouldn't do. Down the hall was a more suitable room, with a brown bedspread and curtains, and a big roomy bureau for the few articles of clothing I had collected on our recent road trip across the continent. I put the Bible and my lucky Buffalo nickel and my Lone Ranger and Tonto pocket knife on the bedside table and carefully set my cowboy hat on top of the bureau. Then I unpacked my socks and underwear and my one extra t-shirt and put them neatly in the bureau. Everything fit easily into one humongous drawer.

I felt hungry, so I went back downstairs and found the kitchen. Aunt Evelyn was still drinking and smoking in the front parlor. I opened a few cupboard doors but found nothing much to eat in them, only a few dusty plates and glasses.

The centerpiece of the kitchen was a big gleaming Frigidaire refrigerator. The latest model, right off the showroom floor. I opened the freezer door and struck pay-dirt: stacks of TV dinners and packages of frozen fish sticks and tator tots. *Eureka!* Just about every kid food group represented here, all in one place. Things were beginning to look up!

I turned the oven on and popped a TV dinner in. Twenty minutes later, I took my royal feast of Salisbury steak and mashed potatoes into the den and gingerly turned the TV on. *Magic touch* – it warmed up and crackled to life with a gentle pop and a whiff of hot cadmium. Good old Motorola – the picture was clear and bright and beautiful. *Wheel of Fortune* and the *$64,000 Question* never looked so good!

When I turned the TV off to go to bed, I went into the parlor to say goodnight to Aunt Evelyn. But she was passed out on the couch, an empty glass and half a bottle of Johnny Walker sitting on the coffee table.

I went upstairs and laid on the bed and stared at the ceiling. I picked up my lucky Buffalo nickel and ran my finger over the smooth, worn Indian head on the front for a while and thought about the old Indian. Unless he wasn't any good at telling the future, he was dead now. Weren't all Indians supposed to be good at telling the future, though? Then I thought about the Old Man. Where was he right now? On his way to Florida, I guessed.

I put the Buffalo nickel back on the bedside table and picked up the Bible. I ran my fingers over its rough leather cover and felt the indented letters of 'Holy Bible' and thought about Reverend Welles and his wife. Why did I run back inside the house to get it that day? Why did I love this book so much? I didn't know the answers.

As was my habit, I let the Good Book open itself. It usually picked a really good part to open to. Tonight was no exception. It was the part where men were multiplying on the face of the earth like rabbits and there were getting to be a lot more people around and a lot more women too, and the Sons of God saw that the daughters of men were beautiful and took as many as they wanted for wives. And the daughters of men bore children with the Sons of God, and these children, called Nephilim, were kinda like super heroes or something because they were half human and half something else.

Then I remembered Reverend Welles giving a sermon about this, and how he said the Sons of God were fallen angels and they weren't supposed to take men's daughters as their wives, and when they did it got things all mixed up down here on earth. So there were giants and super heroes and all kinds of mighty half-lings roaming around causing all kinds of trouble everywhere. Reverend Welles said things got so mixed up and the world got so wicked that God decided to give up on everything and just wipe everybody out and start all over.

I stopped reading and thought about it. Who could blame God for getting so sore about everything that was going on? I mean, here you went to all this trouble to create a world and everything – all the heavens and the firmament and separating the light from the dark and the waters from the heavens and all – only to have all these angels come down and decide they like the looks of these human women so much that they're going to take them as wives and create this super-race of giants and supernatural beings that don't even belong here!

So God decided to send a great flood to wipe everybody out and start over with a clean slate. There was only one guy decent enough for God to spare, and he told that guy he'd better start building a great big boat before the flood started. But, that's a whole other story...

* * *

The next morning, Aunt Evelyn was up early and already engaged in a session when I came down. Curious, I lingered in the foyer outside the parlor with my bowl of corn flakes, trying to hear what was going on over my own crunching.

There was a different woman sitting at the card table with Aunt Evelyn. This woman was younger than the last one, had shoulder-length dark brown hair, and was heavy-set, like Aunt Evelyn. She wore a colorful flower-print cotton dress and sandals. She was just finishing a cup of tea, and sat the teacup down on the saucer.

"That's good, Miss Dupree," Aunt Evelyn said. I watched as Aunt Evelyn took the woman's teacup, put the saucer upside down on top of it, and inverted them both. Then she very deliberately and carefully rotated the cup three times, and tapped the upturned bottom of the cup three times. The woman, Miss Dupree, watched intently as Aunt Evelyn executed each precise action.

Aunt Evelyn then turned the cup right-side-up and peered inside. "There we are," she said quietly. "Oh, my – there's quite a bit of information here!"

"What do you see?" Miss Dupree asked anxiously, her eyes opened wide in anticipation.

"Well, there's quite a bit here, and it's got to be done rather carefully, Miss Dupree," Aunt Evelyn cautioned. Miss Dupree nodded, but stayed silent.

"When the tea leaves are spread out, that's a sign of calmness and peace in your life," Aunt Evelyn began. "But when they're all bunched up like this, it's a sign of anxiety and turmoil."

Miss Dupree nodded vigorously. "I have been quite anxious lately, but I don't know why," she confessed.

"The reason for your anxiety is here in the leaves, waiting to be uncovered and interpreted," Aunt Evelyn calmly assured her. She squinted into the cup, turning it this way and that, and examined it in this manner for a full minute. "Hmmm. Quite interesting..."

"What is it?" Miss Dupree asked in alarm. "What do you see?"

"Who is the man with the beard?"

Miss Dupree looked surprised. "A beard? Well, that's my brother, Oscar."

Aunt Evelyn turned the cup again, still squinting into it. "Why did he go to Illinois?"

Miss Dupree looked confused. "My brother's in Idaho."

Aunt Evelyn squinted harder. "No, no, this is clearly the shape of Illinois. Who is the bearded man in Illinois?"

Miss Dupree shook her head, trying to think.

"He's got horned-rimmed glasses," Aunt Evelyn observed. "And a sleepy right eye."

Miss Dupree went white as a sheet. "Why, that's...that's Alfred."

"Yes, Alfred," Aunt Evelyn repeated. "He is the source of your anxiety."

Miss Dupree did, indeed, look very anxious.

"There is a serpent near his right cheek," Aunt Evelyn continued. "That's a sign of caution. I also see a bridge – yes, a bridge, broken in the middle. That means he took a trip and never came back."

Miss Dupree's eyes were as wide as the saucers on the table.

"Underneath his image is the shape of a fox," Aunt Evelyn observed. "This is the sign of betrayal – and, and scissors, which means a terrible argument, a break-up..."

"Yes, yes – that's right," Miss Dupree said, wiping tears from her eyes. "I caught him with another girl. We broke up, and he went to Illinois."

"But that's not all," Aunt Evelyn cautioned. "I see another bridge – this one intact – he wants to come back to you, he wants to restore your relationship."

"He...he does?" Miss Dupree asked, hopefully.

"Yes, he does. But you must not take him back."

"Why not?"

"Because of the swan," Aunt Evelyn said cryptically.

"The swan?" Miss Dupree asked.

"The swan," Aunt Evelyn repeated.

"But aren't swans good?"

"A swan at the top of the cup is good," Aunt Evelyn agreed. "That means the swan is flying. That signifies good luck and a happy life. But see this swan here? It's at the bottom of the cup. It's not flying. Dead swans signify bad luck, and an unhappy life. And I'm afraid what you've got here is a dead swan."

Miss Dupree became too distraught to go on. She pulled a handkerchief from her purse and blew her nose. Somewhat composed, she finally said, "I'm so glad I came here. I would've taken him back, and that would've been a big mistake. I'm...I'm so grateful to you, Madame Adrienne. Now, how much do I...?"

"With the summer discount, that'll be three dollars and fifty cents."

Miss Dupree took the money from her purse and counted it out to Aunt Evelyn, then checked her makeup in a compact mirror and left the house. Aunt Evelyn stuffed the money into her blouse pocket and looked right at me. "Another day, another dollar, kid."

"Why won't you talk to dead people?" I blurted out, for no real reason.

"Come again?"

"That woman yesterday – Mrs. Waggoner – you told her you never talk to dead people."

"Oh, that. Because it gives me the willies. I used to communicate with the dead all the time, until my – I mean, let's just say I stopped a long time ago."

"Do you believe in God?" I asked.

"Anyone who doesn't believe in God is a fool, kid."

"My Old Man doesn't."

"I rest my case." She lit up a Lucky Strike and took a long puff.

"Are you a witch?"

She looked amused. "A *witch*? Oh, that's a good one, kid. Yeah, I fly around on a broom and commune with Satan and cast spells on people. No, I'm not a witch. I am a psychic. All I do is tell people's fortunes, read their tea leaves, and help them make important decisions. You know – I tell people about themselves and help them solve personal problems and stuff."

"How do you do that?"

"Come here and I'll show you."

I hesitated.

"C'mon, kid. I don't bite."

I walked into the parlor and sat down at the table. "I don't like to drink tea."

"That's not the only way. Come on – give me your hand, like this." She held her hand out, palm up. I reached out my hand. She grabbed it and nearly jerked me across the table. "Your palm can tell a person all about you and your life."

"It can?"

"Sure. But you gotta know what you're doing. See this line here? This is your Life Line. It tells all about your journey through life, what kind of life you're going to have. This line here is your Head Line. It tells all about what's going on up in your noggin – you know, what you think about, what you're curious about, what you like to learn about. This line is your Fate Line, or the Line of Destiny – very important. Ah, and this one here: this is your Heart Line."

"What does that tell about?"

"Affairs of the heart. Relationships, friendships – and *love*."

I blushed slightly. "I don't care about that stuff."

"Well, you should. Look at *your* Heart Line: long and deep. There's a lotta love in your future, kid!"

I blushed some more.

"And you really like the girls. Or you will. See how your Heart Line curves down toward your Mount of Venus down here?"

"What's the Mount of Venus?"

"Never mind, kid" Aunt Evelyn said curtly. "You're still too young to know about such things. But, I don't like this: your Heart Line has some breaks in it."

"What does that mean?"

"Well, let's just say you're going to have a lot of girlfriends when you get older. Just like your Old Man."

"Yuck!"

"You won't be saying that in a few years, kid. Oh, I like this. See how your Head Line passes right through your Plain of Mars and the Mount of Luna?"

"What does that mean?"

"Well, it means that you're going to have an excellent balance between physical strength and perseverance and emotional bravery. Most people have more of one than the other, but this balance will allow you to be successful at anything you try to do with your life. And right here, where it cuts deep into the Mount of Luna? That tells me you've got quite an imagination, intuition, and, well, look at that – a touch of psychic ability of your own."

"What's that?"

"It means you know things other people don't know. And you see things other people don't see. You know what I mean, don't you?"

I nodded slowly. I did understand. She didn't let go of my hand.

"Yes, you do, don't you? You haven't had many friends. Sometimes it's hard to relate to people, especially those your own age. You feel more comfortable around adults than younger people. Most of the time, you just like to be alone. You've felt different all your life, haven't you?"

She had me nailed. I suddenly felt uncomfortable. I wanted to let go of her hand, but she held on tight. "That's right, kid. You and I have a lot in common. A lot in common..."

"I – I don't want to hear anymore right now," I said.

She let go of my hand and I shoved it into the pocket of my jeans. I don't know why.

"Don't be ashamed," Aunt Evelyn advised. "There's nothing to be ashamed about, kid. We're just different from most people, that's all. There's nothing we can do about it."

Still, I looked away, surprised at the unintended connection we had just made. That night, I lay in bed and looked at that palm, the one Aunt Evelyn had read earlier. How could she see so much written there in those lines and creases, the young, un-calloused palm of a thirteen-year-old boy?

Within a week, I realized Aunt Evelyn had no intention of trying to "raise" me. I was pretty much on my own, making my own choices, living like an adult, but without any of the cares of an adult – no bills, mortgages, or taxes. Maybe this was going to work out after all.

She never called me by my Christian name. It was always "Kid." I wasn't exactly afraid of her, but she could be blunt, brash, and rather hard-edged at times.

"I told your Old Man not to marry that nut-job," she said of my mother, not thinking of my feelings. "But would he listen?" That was the thing about Aunt Evelyn: we seemed to get along all right, as long as we stayed out of each other's way, but she seemed to lack sympathy. Or is it empathy? Anyway, one of those. For all her *psychic ability,* she just didn't seem to think of other people's feelings.

Kinda like the Old Man.

I started to notice other things about Aunt Evelyn as time went on. Idiosyncrasies, I guess you'd call them. For instance, I noticed she never left the house. I went to the public library one day and looked it up. It's called *agoraphobia* – the fear of leaving one's home. Yeah, that was Aunt Evelyn. Never left the house. Had all the groceries and other essentials – TV dinners, frozen fish sticks – delivered once a week.

Oh, and the drinking. The Johnny Walker was delivered along with the other essentials every week. *Lots* of it. And the Lucky Strikes. The woman smoked like a chimney. Sometimes I had to go outside into the yard just to get a breath of fresh air.

Other than that, she pretty much left me alone to live my life. Except for one thing.

"When fall comes, you'll have to go to school," she told me one day.

"The Old Man's coming back before then," I told her confidently. "He promised."

She chuckled and exhaled a long stream of smoke. "I wouldn't bet on it, kid."

But after thinking about it, why not go to school? It wouldn't be such a bad thing. Besides, it was still summer, and fall was still a good ways off yet. Yeah – school might be just the ticket, after all.

Like I said – Aunt Evelyn's approach was pretty hands-off most of the time. But one time, we actually (almost) had a real conversation. I asked her who "Madame Adrienne" was.

"She was my high-school French teacher," Aunt Evelyn replied. "She was beautiful, mysterious, worldly – everything I wasn't. I guess the name just always stuck with me."

It made sense, when you thought about it. Who would ever hire a fortune teller named "Aunt Evelyn?"

There was a picture of a sailor on the mantle. I'd been dying to ask her who it was, but had been afraid to. But now that she was a veritable fount of information about Madame Adrienne, I couldn't resist. "Who's that?"

"That's Will, my husband."

"Did he die in the war?"

"No." I could sense her closing up – shoulda stopped there.

"Where is he?"

"Merchant marine. I haven't seen him for a while." She walked out of the room abruptly. Guess I pushed things too far. I didn't mention Will again, it seemed like a thorny issue for her. I just figured he had died in the war, and she just didn't want to talk about it.

Chapter 8

Well, I guess this is the part everyone's been waiting for. So, let's just put it all right out there:

I found the ghost of Joseph Stalin in Aunt Evelyn's cluttered Cleveland attic one day, while I was up there looking for her lost husband's cheap second-hand accordion.

That's a sentence I never thought I'd have to write. But it's the truth, so there it is.

But let me explain.

It all started with Dick Contino. You know, Dick Contino – the darkly-handsome 1950's accordion king and polka music superstar. One day I was browsing through Aunt Evelyn's record collection when I came across Contino's *Polka Craze* album. I put it on the record player, switched it on, and was instantly transported to the transcendent world of polka music. I'd never heard polka before, but it resonated within my soul as if I'd been listening to it my whole life. It was like a missing piece, suddenly restored, and I was finally made complete and whole.

From that moment on, all I did was listen to polka music. It drove Aunt Evelyn out of her mind. "That is the most insipid music ever devised by man!" she declared. But I loved it, especially my new hero Dick Contino, who I became obsessed with and made it my mission to find out everything I could about him. Soon I was a Dick Contino expert, waiting patiently for him to come to Cleveland on tour so I could finally meet him.

Some guys liked Frank Sinatra, other guys liked Glenn Miller. I was an un-abashed Dick Contino man. Nobody was cooler than Dick, slinging his accordion around as he pumped out feverish renditions of *Lady of Spain* or *Swinging on a Star*. And he could sing, too. He lived in Las Vegas and starred in movies. These were the days before Elvis Presley and Chuck Berry. In *my* book, Dick Contino was the first rock star. The only entertainer, to my mind, who ever came close to Dick Contino was Louis Prima.

So, there you have it. I was an unapologetic Dick Contino man hooked on the seductively propulsive rhythm of polka. How does that get me to Joseph Stalin, you ask? Be patient, it's coming.

So, if Aunt Evelyn couldn't stand polka, how did Dick Contino's seminal album end up in her record collection? The answer is simple: it belonged to her husband, Will, the lost merchant marine sailor and fellow polka fanatic. I realized right then and there that Uncle Will was a true kindred spirit, despite never having met the man.

Thank you, Uncle Will, wherever you are, for lighting the flame of polka that sat dormant within me for so long.

One day Aunt Evelyn, in a moment of weakness, confessed that Uncle Will had been such a polka nut that he even took up the accordion at one point. He went to a pawn shop and picked up a cheap, second-hand Hohner accordion for eleven bucks.

"He spent weeks trying to learn how to play it, but he was hopeless," Aunt Evelyn explained. "The man had a tin ear. No musical ability whatsoever."

A few days later, he gave up and squirreled it away somewhere in the attic.

"Then he went to sea for the last time, and never came back," Aunt Evelyn said, pouring herself a stiff glass of Johnny Walker and lighting up another Lucky Strike.

So, that's what I was doing in the attic in the first place. Looking for that old accordion. I never did find it, but I did find Joseph Stalin. Or, at least his ghost.

He was a small man, with a big grey bottle-brush mustache, sitting in an old chair smoking a cigar. He wore a generic kind of brown military jacket, and had a thick head of grey hair meticulously combed up and back from his broad, flat forehead.

He squinted at me through the cigar smoke. I froze.

"Who – who are you?" I asked.

"You can call me Uncle Joe," he said with a thick accent. "That's what FDR used to call me."

"What are you doing in Aunt Evelyn's attic?" I asked.

"Waiting for you," the old man answered. "I want to write my memoirs, and I need you to take dictation. I want to tell my side of the story. They're giving me one year to set the record straight, so we need to get started right away."

"You mean – you're *dead*?" I asked innocently.

"Don't you follow the news? I died in March – that means we have even *less* time!"

"Does this have anything to do with what goes on downstairs?" I asked.

"What, that mumbo-jumbo? No, I'm afraid your aunt is a big fake, my boy."

"Then why did you choose *me*?"

"Because you've got good penmanship," Uncle Joe answered, taking a long puff of his cigar. "And you don't have any friends or pets. That keeps things uncomplicated. And you're not good at sports. That will keep you focused. Plus, I like this attic – cozy. I like the view from the window. The neighbor's backyard is well-organized and the hedges are neatly trimmed."

"You speak English very well."

"Do I? I hadn't noticed. Once you've crossed over, you quickly find the tongue is able to accommodate any language necessary."

We looked at each other a while without speaking. "Well, go get some paper, and something to write with," the dictator finally ordered. "We've got a lot of work to do!"

I ran downstairs and found a Big Chief writing tablet and pencil on a desk in Aunt Evelyn's study. She was reading Tarot cards with a client in the front parlor, and didn't notice me. I went back up to the attic half expecting the chair to be empty, the previous conversation to be a hallucination, but the old man was still sitting there, smoking his cigar and gazing pensively out the attic window. He was so caught up in his thoughts that he didn't seem to notice I was back.

"I've got it," I said, interrupting his reverie. "I've got the paper."

He turned his glare on me. "Do you know anything about me?"

"You – you ran Russia, or something..."

"Russia, ha!" he laughed. "The *Soviet Union*! I built it! With my bare hands and by my sheer will! But, how could *you* know? Your media is too preoccupied with movie actors and singers to worry about important world events."

"Yes, sir."

"Sit down," he ordered. "We'll begin now."

I found an old box to sit on and balanced the tablet on my knee, ready to write. I waited while he puffed his cigar and thought. I began to realize that as much as he puffed on that cigar, it never got any smaller.

"Sir? I'm ready to write," I reminded him.

"I'm thinking," he said absent-mindedly.

"Sorry. Is this going to be a true story, sir?"

"Of course it's going to be true!" he bristled. It was then that I noticed he had a little bit of a short fuse. "These will be my memoirs, the story of my life! To counter-act all of the lies and false information perpetrated by my detractors and enemies!"

"Yes, sir. Sorry again, sir."

"And stop calling me 'sir!'" he blared. "We're going to be spending a lot of time together. I told you to call me Uncle Joe."

"Okay, Uncle Joe," I said.

He puffed on his everlasting cigar in silence a few more minutes before nodding his head ever so slightly and launching in. "I was born in a small village in Georgia, to a humble cobbler and his washerwoman wife. We were very poor, and my father was an alcoholic who beat us mercilessly. My mother was a very religious woman, very close to God. She prayed constantly and read the Bible every day. She taught me how to read the Bible, too. I enjoyed reading it – I remember being fascinated by all the stories and heroes of the Old Testament."

I stopped writing and looked at Uncle Joe in surprise. "I like reading the Bible, too."

"You see, I was a small boy, and weak as a child," he continued. "I had smallpox when I was seven. A few years later, a carriage accident left my arm nearly useless for the rest of my life. And, I was bullied by the other boys."

"*You* were bullied?"

"That's right. But reading the Bible gave me strength. I wanted to be strong, like Samson. I wanted to be confident, like King David. I wanted to be a strong leader, like Moses. I wanted to be cunning, like Jacob. My mother enrolled me in the church school in our village. She wanted me to become a priest. Are you getting all of this down?"

"Yes, Uncle Joe."

"Are you writing neatly?"

"Yes."

"Good. Now, where was I?"

"You were bullied by the other children, and your mother wanted you to become a priest," I reminded him.

"Ah, yes," he nodded, puffing his cigar. "But I was smart. I figured out a way to handle the bullies. Not by fighting them, I was much too small for that. I figured out another way. I simply made friends with the biggest, strongest boys I could find. Soon, I had them all on my side, under my control. Even the bullies came around and became my friends."

"How did you do that?" I asked, genuinely interested.

"Easy. I discovered very early that I had a gift of charisma," Uncle Joe explained. "A seduction, if you will, which I was able to exercise over people and eventually bend them to my will. Not through flowery words, like Trotsky – no, through attitude, determination, *sheer will*. I can't explain it, other than to say I've always had the talent of being able to get people to *follow* me."

"What did your father think about you becoming a priest?" I asked.

"He wasn't around much by that time," the old man said ruefully. "My mother started standing up to his abuse at that point, and he didn't care for that much. So he moved to another town and only visited on holidays. Actually, my mother and I were very happy with this arrangement, as the daily beatings had naturally stopped."

"Gee, things must have gotten a little better after that, huh?"

"For a time," he said. "I was going to church school, where I excelled at my studies and was a top student. I had all the boys in the palm of my hand, I was devout and pious and on my way to becoming a priest, and my mother was very happy and proud of me. I loved music and was a very good singer. I was often chosen to sing the penitential prayers at church fasts. I was a scrawny, dark-haired scarecrow of a kid, but for some reason I was extremely popular. Boys – and girls – all wanted to be around me. Yes, I had several girlfriends hovering around, all vying for my attentions. I began to take it for granted. Yes, things were going along rather well." The old man smiled at the memories.

"What happened next?"

"I was on fire for Christ. I was certain God had chosen me. I knew the Bible better than anybody in my class. In fact, I did so well in church school that I earned a full scholarship to a seminary in a big city called Tiflis. This was unheard of for someone from my village, someone like me. But there I was, in the big city, on my way to my dream of becoming a priest and serving God for the rest of my life."

"Did you really want to be a priest?" I ventured. "Or did you just want to please your mother?"

I was ready to receive a rebuke, but he didn't take offense. "At that time, I did want to be a priest – to start out. Of course, for me, being a priest in some out-of-the-way village wasn't going to be enough. No, I was more ambitious than that. In a few years, I was going to run the whole *Church,* and nothing less. And my teachers at the seminary only fed my ego. I soaked up their knowledge like a sponge. I learned everything they had to offer, and wanted more. My mind seemed bottomless. I was the smartest one there. I was their star pupil. Before long, I was *running* the place.

"But it wasn't enough," he continued honestly. "All of their praise, all of their rewards, all of their accolades – it wasn't enough. There was something missing. The seminary, as large as it was, became smaller and smaller in my mind. Then Tiflis itself – a fair-sized city – became too small for my ego. Soon, thoughts of even running the Georgian Church were not enough. I felt lost – there had to be something *bigger*, something *greater*, for me. I had to have a destiny that *mattered*, that better fit the size of my ambitions. I had learned everything the seminary had to teach, except for one thing: humility. Humility was a concept I'd never been able to grasp. And I began to lose interest in the seminary, in God himself. That's when God became mute, and I fell into a chasm of despair. A crisis of faith. It was a real turning point. I knew one thing: that I had to leave the seminary. But I couldn't tell that to my mother – it would have *killed* her. So I continued on, a non-believing charlatan, a hypocrite, pretending to be the rising star and hating myself for continuing to perpetrate the charade. I was in hell.

"Then it happened. I found my true calling. It dropped into my lap like a beautiful, unexpected gift. You see, for several years, the revolutionaries had been quietly infiltrating the seminary. I had been so caught up in my own clerical ambitions that I hadn't even noticed. Then one day someone gave me a pamphlet, and the Light came on! Of course, the system was rotten, corrupt, rigged against the poor! That was what was wrong with the world! It didn't need more of God – it needed *revolution*! The system didn't need to be fixed – it needed to be utterly *destroyed*, razed to the ground! It was so sick, nothing else would do – nothing but utter annihilation! And from that moment on, I knew what I was to do.

"When I became a revolutionary, I knew I had to leave the seminary. I was always in trouble for insubordination, for reading Karl Marx and other revolutionary materials. I was trying to get kicked out, on purpose, so I wouldn't have to tell my mother that I left voluntarily. Then it happened, and I was a free man! Free to pursue my own agenda, fulfill my own destiny, make my mark on the world. My mother was devastated, of course. She didn't understand the revolution. But I was all in. I knew it was the reason I was born. There was no turning back for me. The Revolution became my religion.

"Listen to me, young man. When you find your true calling, you know it. You *feel* it. Suddenly everything makes perfect sense. The feelings of confusion and uncertainty all melt away in a second. In my boyhood village there was a ruined castle. Near that castle was a huge, perfectly round boulder. It was too large and heavy for anyone to move. Nobody knew who placed it there, or how it became so perfectly spherical. There was a legend that an ancient giant named Amiran was kept chained up in the Caucasus Mountains because he was considered a demon of destruction. But once a year his captors, the gods of the Caucasus, would unchain him and allow him to come down and play with that huge stone like a toy ball. I grew up hearing this story, this myth, and was always fascinated, yet greatly troubled by it. As I grew up, this story, and the anxiety it caused me, never left me. It was like a thorn in my side, and, as much as I tried, I could never forget it or escape its dark fascination.

"But when I left the seminary and became a revolutionary – when I abandoned God and gave my life to the Revolution – the story of Amiran the giant and that great stone was transformed from a thorn in my side to a healing balm that soothed my aching soul. For, you see, I finally understood: *I* was Amiran, and the ball that I would play with like a toy would be the world."

I was still writing frantically when he stopped dictating. "Did you get all of that?" he asked, his mind still racing.

"Yes, I think so..." I said, finishing up.

"What about the part about the giant playing with the ball?"

"Yes, got it."

"Good, I like that part," he nodded, puffing on his cigar. "You don't think it's too over the top?"

"It's a very interesting image."

"Yes. Look, it's very important that you get every word, just the way I say it, do you understand? Do you understand?"

"Yeah, I get it." I put the pencil on the tablet and tried to massage the writer's cramp out of my right hand.

"You're a good boy," Uncle Joe nodded. "I know I made the right choice. That's all for today. We'll continue tomorrow."

Chapter 9

Needless to say, I didn't tell Aunt Evelyn about Uncle Joe. But every day after lunch I would quietly make my way up to the attic and we would continue our work. The old dictator worked chronologically for the most part, although sometimes he would veer off down a rabbit hole about Trotsky's atrocious eating habits (he was apparently a real slob over dinner) or Lenin's often embarrassing attempts at pronouncing the word 'proletariat.'

Being one of the chief architects of the Revolution, of course, he knew where all the bodies were buried (he had personally dug the graves himself) and which skeletons were in everybody's closet. He had hundreds of stories, some of them real side-busters, others not so funny.

One day he stopped dictating and told me to put my pencil down. "This part is off the record. It's about how I won Lenin's confidence and became his right-hand man. It was during the October Revolution, and Lenin had this cozy little flat in Moscow where he liked to entertain the ladies, if you know what I mean. Well, one day he had this cute little revolutionary girl there who he'd been working on for quite a while and it finally seemed like he was going to get to first base with her when I got wind that his old lady, see, was coming in from St. Petersburg to surprise him. Well, when I heard that, I hurried over to the flat to try to beat her there and warn him, but wouldn't you know it his old lady and I arrived at the doorstep at exactly the same time and I really had to come up with something fast! So when she let herself in with her key, I quickly stepped inside in front of her and called out, 'Vlad, I just came by to pick up my sister and look who I ran into – your lovely wife!'

"Fortunately, things hadn't gone as well as Lenin had planned, and they were both still dressed, although they'd managed to kill off half a bottle of French champagne which was sitting on the coffee table with their two glasses. So I rushed in and scooped up the bottle and the glasses and stashed them under a sofa cushion before Mrs. Lenin could see them, then I swirled around and picked the girl up off the couch and kissed her on the cheek and said, 'Dear sister, we shouldn't take up any more of Comrade Lenin's time, he's a very important man and he's got this Revolution to finish so let's get going! Let's go right now so he can spend some quality time with the missus who came all the way from St. Petersburg to see him!'"

"Fortunately, the girl had the wits to play along, and I glanced over at Lenin's old lady to see if she was buying it or not. She looked at poor Vladimir like she was going to pull a rolling pin out of her skirt and start whacking away at him any minute. And whenever Lenin got nervous, he had this habit of sweating profusely and stuttering, and he was just never a good liar in situations like this, so I knew it could go either way at this point. Sweat was already pouring down his face as he stood up and faced his wife and said 'M-m-m-y dear, what a s-s-s-s-surprise!'

"I think his old lady knew something was fishy, but with me insisting the girl was my sister there wasn't much she could say and anyway she ended up not killing him so everything turned out all right in the end. And when things calmed down a bit, Lenin appointed me General Secretary of the Communist Party, and boy you should have seen old Trotsky's face when he heard about it – he turned about as red as a beet and re-fused to talk to me for six months! From that day on, I was aces with the Boss and Trotsky was on the outs. The Old Man hated Trotsky, and just put up with him to get the Revolution going in the right direction. I told him to ditch Trotsky a hun-dred times, but Lenin always said no –'We need his intellect,' he would say. His intellect! What a load of rubbish! Well, when Lenin died and I took over, I fixed that egotistical old Ukrain-ian Jew good and proper and exiled him to Mexico!"

The old dictator shook his head and laughed at the memory. "I tell you, we had to do a lot of unsavory things, like taking property from the rich and sending writers and poets to Siberia and shooting Tsar Nicholas and his family and all, but I sure miss those days sometimes!"

After that, we went back "on the record." He started telling me about what happened after the 1917 Revolution.

"You'd think after launching a successful revolution, you'd have a chance to relax and enjoy yourself a little bit," he told me with a wink. "But boy, the work was just beginning! Af-ter a revolution, everything's topsy-turvy, upside down. Every-thing's broken. Everybody thinks they know how to fix it, but nobody has a clue. You've just got to get to work and start building things up from scratch again. Somebody's got to get the trains running on time. Somebody's got to get the food back in the shops. Somebody's got to get the electricity flow-ing again. And we were still at war with the Germans! Lenin had to hand over Ukraine, Finland, and the Baltics to the Kaiser just to get them off our backs. But as soon as we made peace with the Germans, the White Russians started up, and pretty soon we were in another war – this time a Civil War, Russian against Russian, brother against brother – real nasty stuff."

He stopped short and shook his head ruefully. "It was a big mess. You know the old saying – be careful what you wish for. Lenin took it particularly hard. He couldn't get out of bed for two weeks. I had to step up and take charge until he pulled himself together – Trotsky, as usual, was completely useless, and the others were running around like chickens with their heads cut off. Once again, I was the one with the cool head, I was the one who held things together until Lenin got back on his feet."

The loquacious dictator next related the story of how he met his second wife, Nadya. "In those days after the Revolution, there was plenty of grain down in southern Russia, but none of it was getting to the cities so we had a big starvation problem. So Comrade Lenin sent me down there in my own armored train to get the grain flowing to Moscow and Petrograd. Nadya was my secretary and typist on this trip. We got to Tsaritsyn and pulled into the station and I could tell it wasn't going to be a big problem to get things straightened out. Just like we'd heard, there was plenty of food there, plenty of grain to go around, it was just a matter of the local *kulaks* and their greedy hoarding."

"*Kulaks*?" I asked.

"Peasants who were a little better off than the poorer ones," he explained. "*Kulaks* owned their own land and were getting rich off the grain they produced. Well, I knew right away that we had to put a stop to that. Comrade Lenin had already sent 'food squads' down there to loosen the *kulaks*' grip on the grain, but they were too nice and it wasn't working. So I sent the squads out in the countryside to round up about a hundred of them and bring them back to the city. Then we lined them up in the street and shot them right in front of everybody. There. Problem solved. The grain started flowing to Moscow again, and I was rewarded with another *Commissariat* by Comrade Lenin. It was there, in Tsaritsyn, when we were shooting all the *kulaks*, that Nadya and I fell in love and got married."

"Did you have any kids?"

"Two – Vasily and Svetlana," he answered, smiling slightly. "And then there was Yakov, my son from my first wife, who had died many years before. He came to live with us in the Kremlin after Comrade Lenin died. We were happy, for many years. But as the children grew, we began to quarrel, and Nadya would take them to St. Petersburg for long periods of time knowing I wouldn't be able to leave Moscow. That was her way of punishing me. We grew apart...there were...other women...it hurt Nadya, I know. She began to exhibit signs of mental problems – paralyzing depression, threatening suicide. It was very difficult to watch."

"What happened to her?"

"One night, after a party in the Kremlin, she went up to her room and shot herself in the head."

"Oh. Should I stop writing?" I quietly asked.

"No, keep writing," he sighed. "I promised them I would tell the whole truth this time."

"How did your children take it?"

"Very hard. I told them – and the public – that it was appendicitis. They never knew the truth – that she'd taken her own life." He was quiet for a few minutes, then added: "I tried to be a good husband, a good father. I loved Nadya – I loved my children. But the demands of leadership were all-consuming, and I know they never got as much of me as they deserved. But it was the way it had to be. Mother Russia – the nation I was building – had to come first. It was their sacrifice – it was *my* sacrifice."

"What about your mother?"

The word "mother" brought a smile back to his well-creased face. "Ah, Mama. She lived a good long time. I put her in a palace that used to belong to one of the Tsar's ministers – a real nice place. She had all she needed, or could ever want. Still, she only used one room in that whole palace! Dozens of rooms, and she only used one! Can you imagine? What a waste!"

"Did you see her much?"

"Not much. I tried to get her to come to Moscow, but she wouldn't leave her room. One Christmas, before Nadya died, we did go see her, though. 'Hello, Mama!' I cried, tears rolling down my cheeks. It was so good to see her. But she took one look at me and said, 'Oh, Soso (that was my nickname growing up), who exactly are you *now*?' I answered, 'Remember the Tsar? I'm like a Tsar.' And she said, 'Well, you'd have made a better priest, if you ask me.' Mama – she was just pulling my leg. She remembered everything. But it was true: she was still bitterly disappointed I hadn't become a priest!"

"What happened to your father?"

"I don't know. I never saw him again. There was a story going around that he died in a drunken brawl, but he probably just drank himself to death. I never missed him. The beatings I remember well enough, though. Did your father ever beat you?"

I was taken aback. It was the first time he'd ever asked anything about me. "No."

"That is good. I am glad. Do you have a good relationship with him?"

"Yeah, I guess so."

"I don't know what that is like."

"We took a car trip this summer – across the country, on Route 66 all the way to Cleveland."

"Yes? A boy should take trips with his father," the old dictator perked up. "Vasily and I used to take trips to the *dacha* on weekends, where we did some hunting. We never caught much, but it was good to spend time together. I wish I had had more time...Where is your father now?"

"He's in Florida, trying to find my mother," I replied. "She has...she's like your wife, Nadya was..."

"Oh," Uncle Joe nodded, getting it. It was getting late, the sun already fading outside the attic window. "I think that's enough for today, my boy. You should go spend some time with your aunt now. Family is very important – I wish I'd learned that when I was younger."

"Oh, we don't hang out much," I explained. "She kind of has her routine, and I have mine. See, I'm kind of on my own. I pretty much take care of myself now."

"Does she treat you kindly?" he asked, protectively.

I shrugged. "She's okay. She gets it that I like my space, and she likes hers, too, so it all works out pretty good."

"It sounds like you have a nice arrangement here," he observed, chewing on his cigar.

"Yeah, it's swell," I said. "Hey, what do you do up here all alone when I'm not here?"

He thought a moment, then answered, "I enjoy the peace and quiet. I lived a very noisy, demanding life. It's good to be still and think."

"Don't you ever get bored?"

"Bored? I don't understand."

"Bored. You know, tired of not doing anything."

"A little, but it's all right," he answered. That gave me a great idea.

Chapter 10

The next day, I asked Aunt Evelyn if I could move the TV set up to the attic. She looked at me like I was nutty or something, then said, "Well, as long as you're up there smoking cigars and talking to yourself every afternoon, I guess it wouldn't hurt to watch some television while you're at it. In fact, it just might help you with whatever you're going through right now!" After lunch, it took both of us about twenty minutes to lug the set up the stairs.

"Thanks," I said when we got it up there. We positioned it facing Uncle Joe's chair. He sat there, quietly watching us and puffing on his perennial cigar. I knew Aunt Evelyn couldn't see him.

"My back isn't thanking me much right now, but anything I can do to help out, kiddo!" Aunt Evelyn huffed, and headed back down the stairs. I plugged the TV set in, turned it on, and adjusted the rabbit ears until the reception cleared up.

"What is this?" Uncle Joe finally asked.

"Television," I said proudly.

"I know what television is," he growled. "But why did you bring it up here?"

"I thought you might like to watch the news," I replied. "You know, keep up with what's going on in the world. And the game shows are terrific!"

"Western news is capitalist propaganda," the old dictator said dismissively. "And your game shows are a prime example of materialistic, capitalistic greed run amuck. How can you watch such dreck?"

"Americans love winning refrigerators and new cars," I defended our national pastime. "We even love watching *other* people win refrigerators and new cars. Just try it – you'll get used to it in no time!" I changed some channels, giving a sample of daytime American TV: cigarette and floor wax commercials, some kid shows with puppets, a couple of soap operas, but the dictator didn't seem impressed.

"No Bolshoi?" he scoffed. "Where's the Moscow Philharmonic Orchestra? Soviet television has cultural programming! It educates the masses! It elevates the soul!"

"It sounds boring," I observed.

"What is it with you Americans, anyway – having to be 'entertained' all the time? What good is all this commercial pablum?"

"American TV *sells* things," I boasted. "Not only great products like floor wax and breakfast cereal, but neat things like excitement and adventure, too! Plus, it helps parents by letting the kids see all the neat things they want for Christmas and stuff."

"That's the problem with your culture," he explained. "You *have* no culture. It's all buy, buy, buy, sell, sell, sell! Carnivals, fairs, circuses, game shows – faster, higher, better! How does that feed the soul?"

I just looked at him and shrugged. I didn't know from feeding the soul – all I knew was TV was fun and addicting, and I couldn't find anything wrong with that. "It's just harmless fun."

"Fun!" he scoffed again. "Mark my words: Fun is what's going to bring your country to its knees!"

To underscore his resolve, Uncle Joe refused to watch anything I was able to tune in that afternoon. But he was whistling a different tune a couple of days later after just one episode of *The Guiding Light.* Another episode of *Search for Tomorrow,* and he was hooked. Yes, I was thrilled to discover that the crusty old dictator had become hopelessly addicted to daytime American television – specifically the soaps.

I would come up to the attic with my Big Chief tablet and freshly-sharpened pencil ready to work and he would be so absorbed in his shows that he'd barely even notice me.

"Umm, don't you think we should be getting to work now?" I would quietly ask.

"Yes, yes, just a moment – right after this show," he would say, waving his hand in the air and never taking his eyes off the screen. Of course, he would never admit it, insisting they were "silly trifles," but, as far as I could tell, he never missed an episode. I even noticed him paying more attention to the commercials, as well – possibly secretly wondering if Russian housewives could wear pearl necklaces and high-heeled shoes while they waxed their kitchen floors to a brilliant shine, just like American housewives did. Just imagine a Moscow party *apparatchik* coming home from a hard day at the Politburo, being met at the door by his perfectly-coiffed wife wearing a designer dress and holding his slippers, a freshly-poured highball, and a neatly-folded copy of Pravda. Yes sir, things could really be looking up in the old U.S.S.R.!

When his show was over, I turned down the sound on the TV and sat down on my crate to get to work. But before we started, I had a question that had been nagging me.

"What's it like?" I asked.

"What's what like?"

"You know – death."

"It's over-rated. Like reading a Dostoevsky novel – bleak, joyless, and none of the characters can cook."

"No, really. I'm serious. What's it like?"

Uncle Joe shifted in is chair. "What's with all the questions? I thought *I* was the one dictating my story."

"Okay, okay – settle down," I said calmly. "I was just asking."

The soaps were over, but I could tell he was still not ready to get down to work. He seemed distracted, and kept looking out the attic window every few seconds.

"What are you looking at?" I asked, absent-mindedly.

"Nothing!" he blustered. "Can't a fellow look out a window if he wants to?"

I got up and looked out the window myself. It was just a typical summer's day in suburban Cleveland – blue sky, clouds, trees and birds. And the neighbor lady sunbathing in a two-piece suit in her backyard. Was *that* what he was looking at? I shrugged my shoulders and sat back down.

"What's on the docket today?" I asked cheerfully, ready to work.

The old man felt like talking about his legacy. "Today, the Soviet Union is the greatest and strongest power in the world. When I started out, Britain and France were the big boys on the block. But not anymore. Britain lost her empire and France was never the same after Germany got through with her. And look at the United States, a great power, yes – but crumbling and rotting from the inside with materialistic greed and political corruption. No, the Soviet Union stands alone, the greatest superpower the world has ever known!"

He was boasting – like a guy at a bar trying to impress the ladies. Only there weren't any ladies here, just me. He looked at the window again, briefly, then quickly swiveled his gaze back to me. *Was he thinking about her? The sunbathing neighbor next door?*

"I did that! I built it – all of it – from the sweat of my own brow and by my own sheer will!" I was a bit taken aback. I'd never heard him so bellicose, so worked up before.

He talked of how, after his mentor Comrade Lenin kicked the bucket, he consolidated his power in the party and seized control before anybody even realized what had happened. Uncle Joe had been preparing for this for years, waiting patiently for the Boss to die, quietly building a party machine that was completely loyal to him and to him alone. And once Lenin was kaput, it was just a matter of carrying out the plan.

"I could have killed him anytime I chose, you know," he said of Comrade Lenin. "When he was really sick, he begged me to bring him poison so he could end his agony. It would have been easy. But I didn't. Out of respect for him, I waited."

He spoke passionately of the condition of Russia when he took power – the poverty, the economic chaos, the poor distribution of food, and the starvation and disease rampant everywhere. He had to act, he had to do something fast. In order to save the patient, he had to take drastic action. Yes, he had to do some terrible things to weed out the corruption and get control of his country. Any leader would do the same, under those conditions.

Russia was an agrarian society, fifty to a hundred years behind the West. He was determined to close the gap in an astonishing amount of time. There was food in the countryside, but the cities were starving. He needed to industrialize, and industrialize *now*. So he built factories in every city, and brought farm workers in from the countryside to man them. Then to feed the millions of new workers in the cities, he took the farms away from the peasants and nationalized them. The first priority was to feed the cities and thus keep the factories churning out iron and steel to rebuild the country. If people in the countryside had to go without food, there was nothing that could be done about that. Famines became common place, as the cities and factories grew.

He knew he had to rebuild the infrastructure – bridges, roads, highways, apartment buildings – so he began an unprecedented building boom that lasted throughout the 1930's. Many people suffered, many people starved, but they died for the Motherland, they sacrificed for Mother Russia. There was political resistance, he had to do away with it. He had to get rid of everyone in the political structure who remembered Lenin and replace them with younger men who knew only him as the Boss. That would ensure loyalty – that would ensure Russia's future. So the show trials and executions began – a whole generation of Bolsheviks had to be erased. All of his contemporaries from the Revolution were gone – either hanging from ropes or being worked to death in the Siberian gulags. It was all necessary. They would've gotten in the way, they would've impeded progress towards Uncle Joe's dream. Only he saw the big picture. Only *he* understood.

Then there was a need for more farmland, more cities, more factories, more people. So the dictator started adding countries to Russia, sticking them on like new pieces of clay being added to an already existing sculpture. Ukraine, the Baltics, Armenia, Georgia, Azerbaijan – one after another, he built the Soviet Union. He dreamed it. He spoke it. He made it happen. He willed it into being.

"There was no other way to do it," he swore. "It had to be done and it had to done quickly. The re-birth of Mother Russia had to be completed in ten years! Yes, people suffered greatly, so their sons and daughters and grandchildren could live a better life in the new Soviet Union. There was no other way.

"My detractors – I know what they say about me. They talk about all the people who died, all the people in the gulags. The trials and executions. They never had to lead. A leader who does not instill discipline is worthless. Do you think I enjoyed having people shot? It was to restore order! There's no more effective way to get control of a rebellious population than to line them up in the streets and shoot them. It's just a fact. They respect that, you see. They respect order! Even Comrade Lenin said it – 'You can't have a revolution without shooting people.' Even *he* knew!"

I was writing furiously to keep up. He seemed to notice, and got quiet for a spell. I took a moment to re-read the last few pages, and saw a problem. "Umm, if you wanted to set the record straight, win people over – I'm not sure this is really going to help you that much..."

"I'm telling the truth," he said, calmer now. "It's the truth, and they will understand it."

"If you say so," I said.

He had more to say. "You will remember I told you I went to seminary. I studied the Bible. I feel a kinship with certain figures, especially the Apostle Paul. Like him, I have no eloquent tongue, no gift for speech-making. Yes, like him I was beaten. I was imprisoned. I was exiled, went without food, went without shelter and warmth. I languished in sickness. I suffered, just like the Apostle. He suffered for his gospel, and I suffered for mine: Russia. Look at Moses, when he went up on the mountain to bring down the stone tablets and Aaron let the sons of Israel get out of control – what did he do? He had the Levites kill *three thousand* of them, just to set an example. The others saw that and fell right into line! See, he knew! He wasn't a good speaker, either – but he knew what it takes to be a leader! How is that different from what I did?"

I knew it was a rhetorical question, and he didn't expect an answer from me. He was really talking to the people who sent him here, and the future historians who would be judging him for hundreds of years. I decided to try to lighten the mood by changing the subject.

"Uh, what was FDR like?" It was the first thing that popped into my head.

He looked at me in surprise, as if to say *that's an abrupt left turn!* Then he cocked his head and thought a moment.

"He was a very reasonable man," the dictator remembered. "I first met him at Tehran in 1943. I knew right away he was a man I could do business with. But the poor fellow had a habit of talking in his sleep."

"Talking in his sleep?" I asked. "How – how do you know?"

"Oh, we had his quarters bugged," Uncle Joe admitted. "Very light sleeper. Carried on conversations with Lana Turner and Betty Grable all night. At one point, he thought he was on the phone with Adolf Hitler, and kept insisting to the *Fuhrer* that the Yankees were going to win the World Series and offered to sell New Jersey to Germany for half a million dollars and two balcony tickets to the musical *Oklahoma!*"

"What about Winston Churchill?" I asked.

"Well, I had heard that Winston fancied himself a real practical joker," Uncle Joe said. "But with me, he'd met his match. The first night in Tehran, I slipped the porters a couple of rubles to have his bed short-sheeted. He must have known we were bugging his room because he shouted 'Damn you, Joe! This has got your fingerprints all over it!' Now, Winston was a very heavy sleeper, so the next night I snuck into his room and emptied all of his expensive Cuban cigars out of his box and replaced them with cheap Turkish ones. For the rest of the conference, he had to watch me light up Cuban after Cuban while all he had to chew on were those little black Turkish dog turds!" The dictator rolled his cigar between his lips, smiling warmly at the memory.

My head was spinning with the seeming contradictions embodied in this man. The devout seminary student who enjoyed reading the Bible, eager to please his mother by becoming a priest. The ruthless revolutionary who had people lined up in the streets and shot for hoarding grain. The ambitious party boss who rounded up political opponents and sent them to Siberian work camps for the rest of their lives. The enigmatic leader who let millions starve to death in order to modernize and industrialize his new nation. The merry prankster of the Tehran Conference, playfully teasing and playing jokes on his

Allied partners as World War II raged across the globe. Which one was the *real* Joseph Stalin?

I could tell he was in a much better mood now, and I was glad to leave things on a lighter note. "Can we knock off a little early today?" I asked. I had something else I wanted to do.

"That's fine," he agreed. "We can pick it up tomorrow."

I left him watching television and scrambled down the stairs to the den. I put Dick Contino's album on the record player and carefully lowered the needle onto the first track. The sweet dulcet sounds of Dick's accordion emanated from the speakers with a warm crackle, putting me in just the right mood for what I wanted to do now. All of this writing for Uncle Joe had given me the idea of writing my own story. Not about me, I mean. A short story – fiction. I knew what I wanted to do now – aside from learn how to play the accordion and join Dick's touring band, I mean.

I wanted to be a writer.

And I thought I had just the right idea to get started. A story about my hero and soon to be friend, Dick Contino. In this story, I imagined myself replying to an ad in the paper to audition for Dick's band. I had already studied and mastered the accordion, of course, so as not to make a fool of myself. So Dick calls me back and suggests we meet and discuss things over lunch at a fancy restaurant. I would get dressed up in my best clothes and wear a silk ascot and arrive at the restaurant fifteen minutes early, to scope the place out and have time to calm my nerves. When I arrived, I would tell the maître d' in a casual tone that I would be dining with Mr. Dick Contino, Esquire, when he arrived, and that I would be happy to wait in the foyer so Dick would be able to pick whatever table he chose when he got there. Of course, he would be late, but fashionably so, because, as everybody knows, all real stars never arrive on time and the bigger the star, the later they arrive.

When Dick got there he would have a beautiful girl on each arm and he would be wearing a silk ascot, just like me. We would both tilt our heads back and point at each other's ascots and laugh heartily at how alike we already were, and everyone in the restaurant would turn and see us and wonder who that dashing young man who was about to have lunch with Mr. Dick Contino was. Some rising Hollywood star, perhaps? A brilliant, unknown musician? Or a writer of espionage novels who just flew in from London? The restaurant would be abuzz with speculation.

At the table, we would order the same thing at the same time and both laugh again, while the girls hung on our every word. During lunch we would sip tea and engage in witty urbane banter, and find that we had an uncanny amount of things in common. After dessert, Dick would wipe custard from his handsome Italian lips with a cloth napkin and say, "Well Sport, don't you think it's time I heard you play?" Then he would snap his fingers and the maître d' would produce two accordions for us and we would serenade the enchanted restaurant patrons with an impromptu duet of *Lady of Spain*.

Pleased with the outline I had just formulated in my head, I picked up a pencil and began to commit it to a new Big Chief tablet while each and every nuance was still etched in my gray matter.

Chapter 11

Like I said before, I never did find Uncle Will's old accordion. I went through that attic from one end to the other, but it wasn't there. Maybe Aunt Evelyn had thrown it out and just forgotten about it. It didn't matter anyway, because I won a brand-new accordion in a contest I read about on the back of a cereal box.

The contest caught my eye because it was all about Bible trivia, and I thought I was a shoe-in for first place, which was a new Schwinn bicycle. I shoulda been more careful with the answers though, because I got one wrong: "Who was the oldest living person in the Bible?" It was Methuselah, and I got that part right, but the second part was "And who was he the grandfather of?" I answered Lamech, but the real answer was Noah, and I shoulda known that because of the ark and everything but I didn't kick myself too much because I came in second place and won the accordion, which was better than a new Schwinn bike and what I really wanted all along anyway.

The prize accordion came on the morning I had decided to go to the public library to do some research on history so I would have something to talk to Uncle Joe about without sounding like a complete idiot all the time. It was all wrapped up in a big box with my name on it and I tore it open and pulled it out and it was so beautiful I could hardly believe my eyes. I knew it wasn't nearly as good as the accordion Dick Contino played because it had plastic keys and buttons and a fake leather strap, but it came with a lesson book and a record so I could start learning how to play songs right away.

Anyway, my first lesson would have to wait because I wanted to get to the public library early enough to do a bunch of research and get home by lunchtime to work with Uncle Joe. I hopped on the number 13 bus on the corner and got off at the library a few minutes later. It was a weekday so there were only a few people there that early. I walked right up to the librarian's desk and the librarian asked if she could help me.

I told her I was looking for books on Russian history, and maybe a book or two about World War II.

"Do you know how to use the Dewey Decimal Classification System?" she asked. It sounded like a challenge.

"I don't think so, Ma'am."

"Well, our books are organized according to the Dewey Decimal Classification System," she explained. "The Dewey Decimal Classification System was created by Melvil Dewey in 1876. Mr. Dewey was a pioneer in American librarianship, or, as I like to call it, the library arts. He was also one of the founders of the American Library Association, and served as its president in 1891 and 1893. In his hallowed system, each book is assigned a particular number. That number combined with the first three letters of the author's last name represents the book's call number."

"I'm looking for books on Russian history, and maybe a book or two on World War II," I repeated calmly.

She pointed to a row of shelves in the corner. "Over there. Nine hundred forty."

I found a couple of books that looked interesting. One was about Tsar Nicholas and his family. Another one was about the Bolsheviks. Since Uncle Joe had been a Bolshevik, I thought that one would really come in handy. I sat down at a table where a middle-aged couple were sitting and started to read quietly.

Immediately, the woman's gum-clacking drew my attention. She had a round face, short dark hair, and very red lipstick. The man wore round wire-rimmed glasses, a suit and tie, and had a small mustache on his upper lip. Although they were both very average-looking, I had a nagging feeling I'd seen them somewhere before. The man was methodically skimming through a stack of legal books, but the woman was reading a book called "Be the Best You Possible, in Three Easy Steps." She looked up and saw me staring at them.

"Sad, isn't it?" she said to me, clacking her gum. "I keep telling him he's wasting his time, going through all those legal books, looking for some kind of loophole that doesn't exist."

"What does it hurt, with all this time we've got now?" he retorted, picking another book out of the stack. "It's got to be here somewhere – I just know it!"

"Julius, dear," she replied. "Even if you found it, it's too late. We've already been executed. No loophole in the world can undo that."

"Well, Ethel, I've been stuck in this library for nearly two months," he complained. "You know as well as I do that we can't leave until we find it. So you go ahead and enjoy your positive thinking self-help books, but I'm going to keep looking!"

They were talking rather loudly, but nobody seemed to notice. I looked over at the librarian behind her desk, but she didn't seem to notice, either. It was like I was the only one in the library who could hear them.

Then it hit me where I'd seen them before. On TV, back in San Diego at the Welles's house. During my ill-fated birthday party.

"Excuse me, but you're the Rosenbergs, aren't you?" I timidly asked.

The woman looked surprised. "Hey, that's pretty good, kid! We've been here almost two months, and you're the only one who's ever noticed us!"

"I have this thing where I, um, can see dead people – well, not all the time, but there is this one guy in my aunt's attic that I'm kind of helping out right now, and he's pretty dead, too."

"You hear that, Julius?" she asked her husband. "The kid says he's seen other people like us."

"Uh-huh," Mr. Rosenberg grunted, still skimming furiously through the book.

"Never mind him, kid," Mrs. Rosenberg said, chewing her gum and smiling. "He's always got his head in a book. I get pretty lonely around here with no one to talk to. So, what are you doing here, anyway?"

"I'm studying history," I said. The librarian shot me a dirty look, so I lowered my voice. "So I can understand what my friend in the attic is talking about."

"You mean the other dead guy?" Ethel asked. "What is he, some kind of historian or something?"

"Well, he knows quite a bit about history, that's for sure," I answered.

The librarian looked at me again. "Young man, talking is strictly forbidden in this library – even if you're talking to yourself!"

"Sorry, Ma'am," I said.

I continued in a whisper, and Mrs. Rosenberg and I had a very pleasant chat about their life together. She told me they were both born in Manhattan, and when she was younger she wanted to be an actress and singer but ended up taking a job as a secretary at a shipping company. Then she joined the Young Communist League and met Julius at one of the meetings in 1936. They were both active in the League, organizing labor and important community events. They got married in 1939 and had two sons.

When World War II broke out, Mr. Rosenberg, who was an electrical engineer, joined the Army Corps of Engineers and started working on some top secret projects having to do with radar and guided missiles. In 1942, she said, Mr. Rosenberg was recruited by the Soviets to pass along classified information to Moscow. Over several years, Mr. Rosenberg recruited other communist sympathizers to spy for the Russians. Then Mrs. Rosenberg talked her brother, who was working on the Manhattan project to build the first atom bomb, into passing secrets to the Soviets as well.

"Didn't you feel like traitors?" I asked.

"Why should we? Look, being a Communist in 1942 wasn't that big of a deal," she explained. "It wasn't like we were selling secrets to an *enemy*. The Russians were the good guys back then – they were on *our* side!"

"But all that stuff, wasn't it still top secret?"

"Technically," she said. "But the government was sharing so much military information and weapons with them already – with the British, with the Russians – what did it matter? We were all on the same side, anyway!"

"Now, don't get upset, dear," Mr. Rosenberg cautioned. "The boy is simply asking a question."

"I'm not upset! All I'm saying is they had no right to execute us for sharing a few things with friends and allies."

A few things. Like the atom bomb.

Still, I felt kinda sorry for them, stuck here in this library until Mr. Rosenberg found whatever it was he was looking for in all those books. They seemed like a real nice Jewish couple.

I stayed a couple of hours boning up on Russian history, and it was pretty interesting stuff. For instance, I'll bet you didn't know that Nicholas became Tsar of Russia when he was only twenty-six years old, and that he married a Danish princess who had to change her name to a more Russian-sounding name like Alexandra Feodorovna. On paper, Tsar Nicholas looked like the real deal: all handsome in his dashing military uniform, beautiful wife, five good-looking kids, religiously devout – he appeared to have it all. But apparently, the truth was he was a terrible leader. No matter how hard he tried, he just couldn't seem to do anything right.

"He was out of touch with the Russian people," Uncle Joe told me when I got home that afternoon. "He was weak and ineffective, and he refused to make concessions and reforms that the workers demanded. He was tone-deaf. When the workers marched on the Winter Palace demanding reforms, he was off on a hunting trip. His Cossacks fired on the crowd, and it was all over. The Revolution had begun, and he didn't even know it."

"Who gave the orders for Nicholas and his family to be shot?" I asked.

"I was not privy to those discussions," the old dictator said gravely. "But nobody would have dared shoot the royal family without direct orders from Comrade Lenin himself."

"Wasn't there any other way?" I asked.

He puffed on his cigar a moment, thinking. "You Americans see everything – what's the expression? – through rose-colored glasses. History isn't always wrapped up in a nice neat package with pretty pink bows. It's messy. There are winners and losers. The Tsar was a loser. He ran Russia into the ground. It took me twenty years to repair the damage."

"Is that what it's all about?"

"By the time I was through, people had jobs, warm clothes to wear, food on the table," he said. "I took a backward, third-world country and made it into a modern industrial powerhouse. People could take pride in their country again. I was looked up to, as a savior of the people. Hey, this is pretty good copy – shouldn't you be getting this down?"

"Oh, yeah," I said, picking up the legal pad and pencil. I quickly scribbled down his last few lines. "What about World War II?"

"Well, that was a tough time," he admitted, grimacing slightly.

August 23, 1939. The Treaty of Non-Aggression was signed in Moscow by Germany and the Soviet Union, thus guaranteeing a German invasion of Russia would never take place.

September 1, 1939. Germany invaded Poland from the west while Soviet forces invaded from the east. Adolf Hitler and Uncle Joe split up Poland like they were sharing a birthday cake.

"It was a pretty sweet deal," Uncle Joe remembered fondly.

"So, you were actually partners with Hitler for a while?" I asked.

"On paper, at least," he confided. "But I never trusted him, and he never trusted me."

"Did you ever meet him?"

"Hitler? Strangely enough, for a time before the Great War, Hitler and I both lived in Vienna," he divulged with a sly grin. "Along with Trotsky and Josef Tito, the future dictator of Yugoslavia. Trotsky and I were hiding out until things back home cooled down a bit. Vienna in those days was the kind of place for outlaws on the run, revolutionaries looking for a cause, failed despots, and future dictators planning their great conquests. The streets were full of guys like us. So, yes, there's a good chance Adolf and I ran into each other in a café or brothel without knowing it."

"Gee, that's fascinating," I commented.

"Yes, now that I think of it, Trotsky must have known him," Uncle Joe continued, rubbing his chin. "Leon had this girlfriend he saw every night at the Café Central, and I remember him telling me about this irritating little man with paint under his fingernails and a funny mustache who was always trying to steal her away from him. He was a wild-eyed Austrian who

put everybody off with his talk of 'racial purity' and 'social order.' He would get so wild when he talked that flecks of spittle
would fly out of his mouth and into everyone's coffee. He was
always carrying a rolled-up canvas and dirty paintbrushes under his arm, and always trying to get someone else to pick up
his tab. Yes, I'm sure that was the *Fuhrer*."

"How did you feel when he invaded Russia?"

"I realized I had made a deal with the Devil, and got burned."
Uncle Joe's face turned dark. "He thought his *blitzkrieg* would
shock my armies into deserting. He thought his dive bombers
would frighten the population into giving up and over-throw-
ing me. But he was wrong. He didn't know the Russian people.
He underestimated the punishment Russians could endure for
their country and their leader. And they did. They suffered
greatly in that war."

He went on to explain the whole thing. It was Russia's dark-
est hour. He had to save the homeland once again. The Red
Army was falling back, retreating along the whole front. The
Germans were driving hard and deep into Russian territory,
and they seemed unstoppable. There was panic in the streets,
refugees, civilians, and defeated troops fleeing east to get away
from the Germans.

"When we realized we couldn't stop them at the border, I
got an idea," the dictator said. "Let them come. Russia is a
huge country, there wasn't enough of them to fill it up. So, let
them come. Draw them in so deep that they'll never be able
to get out. Let the vastness of Russia swallow them up. And
it worked. The farther they drove into Russia, the smaller they
became. And I still had a few tricks left up my sleeve..."

He told me how he disappeared for several days, hold up in
his *dacha* in the countryside. His ministers and generals didn't
know where he was. Years later, historians would write that he
was despondent, that he couldn't show his face at the Kremlin,
that his confidence was shaken. But he had a plan.

"It was a test," he told me. "I was testing my ministers, my generals. I was trying to see who would betray me, and who would stay loyal in my great time of trial and doubt. If I were sick, or incapacitated, that would be seen as a sign of weakness, the perfect chance to take me out. So I waited, alone, isolated in my *dacha*, to draw my enemies out, to see what they would do. But there was no coup, no insurrection against me, no talk of replacing me. Quite the opposite: my absence taught them how much they *needed* me."

But the old trickster wasn't through yet. When he emerged from his isolation, he looked haggard and unwell, on purpose. He dressed and acted like a lost, defeated man. His ministers were shocked at his appearance. He played along with his own game, confessing that he'd let them down, that he'd brought catastrophe upon Russia, that Comrade Lenin would be ashamed of him if the great man were still alive. His ministers were distraught at his words, speechless seeing their Boss in such a state.

"That's when I told them I was going to quit," he said. "Resign. Leave Moscow forever. I told them any one of them could take my place – any man, just step forward, and the job would be his. That was his chance – if there was a traitor among them, he would not be able to resist such an offer. And do you know what they did? They *begged* me to stop talking like that. They told me no one among them could take my place. They said I and I alone could save Russia. That's right: nobody wanted my job after all. They had passed the test. I was relieved, because if any man had stepped forward, I would have had to have one of my friends shot. Maybe they knew I was bluffing, who knows? But it worked: I stayed in power, and they were more loyal to me than ever."

But there were still the Germans, who were approaching Moscow with so sign of slowing down. Dust clouds from columns of German panzers blacked out the western skies.

Muscovites were packing up and getting ready to abandon their capital. The government was moving east to the Urals for safety.

"We had to do something with the Sacred Body," Uncle Joe said. "We couldn't let the Germans capture Comrade Lenin and have Hitler put him on display at the *Reichstag* or a carnival. It was unthinkable, so I had a special railway car fitted out for him, to keep him at just the right temperature and humidity, so he could be taken to a safe place in the east. But I didn't want the people of Moscow to lose hope, so we took him out of his mausoleum in the middle of the night and replaced him with a wax dummy, so no one would know. The people of Moscow had to go on believing that 'Lenin is with us.'"

"Did *you* leave Moscow?" I asked.

"My staff wanted me to. But I decided to stay. What kind of leader deserts his people? Besides, I was determined to stop the Germans at Moscow. And that's just what we did."

He went on to explain how. First, he called in all the commanders of the retreating units of the Red Army and had them shot – in front of their replacements.

It had an immediate affect: the Red Army stopped retreating.

Second, he called up dozens of divisions of troops he'd been hoarding and safekeeping in Siberia, and brought them to Moscow. He'd been saving them for last, letting the Germans bleed themselves dry on his older, more depleted units, which were now almost completely exhausted.

The waves of fresh troops were able to stop the Germans cold at Moscow, and the bitter Russian winter did the rest. The capital was saved.

"When I saved Moscow, and the news of the German atrocities on our civilians reached the capital, the people rallied behind me like never before," the war hero beamed. "I became like a god to them. I was invincible."

It was his finest hour. He was Stalin – Man of Steel. He was now a member of a very exclusive club: FDR, Winston Churchill, perhaps even Charles De Gaulle.

He was now the mythical giant Amiran, playing with his magnificent rock ball.

But this triumphant moment was also a time of great sorrow: Uncle Joe's eldest son, Yakov, was captured by the Germans and taken to a POW camp in Germany.

"He was a lieutenant in the Army, and I was too busy trying to save Moscow to notice that somehow he'd been sent to the front lines," the old dictator recounted gravely. "The Germans used him for propaganda, announcing that he had defected because Russia was going to lose the war due to my poor leadership. It was all lies, of course, but I believed it. Because of what they were saying, I had to disown him. I put him out of my mind as if he were dead. The Germans offered to trade him for one of their generals we had taken prisoner, but I wouldn't do it – I didn't want it to look like he was getting special treatment because he was Stalin's son. Later in the war, we got the news that he was shot while trying to escape. And that was it.

"It wasn't until the end of the war that I learned the truth. When Germany surrendered, we got the records from his POW camp and found out that he had not defected – he was captured while trying to rally his men to attack a German panzer column. He had acted honorably and heroically. He had not collaborated with them. I believe he wasn't trying to escape when they shot him. The records said the guards shouted several times for him to stop, but he kept walking toward the electrified fence. When he got to it, he simply reached out and grabbed it with both hands – they shot him while he was simultaneously being electrocuted. I believe it was suicide."

Uncle Joe bowed his head slightly, resting his chin on his chest. He looked old and small and deflated.

He wasn't the giant playing with the great boulder anymore.

Chapter 12

On the way to the library the next morning, it happened again. The bus stopped to pick up three people waiting on the corner: a man, an old lady, and a younger, elegantly-dressed blond woman. When they all three got on, the man and the old lady paid their fares and were greeted with a cheerful "Hello!" from the bus driver. But when the blond woman got on, she didn't stop to pay her fare and just walked right past the driver without a word. And the driver didn't say anything, either. He acted like he didn't even see her.

Oh no, not another one! I thought. And wouldn't you know it, she walked down the aisle and sat on the seat right next to me! What was I, a ghost magnet or something?

I looked her up and down. She was attractive, her hair pulled back into a bun, and she wore expensive Italian shoes. She looked like a movie star or something.

"How did you die?" I couldn't resist asking. She looked startled.

"You – you can see me?"

"I've been seeing a lot of people like you lately – you know, *dead* people," I told her matter-of-factly.

"Oh, I'm just a little surprised," she explained. "Most of them, you know, can't..."

"It's a gift," I said.

We got to talking, and really hit it off. She was a bright, funny, charming lady, and I was right about her; she had indeed been a movie star – in Argentina.

Her name was Eva, and each day she would get on the bus at the same stop and tell me a little bit more of her story.

The first day, she told me all about her upbringing in a small, poor town in the Argentine countryside. Her family was doing okay, though, because her father took pretty good care of them and seemed to have plenty of dough. But when Eva was very young, she found out that her mother wasn't really married to her father, and that his "real" family lived in a nearby town. Her mother was her father's "mistress." Her father abandoned them and returned to his first family, leaving them with nothing. Life was tough, and to make ends meet, Eva and her sisters had to do cooking and cleaning in other people's homes. Eventually, the little family was able to open a modest boarding house and Eva started school. She said she loved school, especially the plays the children got to put on. She also loved going to the movies because Argentina had a thriving movie industry with all kinds of glamorous and exciting stars. That's when she first realized that she wanted to be an actress. Eva said that when her father died, her mother packed them all up and took them to his funeral in the other town, but there was a real ugly scene when the "real" wife threw a fit and wouldn't let them stay. "Get those bastard children out of here!" she screamed at Eva's mom. So they didn't get to be in his funeral at all. Eva said she didn't know what "bastard" or "illegitimate" meant, and would only find out a few years later when she started making a name for herself and hobnobbing with rich people.

The second day, she told me all about how she ran away to Buenos Aires to become a movie star when she was fifteen years old. She said she immediately loved the capital city, with its cinemas and stage theaters and restaurants and cafes, and all the people bustling around the lively city day and night. She said it was the "Paris of South America." She started auditioning for acting jobs and refused to give up even though she faced a lot of rejection. That's when she got the idea to bleach her black hair blond. The change made her more confident and she began to stand out at auditions, finally landing some small roles in a series of Argentine B-movies. To augment her meager income, Eva also took a few modeling jobs and toured with a national theater company. Then she landed a steady gig on a national radio show called *Muy Bien*, which brought her to a wider audience. For the next few years, she had steady work in radio and the movies, and was able to move into a very nice apartment in a ritzy Buenos Aires neighborhood. She said she felt like her dreams were finally coming true.

The third day was all about how Eva broke into management and became a co-owner of a radio production company and co-founder of a national radio syndicate. This, she said, gave her political clout and brought her lots of attention from the rich people, which was kind of a good thing and kind of a bad thing. Eva said when she was just an actress, the rich people treated her okay and didn't bother her much, but as soon as she started rubbing elbows with them as a business-woman, they got all snobby and snooty and didn't want to invite her to any swanky shindigs because she didn't have a formal education or fancy connections. People talked behind her back and said she would never be accepted because of her poor background. She said this really hurt her feelings, but she stayed in Buenos Aires and kept building her radio empire. That's about when she met a dashing army colonel and fell in love with him. His name was Juan Peron, and he was a real mover and shaker in Argentina.

On the fourth day, I was dying to find out what happened next. Eva didn't disappoint. She seemed to like talking about her life in Argentina, maybe because she was so far away from that time and place now. At any rate, the story continued with Juan being thrown into jail by his political enemies for being too popular. They thought Juan was becoming more popular than the president, so they put him in jail. But when Eva heard about it, she went out and got thousands and thousands of people to come and rally at the president's house for Juan's release. There were so many people there, that Eva said the president had to let Juan out of prison. As soon as Juan was a free man, he and Eva got married and then Juan turned around and ran for president of Argentina and actually won in a landslide!

"That's when things really got crazy," Eva told me. "We were very popular with the workers and the poor people, but the rich people hated us because of the direction my husband wanted to take the country. And because he let some of his German friends come to Argentina after the war, when they had nowhere else to go. No, they didn't like that one bit."

These "German friends" were actually Nazis on the lamb after things didn't go very well for them in World War II.

"Was your husband a Nazi, too?" I asked.

"Goodness, no!" she exclaimed. "Juan wasn't political like that! He just wanted to help people. And his German friends had nowhere else to go, so he couldn't just turn them away…"

So I took her word for it – her husband was just a nice guy who cared about people and wanted to make his country a better place to live. For his own people. And for a few poor Nazis. But I liked Eva. She had a real genuine quality to her. She was a real popular first lady, maybe even more popular than Mamie Eisenhower, and her people loved her. In fact, to show their affection they nicknamed her "Evita." Her husband let her do whatever she wanted, so she gave up acting on the radio and started a foundation for poor people and took care of orphans and lepers and other sick people and everyone loved her even more for all that.

Everyone but the rich people, who couldn't get over her humble beginnings and the fact that her mother was never married to her father. I guess rich people have a hard time dealing with things like that.

To be honest, her story was so fantastic that sometimes I wondered if it was even true. But then I remembered one time Uncle Joe told me that ghosts can't lie, and I was relieved and a little ashamed of myself for doubting the story of such a kind, caring lady. I looked forward to our morning chats on the bus even more than I did talking to the Rosenbergs at the library each day. Of course, Mr. Rosenberg wasn't much of a conversationalist, but boy did Mrs. Rosenberg make up for him – and how!

Every morning she asked me if I'd talked to my mother lately.

"My mother is in Florida," I would remind her.

"A boy should call his mother every day," she would say.

"I don't know where my mother is."

"That's no excuse. You're breaking her heart."

"Ethel, the boy says he doesn't know where his mother is," Mr. Rosenberg would pipe up, poring over another thick legal volume.

"Well, he should ask his father."

"My father doesn't know where she is, either," I would try to explain. "He's in Florida looking for her."

"Hear that, Ethel? The boy's mother and father are both in Florida, looking for each other," Mr. Rosenberg would say, without looking up from his book.

"Well, Florida's a very big state!" Mrs. Rosenberg would observe. "I don't know how they expect to find each other in a big state like that!"

"Well, my mom may not be looking for *him*," I would try to clarify. "I don't think she knows he's in Florida at all."

"And then there's the *everglades*," Mrs. Rosenberg would point out. "Very dangerous! You wouldn't find *me* in Florida."

"I don't think my mom would go to the everglades."

"What kind of crazy mixed-up family *is* this, anyway?" Mrs. Rosenberg would demand. "When we were all together, I never let my boys out of my sight for a second! Let alone run off to Florida on my own!"

"The boy told you, his mother has some issues," Mr. Rosenberg would say, pointing to his head. He would try to be discreet, but I knew what he meant.

I felt a little hurt. Maybe my mom was a howling-at-the-moon whacko, but at least my parents never sold atom bomb secrets to the Russians. That I know of, at least.

But I didn't say anything. I know Mrs. Rosenberg meant well, in her own way.

When it was time to go home, I put the books I was reading back on the shelves and walked quietly past the librarian's desk to the exit. She gave me the eye as I passed by. I got it. I was the weird kid who sat all alone and talked to himself in the library. That was okay – I owned it.

Back home, I made a baloney sandwich in the kitchen and grabbed a bottle of Dr. Pepper from the fridge and went upstairs to see what Uncle Joe was up to. *The Guiding Light* was just ending, and I caught him looking out the window at the neighbor lady's yard again. Sure enough, like clockwork, she was just coming out of her house to sunbathe on her chaise lounge on the lawn.

Uncle Joe watched her arrange her towel in a fussy way and lay down on her back, stretching out her long, smooth legs. She sipped a glass of lemonade and read a copy of *Life* magazine.

"Tell me about your neighbor," Uncle Joe calmly requested, as if he were talking to one of his KGB agents.

"Mrs. Riley? I don't know anything about her."

"Well, be a good lad and find out, won't you?" It wasn't merely a suggestion.

"Okay, I'll go over there later this afternoon," I said, as if what he was asking me to do – indeed, this whole situation – was just a routine part of any boy's life. "Do you want to work a while, or not?"

We worked a couple of hours, then knocked off for the day. I wanted to kick back and watch some TV, but Uncle Joe looked anxious.

"Don't forget about what I asked you earlier," he said.

"Huh?"

"You know – about the *thing*." He cocked his head toward the window. I don't know why we were speaking in code all of a sudden. A trick of the trade for him, I guess.

"Oh, yeah." I picked myself up off the crate and lazily made my way down the stairs. I found Aunt Evelyn in the front parlor, doing her nails.

"Hey, kid," she said, not very interested. "What's up?"

"Nothin'."

"How's things in the attic?"

"Uh, fine."

"You sure spend a lot of time up there."

"Uh-huh."

"Doing God-knows-what."

"Yeah."

"Probably just as well I don't know."

"Mmmm."

"This is a fascinating conversation, but why don't you get to the point and ask me what you want to ask me. Because, you're really starting to bug me."

"Okay." I didn't know how to say it. "It's...it's about Mrs. Riley."

Aunt Evelyn's eyes narrowed suspiciously. "What about her?"

"Oh, nothin'. I mean, does she have a husband or anything?"

"Isn't she a little old for you?"

"It's not for me – I mean, *I* don't need to know..."

"Who does?" she asked. Darn Uncle Joe. This was gonna be more difficult than I thought.

"I mean, I was just wonderin' and stuff..."

"There is a Mr. Riley, but he travels a lot," Aunt Evelyn explained, still suspicious. "You know, for business. Other than that, I don't know much about the lady. I'm of the opinion children and neighbors should be seen and not heard."

"Oh."

"Look, if she chooses to sunbathe out in the open for all the prepubescent neighborhood boys to see her in all her glory, so be it," she declared. "That's her choice. I'm strictly hands off when it comes to telling people how they should live their own lives. And that goes for you, too. All I'm gonna say is, be careful kid. We don't need any salacious neighborhood sex scandals around here, if you get my drift. Now, am-scray and let me have some peace and quiet before slowly slipping into my customary evening oblivion."

I went out into the backyard and stood there looking at the unmown lawn in a funk. Aunt Evelyn was definitely onto something, but she still had no way of knowing about Uncle Joe and my mission to build a dossier on Mrs. Riley for him. Maybe she thought I was a sex-crazed peeping tom with some creepy obsession with middle-aged sunbathing housewives. Or maybe she thought I was just a loner kid with no friends, living all alone in my own fantasy world of imaginary people and non-existent plots. For all she knew, I was as batty as my mother.

I decided to go over to the fence and peer over the top to see if Mrs. Riley was still in her yard. She was. I ducked down immediately. She hadn't seen me. I poked my head up again, slightly, straining for a view between the slats. She put her magazine down and looked directly at me. I ducked again.

"Hello!" I heard her call. I waited, hoping she hadn't seen me. "Hello! Young man!"

I was burned. Slowly I raised my head above the fence. I raised my hand and waved half-heartedly.

"Come on over!" she called. "Just through the gate there!" There was a small gate in the fence between the two yards. She'd caught me. I felt like bolting into the house. Out the front door and down the street and just keep running. "Yoo-hoo! Come on over, neighbor!" She didn't sound angry. Like a tractor beam I felt myself, unwillingly, pulled towards the gate. *What was I doing? This is crazy!* But still I walked on. I opened the gate and walked through into Mrs. Riley's immaculate backyard. I expected the police to arrive and take me into custody any moment.

"Come here," she beckoned. "I want to talk to you!"

I walked across her lawn toward her. It was a nice backyard – nicer than Aunt Evelyn's. The grounds were nicely kept, and there was a pool house and a kidney-shaped swimming pool. Then I was standing over her, in her yellow chiffon two-piece bathing suit. I looked away, my face burning, blushing as red as a beet.

"Hi. What's your name?" she asked.

"Calvin," I replied. I looked at her briefly. She was a brunette with soft, pink shoulders. She was wearing eyeliner and false eyelashes. My eyes darted away again. I glanced over at Aunt Evelyn's attic window. Uncle Joe was there, giving me a hearty wink and a thumb's-up.

"Sit down, Calvin," she ordered. I launched myself violently into a lawn chair, putty in her hands. "I always like to know who my neighbors are."

"I'm Calvin."

"So you've said." She smiled in a friendly way. I felt like an idiot.

"How has your summer been so far, Calvin?" She asked, sipping lemonade through a straw. She spilled a little bit of it on her swimsuit top, and brushed it away with her hand. I looked away again.

"Summer. Fine." I could barely produce words.

She looked at me and smiled. "I know what a young boy wants more than *anything* on a hot summer day."

I felt my face turning crimson again. I almost blurted out, *I'm sorry for looking at you over the fence! Please let me go!* But I couldn't animate my tongue – it was as thick as a Persian rug.

"You wait here, I'll be right back." She got up and walked into the house. I tried to stand and run away, but my legs felt like heavy rubber. I looked at the attic window again. Uncle Joe was smiling and giving me the "okay" sign.

Mrs. Riley emerged from the house with a tray of chocolate chip cookies and a glass of ice cold milk. She set it on a small round table between us.

"Help yourself," she said.

I began to realize that I wasn't going to prison after all. My throat opened up and my tongue shrank to its normal size. I picked up a cookie and took a large bite. Mmmmm – homemade. I grabbed the glass and chugged ice-cold milk, letting it hydrate my parched throat.

"Now, that's better, isn't it?" she asked cheerily. "I didn't know there were any children living next door to me. Have you been there long?"

I swallowed chewed up cookie and took another swig of milk to clear my throat. "I'm living with Aunt Evelyn temporarily. My dad left me here while he's...away working."

"Oh, he's a traveling man, is he?" she asked. "Just like my husband." I tensed at the word *husband*. "Howard's always gone. It seems I never see him anymore. But, you know what they say: work is work."

"Uh-huh," I said, nervously biting off another piece of cookie.

"So. Why were you looking over my fence, Calvin?"

"I wanted to know if... if you needed me to mow your lawn for you." It was the first thing that popped into my mind.

"Oh, that's so sweet of you, Calvin!" she exclaimed. "But I already have a gardener."

"Okay," I said.

"But I would like you to come over any time you like," she said, smiling again. "For more milk and cookies. I think you're a very charming young man, Calvin. You're welcome here anytime!"

"Thank you, Ma'am," I said shyly. "Can I go now?"

"You can go now. But remember: come over anytime for more milk and cookies. I could certainly use the company of a charming young man like yourself!"

I put a cookie in my pocket and got up to leave. Then I thought better of it and pulled the cookie out to put back on the plate.

"You may take the cookie, Calvin," she said. "There's plenty more where that came from!"

Chapter 13

The next day, as soon as I stepped foot in the attic, Uncle Joe began pumping me for information about Mrs. Riley.

"What is she like?" he asked, eyes wide. "Is she nice?"

"Yes, she's very nice."

"Well, what else?"

"She's married."

His face darkened.

"But her husband is always away, working," I qualified. "His job requires him to travel."

The old dictator's face brightened. "Then she's lonely."

I thought about it. "Yeah, maybe she is."

"What did you talk about?" he demanded.

"Well, we talked about her yard," I replied. "She has a professional gardener take care of it."

"Oh, yes. That's why it looks so neat and orderly," he said approvingly.

"And then she brought me milk and cookies."

"That's a good sign," he nodded his head. Then, as if remembering something, he pulled a small piece of paper out of his jacket pocket and unfolded it. "I wrote a poem for her."

"Wait. You wrote a *poem*?" I asked.

He looked uncharacteristically defensive. "Yes. Why? Do you think it unlikely that I have true feelings, like any man in love?"

"No, no. It's just – it's a little bit unexpected. That's all."

"I'll have you know that in the days before the Revolution, I was on my way to becoming a well-respected poet."

"Really?"

"Yes. I see your surprise." He wasn't pleased. "I had my poems published in many poetry journals – very prestigious literary journals, I'll have you know!"

"Okay. I wasn't aware of that."

"Now you are!" He calmed down a bit. He handed me the poem.

It read:

Morning
The pinkish bud has opened,
Rushing to the pale-blue violet
And, stirred by a light breeze,
The lily of the valley has bent over the grass.

"Well, what do you think?" he asked expectantly.

Knowing the kind of answers he was accustomed to, I said, "I think it's great. It's about the morning."

"Yes, on the surface," he explained, slightly irritated. "But the whole thing is a metaphor for the blossoming of a new love. So, do you think you could get it to her?"

"Get it to her?"

"Yes. Give her my poem."

"To Mrs. Riley?"

"Yes. To Mrs. Riley!"

I thought about it a moment. "And who do I say it's from? My friend, the former head of the Soviet Union, who has fallen madly in love with you?"

"You'll think of something," he said. That's right – the man who built the Soviet Union and defeated Nazi Germany was used to having other people solve these little problems for him.

* * *

The next day, I was practicing playing my accordion in the backyard because Aunt Evelyn said she would take a butcher knife and fix my cheap plastic accordion for good if I ever played it in the house again. I can't really blame her – the first few weeks of practice consisted of squeaks and squeals that probably would have driven any music-lover over the edge. But I was slowly getting better. I could play *Twinkle, Twinkle, Little Star* pretty well now and could almost play *Deep in the Heart of Texas* all the way through without hitting any clunkers.

I was working my way through the second verse of *Texas* when Mrs. Riley popped her head over the fence and called out, "Hey! You're getting pretty good at that thing, Calvin!"

"Aw, jeepers," I said sheepishly. "I didn't know anyone was listening..."

"No, no – I can tell, you're really making progress!" she said brightly. "Why don't you come on over? I might have some chores for you to do after all. Bring your accordion!"

I walked through the gate with my instrument and sat it down gingerly on a patio chair. She wanted me to trim her hedges, and handed me a big, sharp pair of trimming shears.

"What happened to your gardener?" I asked.

"Oh, I had to let him go," she said. "How long have you been playing the accordion?"

"About two weeks," I replied.

"You sound great," she said, smiling brightly. "Why did you choose the accordion?"

I told her all about my hero, Dick Contino, and polka music, and how I won the accordion in a contest on the back of a box of breakfast cereal.

"I like polka music, too," she said. "It's so cheerful and full of life!"

Mrs. Riley seemed like a really nice lady. She was real easy to talk to and seemed interested in me. It started to look like we were going to be really good friends after all.

I trimmed her hedges – badly. There were cookies and milk afterwards.

"How do you get your milk so ice cold?" I asked admiringly.

"It's not rocket science, Calvin," she explained, ruffling my hair. "I just turn the Frigidaire up to 10."

I remembered Uncle Joe's poem and pulled it out of my pocket. I unfolded it and gave it to Mrs. Riley. She read it and smiled.

"Did *you* write this, Calvin?"

"No. My friend wrote it."

"Well, tell your friend it's lovely," she said, beaming. "I'm going to keep it forever."

The next day, she called me over to mow her lawn. She lounged and sunbathed in her two-piece and watched me work the whole time.

The day after that, she had me pulling weeds. Again, she was sunbathing in her swimsuit the whole afternoon.

It was like that every day: *Calvin, can you come trim the roses? Calvin, I need you to rake the mulch...*All the while, her sunbathing in her swimsuit and watching me work.

And after each chore was done, there were milk and cookies and conversation with Mrs. Riley. She wanted to talk. She wanted to know all about me and my family. I told her everything, and she still wanted to know more. I told her everything about me except how I was able to see dead people because I didn't want her to think I was weird or anything.

"How come I never see your aunt?" she asked.

"She doesn't like people," I said bluntly.

"When is your father coming back to get you?"

"I don't know."

"How come your mother ran away?"

"She felt sad."

"Is she ever coming back?"

"I don't know."

"I have a son, you know," she suddenly announced. "A little older than you."

"Is he with his dad?" I asked.

"No, we put him in military school. To straighten him out."

"What was wrong with him?"

"He was belligerent. Disobedient and belligerent. My husband said military school would straighten him out."

"When will you let him come home?"

"When he's good and straightened out."

Mrs. Riley giggled. "I've got a little secret to tell you." She was acting kinda funny. I think there was something in her lemonade. The more lemonade she drank, the sillier she seemed to get. "You wanna hear my secret?"

"I guess so."

She leaned over closer to me, spilling a little lemonade and not noticing. "I steal things," she whispered. Gee whiz, there was no one else around and she had a big backyard and all. I don't know why she had to whisper all of a sudden.

"Why?" I asked, a little shocked.

"For kicks," she explained. "I've got plenty of money. It's not that – it's the rush you get walking out of the department store, right past the security guard, with a scarf or a pair of nylons in your purse that you didn't pay for. You feel so alive. You feel, I don't know – *invincible!*"

Funny, I never figured Mrs. Riley for an adrenalin junkie. Church on Sunday morning maybe, but *shoplifting?* It just didn't add up.

"Have you ever, you know, shoplifted?" she asked me.

"No," I said.

"Really?" she asked. "Come on – you can trust me. I told you *my* secret."

I was about to say I'd never stolen anything, then remembered that wasn't exactly true. "I stole a Bible once."

"A *Bible*?" she asked, scrunching up her nose. "What did you do that for?"

"I wanted it."

"Who did you steal it from?"

"A preacher."

"You stole a preacher's Bible!" she exclaimed in approval. "So, tell me John Dillinger – did you feel the adrenalin? You know, the *rush*?"

"Well, I remember being real excited," I replied. "But it wasn't because of stealing something. It was because my Old Man was waiting in the car outside. We were about to take a road trip together on Route 66."

"I'll bet it was a real crime spree," she nodded, sipping more lemonade.

Actually, when you thought about it, she wasn't far from the truth. But all I said was, "It was pretty exciting. Have you always been a, you know, shoplifter?"

"Heavens, no!" she laughed. "No, I was a perfect young lady growing up. My parents were the straight-laced type. They would've killed me for something like that."

"When did you start?"

"About two years after getting married," she replied. "About the time my son was born, and my husband started travelling more for work. He kept making better and better money, and being gone longer and longer as the years went by. I had every-thing I'd always dreamed of – you know, cars, appliances, fancy clothes and shoes. The real American Dream. But I just started feeling dead inside. When you're just a girl growing up in Wis-consin they never tell you that the American Dream will make you feel dead inside. But I discovered the truth: the *real* Amer-ican Dream is having a secret. A dangerous secret, and it's all *yours*. It changed my whole life!"

"But what if you get caught?" I asked.

"Well, I suppose they'd put me in jail."

"What do you think your husband would say about that?"

"Oh, he'd have plenty to say! But at least he'd have to notice me, for a change!"

"Wouldn't there be a scandal?"

"Oh, a terrible scandal, I should hope!" her eyes gleamed. "But I never get caught. I'm too good at it."

"But what if you slip up – just once?"

"There are worse things than going to jail, Calvin. Like boredom. Like being married to a man who doesn't notice you, and stays away from home as long as he can get away with. Like feeling like you're nothing, like you're not even there."

I went home that afternoon with mixed feelings about Mrs. Riley, and feeling a little sorry for her.

I mean, she was awful good-looking and everything, but she was really clingy and needy and messed-up and to tell you the honest truth it was kind of getting on my nerves a little bit. And she started touching me more – rubbing my back and neck, caressing my cheek or shoulder. It didn't feel right. It was getting kinda creepy.

I began to realize that poor Mrs. Riley was a very lonely woman. When she called over the fence for me to come help her with something, it got to where I would actually pretend I didn't even hear her, just so I didn't have to go over there anymore. I was kinda sorry Uncle Joe ever got me mixed up with her.

Then one day, desperate to practice the accordion, I snuck into the backyard when I thought she wasn't out there and started playing my signature song, *Deep in the Heart of Texas*, very low and quiet. Sure enough, her head popped over the fence and she caught me.

"Calvin! I really need your help today! There's some kind of animal in the pool house, and I need your help to get it out!"

"What kind of animal?" I asked.

"I don't know – a raccoon or badger or something. Please, help me!"

Reluctantly, I put the accordion down and walked through the gate into her yard. At least she was wearing a robe tied at the front, covering her whole body. Taking heart at that, I followed her into the pool house. When we were inside, I saw her lock the door. I thought that was weird.

"Umm, Mrs. Riley, what are you doing?" I asked.

She stood in front of the door, blocking it. Then she opened her robe and dropped it to the floor, revealing the tiniest two-piece bikini I'd ever seen her wear. It was so scanty, I thought she must have ordered it all the way from Paris or something.

"I *need* you, Calvin..."

It was then that I realized what Mrs. Riley needed most was love. But I just wasn't equipped to give her the kind of love she needed so desperately. "Mrs. Riley, I think you should let me out now," I suggested.

"Please hold me," she pleaded. I looked away. "It's all right, dear. I'll show you what to do. I'll lead you through everything..."

I didn't move.

"I know I'm older. But am I *that* hideous?"

"You're not hideous," I said. "In fact, you're very beautiful. I just don't think it would be a good idea."

I reached around her soft bare waist and fumbled to unlock the pool house door. Then I was out and running back to Aunt Evelyn's backyard. I heard Mrs. Riley calling "Wait, Calvin! What about the milk and cookies?"

* * *

Next time I saw Uncle Joe, he was eager to hear the latest about Mrs. Riley.

"I saw you go into the pool house with her," he said. "What happened in there?"

"There was some kind of animal in there," I said. "She wanted me to help her get rid of it." I couldn't tell him what really happened. I was much too embarrassed to ever tell *anyone* about that.

"I didn't see you with an animal when you came out," he observed.

"We couldn't find it," I lied. "It must have crawled out some hole in the wall or something."

"Did you show her my poem?"

"Yes."

"Well, did she like it?"

"She said it was 'lovely.'"

"She did?" he asked, excited. "It is lovely, isn't it?"

"She thought I wrote it," I told him.

"What did you tell her?"

"I told her my friend wrote it."

"She knows about *me*?"

"I didn't tell her your name. Or that you're dead. I didn't want her to think I was crazy."

"I want to meet her."

"I don't see how," I said. "You can't leave the attic."

"Invite her up here."

"I can't do that," I shook my head. "What would I tell Aunt Evelyn?"

"You can sneak her in."

"But she won't even be able to see you."

"It doesn't matter. You can bring her up here and talk to her while I get a good look at her. I will enjoy her company vicariously, through you."

After what happened in the pool house, this was unthinkable. I knew I had to find a way to talk him out of it. "I don't know. She told me a lot of weird stuff the other day. I think she's pretty messed up."

"I like messed up women," he said, enthusiastically. "I'm quite used to it."

"I just don't think it'll work out."

"What do you mean?"

I had to think fast. "She told me she has a fear of attics."

"A fear of attics?" he scoffed. "That's ridiculous! Nobody has a fear of attics!"

"She does," I said. "I told you she was messed up."

He rubbed his chin thoughtfully. "Well, I'll just have to think of another way..."

In an attempt to change the subject, I suggested we get to work. He asked to see yesterday's pages, and I handed him the tablet.

He read it and said, "What's this?"

I realized I'd handed him the wrong tablet. "Oh, sorry — that's just a short story I've been working on." I tried to take it back before he could read any more of it, but he wouldn't let go.

"Wait a moment. Let's take a look at this..." He read the title, "*Sandwiches and Tea with Mr. Contino?*"

"It's just a story about meeting Dick Contino," I said lamely.

"The accordion guy?" Uncle Joe started reading the story. About half-way through, he said, "I don't get it."

"Dick Contino's a big star," I tried to explain. "In the story, I'm just an admirer inspired by him to learn how to play the accordion. Then I get a chance to audition for his band, so we meet for lunch and realize how much we have in common, even down to how we dress and what we like to eat."

"But polka music is not as noble as, say, classical music," he argued. "Why couldn't you meet Shostakovich, or Tchaikovsky, instead?"

"Because I don't like classical music," I said. "I like polka music."

"And it doesn't have an ending. Every story needs an ending, you know."

"I'm still working on it."

He shrugged and handed the story back to me. "I've seen enough."

"You don't like it?"

"It shows promise," he replied. "But it needs a lot of work."

I have to admit, I was a little bit sore about his appraisal of my story. I thought it was pretty good, myself. But the next time we met, he brought some back-up.

Uncle Joe was sitting in his chair, puffing on his cigar, as usual. He was flanked by two men about his own age. They both had long beards and craggy, weathered features. I looked the two men over. They didn't say a word.

"The boy wants to be a writer," Uncle Joe said to the man on his left. "Help him."

I handed my short story to the man Uncle Joe had spoken to. His name was Fyodor Dostoevsky. The writer sat down on a box and read my story. When he was finished, he handed it to the other man.

This man's name was Leo Tolstoy. He sat down on an old chair with a broken back and read my story, too.

"Well?" Uncle Joe demanded, puffing on his cigar.

Dostoesvky spoke up first. "The deep longing in the heart of the protagonist to produce sublime music is very powerful and tangible to the reader. The reader senses the acute feeling of loss the protagonist would endure if he were denied the opportunity to join Dick Contino's band and produce the uplifting music his spirit yearns for. The virtuoso Contino, on the other hand, embodies the seasoned professional who has traded his simple joy for playing music in exchange for wealth and fame, and now feels an existential emptiness that gnaws at his very soul. In the young protagonist he recognizes an innocence and wonder that he knows he left by the wayside many years before and that he thought would remain beyond his grasp for all eternity. In this story, the human spirit rejoices and triumphs, overcoming and pushing back the darkness of ignorance and neglect."

Gee, I thought he made my story sound pretty good. But the dictator wasn't satisfied. "How can the boy improve it?" Uncle Joe demanded.

Dostoevsky rubbed his chin and thought a moment. "It needs more suffering, more spiritual repression. The tone is all wrong – too joyful, too much hope."

"Don't listen to him," Tolstoy sniffed. "What you need is a great battle scene. Two great armies, facing each other across the battlefield, led by desperate men willing to risk everything and face oblivion itself for the sake of honor!"

"Are you going to take this hack seriously?" Dostoevsky responded. "The soul of man is bankrupt. The plight of humanity is spiritual death. Suicide is the only noble act."

"Suicide is an illusion, a clever conceit employed by cowardly men unwilling to face their destiny!" Tolstoy countered passionately. "Men must fight, nations must clash in the grand arena, in order to purge the stain of their own iniquities – both from this generation, and from generations past!"

"You are an imposter!" Dostoevsky spat. "The joy in this story is a *murderer* – strangling the very life out of Truth itself, and then casting the bloated corpse into a river of mediocrity and remorse!"

"You are wrong as usual," Tolstoy declared, shaking his head. "This story is a celebration of the artist's will – an affirmation of the creative mind and its ability to rise above the mundane and conquer the fear and doubt that has so long crippled it."

"If you had read it more carefully, you would have seen that it's a sermon of atonement," Dostoevsky argued. "A buoyant hymn of spiritual re-awakening, an optimistic Utopian anthem of elation and bliss, tempered by the bleak reality of music's innate inability to pluck man's soul from the abyss."

"But, gentlemen, how can the boy improve it?" Uncle Joe asked again.

"It needs more conflict," Tolstoy suggested.

"Exactly!" Dostoevsky exclaimed. "That's just what I've been trying to tell you!"

The novelists hung around arguing about each other's books, while Uncle Joe smoked his cigar and watched another soap opera. It got particularly heated when Dostoevsky called *War and Peace* perfect for summer beach reading, and Tolstoy countered by asking why Dostoevsky had named his book *The Idiot* after himself.

I sat on my box thinking about how I could imbue my masterpiece with more conflict, as Tolstoy had suggested. He was right – in the story, everything came too easily for me. I met Dick Contino and we hit it off immediately. We played *Lady of Spain* and I passed the audition without a hitch. Dick had me move into a room in his big Las Vegas house so we could hang out and write songs together. We flew to L.A. and went shopping for new stage clothes on Rodeo Drive, and had brunch with the record label A&R man at the Beverly Hills Hotel. We ate dinner with a couple of young starlets from Paramount at Musso and Frank's. We rehearsed together and did radio spots in preparation for our upcoming world tour. Everything was going too swell in my story.

It was boring.

What if I'm stricken with a rare disease that paralyzes my right arm on the eve of our world tour? I wouldn't be able to play the accordion, and I'd miss the whole tour!

But, knowing Dick, he'd take me on tour anyway. "You've got great pipes, kid. You'll be my lead singer!"

Okay, so what if another side effect of the disease is laryngitis? No singing, no tour.

But Dick still wouldn't leave me home. "You can play the triangle with your left hand. I've always wanted a triangle player in the band, anyway."

That Dick – such a swell guy, always thinking of others like that!

Then what if another side effect leaves my left arm paralyzed, too?

But Dick was adamant. "I can't leave you behind, kid. You'll miss out on all the fun. I'm still bringing you along to inspire me, to be my moral support."

I've got it now. Right as we're about to leave on the tour, another hidden side effect emerges – a fear of traveling on airplanes, ships, and trains. That's it – there's no way I can go now, no matter how nice Dick is.

There. That had to be enough conflict to satisfy even a picky guy like Tolstoy. *But wait – every story has to have a happy ending, doesn't it? So Dick goes out and scours the whole world for the one doctor who knows how to treat my disease, and brings him back to cure me. One by one, the side effects disappear, and soon I'm able to go on the tour after all!*

There was so much noise from TV commercials and the yelling of the two novelists that I had to go downstairs to the den to finish writing my epic. Now that my story was going to be fixed, I hoped the quarrelling Russian writers would be gone when I came back to the attic the next afternoon.

Chapter 14

When school started that fall, I had to go down and enroll myself. When I got there, wouldn't you know it, the name of the school was *Calvin Coolidge Junior High*. My name, only without the "Jefferson." It was like a sign or something.

The front office was as chaotic as a train station at rush hour on account of it was the first day of school and all. The insufficient school secretary was doing her best to keep up with the ringing telephones and kids who'd lost their class schedules and needed new ones. When I finally got up to the counter I told the secretary I wanted to enroll in school.

"You need a parent or guardian with you to do that," she informed me.

"They couldn't come," I said.

"Well, you can't enroll yourself," she huffed. "You'll have to talk to the principal, Mr. Hayvenhurst. Have a seat over there until he can see you."

I sat on a chair in the corner until the principal could see me. It took an hour. Finally, the secretary showed me into his office. Mr. Hayvenhurst was sitting behind his desk. He wore a suit and tie and shiny horn-rimmed glasses. His face was so narrow that when you were looking at him straight-on you nearly lost sight of him. He asked me to take a seat.

"What can I do for you, young man?" he asked.

"I'd like to enroll in your school," I said.

"The secretary can enroll you at the front desk," he told me.

"She sent me in here on account of I don't have a parent or guardian with me."

"I see," he said gravely. "And why is it you don't have a parent or guardian with you?"

I explained to him that my guardian, Aunt Evelyn, couldn't leave her house on account of her agoraphobia.

"My, that sounds serious, doesn't it?" Mr. Hayvenhurst looked like he wasn't exactly sure what agoraphobia was.

So I said, "It's a fear of leaving your house. Aunt Evelyn stays inside all of the time. She never goes outside for anything."

"I see," Mr. Hayvenhurst said for the second time. "Is she your only guardian?"

"Yes."

"What about your parents?"

"They're in Florida."

"Well, they certainly won't be able to enroll you in school from Florida, will they?" he asked. "Under the circumstances – I mean, considering your aunt's serious condition and all – I think we can make an exception. I'm certainly not going to be the one to deny a young man such as yourself the benefits of a first-class education because of a mere technicality."

One of the first things I noticed about Mr. Hayvenhurst, besides his abnormally narrow head, was that he seemed very confident and he said "certainly" a lot. He opened a desk drawer and pulled out a blank enrollment form. "Now, what is your name, young man?"

"Calvin Jefferson Coolidge."

He started to write, then stopped and put the ballpoint pen down. "Umm, that's the name of our school. Except for the 'Jefferson' part."

"Yes, I know," I said.

"Listen, you aren't – I mean, you aren't pulling my leg or anything right now, are you son?"

"No, sir. That's really my name."

"Well. That's certainly a coincidence, then." He picked up the pen and wrote my full name on the form. He asked me all the other important information, like date of birth and place of birth and previous school and everything, and I answered truthfully with what I knew and just fudged the rest. As far as I could tell, he bought it.

"Well, I guess that does it," he said, finishing up the form with a flourish of his pen. "But you'll have to take this form home and have your aunt sign it. Don't forget to bring it back to the office first thing tomorrow morning." He carefully folded the form and stuffed it into an envelope with the school's name printed on it. Then he handed it to me and said, "Welcome to Calvin Coolidge Junior High School, Calvin!"

I thanked him and stuffed the envelope into my pocket.

"Mrs. Hackle will take care of the rest of the details for you," Mr. Hayvenhurst said. That was the school secretary's name – Mrs. Hackle.

He shook my hand and patted me on the back and guided me back out to the front office area where Mrs. Hackle assigned me a locker and a P.E. uniform and my class schedule. Then she led me out of the office and down a long, locker-lined hallway. The halls were empty because all the other kids were already in class. Mrs. Hackle stopped at Room 112.

"This is your first class," she said. "The times for the rest of your classes are on your schedule. Here at Calvin Coolidge, we expect punctuality and diligence." Then she turned and walked back towards the front office.

I opened the door and quietly slipped into an empty seat in the back of the room. There was a man at the front scribbling equations on a chalkboard. The other students were busily scribbling the equations down in their notebooks, and hadn't even noticed me. I suddenly realized I didn't have a notebook, and scrunched down in my seat hoping the teacher wouldn't notice. I looked at my schedule: the class was Algebra 1, and the teacher's name was Mr. Best.

I'd never seen algebra before, but I started to catch on when Mr. Best turned around and explained what all the X's and Y's meant. "You get your X's and Y's straight, and algebra's a piece of cake!" he told us, trying to be encouraging. Then the bell rang and I left class feeling like with a little work I'd be able to catch up with math all right.

My next class was P.E., and we were practicing rope-climbing. The gym ceiling was very high, and the ropes went all the way to the top where they were tied to beams. The P.E. teacher, Coach Axelrod, wore a baseball cap with the school's name on it and had a large, round belly and skinny stick legs shooting out down to the ground.

"Don't worry about a thing, boys," Coach Axelrod assured us. "All you need to remember about rope-climbing is to never look down."

He called two boys up to try it. One boy made it all the way to the top, but the other one gave up two-thirds of the way and pathetically slid back down.

"Not bad, not bad," the Coach said. Then he pointed at me. "You. What's your name, son?"

"Calvin Jefferson Coolidge, sir," I answered.

He looked at me funny. "Why, that's the name of our school. You aren't pulling my leg, are you, son?"

"No, sir."

"Then come on up here and show us what you've got."

I walked to the first rope and started climbing it. Halfway up, I froze.

"You're doing great, son!" Coach Axelrod called up to me. "Just don't look down!"

I wish he hadn't said that. Didn't he know that when you're climbing a rope and someone tells you not to look down it's nearly impossible not to?

I looked down and got dizzy and fell all the way down, landing flat on my back on the hardwood gym floor. I heard all the other boys gasp. "Is he dead?" someone asked. Then it was silent.

Coach Axelrod knelt down and put his sweaty face very close to mine. "I *told* you not to look down, son!" he bellowed.

He had the two boys who had already climbed pick me up and carry me to the nurse's office. There were three or four other kids there with P.E. related injuries like twisted ankles and scraped knees and jammed fingers. The nurse had me lie on my stomach on the couch while she applied a cold-pack to my back.

"You looked down, didn't you?" was all she said, shaking her head. Then, for some reason, she jammed a thermometer into my mouth to take my temperature.

A little while later she told me to get up and she gave me a note to get out of P.E. for a whole week and told me to go to my next class. My back still felt a little stiff, but I wasn't dizzy anymore so I went back to the locker room and changed out of my P.E. uniform and went to my next class. It was English.

Ah, English. I finally felt like I was on my home turf. I was late, of course, but the teacher, Miss Underwood, didn't seem to mind. She was young, and seemed real nice and gentle and stuff – not like the older, grumpier teachers. The kind of teacher that boys and girls would sit down and be quiet for just to hear her voice.

I liked her immediately.

The class was reading *A Tale of Two Cities*, and Miss Underwood gave me a book and asked me to read a passage out loud. I read about half a page and she said to stop. I was worried, and wondered what kind of egregious error I'd made, but Miss Underwood smiled at me and said, "That was very nice. What is your name, young man?"

"Calvin Jefferson Coolidge, miss," I replied.

"Oh, like our school!" She didn't even ask me if I was pulling her leg. Then she looked at a clipboard on her desk. "Hmmm. You're not on my roster."

"I'm new," I confessed breathlessly. "I just enrolled this morning."

"That explains it," she smiled. "Well, I liked several things about your reading, Calvin. Foremost, I liked the way you pronounced both *indictment* and *abominable* correctly. Have you encountered those words before?"

"Yes, miss."

"Oh, then you must be an avid reader!" she said, visibly pleased. "I wonder if you could tell us the meaning of *indictment*, then."

My heart was beating out of my chest. I took a deep breath and said, "An indictment is when someone is charged with a serious crime." Her eyes got wide.

"Yes, that's right," she beamed. "And what about *abominable?*"

That one I wasn't as sure about. "Umm, intolerable?"

"Yes, right again," Miss Underwood said. "Class, it looks like we have every reason to expect great things from our new pupil, Calvin."

I felt my face getting all hot, but inside I felt proud. Miss Underwood used words like *foremost* and *penultimate,* and she was already aces with me. This class had certainly gone much better than P.E.!

When the bell rang, I didn't want to leave, and already started looking forward to tomorrow's English class.

At lunch, the cafeteria served Salisbury steak with mashed potatoes and gravy. It tasted just like the frozen TV dinners I'd been eating since I came to live with Aunt Evelyn. Which is to say, *good.* I sat down next to a skinny boy with glasses who was sitting all alone and decided to strike up a conversation with him.

"Hi, I'm Calvin," I said.

"Hi, I'm Allen," he said.

"You new to the school, too?" I asked.

"New? No, I've been going to this school for two years."

"Oh, I just thought because you're sitting all – I mean, never mind." I didn't want to make the kid feel bad by saying I thought he was new because he was sitting all alone at lunch. I noticed he wasn't eating the cafeteria food. He'd brought his own sack lunch from home: a tuna fish sandwich wrapped in wax paper, raw carrot sticks, and some raisins. Yuck! The only thing he had that looked halfway edible was a Moon Pie.

"How come you don't eat the cafeteria food?" I asked, tucking into my Salisbury steak. It had a delightful processed-meat consistency that simply melted in your mouth.

"My mom says it's not healthy," Allen said, snapping into a raw carrot stick.

"Oh." Admittedly, I'd never considered the health question when choosing food. I probably hadn't eaten a legitimate vegetable in years.

We talked a little bit, and Allen seemed like a really nice guy. He told me his father was a dentist, and offered me some dental floss when I finished eating. I'd never used dental floss in my life. I didn't even know what it was.

"Umm, no thanks," I said.

He unspooled a piece and broke it off. I watched with a mixture of dread and fascination as he worked it between each of his teeth right there at the table. I felt as if I were witnessing some indecent primitive custom from somewhere outside the civilized world. Some girls nearby picked up their trays and fled in horror.

After he was finished, he wiped the floss on his pant leg and wound it back onto the spool. I didn't say anything. I *couldn't* say anything.

Gee, why didn't Allen have any friends at school?

At last, I said, "Well, nice talking to you." I stood and picked up my tray.

"Yeah, you too," Allen said. "Maybe we can sit together at lunch again sometime."

"Right." I turned around and took my tray to the drop-off table, trying desperately to "un-see" what had just happened.

After lunch was science class. The only exciting thing that happened was when a girl named Amy fainted when the teacher was showing us how to chloroform and dissect a frog. I helped carry her to the nurse's office, where I noticed six or seven new kids with P.E. related injuries sitting around waiting for the nurse's attention. The nurse revived Amy with smelling salts, but on the way back to class she threw up in the hallway on account of the smelling salts, so I had to carry her back to the nurse's office to be treated for nausea. All on account of a chloroformed frog.

It wasn't a good day for Amy.

The last class was shop, where we got to wear protective goggles and thick rubber gloves and sand and plane big blocks of wood for an hour. I saw Allen in the same class. He waved to me. I waved back. At the end of class, the shop teacher, Mr. Dugan, told us all we would be doing a term project that would be sixty percent of our grade, and I decided to make a pewter salad bowl for Aunt Evelyn, in case I was still living here when Christmas came along.

All in all, it was a pretty good first day of school, even considering my humiliating failure in P.E. and the dental floss incident. Oh well – I was never great at sports, anyway.

Chapter 15

English was my favorite class at school, and it was no secret why. Miss Underwood was a wonderful teacher – kind, gentle, generous – and she genuinely cared about all of her students. But as the days went on, I could see that she began to take a special interest in me.

One day she asked me to stay after class to take a test. It wasn't the kind of test that every student takes – she said it was a special test. It had questions like "Book is to reading as fork is to _____, then it had a bunch of words to choose from. It also had questions about which numbers completed a certain pattern, and questions where I had to read long lists of words and find pairs of words with similar meanings. It was pretty easy, and I finished it in twenty minutes while she graded papers at her desk. When I told Miss Underwood I was finished, she looked surprised.

She checked my answers and said there must be a mistake. She said I would have to take it again, so I did. This time I finished in fifteen minutes.

Miss Underwood checked the new test and looked even more surprised.

"Do I have to take it again?" I asked.

"No, Calvin."

"Is there something wrong, Miss Underwood?"

"No, Calvin. There's nothing wrong. You got a perfect score – both times. There's no mistake."

She said the test was an IQ test, and only real smart people had to take it.

"Calvin, I believe in all of my students, and I think they are all very bright. But I have to say – and I don't want you to take this the wrong way – there is something different about you that I haven't quite been able to put my finger on."

"You think I'm different?" I asked.

"Yes. But not in a bad way." It was uncharacteristic of her, struggling to express her ideas like she was now. "What I mean to say is...I think you may be a *savant*. Do you know what that means?"

"Well, I don't remember learning to read. I could just always do it. I didn't have to learn the letters or the words. I just *knew* them. But I just thought everyone was like that."

"They're not – *we're* not – all like that, Calvin."

"And, also, everything I read is like...recorded, up here, forever..." I tapped my head.

"Everything?"

"Yes. And when I read a new book, it's like it completes a part of me that was already there, but covered up. It's like I knew it before, but I'm just remembering it again. Like missing puzzle pieces, but you knew their exact shape and size and you were just waiting for those exact pieces to appear and fill in those spots. And when they do – when you read that book for the first time – the pieces fit perfectly and then it all makes sense."

Miss Underwood was speechless. Finally, she said: "I – I think that's the best definition of 'savant' I've ever heard, Calvin. Tell me, what was the first book you ever read?"

"The Bible."

"The *Bible*? Have you read all of it?"

"Yes."

"All the way through?"

"Yes."

"How many times?"

"Twelve. But I don't have to read it anymore."

"Why not?"

"I remember it pretty good now."

"Do you believe the stories in the Bible, Calvin?"

"Well, my Old Man said it's just a book of fairy tales. But the more I read it, the more I got to thinking: how could a book of fairy tales have such a big impact on Western Civilization?"

"Good point, Calvin." She walked to a bookcase and pulled a book off a shelf. "I want to try something, if you don't mind. Read this and write a book report for me, won't you?" She handed me a copy of *Crime and Punishment*.

"Sure."

"Take your time, there's no rush. Just hand it in whenever you finish."

"Okay."

The next day, I brought the book report back to Miss Underwood.

"What's this?" she asked.

"The book report on *Crime and Punishment*."

"You read the book?"

"Yes."

"And wrote the report?"

"Yes."

"When did you do this?"

"Last night, after watching *The Lone Ranger*."

She sat down and read the book report, right there in front of me. When she was finished, she said, "You noticed things in that book – metaphors, symbolism – that I never saw. You are extremely gifted, Calvin."

The next day, I brought in my short story about Dick Contino for Miss Underwood to read. She was somewhat less impressed.

"This is all right, Calvin," she told me. "But it's fantasy. If you want to be a writer, you've got to write about real life. Write about your life. Write *your* story, Calvin."

"Who would want to read *my* story?" I asked.

"I would," she smiled. "A lot of people would."

"But there's just some things I *can't* write about," I said, thinking about Uncle Joe in Aunt Evelyn's attic and Mrs. Riley in the pool house and the Rosenbergs at the library and the Old Man's con games on Route 66. "There are things that happened to me that people wouldn't understand."

"They'll understand," she promised. "You're a very intelligent human being. They'll relate to your experiences. They'll get it. You've just got to have the *courage* to write about it."

She just didn't understand. She was talking about someone with a *normal* life. She couldn't imagine someone like me – she had no idea what I was going through.

It certainly wasn't normal.

* * *

When I got home from school that day, there was a new surprise: Aunt Evelyn's son Buck was there. He'd just gotten back to the States from Korea. The war was over and the Army had discharged him.

And now he was moving back into Aunt Evelyn's house.

I didn't even know she had a son.

"Meet your older cousin, kid," Aunt Evelyn said when I stepped through the door and saw him. My *cousin?* He was a complete stranger to me. Worse yet, I had been sleeping in his old room. So now I had to move into the bedroom with the frilly pink bedspread and curtains.

Buck was twenty-two, twenty-three years old. He had been in combat in Korea. He was tall and dark-haired, with bulging biceps and bushy, caterpillar eyebrows over sharp, penetrating eyes. He was just out of the Army, but his hair was already growing out and he was combing it into a kind of ducktail style.

He was the kind of guy who would have a cigarette over one ear and a whole pack of smokes rolled up in his tight, short shirt-sleeve.

You know the type. He reeked of trouble.

Buck turned my whole world upside-down, in the snap of a finger.

"Where's the TV set?" he barked at Aunt Evelyn.

"You know I don't watch TV," she told him. "The kid took it up to the attic."

"How could that pipsqueak get it up there by himself?"

"I helped him," she replied.

"Why the hell did you do that?" he asked.

"Because I don't watch TV," she repeated.

I got the idea the TV set would have to come back down to the den. Uncle Joe wouldn't be happy about it, but he'd have to understand. There was a New Order in the house.

"What's the kid doing here, anyway?" Buck demanded.

"He's my brother's kid," she said.

"You have a *brother?*" Buck asked, eyebrows raised. Apparently, there wasn't a lot of communication in this family's history.

"He dropped him off here while he's looking for his runaway, nut-bag wife in Florida," Aunt Evelyn explained, pouring herself a stiff glass of Johnny Walker. Buck pulled a cigarette from behind his ear and lit it, one-handed, with a Zippo lighter that had his Army unit's insignia on it.

Who are these people? I thought.

"He's only gonna be here for a while," Aunt Evelyn went on. "He's just a kid, he doesn't take up much space. And he keeps to himself pretty well – hell, I hardly know he's even around here most of the time, except when he's talking to himself in the attic."

"He talks to himself in the *attic?*" Buck exclaimed, exhaling a thick cloud of smoke. "Joseph, Mary and Jesus. He's as crazy as his mother!"

The first few days, I went to school early each morning and generally tried to stay out of Buck's way. One day, I came home from school and went into the kitchen to make a peanut butter sandwich for a snack. He was sitting at the kitchen table, smoking and reading the newspaper.

"Who the hell are *you?*" he barked when he saw me.

"Calvin. Your cousin," I replied, getting the peanut butter jar from the cupboard.

"Oh yeah," he said, distractedly. I got out the bread and a butter knife, and started making my sandwich.

"How long you been living here?" Buck asked.

"Most of the summer," I said.

"Where you from?"

"California." I spread the peanut butter nice and thick on the pale white bread, then carefully placed another piece of bread on top.

"Is your mom really nuts?"

"I guess so." I took a bite of the sandwich, most of it sticking to the roof of my mouth.

"What's that like?" he asked.

"Sad," I said, through thick wads of peanut butter and white bread. Desperately needing lubrication, I got a quart bottle of milk out of the fridge and poured a glass.

"You don't talk much."

"I'm eating."

"Yeah, I can see that," he said, stubbing his cigarette out in a plate of uneaten, congealed eggs.

"How about your Old Man? He crazy too?"

I drank some milk to clear my throat. "No. He's in Florida trying to find my mother. When he finds her, he's coming back to pick me up and we'll be a real family again."

"Don't hold your breath, kid." That was what Aunt Evelyn said to me when I first got here.

"A *real* family?" he continued. "What does that *mean*, anyway? Sounds like a fairy tale to me."

"Well, my Old Man's coming back for me," I said defiantly. "He promised."

"Let me tell you about promises, kid," Buck said, lighting another cigarette. "Promises are no better than the people making them. Take, for instance, Uncle Sam. Uncle Sam promised me lots of things when I signed up. Money in my pocket, a roof over my head, three squares a day. They even said I'd be able to get any job I wanted when I got out. But what really happens? The war ends, I'm out on my ear, I got no money, I got no job."

"Were you really in the Korean War?" I asked, taking another bite of my sandwich.

"Hell yes I was in Korea!"

"What did you do?"

"We killed a lot of gooks, that's what we did," Buck said, leaning back in the chair and putting his hands behind his head. "That's what Uncle Sam paid us for, so that's what we did."

"Did you hate them?"

Buck thought about that a moment. "No, not really, I guess. We just killed 'em because they were trying to kill us."

"Why were they trying to kill you?"

"That's just what wars are like, kid," he said, puffing on his cigarette. "There's just lots of killing."

"Did it affect you?" I asked.

He shook his head. "No. No way. The old noodle's as clear as it was the day I shipped out. You can take it to the bank."

"What are you going to do now?"

"Try to find a job," he replied. "Make some money. Maybe find a girl and settle down, you know?"

It was quiet for a moment, while I finished my sandwich and glass of milk.

"Hey kid, you really talk to yourself in the attic?" he finally asked.

"Yeah, I do," I admitted. "But I'm not crazy. There's a good reason for it."

But that night as I lay in bed, I began to wonder myself if this was real or just a wild hallucination. Was I really seeing ghosts? Or was I actually going mad? The casual reader may believe I'm just lying. But more discerning readers will notice the great amount of detail included in my "hallucinations." Therefore, we can rule out lying. So that leaves two possibilities: either I'm crazy like my mother, or it's all true. And if I'm just bonkers, I sure have one heck of an imagination.

I mean, my "hallucinations" sure give a lot of information and details. And I've checked it all out at the library, so I can't be just making it all up, can I? So, I *must* be telling the truth.

Or am I?

* * *

Calvin Coolidge Junior High School was a very nice school. It had a great library, nice clean facilities, and the cafeteria food was swell. Everybody had a smile on their face and a spring in their step. All my teachers seemed to take a personal interest in me – especially the school psychologist, Mr. Stone. One day he called me into his office for a talk.

"Hello, Calvin. Thank you for coming," Mr. Stone smiled warmly. "Please have a seat, I'd like to have a little chat with you."

I did as he asked.

"Whenever we get a new student, I like to do a little screening. It's routine procedure, usually nothing to be alarmed about."

"Okay."

"How are you adjusting to our school? Everything all right? People treating you well?"

"Yes, sir," I said. "Everyone's just swell."

"Good, glad to hear it," he said. "And how are you doing? You feeling all right?"

I couldn't tell what he was driving at. "Sure, I guess."

"It's just that sometimes a new environment can be a bit overwhelming, intimidating," he elaborated. "It's perfectly normal to feel out of place at first."

"I don't feel out of place," I said.

"Good. How's your appetite? You sleeping all right?"

"Yes, sir."

"So you feel good, nothing's bothering you, is that what you're saying?"

"I guess so."

His face became more serious. "Calvin, sometimes we have a tendency to downplay what we think are small things, but they actually may turn out to be big things later on. Sometimes we tend to cover up or deny unpleasant realities because we just don't want to face them right now. But putting them off, or denying them, can just make things worse. Do you follow me?"

"I think so."

"Then you understand that denying things like these, or lying about them, doesn't really make them go away?" he asked.

"Yes, sir."

"Good. As part of the routine screening, I talked to your aunt yesterday. And I have to admit that what she told me was a tad troubling. She says you spent all summer up in the attic talking to yourself. To be honest with you, that doesn't sound normal to me, Calvin. That puts up some real red flags. Can you tell me what's going on up there? Are you hearing voices? Do you have imaginary friends or something?"

"They're not imaginary," I said.

"Why don't you tell me about them, then?"

So I did. I spilled everything – Uncle Joe, the Rosenbergs, Eva Peron. I'd never told anyone about it before. I have to admit, I felt relieved. It felt good getting it all off my chest. I was tired of holding it in. And I thought that if anybody would understand, it would be Mr. Stone.

Mr. Stone scribbled notes on his pad while I talked. He didn't look very surprised.

"When did you, umm, first start seeing dead people, Calvin?" he asked.

"When the Old Man left me at Aunt Evelyn's house this summer."

"That was the first time? You're sure?"

"Yes."

"Don't you find corresponding with a monster like Stalin – or his ghost, as you say – unsettling?"

"He's misunderstood."

"Misunderstood?"

"That's right. He says he's gotten a bum rap. He wants to set the record straight."

"Doesn't your mother suffer from similar delusions?"

"These are not delusions. I'm not crazy."

"Calm down, I'm just asking –"

"And leave my mother out of this!"

"All right, just calm down."

Mr. Stone said that was enough for one day, but he wanted to meet with me for weekly "therapy" sessions from now on. I didn't know if telling him about all these things was the right thing to do or not, but he sure seemed worried after hearing about them.

Chapter 16

The more time I spent around Buck, the more I began to see that something just wasn't right with him. He insisted the war hadn't affected him, but he must have been in denial because strange behaviors began to emerge almost immediately. I could tell he had trouble sleeping because he woke me up several times pacing in the hallway outside my room in the middle of the night. I think he didn't want to fall asleep because he was afraid of having nightmares about Korea.

One night, I woke up to tapping sounds coming from inside my closet. It was Buck, on his knees, testing for loose floor-boards. He said he thought the North Koreans were digging an underground tunnel to my closet.

"An underground tunnel to the second floor?" I asked in confusion.

Another time I caught him on his hands and knees in the front parlor with a revolver, looking for North Koreans under the sofa. When he saw me, he calmly stood up, walked into the kitchen, and put the revolver in the freezer.

He kept his car keys buried in the flour canister and his underwear in the oven so the North Koreans wouldn't find them. He told me the "gooks" were involved in a conspiracy to steal his underwear because theirs was made of horsehair fibers and was very uncomfortable to wear.

Every day when the mail came, he peeked out between the curtains suspiciously because he was convinced the mailman, who was Japanese, was a North Korean POW camp commander who was trying to kidnap him.

He even switched cigarettes because he believed they were slipping substances to chemically castrate him into his brand.

And he never talked at the breakfast table because he believed the butter dish had been bugged by – you got it – the North Koreans.

But then I found out it wasn't just the North Koreans who gave Buck the jitters. I noticed several nights in a row he went out and stood in the backyard in the middle of the night, looking up at the sky for hours on end. One night I went out there and asked him what he was doing.

"Looking for *them*," he said quietly.

"The North Koreans?"

"No," he said. "The little men from Mars."

With great detail, he told me of how one night in Korea his platoon was on patrol and got completely surrounded by a superior enemy force.

"They were everywhere," he said. "There was no way out. We knew we were goners."

They talked it over amongst themselves and decided not to surrender. They didn't want to spend the rest of the war rotting away in a North Korean POW camp. So they decided to go down fighting.

"We were going to take as many of them to hell with us as we could," he said.

But just as the enemy approached from all directions to wipe them out, there was a blinding, pulsating light from above and a large spherical craft came hovering right over them.

"Then red and green laser rays started shooting out of that ball in all directions," he said excitedly. "But they weren't shooting at us. They were shooting at the *gooks*."

He said the UFO wiped out the North Koreans, but didn't harm his platoon. "It just hovered there right over us, protecting us. Those death rays *vaporized* those gooks. They didn't stand a chance."

When all of the North Koreans were dead, big glass tubes came down from the belly of the craft and "vacuumed" Buck and his friends up into the UFO. Buck said he doesn't know how long they were inside the spaceship, because everything was like a dreamlike state and time seemed to stand still. He said it could have been days or it could have been only minutes.

"What happened inside the UFO?" I asked.

"Unspeakable things," he shuddered.

First, they were stripped naked and strapped to cold metal tables. Then they were coated with a slimy gelatinous substance that burned off all their body hair and made their skin itch and burn. Then rubber tubes and hoses were stuffed into their bodily orifices and they were pumped full of nitrogen and helium and a thick, black, foul-smelling substance kind of like motor oil. They were pumped full of that until it oozed out their noses and ears.

"One poor bastard – Gillespie – couldn't take it," Buck said, visibly shaken. "They pumped him so full of the stuff that he just popped like a tick – all over the walls and ceiling and all over us!"

Then the hoses were removed and flexible metal arms like tentacles were inserted and they could feel the little rubber fingers on the tentacles pinching and squeezing and plucking their guts and organs just like shoppers in the produce section looking for ripe fruit. Tiny tentacles held their eyelids open, and if they passed out or tried to sleep they would be shocked awake with electrodes.

After that, flexible probes were stuck up their nostrils all the way to their brains and everything they knew was downloaded and stored on a bank of machines in the UFO.

"I felt like they were stealing my memories," Buck said.

Finally, they were stuck, probed, impaled, and experimented on in ways that Buck wouldn't talk about. He had to turn away for a few minutes to compose himself.

"Did – did you ever *see* them?" I finally asked.

"Just once. I got a glimpse of one of 'em out of the corner of my eye. It was...terrifying. It was about four feet tall and had big bug eyes, but it didn't look human at all. To me, it looked just like a giant crayfish. To this day, I can't eat seafood."

Then Buck told me how they were unstrapped from the tables and allowed to put their uniforms back on. They were given their rifles back, but all the ammunition had been taken out.

Then they were released – all except the guy who exploded – and the UFO flew off just like nothing had ever happened.

"But it wasn't over yet," Buck said ominously.

When they made it back to their unit, they told their captain what had happened. The captain separated them from the rest of the unit and locked them in the infirmary. Then he called HQ.

Sometime later, three generals entered the infirmary and interrogated them for several hours. The generals listened to their story but strongly implied that the platoon may have misconstrued events.

"During wartime, the mind can become fatigued and play many tricks on us," they were told. "Why don't you boys take some time and decide whether you might be mistaken or not?"

When they told the generals they were sure of their story, the generals shook their heads and left. Warm food was brought in and they were allowed to sleep for a few hours.

Then the generals came back and woke them up. With the generals were two men wearing black suits and sunglasses – indoors. The generals stayed quiet this time, and seemed to defer to the two men in black suits.

"They were definitely calling the shots," Buck testified.

The men in black suits grilled them for countless hours, but their story never changed. Finally, one of the interrogators said, "This is *not* a story you want to stick with, if you get my meaning."

"It was a direct threat," Buck said.

One of the government men opened a briefcase and pulled some typed pages out. "Here is the *real* story," he told them. "All you have to do is sign it, and all this will be over. No harm, no foul, you can go back to your normal lives. All forgiven. We promise."

Then the men left the room to give them time to think about it. "We read their statement and it said nothing about the UFO," Buck said. "It was a lie. So we talked about it, and decided we were sticking with the truth."

Well, the government men came back a few minutes later and the platoon told them to stuff it. The men in black told them if they didn't sign the statement and forget about the whole thing, they would be sorry – very, very sorry.

They didn't sign it.

"We were all put on an airplane and shipped back to the States," Buck said. "The Army discharged us and put us in a mental hospital and said we'd never see our loved ones again. They gave us electroshock therapy and psychotropic drugs, but we never broke."

"How did you get out?" I asked.

"I broke out," he said. "That's right, I waited for an opportunity and ran like a rabbit when I had the chance. That means someday there could be a knock on the door and I could just *disappear*. If that happens, now you'll know why."

"Why didn't you just sign the statement?" I asked.

"Because it wasn't the *truth*," Buck explained. "They called us liars. Sometimes you gotta stick to your guns no matter what, kid."

But even though Buck was slowly cracking up on account of what happened to him in the war, he didn't exactly act crazy all the time. Mrs. Riley, for instance, apparently didn't notice anything strange about him, since he'd been over at her house about a dozen times already since coming home from the war.

Aunt Evelyn noticed what was going on right away. "Why do you go over to Mrs. Riley's every afternoon?" she asked him one day.

"She's having me do some work in her pool house," Buck answered.

"While she's in there with you?"

"She's very involved in the details," he replied with a wicked grin.

Well, I thought, *at least Mrs. Riley isn't lonely anymore.*

* * *

The next day at school started off just swell. It was the day of the Talent Show and there was going to be an assembly and I'd been practicing *Deep in the Heart of Texas* on my accordion all week to get ready for it. The winner was going to get a trophy and a "No Homework" pass for a whole week and second helpings of dessert in the cafeteria for a whole year. Boy, I sure wanted to win that prize!

I brought my accordion to school with me and stuffed it in Miss Underwood's classroom on account of the Talent Show wasn't until the end of the day. I spent most of the time in class daydreaming about how I was going to dazzle the entire school with my cool accordion playing and win the grand prize. I was certain the abundance of accolades from my teachers and peers would be truly humbling, and was more than ready to play the part of the modest winner.

At lunch I got my tray and was looking for a place to sit when wouldn't you know it there was that gross skinny kid Allen what's-his-name sitting all alone again. I tried to pretend

I didn't see him but he kept calling out my name and wouldn't stop so I had to sit down across the table from him.

"Hi, Allen."

"Hi, Calvin," he smiled. There was something different about him. He kept smiling, longer than any reasonable person would. Then I realized what it was – he had braces.

"Just got 'em," he beamed, pleased with himself.

"Don't they hurt?" I asked.

"Yeah, but Dad says when I'm older I'll be glad because I'll have straight teeth and a dazzling smile."

Spoken like a true dentist's son.

Allen cheerfully unwrapped his sandwich and took a gigantic bite. Today it was watercress, with celery sticks and some mixed nuts on the side.

"No Moon Pie today?" I asked casually.

"Too gooey," he replied. "Mom says it would gum up my new braces."

At least with the braces I won't have to watch him floss, I thought. But when he was finished eating he took out a small metal scraper with a hooked end and started picking the food out of his braces with it. Not surprisingly, it was much worse than watching someone floss.

The rest of the day was uneventful except for P.E. Coach Axelrod had us doing the shot put, and while he had his back turned two kids recruited me to help them form a human slingshot using a jockstrap. They each held one end of the strap while my job was to create the tension necessary to catapult the shot put into the air.

They wanted to see how far we could get it to go. In hindsight I should have declined, but I guess I was in a playful mood on account of the Talent Show, so I said "okay." Anyway, they held on tight to each end of the strap while I stretched it back with the shot put in it, as far as I could stretch it. Just when I couldn't pull it back anymore, one of the kids said, "Let 'er rip!"

and I let go of the strap just as Eddie Brockelman stepped right in front of us.

I yelled "Watch out!" but the shot put was already airborne and it hit Eddie Brockelman square in the middle of his forehead and he went down backwards just like a redwood tree.

"Holy cow, we *killed* him!" I heard one of the other boys say. They quickly tried to ditch the jockstrap in some bushes.

Coach Axelrod and the rest of the class crowded around Eddie, trying to revive him, but we stayed right where we were.

"I've got a pulse!" someone shouted triumphantly, but we weren't out of the woods just yet.

Boy, was Coach Axelrod sore. He yelled at two kids to pick Eddie up and carry him to the nurse's office. Poor Eddie was still seeing birdies when they carried him away.

Then Coach Axelrod turned on the three of us. "Of all the hair-brained, dim-witted stunts I've ever witnessed, this one takes the cake!"

Boy, he was really steamed.

First, he made us run the Axelrod Gauntlet: we had to run between all the boys formed up into two rows while they threw jelly balls at our heads. Coach Axelrod felt that everyone should share in the meting out of discipline in order to build class comradery and team unity.

He made us run the gauntlet three times. Then he sent us to the office.

Sitting in the office, I was despondent and regretful over the possibility of missing the Talent Show. And, of course, I hoped Eddie Brockelman would be all right, too.

Mr. Hayvenhurst, the school principal, called everyone's parents in. Of course, Aunt Evelyn couldn't come on account of her agoraphobia and all, so she sent Buck instead. Buck got there just as Mr. Hayvenhurst was finishing up with the other boys and their parents. Sitting outside the principal's office I could hear all the shouting, cursing and crying going on inside, from both the kids *and* their parents.

When it was our turn, Buck and I filed into Mr. Hayven-hurst's office and sat down. Buck's hair was messy and needed to be cut. He had his pack of smokes tucked inside in his shirt-sleeve, bicep-high.

When Mr. Hayvenhurst told him what had happened, Buck broke out laughing, then caught himself.

"I don't think this situation is funny at all," Mr. Hayven-hurst chided.

"I'm sorry, it's just the mental image I got when you said it," Buck half-heartedly apologized. He took the pack out of his sleeve and pulled a smoke out with his lips. Mr. Hayvenhurst looked at him in horror.

"I hope you're not thinking of smoking in here!"

"Oh, yeah – force of habit," Buck smiled, tucking the ciga-rette over his ear. "I just got back to the world from Korea. I'm still re-adjusting."

"Well, I guess I can understand that," Mr. Hayvenhurst said. He was an awful nice guy, after all, even though I could tell he was still pretty sore about what happened in P.E. and he didn't think much of my uncouth cousin.

"Eddie Brockelman has a lump on his forehead roughly the size and color of a PGA regulation golf ball," Mr. Hayvenhurst reported. "But the doctor said there's no lasting brain damage and he should be able to return to school in a few days."

"So what's the big deal?" Buck demanded.

"The 'big deal' is that it could have been much worse," Mr. Hayvenhurst tersely replied. "You're a very lucky young man, Calvin. You very well could have made Eddie Brockelman a vegetable for life. Then how would you feel, son?"

I expected Buck to burst out laughing again, but he some-how managed to hold it in.

"Your compatriots in this appalling misadventure have been suspended from school for two days," Mr. Hayvenhurst told me. "I'm still weighing just what *your* consequences should be."

There was a knock on the door. "Come in," the principal said. The door opened and Miss Underwood stepped inside. She looked at me, and then at Buck. Buck looked back at her and winked.

"Hello, I'm Miss Underwood, Calvin's English teacher," she said to Buck.

"I'm his cousin, Buck," Buck replied. Then he leaned over and whispered to me, "You never told me your English teacher was such a dish." It was loud enough for her to hear. I could have crawled beneath Mr. Hayvenhurst's desk and stayed there the rest of the day.

"What can we do for you, Miss Underwood?" Mr. Hayvenhurst asked.

"I heard about what happened earlier today, and I'd like to offer my two cents worth," she told the principal.

Good old Miss Underwood. I knew I could count on her — she'd come to plead my case.

She told Mr. Hayvenhurst I was her star pupil and that, unlike the other boys, I'd never been involved in any mischief like this before. She told him I'd been looking forward to taking part in the Talent Show and had been practicing the accordion for weeks (she knew it sounded better than days). She told him that denying me the chance to put my musical talent on display could have a negative effect on my self-esteem and possibly lead to further delinquent behavior. She told him that mercy was an honorable and noble trait and that true leadership required wise and measured judgments.

It was a pretty good speech.

And he bought it.

"Well, that was very impassioned, Miss Underwood," he said. "And it's no secret that your words carry a great deal of weight with me, given the high level of esteem I hold you in."

It sounded good so far.

"And, given the fact that the other boys involved admitted it was their idea and that they had recruited Calvin, under a great deal of pressure, no doubt, to take part in their shenanigans, and that none of the boys, Calvin included, had any intentions of harming anyone, I think we can all agree that this momentary lack of judgment on Calvin's part shouldn't result in his being suspended from school or missing the Talent Show."

It was sounding a whole lot better.

"However, consequences of some sort are required in a matter such as this," the principal went on. "But I believe perhaps one week of cleaning the cafeteria during lunch break should be sufficient punishment."

"Thank you, Mr. Hayvenhurst," Miss Underwood smiled.

"Thanks, pal!" Buck said.

"Don't mention it," Mr. Hayvenhurst responded.

Buck and I got up to go.

"It was nice meeting you," Miss Underwood said to Buck.

"Nice meeting *you*," Buck replied, with another wink. "See you at Open House."

I cringed, but Miss Underwood didn't look offended at all. In fact, if I didn't know better I'd swear Miss Underwood actually batted her eyelashes at him.

Oh, no. Not Miss Underwood, too...

Nevertheless, I walked out of Principal Hayvenhurst's office feeling like a weight had been lifted off my shoulders. After the morning's excitement, though, the rest of the day was sort of anti-climactic. Even the Talent Show.

I was fourth up in the show. The act before me was Amy, the girl who fainted in science class and threw up in the hall. Her act was playing *How Much Is That Doggie in the Window?* On the saxophone, but half-way through the song she ran out of wind and fainted right there on the stage. Two kids in the front row volunteered to carry her to the nurse's office.

Then it was my turn. I took the stage expectantly, even exuberantly – but there was a problem. I'd never played on a stage in front of an audience before, and was stricken with a sudden and severe case of stage fright. I hadn't anticipated this. My mind went blank and the sea of faces out in the audience began to swim before my eyes. The emcee had to announce me and my song three whole times before I snapped out of it. Finally, I regained control of my brain and fingers enough to form the "D" chord on my instrument's keyboard and belatedly launched into the song.

From that point on I did all right until I hit a couple of flat notes when I got to the "rabbits rush around the brush" part of the song. It was an admittedly ragged performance, but unlike poor Amy, at least I was able to finish the song.

Needless to say, I didn't win. The first place winner was a kid who picked up a twelve-pound bowling ball suspended from a rope with his teeth. I won second place though, and got my very own copy of a book titled "Personal Hygiene: A Boy and Girl's Guide to Cleanliness and Healthy Living."

Chapter 17

Mr. Stone, the school psychologist, was convinced I was experiencing some kind of mental breakdown. He told me he thought I had a "death fixation' that wasn't healthy for a normal 13-year-old boy. In between sessions, he had been gathering evidence about my mother's condition and stays in various psychiatric wards, and Aunt Evelyn's fortune-telling endeavors.

He was building a dossier on me.

One day when I arrived for one of our regular sessions, he told me "I think you're in a lot of trouble, Calvin. I think you have a deep-seated anger down inside you because you were abandoned by both your parents. You are receiving no guidance or love from your aunt whom you now live with. Your only friends are famous 'dead' people with whom you carry on imaginary relationships and conversations. I think you are going through a severe identity crisis, crying out to a world which you feel not only doesn't acknowledge your existence but is rapidly leaving you behind. I feel we need to take action before your anxieties and delusions completely take over and drive you to even more reckless and self-destructive behavior."

He stood up and opened his office door, waving a middle-aged woman inside. "This is Mrs. Ardmore. She is here to talk with you about making a big change, Calvin. A necessary change."

Mrs. Ardmore was a social worker with the State Child Welfare Office. She proceeded to tell me that Mr. Stone had contacted her because he felt our sessions were ineffective and I wasn't making any progress and he was extremely concerned for my well-being. She said that she and Mr. Stone had decided that the best thing for me was to remove me from my current surroundings so I could get the help I so desperately needed.

"Where would I go?" I asked, in shock.

"We have a nice, nurturing place in mind for you to relax and rest and get better, Calvin," she said in a soothing voice. "It's run by the state, and it's especially for troubled and possibly violent children like yourself."

"I'm not a violent child," I protested.

Mr. Stone picked a report up off his desk. "Last week you injured another student with a shot put during P.E. Coach Axelrod made a full report of the incident. The student, one Eddie Brockelman, required emergency medical attention at a hospital."

"That – that was an accident!" I said.

"Was it?" Mr. Stone asked sardonically.

"Why can't I just keep living at Aunt Evelyn's?"

"Your aunt's home is an inappropriate environment for a child," Mrs. Ardmore said. "She is an alcoholic and her vocation is not a wholesome influence. You have been abandoned by both your mother and father. You have been neglected and left to raise yourself. The institution you will be placed in will provide the type of structure, discipline, and supportive environment that a child needs while you heal from these...hallucinations and delusions you're suffering from."

"I don't want to go."

"As a minor, I'm afraid it isn't your decision, Calvin," the social worker said.

"My aunt won't allow it!" I said.

Mr. Stone spoke up this time. "As a state child welfare official, Mrs. Ardmore has the authority to remove you form your aunt's home and place you in a safe environment. I'm afraid it's the law, Calvin."

I could see that there was no arguing with them. So I said goodbye to Calvin Coolidge Junior High School, and Mrs. Ardmore and a police officer drove me to Aunt Evelyn's house to pick up my things. "Don't worry, Calvin," Mrs. Ardmore cheerfully told me as we drove away from the school. "Your new facility has a school with teachers and other children just like you. I'm sure you'll like it very much!"

When we got home, Aunt Evelyn and Buck let us in. "I'm sorry, kid," Aunt Evelyn apologized. "You know I'd let you stay as long as you wanted, but they've got a court order."

Mrs. Ardmore went upstairs with me to pack my things. In the hall we passed the closed attic door, behind which sat Uncle Joe smoking his cigar and waiting for me to come home from school. But now it looked like I'd never see him again.

In my room we packed my suitcase with my clothes and underwear and the Bible and my Dick Contino records. I also packed my short story and all the pages Uncle Joe and I had written together. I put my Buffalo nickel and my Lone Ranger and Tonto knife in my pocket. Then I put on the Route 66 cowboy hat with the red drawstring the Old Man had bought for me, and that was that.

"Can I take my accordion?" I asked.

"Of course," Mrs. Ardmore said.

We went back downstairs with my suitcase and accordion to say goodbye to Aunt Evelyn and Buck.

"Take care of yourself, kid," Aunt Evelyn said, shaking her head. I was pretty sure she was going to miss having me around after all.

"Tell my Old Man and mother where I am when they come to get me," I said.

"Sure thing, kid."

"'By, Buck," I said.

He shook my hand. "I'm gonna come visit you, kid," he promised. "Don't forget that."

And then we were in Mrs. Ardmore's car, driving away from the big yellow house in Cleveland. I was numb. It really hadn't registered yet what was happening.

"I've had to do this many, many times, Calvin," Mrs. Ardmore told me. "Believe me, the best way to do it is quickly – like pulling off a band aid."

* * *

I was under no delusions about where they were taking me, of course. I knew full well it was a funny farm for kids like me. I even felt relieved, in a way. At least I would be around other kids like me. And I wouldn't have to pretend to be "normal" anymore just to fit in.

It was called Sunnybrook State Institute for Children. Sounds like a real nice place – if you like crumbling, one-hun-dred-year-old brick buildings with bars on the windows and tall iron fences around them. Not that it didn't have its own peculiar charm. A certain Edgar Allen Poe quality quickly came to mind.

But it wasn't too bad on the inside – it was clean, orderly, structured – just the way a lot of the patients liked things. Mrs. Ardmore helped me lug my suitcase and accordion inside to the reception area. A nurse behind the counter checked me in, and a lean, straight, balding man in a white coat came down the corridor toward us.

"I'm Dr. Spielman," he said, reaching out a hand. I politely took it but didn't say anything.

"This is Calvin, the boy I told you about on the phone," Mrs. Ardmore told him.

"Glad to meet you, Calvin," the doctor said. He was cheerful and well-groomed, but I noticed that he avoided making eye contact with me.

"Well, I think you have all the documents, and the school psychologist's notes," Mrs. Ardmore said. "So I will just leave you two gentlemen to it and be on my way. Goodbye, Calvin. Don't worry, you'll be in good hands here. Won't he, Dr. Spielman?"

"Entirely," the doctor concurred, and Mrs. Ardmore smiled one more time at me and she was gone.

The nurse behind the counter reached across and handed me two tiny paper cups. One had water in it and the other one contained two little white pills.

"It's just your medication, Calvin," Dr. Spielman said calmly. "Go ahead, it just relaxes you – you know, evens things out a bit."

"I'm already relaxed," I said.

"Well then, you'll feel *more* relaxed," he insisted. "Go ahead, it'll make you feel better."

I guessed there was no use in resisting, so I took the pills and swallowed them with the water.

"That-a-boy," the doctor said. "Now, we're just going to do a few tests, then we'll show you to your room and you can get settled in and get some rest."

I started to pick up my suitcase and accordion, but he said, "You can leave them here. An orderly will take them to your room."

Doctor Spielman took me to an examination room, where a different doctor gave me a full physical. Then Dr. Spielman came back and took me to a different room with a table and chairs and did some other kinds of tests. He showed me pictures and ink splotches and numbers and letters and asked me what I saw, while a nurse scribbled down notes on a clipboard. I was feeling awfully light-headed from the pills but I think I

did a good job on all the tests because Dr. Spielman seemed
pleased and he didn't yell at me for making any mistakes or
anything.

Then he took me to another room that looked just like the
last room and gave me a bunch of tests with all sorts of differ-
ent-shaped blocks and puzzle pieces and I had to try to make
them all fit in their correct slots and holes while he timed me
with a stop-watch. The same nurse was there scribbling notes
on her clipboard.

Then he took me back to the first room and gave me a
whole bunch of word puzzles and analogies and grammar
games to do. The nurse was there too, scribbling down notes
on her clipboard the whole time.

When the games and puzzles were all done, Dr. Spielman
said it was time to show me to my room. He said I would live
on C Ward, and led me upstairs to the second floor. We walked
down a long, dreary corridor of closed doors until we came to a
door marked "C 7."

"Well, this is it," Dr. Spielman said brightly, opening the
door.

It was a drab little room with two of everything: two beds,
two desks, two wardrobes – but only one window, with bars
criss-crossing it. My suitcase and accordion were sitting on one
of the beds.

"Well, what do you think?" Dr. Spielman asked.

"There are two beds," I observed.

"Yes, your roommate is in class right now," Dr. Spielman
replied. "Why don't you unpack and get settled in and get a
little rest, and I'll bring him up in a little while to meet you?
Sound like a plan?"

"I guess so."

So he left and I unpacked my suitcase and put my clothes in
the wardrobe and my writing stuff in the desk and left my accordion on the bed because I didn't feel like resting right now

so I just sat down in a chair and stared through the bars at the trees outside the window. Then I got out Uncle Joe's memoirs and leafed through the pages remembering all the stuff we'd worked on together and wondering what he was gonna do now that I wasn't there to help him finish it and all. Then I got out my short story and leafed through its pages and remembered what Miss Underwood had told me about real writers write true stuff about their own lives and how I should write about my life, and then I thought *who would want to read that?*

But she said people would want to on account of it's *true*, and I trusted and believed Miss Underwood so I decided right then and there that I would start writing about my *real* life and all the *real* things that happened to me and just trust that she was right and knew what she was talking about when she said people would want to read about *me.*

By that time it was getting late and I was just beginning to wonder when Dr. Spielman would be coming back to introduce me to my roommate when there was a knock on the door and I opened it and Dr. Spielman stood there with a blond, shaggy-haired, pudgy boy about my age. Only something was wrong.

The boy looked like a zombie. His eyes were red-rimmed and half-closed. His mouth was slack and drool dripped from its right corner. He shuffled into the room like he'd just under-gone a lobotomy. I was horrified.

"Cut it out, Orson," Dr. Spielman ordered. "It isn't funny. Calvin just got here."

Orson snapped out of his zombie act and wiped the drool from his chin with his sleeve. He winked and smiled at me. He looked almost completely normal now.

"Orson is a real joker," Dr. Spielman said. "He has an obses-sion with shoving screwdrivers into other kids' ears, but we're working on that, aren't we, Orson?"

Dr. Spielman must have seen the look of horror on my face, because he quickly added, "Don't worry, Calvin. We don't allow any screwdrivers in *this* facility."

"I like to break things," Orson told me.

"*Orson!* Such a kidder!" Dr. Spielman said. "Well, why don't you two get acquainted now, and Orson can bring you down to the afternoon group therapy session where you can meet the others before dinner time."

"You're – you're not going to leave me here with *him*, are you?" I asked.

"You're roommates now, Calvin," the doctor said. "We'll see you two at the session. Be sure and get him there in one piece, Orson!" And Doctor Spielman turned and left the room.

"Is that your accordion?" Orson asked, pointing to my bed.

"Yes..." I said apprehensively.

"I like to smash things."

"I won that in a contest," I said. "I won second place in my school Talent Show with it. Please don't smash my accordion."

"What else you got?" he demanded.

I showed him my cowboy hat with the red drawstring. "It's just like the one the Lone Ranger wears," I told him. "My Old Man bought it for me at a trading post on Route 66."

"Can I try it on?" Orson asked.

"Sure."

He put it on and drew the string up tight under his chin. I showed him my Lone Ranger and Tonto pocket knife and my Buffalo nickel.

"Can I have these?" he asked me.

"No. I got them on my road trip with my Old Man last summer. They mean a lot to me."

"Oh, okay," he said.

I guess Orson wasn't such a bad kid after all. Just a little different. And really immature. He told me that his parents owned a hardware store in Columbus and they never came to see him, but sent him a lot of gifts at Christmastime to make up for it. He admitted to being enamored of screwdrivers, but swore that he'd only plunged a screwdriver into one kid's ear at school, and that's what got him sent here.

"What do you like to break?" he asked.

"I don't like to break anything," I replied.

"What do you like to do?"

"I guess I like to write."

"Oh," he said.

"So, whose ear did you shove a screwdriver into, anyway?" I asked.

"Some kid in History class."

"What did he do to make you mad?"

"Who said anything about being mad?"

It was time for the afternoon therapy session, so Orson took me downstairs to the first-floor therapy room. Dr. Spielman was there, with seven or eight kids sitting in chairs arranged in a circle.

"Ah, here comes our newest member now," Dr. Spielman announced as we entered and took a seat. "Everyone, this is Calvin. Please welcome him and say hello."

There was a half-hearted chorus of "*Hello, Calvin*" from the whole group.

"Calvin likes reading and writing and music," Dr. Spielman continued. "He just arrived today, and I'm sure everyone will do what they can to make him feel right at home."

"What did he do to get sent here?" a mousy little girl with long dark hair and glasses demanded.

"Now, let's remember our manners, Nell," Dr. Spielman gently chided.

The little girl gave him a stony glare. "My name's not Nell. It's *Dot*."

"My apologies, Dot. My point is that Calvin hasn't even had a chance to settle in yet. Let's give him some time before we start asking him personal questions like that."

"I bet he's got hodophobia," Dot declared. "Or maybe helio-phobia. That would make him a vampire. How about it, Calvin? You a vampire, or what?"

"Don't worry about Dot," Orson leaned over and whispered to me. "She's a lot quieter when she's Nell."

"Remember what we said about monopolizing group ther-apy time, Dot," Dr. Spielman reminded. "Everyone must have a chance to speak, so we must take turns."

"Oh, all right!" Dot said, crossing her arms in a huff. "But I think this hospital has stupid rules!"

"You are entitled to your opinion," Dr. Spielman allowed. "Now, I would like to talk about what happened at dinnertime last night."

A pasty-looking kid with meticulously-combed black hair and the kind of eyeglasses that have a strap going around the back of the head started rocking back and forth in his chair. Dr. Spielman seemed to ignore it.

"That's Stuart," Orson whispered to me. "He threw a fit last night because his peas got mixed up with his carrots. Bart had to come take him out of the cafeteria and they had to give him sedatives to calm him down."

"Does anyone have a comment to make about the incident?" Dr. Spielman inquired.

"I don't see why Stuart gets special food just for him," Dot complained. "That's special treatment. That's not fair."

"Dot, you know Stuart is very particular about how his meals are prepared," Dr. Spielman said, trying to sound patient and controlled.

"They have to cook all of his food separately so none of the juices intermingle," Orson explained to me.

"But it's not fair!"

Stuart began to rock harder in his chair.

"Dot, I think you need to leave the circle now," Dr. Spielman said.

"I'll be quiet now," the little girl promised.

"Dot..."

"Oh, all right," Dot agreed, and a very strange transformation came over her. Her whole demeanor changed from a confident posture of sitting up in her chair to one of total meekness and submission.

"Welcome back, Nell," Dr. Spielman said warmly. "Now, would anyone else like to comment on last night's incident? Anyone except Nell, who has already ceded her allotted time to Dot."

A girl with stringy dark hair and bangs covering her eyes spoke up. "I don't know why we all have to go to bed early whenever Stuart gets his vegetables mixed up." She spoke very quietly and timidly, and seemed a little depressed to me.

A red-haired boy with freckles and deep blue eyes interjected, "It wouldn't have happened at all if Trevor hadn't fooled with his plate!"

"I was only trying to cut his Salisbury steak for him," Trevor, a sensitive-looking boy with curly brown hair, explained. "The cook forgot to do it."

"You know you should've sent it back to the kitchen," the boy with red hair and freckles argued. "That's what we always do when they forget!"

"I was only trying to help," Trevor said.

Stuart, still rocking back and forth, began to moan.

"Should I go get Bart?" Orson asked Dr. Spielman.

"No, Stuart is a member of this group," the doctor said firmly. "He should be a part of this discussion."

"You know he doesn't like anyone messing with his food!" the boy with freckles said again.

"I said I was sorry!" Trevor cried out emotionally. "What else do you want me to do?"

"Why don't you just kill yourself?" the boy with freckles suggested.

"Now, that's enough!" Dr. Spielman ordered. "That was a very inappropriate thing to say, Edmund."

"I'm sorry," Edmund said. Stuart moaned louder.

"I think I should go get Bart now," Orson said to Dr. Spielman.

"Not yet," Dr. Spielman said. Nell brought her feet up and curled herself into a ball in her chair. The girl with stringy bangs sat impassively. Trevor started crying.

"Pointing the finger at others is misguided and unproductive," Dr. Spielman declared. "I think the lesson we can all learn from this episode is to respect the sanctity of Stuart's plate and mind our own bee's wax at dinner time!"

Edmund stood up and began screaming loudly, looking in terror at his arms and legs as if he were in great pain. Stuart moaned louder, and Trevor wouldn't stop crying. Dr. Spielman looked ready to throw in the towel.

"Go get Bart now," he said to Orson.

Bart was the orderly on our floor. He was tall and strong and as thick as an oak tree. When he got there he picked Stuart up and tucked him under one arm, and Edmund, who was still screaming bloody murder, under the other arm. He carried them off to the nurse's station to have them sedated.

It was my understanding that places like Sunnybrook were meant to be calm and quiet and peaceful – a place where kids who had trouble dealing with the stresses and burdens of everyday life in the outside world could rest and get better. But from what I'd seen so far, it was just as stressful in here as anywhere else.

Dr. Spielman said the therapy session was over. He told us to line up at the medication window and get our evening pills.

He watched each one of us carefully as we passed by the window to make sure we swallowed both pills. Then he told us to go to the cafeteria for dinner and "for God's sake don't touch anybody else's plate!"

After dinner, we got to go to the recreation room for free time until lights out. There was a TV set and tables set up with all kinds of magazines and jig-saw puzzles and board games. There was even a ping-pong table and an old, beat-up pinball machine.

"The pinball machine is set up to play without putting any nickels in," Orson told me. "Otherwise, no one around here could afford to play it."

I didn't feel like playing pinball or ping-pong. Orson suggested chess, so we sat down at a table and had a great game. He was much better at chess than I was. In fact, I thought he was quite good. He knew moves I'd never even heard of. Of course, he beat me every time.

While we played, he filled me in on all the other kids. He told me that Edmund, the kid who started screaming during the therapy session, had a super rare condition that caused him to believe he was on fire. It was usually triggered by a stressful situation, like a group therapy session. When it happens, he starts screaming hysterically until someone is able to prove to him he's not on fire. Other than that, Orson said Edmund was completely normal.

Then he told me about Stuart, the kid who was so particular about his food. Orson said Stuart suffered from crippling obsessive compulsive disorder. If there was any deviating from the schedule, Stuart would completely fall to pieces. If he believed somebody tied their shoelaces the wrong way or parted their hair on the wrong side, it would cause severe anxiety and he would end up a rocking, moaning basket case. Anything could set him off, and it was anybody's guess what it would be next.

Next was Trevor, the kid who cried during the session. Trevor was an artistic type and very sensitive. He was also bipolar. Orson said Trevor couldn't have a roommate because he stayed up for days on end painting – not eating, not sleeping – only to tear up the painting in frustration when he wasn't satisfied with it. He would stay in bed for days afterward, only to get up and begin the whole process over again.

The girl with the stringy bangs in her eyes was named Minnie. She was obsessed with Lord Byron and death. She was on continual suicide watch.

Bertram had possibly the strangest phobia of all. He had a paralyzing fear of implements meant to temporarily hold or store clothing items, such as hat racks, coat hooks, hangars, and shoe horns. All such items had to be carefully removed from his room. It was the *temporariness* of their function that particularly terrified him, for some reason. Garment bags were especially horrifying to him. Strangely enough, according to Orson, Bertram was a haberdasher's son.

Then there was little Nell. She was quite possibly the most messed up of all. The little unassuming dark-haired mousy girl with glasses was a dangerous arsonist with multiple personalities. Nell was shy and reclusive. Dot was assertive and argumentative. Nina was a thief and a con artist. Kat was a chain-smoker and gambling addict. Sarah was a devout evangelist. On any given day, you never knew what you were going to get with little Nell.

Oh yeah, Nell was in here with no possibility of release for trying to burn down her own house while her parents were asleep in their bedroom.

What happens to the human mind when it breaks is sometimes a very mysterious thing.

"What about you?" Orson asked when he was finished filling me in on all the others.

"I see dead people."

"No kidding?" he smiled. "I haven't come across that racket before."

That night at lights out I brushed my teeth in the shared bathroom down the hall and got into bed. Bart came by each room to make sure everyone was accounted for. Edmund and Stuart had been sedated for the night and all was quiet on the floor.

"Hey, Orson – you still awake?" I asked.

"Yeah, what is it?"

"What's in those little white pills they give us, anyway?"

"I dunno," he replied. "Probably lithium or something. You know, something to take the edge off."

"Oh," I said. "Good night."

"Good night," Orson said. I was tired but I couldn't go to sleep. I kept thinking about screwdrivers, and it kept me up half the night.

Chapter 18

The daily schedule was rigid, predictable, and unchanging – just the way most of the patients liked it. At 7:00 a.m. it was morning medication time, followed by breakfast at 7:30. School started at 8:00 and we had lunch at noon. After lunch, there was more school until 3:00, when we got a thirty-minute break in the exercise yard. At 3:30 we had afternoon group therapy, then evening medication at 5:00, followed by dinner at 5:30. After dinner we had two hours of recreation time, then lights out at 8:30.

School took place with all the kids in one classroom with one teacher. It was easy for me – it was easy for most of us, although some were less motivated than others. I missed Miss Underwood every day.

Right after school was out, we got thirty minutes to play outside in an enclosed yard before afternoon therapy. That's when we got to play stickball or football or just run around the yard playing tag or hide and seek.

We had two orderlies on our ward. Raoul was from Puerto Rico, and Bart was a former ranch hand from Montana who entertained us with rodeo rope tricks. He even taught me a few, including the "Texas Skip" and some others Montie Montana and Will Rogers did in the movies.

Every Saturday the kids who were good all week got to pile into the hospital bus and go to a double-feature movie. Since Bart was always the one who took us, it was usually a pair of

Westerns starring either Gene Autry or Hopalong Cassidy. We even got free popcorn and soda.

No knives or sharp objects were allowed at Sunnybrook, so I had to surrender my Lone Ranger and Tonto pocket knife. Dr. Spielman put it in a large manila envelope with my name on it and said they would keep it safe and return it to me when I was discharged.

That rule also applied to pencils, which presented a problem for me. At school, they had these big blunt things that barely wrote neatly, but the teacher counted them carefully at the end of each day to make sure we weren't pinching them to use in our rooms. So I either had to do my creative writing with crayons or learn to use an old typewriter that was in the recreation room. Since no one ever used it, Dr. Spielman let me take it to my room so I could work in peace and quiet so I lugged it upstairs, set it on my desk, and dusted off its well-worn keys.

Miss Underwood wrote me a nice letter telling me all about the happenings at Calvin Coolidge Junior High School, and how much she missed having me in her English class on account of I was just about the only one who ever really understood the books we read and I always had insightful answers to offer whenever she asked questions about them. I wrote back to her thanking her for her letter and letting her know that I was taking her advice and writing about my *real* life, and she wrote back to me right away and said she would love to read it if I could mail it to her so I wrote back that I would do that when it was finished.

It was slow going with that old typewriter at first, but after a while I got the hang of it and memorized where all the letters were and which keys I had to punch extra hard because they always made the letter too light and after that it wasn't so bad anymore. I started at the beginning back in San Diego with the Old Man getting kicked out of the Navy during the war and all my mother's personal problems and then her running off to

Florida and the Old Man getting put in jail for fighting and me ending up in foster care with Reverend Welles and his wife, and then I just kept typing and continued the story from there.

Aunt Evelyn and Uncle Joe and Mrs. Riley and Buck and the Rosenbergs and the old Indian guy who gave me the Buffalo nickel on Route 66 were all in it, and I was accumulating quite a stack of papers so I decided to send it to Miss Underwood in parts instead of all at once. I knew she would take good care of it and send it back to me when she was finished reading it, so I wasn't worried about losing it unless some freak accident happened and it got lost in the mail or something. But I'd always heard good things about the good old U.S. Postal Service so I wasn't too worried about that happening.

All of us kids at Sunnybrook had to have one-on-one time with Dr. Spielman a few times a week, in addition to group therapy. The first time I talked to Dr. Spielman alone, he just asked me how I liked Sunnybrook and how I was getting along with the kids and then he asked me some general things about my life and Aunt Evelyn and Buck and how I liked Calvin Coolidge Junior High School. He didn't ask me anything about the crazy stuff at all, and when we were through he said I did a real good job and that he looked forward to our next conversation.

The second time we talked, he got into the crazy stuff a little more and there was another older man with a beard sitting quietly in the corner smoking a cigar. He didn't say anything and Dr. Spielman didn't introduce us, so I figured he was just another psychiatrist sitting in on the session, or maybe Dr. Spielman's boss or secretary or something.

Anyway, Dr. Spielman asked me to tell him about Uncle Joe. I just told him that I needed to get cured fast so I could get back to Aunt Evelyn's attic before Uncle Joe runs out of time.

"Runs out of time?" he asked, confused.

"Yes. You see, he's only got a year to set the record straight."

"Who told him that?"

"Whoever's running the afterlife."

"And that would be God?"

"I suppose so."

"Why can't he come here, and dictate his memoirs to you while you're here?"

"He can only appear in my aunt's attic," I explained. "He can't leave it, he can't go outside or go anywhere else. He's fallen madly in love with the neighbor, Mrs. Riley, who sunbathes in her swimsuit in her backyard. But he can't even leave the attic to talk to her."

"Tell me about this Mrs. Riley," the doctor said.

"Well, I do—did—odd jobs around the house for her last summer, but that was just to find out more about her for Uncle Joe."

"So, you did odd jobs around her house for her. While she sunbathed in the swimsuit?"

"That's right."

"What did you find out about her, Calvin?"

"She seemed lonely."

"Why did you think that?"

"Because one time she cornered me in the pool house, and wouldn't let me out. She seemed...desperate."

"I see. Did anything...you know...*happen*?"

"No, I finally managed to get away."

"Calvin. Are you sure it isn't *you* who is in love with Mrs. Riley?"

"Yes, I'm sure. She's a grown woman. It was definitely Uncle Joe who was in love with her."

"But, Uncle Joe doesn't really exist, does he? Wasn't he just a delusion?"

"No, he was real, all right."

"How do you know? Did you ever touch him?"

"He spoke to me. We had conversations. He told me things about his life, things I couldn't possibly have known..."

"But he wasn't a real person."

"I told you before, he was a ghost. Aren't ghosts real?"

"No, Calvin. Ghosts are not real."

"But what about the conversations?"

"Calvin, the mind is a tricky thing. We can think what we're seeing and hearing is real, when it's not. We can project our own desires, such as your desire for Mrs. Riley, on fictitious persons in order to alleviate feelings of shame or guilt."

"I'm not in love with Mrs. Riley!"

"You say that because you know your desire for an adult woman is taboo in our culture," the doctor explained. "So you invented Uncle Joe, an adult, so you could live out your sexual fantasies vicariously through him. It's quite a common occurrence in over-sexed boys of your age. The line between fantasy and reality becomes blurred and then completely disappears as you fall ever deeper into the chasm of your own illicit feelings for an adult woman you know you can never possess. How many times a day do you fantasize about her, Calvin?"

"I told you, I don't think about Mrs. Riley like that."

"Calvin, we're never going to get anywhere until you decide to stop lying and be honest with yourself. There is no 'Uncle Joe.' You invented him as a means of escape from a life that you cannot control. From the feelings of abandonment you have towards your parents, and the obsessively dirty thoughts you have about Mrs. Riley."

He had my head all twisted around in knots. He was telling me stuff that sounded true, but I knew wasn't. Most of all, he was trying to get me to say that I made it all up, as a defense mechanism against abandonment and loss. But deep down I knew it wasn't that way at all. I knew I could save myself a lot of trouble and just tell him what he wanted to hear, but it wouldn't be *true*. Why wouldn't he believe me?

The older guy just sat there the whole time, listening intently and puffing away on his cigar like a silent exclamation mark for Dr. Spielman's accusations.

To make matters worse, it started happening again. A tall, dark man with a neatly-trimmed mustache started hanging around the recreation room after dinner. He looked a little bit like Clark Gable, but had a more dangerous gleam in his eye. At first I just ignored him. If he thought I couldn't see him, maybe he'd just go away. Then one time he pulled up a chair and watched me and Orson play chess. He was quiet for a long time, then he said, "He's gonna take your Queen, kid."

"How did you know I can see you?" I asked.

"What?" Orson asked, confused.

"It's just one of those things," the guy said. "A sort of tingling feeling."

"What are you doing here?" I asked.

"I'm about to take your Queen," Orson replied.

"I'm not talking to you," I said to Orson.

"Then who *are* you talking to?" Then he thought about it. "Oh, one of *them*, right?"

I nodded. There was nothing judgmental about his comment. This was a looney bin, after all.

"What are you doing here?" I repeated to the ghost. Orson, catching on, stayed quiet.

"Do I have to have a reason?" the ghost asked.

"There's always been a purpose – with the others, I mean," I said.

"It's not always like that, kid," the ghost said. "Sometimes it's just random."

It was really bugging me – I couldn't put my finger on it. There was something charming and something commanding and at the same time something very desperate about him.

"Are you gonna move, or what?" Orson finally said.

"Oh, sorry," I said, pushing a pawn forward without thinking. That opened a path for him to take my Queen with his bishop.

"I told you he was gonna knock off your Queen, kid." It was something about the words he used – *knock off*. Then I had it.

"You're John Dillinger."

"Very good, kid."

"John Dillinger? *Really?*" Orson asked, looking around the room. "Gee, I wish I could see ghosts!"

"Look, you hanging around here is just going to cause a lot of trouble for me," I said.

"What can I say? Trouble's my middle name, kid."

I tried to ignore him again, but he followed me around everywhere. He even tried to carry on conversations with me. At breakfast the next morning he sat down across the table from me and watched me eat my scrambled eggs.

"Why don't you wanna talk to me, kid?"

"Because I don't want people to think I'm talking to myself."

"Like it matters in here."

"Please go haunt someone else," I pleaded.

"That hurts my feelings, kid. But I'm gonna let it go. So, how long have you been seeing, you know, people like me?"

"Since August." That was when the Old Man dropped me off at Aunt Evelyn's.

"What's it like being crazy?" he asked.

"I'm not crazy."

"What about your mother?" he asked, watching my face intently. I couldn't hide it. "See, I knew it! It always runs in the family."

"You're a very tactful guy," I observed.

"It's all right kid," he went on. "Nothing to be ashamed about. We're all a little crazy in one way or another, you know. You shoulda known Pretty Boy Floyd – that guy was completely bonkers!" He laughed heartily at some unspoken memory.

I had never realized John Dillinger was such a blabbermouth.

"I gotta go," I said, standing up and picking up my tray. Dr. Spielman had come in, and I was sure he saw me talking to myself. I could tell by the look on his face. That was definitely not good.

"Stay away from me!" I hissed, and walked away. But he followed me everywhere – even to school, where he sat next to me and made derogatory comments about the teacher the whole time.

"Hey, you're one of those egg-heads, aren't you?" he asked. "There's nothing wrong with being smart. I'm pretty smart myself, you know. I never had my IQ tested, but I bet if I did it would be off the charts!"

That night during recreation I elected to stay in my room and write. Sure enough, there was Dillinger, lounging on my bed thumbing through a *Look* magazine while I typed away.

"What are you writing anyway, kid?"

"It's about my life."

"Why would you want to do that?"

"Because my English teacher, Miss Underwood, said I should write my story."

"Miss Underwood, huh?" he mused. "Is she a real dish?"

"My cousin Buck thinks so," I answered.

"Well, what do *you* think?"

"I'm just a kid," I said. "But I think she's the most supportive, inspiring teacher I've ever had."

"Ugh – don't make me puke, kid," he grimaced. "Cut the inspirational crap and tell me about this Buck character. He sounds like a real He-man type."

"He just got back from the war in Korea," I said.

"That must've really messed him up, huh?"

"Not the war so much," I clarified. "But while he was over there fighting the North Koreans, his whole platoon got abducted by men from Mars and taken up into their spaceship."

"No kidding?" Dillinger stopped leafing through the magazine. He really seemed interested in this part.

"Yeah, he said they stripped them down and probed them and penetrated them and experimented on them but he didn't know if it lasted for hours or minutes on account of it seemed like time stood still."

"You don't say..." the outlaw was enthralled.

"Then they let them all go – except for one guy, Gillespie, who exploded when they pumped him too full of all these special gases and oils and stuff."

"Oh my God!" the outlaw was repulsed.

"But when they got back to their unit and told their story, nobody believed them and these generals and top secret guys from the government threatened them that if they didn't say they were lying, they'd never be heard from again."

"What did they do?"

"They wouldn't back down," I said proudly. "Then the government guys called them all crazy and put them in an institution and they were never going to get out, but Buck escaped and made his way back to Cleveland and now he lives there with my Aunt Evelyn."

"Gee, that's a peach of a story, kid," Dillinger said. "You gonna put that in your book?"

"Yes."

"Well, I'm not much for books, but that sounds like one book I'd like to read, Shakespeare."

"Thanks," I said, and went back to typing.

Chapter 19

I first met Sigmund Freud in the hospital cafeteria on a Tuesday morning when they were serving flapjacks and maple syrup and fresh strawberries with whipped cream on top. Tuesday was always flapjack day, but the strawberries and whipped cream were subject to availability and were, sadly, never a sure thing around here.

But I digress.

He was a small old man with a white beard and a neat bow tie and kindly smile. And, of course, the ever-present cigar. And yes, he *was* the guy I saw in Dr. Spielman's office during therapy time – the one sitting silently in the corner listening to everything we said.

I'd seen him several times since then, wandering the hospital corridors looking lost in thought, or sitting in the rec room in the evenings reading a book and smoking his cigar.

Dr. Freud had died in London in 1939 of jaw cancer on account of that cigar, and many, many others like it. Maybe that's why he still held on so tightly to it in death.

He sat down at my table and said, "That looks wonderful. I used to enjoy strawberries and cream on Sunday mornings in Vienna." He spoke with a thick Austrian accent, but every syllable was meticulously delivered.

"Hi, I'm Calvin," I said.

"I know," he said. "I've been observing you."

"Why?"

"It was my life's work," he shrugged, and smiled. "Old habits die hard, as they say."

Then he asked me what I thought of Dr. Spielman.

"I think he's a great doctor," I said without even thinking.

"No, Calvin," Dr. Freud said. "Don't say what you *think* I want to hear. Tell me what you *really* think."

"Well, I think he's a little frustrated with me, to be honest."

"Why do you think he's frustrated with you?"

"He thinks I'm not making enough progress."

"What do *you* think?" he asked me. "Do you think you're making enough progress?"

"I guess not."

"Why?"

"Because I'm still having the delusions."

"But you don't believe they're delusions, do you?" he asked. "Aren't they real to you? Aren't *I* real to you?"

"I know they're real," I admitted. "But Dr. Spielman keeps calling them delusions."

"How does it make you feel when he does that, Calvin?"

"Anxious."

"That's exactly right," the doctor said. "And anything that makes you feel anxious is not good."

"So Dr. Spielman calling my ghosts delusions isn't good," I said, catching on. "Because it makes me anxious."

"Smart boy," he smiled. I was beginning to feel like Dr. Freud, unlike Dr. Spielman, just might be on my side.

I asked him what *he* thought of Dr. Spielman. He got a very serious look on his face and puffed his cigar. I realized his cigar was just like Uncle Joe's: no matter how much he smoked it, it never got any smaller. Finally, he spoke.

"I don't make a habit of criticizing colleagues, but in this case I'll make an exception. I'm not very impressed. His technique is sloppy and his methods are amateurish. He doesn't get any of my theories right because he doesn't fully understand them. Worst of all, he makes his patients feel like they've done something wrong when he fails to help them. He sees them as broken objects that need to be fixed, like a broken watch or an umbrella that won't open."

"How do *you* fix people?" I asked.

"In my old job, I just listened to people talk and they paid me for it," he replied.

"And that's supposed to make me better?"

"I don't think we need to make you better, because I don't believe there's anything wrong with you," he told me. "I don't believe in 'fixing' people, especially people who aren't broken. What we need to do is simply make you *feel* better about yourself the way you are. Then the anxiety will go away, and when that happens, you don't have any more problems."

Gee, talking to Dr. Freud was easy, just like talking to an old friend. I was starting to catch on to his method. He believed people's problems came from anxieties that they didn't even know the cause of. It could be things that happened when they were children or little babies even. Things they didn't even remember. He called that the *unconscious* mind. He said traumatic things in the unconscious caused anxieties that came out in different ways: some people developed phobias, others severe physical symptoms, and still others hallucinations or delusions.

But by getting people to relax and talk about their feelings and memories, it made them remember the traumas and he called this the *conscious* mind. And when the memories entered the conscious mind, it made the anxieties go away.

"Moving those pesky old memories from the unconscious to the conscious mind is like shining a big, bright spotlight on them," he explained. "Out in the light where you can *see* them they don't seem so scary or intimidating anymore."

It all seemed so simple, but he came up with a very complicated word for it: *psychoanalysis*. He invented it, and it pretty much changed the world.

Anyway, it made a lot of sense to me, so I agreed to have regular chats with Dr. Freud in addition to my regular therapy with Dr. Spielman. Dr. Freud promised he would do his best to undo the damage Dr. Spielman was doing to my psyche. He was pretty sure he could help me get rid of the anxiety and feel better about myself, even with Dr. Spielman mucking things up so bad.

Dr. Freud's treatment was much more pleasant than Dr. Spielman's. He said he didn't believe in giving patients medication unless they were a danger to themselves or others. But at Sunnybrook, they kept us doped up pretty good all the time, for good measure.

Talking to Dr. Freud wasn't like going to the doctor at all. He just talked to me like we were having a normal conversation, that's all. Not like Mr. Stone back at school, or Dr. Spielman here, who both made you feel like you were in trouble or something.

Dr. Freud liked to talk about feelings. He said feelings never lie. I think what he meant was that feelings are clues about what was really going on inside us. We talked about my feelings a lot. By asking me questions he made me think of feelings I never really thought about much. Like about my parents.

Instead of telling me I was abandoned like Dr. Spielman did, Dr. Freud asked me questions that coaxed out my own feelings about my mother running off and my Old Man leaving me at Aunt Evelyn's. Dr. Freud agreed with Dr. Spielman that this was a very important issue for me, but his approach was completely different.

For instance, instead of just saying "You feel mad because your mother ran off," Dr. Freud's method was designed to get to the buried feelings *behind* the anger.

"Tell me about your mother," he instructed me. By this time, I trusted him enough to reply honestly, even though I really didn't want to talk about my mother leaving.

"She was pretty messed up."

"Go on."

"She had trouble taking care of me."

"Why was that?"

"She would get drunk and stay that way for days," I said without emotion. "I had to learn how to take care of myself."

"Why did she get drunk?"

"Because she wasn't happy."

"Were you angry because of this?"

"Not that. I didn't mind taking care of myself. It made me more independent."

"And you like being independent."

"Sure."

"Because independent people don't need friends," Dr. Freud said. "Independent people don't even need parents."

"I suppose."

"So you weren't angry when she didn't take care of you and you weren't angry when she got drunk."

"That's right."

"When did you get angry?"

"When she went to Florida."

"And why did that make you angry, Calvin?"

"Because she left me," I said, getting upset. "Mothers aren't supposed to leave their children."

"Would you have felt better if she had taken you with her?"

"Of course."

"Why do you think she left you behind?"

That was somewhere dark and scary, like a closet in the middle of the night, and I didn't want to go there.

"Can – can we talk about something else now, please?"

"If you want to feel better, sometimes it takes courage, Calvin," he said reassuringly. "I think you can do it."

I opened the closet door and got inside. It was dark and I felt like I was going to suffocate.

"Why do you think she left you behind?" he repeated.

"Because I must've done something wrong." I felt the tears beginning to sting my eyes. "I must've done something to make her not love me anymore..." I wiped my eyes and choked back the sobs.

"Can you think what you might have done, Calvin?"

"No. I don't...I don't know..."

"Think hard, Calvin," he encouraged. "Try to remember."

"Maybe she resented me because she didn't want to have a kid. Maybe she thought I wanted her to be a better mother." I couldn't hold back any longer. The floodgates opened and hot tears poured down my cheeks.

"But I didn't think that," I wept. "I was willing to take care of myself. I didn't hold it against her at all!"

"I believe you, Calvin," Dr. Freud said. I began to calm down and wiped the tears on my sleeve. "Now tell me why you were angry at her for leaving."

"I already told you. Parents aren't supposed to leave their children..."

"But that's an abstract reason," he argued. "Tell me why you're really angry."

"What do you mean?"

"Dig deep, Calvin," he urged. "Find a memory – find *any-thing* – that will help explain the anger."

"Because I missed her."

"That's better," he said. "But be specific – what do you miss about her?"

"Her not being there."

"More specific."

"The smell of her perfume."

"That's better. Keep going."

"Playing games with her," I remembered. "We used to build forts and tunnels out of blankets and sofa cushions and pretend we were cave explorers."

"Good. Keep going."

"Playing hide and seek all over the house," I said. "Eating watermelon on the front porch in summer."

"More, Calvin."

"Her giving me a penny from her wallet for the gumball machine at Woolworth's. Taking me out to the movies on Saturday night. Going to the beach and building sand castles together."

"These are all wonderful memories, Calvin," Dr. Freud said. "It doesn't sound like you did anything wrong at all. It sounds like she loves you very much. Sometimes the choices others feel they have to make aren't really our fault at all."

He was right. I had kept those memories hidden, put away in that dark closet for so long. Taking them out and experiencing them again took away a lot of the dark feelings I had for my mother. I was starting to feel better already.

"She's not a bad person," I told Dr. Freud. "I think she was doing the best she could."

"I'm sure you're right, Calvin," he said.

Every time Dr. Freud and I had one of these little "chats," more nice memories emerged and I felt a little bit better about myself. Dragging the past out into the light — even the bad stuff — sure helped you understand things better. Most of all, I think Dr. Freud helped me to understand that "crazy" didn't mean bad. He told me there was no such thing as "normal."

I guess it was okay to be the way I was — there was nothing wrong with me after all.

* * *

But, most of all, Dr. Freud liked talking about dreams. He told me that ever since he was a child he had been fascinated with dreams and the dream-world.

"I was different than all my brothers and sisters," he said. "And all my peers."

Boy, could I relate to that!

"I was interested in the mind," he explained. "Where did all these dreams come from? Why did all of this happen while we were sleeping? It was my first inkling of the *unconscious*."

Dr. Freud said he started writing his dreams down because he felt like his unconscious was trying to tell him something. "I needed to solve the puzzle. I needed to know what my unconscious was trying to tell me."

Then one night he had a dream about one of his patients. In the dream, his patient was dying and there was nothing he could do to save her. He felt completely helpless. The next day he realized the dream wasn't about the patient at all – it was about *him*. It was about the kind of guilt all doctors face when they can't save a patient.

And that got him writing a famous book about dreams. He said that before he wrote the book everybody thought dreams were just random funny or scary stories that didn't mean anything. But he said he believed dreams have meaning. It was another simple idea that he made up a complicated name for: *interpretation*.

He said it wasn't good enough just to write your dreams down the next morning and think about them. You have to *interpret* them.

Well, I had a couple of doozies for him.

My hands and feet are tied. I'm in the bottom of the baptismal tank at Reverend Welles's church. It's empty, but slowly filling with water. Reverend Welles looks down over me with no expression on his face. Mrs. Welles stands next to him, holding a birthday cake and smiling down at me. She seems unaware that

I am in any danger. I try to ask them to turn the water off, but I can't speak. The water continues to rise, but they do nothing to save me.

It's almost over my face, I start to panic. "Where's my Old Man?" I wonder. Then the water covers my face and I can't breathe. I struggle but the ropes are too tight. I hold my breath but I know I can't last long.

Then somebody shoots Reverend Welles and his wife with arrows, and they fall. Somebody reaches in and pulls me out of the tank. It's the Old Indian. He unties me and I am free. He hands me a Buffalo nickel. Then he turns and walks out of the church. I follow.

Outside, I see we're in the middle of the desert. Off in the distance, his people are slowly marching away to some unknown land. There are two horses. The Old Indian gets on one and motions for me to ride the other one. It's got my Lone Ranger cowboy hat hanging from the saddle. I climb up and mount the horse. I put my cowboy hat on. The Old Indian rides off towards his people. I try to get my horse to go, but it won't move. I kick it but it won't go.

I realize it's not real. It's one of those big fake plastic horses like they have at trading posts. The Old Indian keeps going towards his people. "Wait!" I call out, but he doesn't hear me. I'm left all alone. Now the church isn't there anymore. I get down off the plastic horse and start walking.

All the Indians are gone. I don't know which direction I'm going in. I just walk, over miles and miles of endless desert. I'm tired and hungry and thirsty.

Finally I come to a trading post on a highway. There are some people inside shopping for souvenirs. It's a man and a woman. They come outside and walk toward me. It's Dick Contino and Miss Underwood, my English teacher. They are dressed casually in tourist clothes and look like a very happy couple. They see me.

"We've been waiting for you, Calvin!" Dick calls out. They give me a pecan log and a cold bottle of Dr. Pepper. We get in a nice, shiny convertible – Dick and Miss Underwood in the front, me in the backseat. My shiny plastic accordion sits on the seat next to me. The car drives away from the trading post and onto the highway, past a sign that says "Route 66."

"Why don't you play us a tune, Calvin?" Dick calls back to me. I pick up the accordion and start playing "Deep in the Heart of Texas," but it comes out as "How Much is that Doggie in the Window?" and at half-speed. I try to speed up my fingers and play the notes for "Texas," but it always comes out as the other song and very, very slow. It sounds like a 78 rpm record set on 33 and 1/3. It's disturbing, but Dick and Miss Underwood like it for some reason.

I stop playing and watch the scenery whizz by outside the car. Dick Contino and Miss Underwood act very happy. He leans over and gives her a big smooch on the cheek. We're just like a real family. Then I see a state trooper patrol car behind us. Its red lights and siren come on, only the siren plays "Deep in the Heart of Texas."

"Don't worry," Dick says. "I'll give him a pecan log!" Then he pulls over on the side of the road. The state trooper stops behind us and gets out of his car. He walks up to the side of our car and it's Coach Axelrod in a state trooper uniform. He's carrying a shot put.

"Calvin forgot this," he says, handing it to Dick. Dick hands him a pecan log.

"Thanks," Coach Axelrod says. "You folks have a nice trip, now!" He goes back to his car. Dick hands me the shot put and I hold it on my lap. It feels nice and smooth and cool in the hot sun.

We keep driving. We are a family, enjoying a summer road trip on Route 66. I feel happier than I've ever felt in my life. Then a dark cloud forms over the road up ahead. We watch as light-

ning flashes from it, but no thunder. Then a brightly-glowing flying saucer emerges from the cloud and hovers over the desert to our right. The flying saucer comes low to the ground, and a long metal ramp extends out of it to the desert floor.

A dozen alien creatures on motorcycles race down the ramp and start chasing us.

"Faster, Dick!" I cry.

"Don't worry, I'll just give them a pecan log!" Dick calls out confidently. The aliens are gaining on us. I get a good look at them. They look like giant crayfish, with big beady eyes. They swarm around us on the highway. We pass Coach Axelrod leaning up against his state trooper car, casually smiling and waving at us as we pass by. "Don't forget to stop at the Grand Canyon!" he calls out to us just like nothing's wrong.

The aliens pull out ray guns and shoot the car. It disintegrates all around us and now we're running along the highway. They quickly capture us and giant glass tubes suck us up into the flying saucer. I am separated from Dick and Miss Underwood and taken to a room full of people. They're all strapped to cold metal tables. I see Eddie Brockelman, passed out on one of the tables, with a white knot in the middle of his forehead. I see Mrs. Riley, strapped to a table in her swimsuit, and Amy, the girl who fainted during science and threw up in the hallway.

The aliens strap me to a table, too. An alien in a white doctor's coat talks to me.

"I'm just going to give you a few tests now, Calvin." It's Dr. Spielman's voice. He starts showing me pictures of ink splotches and weird shapes I don't recognize. He asks me what they are.

"I don't know." I look over at some of the other captives. Aliens are chloroforming them and starting to dissect them like frogs. But they don't cry or scream. Some of them just watch the procedure being done on them with great interest.

"Are, are they going to do that to me?" I ask.

"Of course," the Dr. Spielman alien says cheerfully. "We've got to find out what makes you tick, Calvin!"

I remember the shot put. It's still in my hands. It still feels smooth and cool. Only now it's pulsating and vibrating. Something's happening. The aliens gather around me. They're all jabbering, but I can't hear them. Lights flicker, the flying saucer starts to lose power.

The shot put is doing something to them. They cover their ears and eyes. The flying saucer wobbles and weaves. Then it loses all power and crashes violently into the ground.

I wake up sometime later. I pull myself from the smoldering wreckage. I am the only survivor. I have the shot put in my hands. The one that gave poor Eddie Brockelman a knot in the middle of his forehead. It's not pulsating anymore.

I walk across a vast, white plain. It looks just like the Bonneville Salt Flats. I see something in the distance. I keep walking. It gets bigger.

Finally, I recognize Aunt Evelyn's yellow wood frame house. It's the only thing there, standing erect on that vast, flat plain.

I keep walking. It's still so far away.

I walk and I walk. It stays in the distance.

"Uncle Joe!" I call out as I trudge toward it, holding on tight to the shot put.

"That's it?" Dr. Freud calmly asked when I was done.

"That's it."

It took us a full week to unravel that one. The most obvious part was feeling trapped and needing to be rescued from Reverend Welles, and me and Dick Contino and Miss Underwood forming the family that I so desperately craved. Then there's the Buffalo nickel being a symbol of hope and the shot put being a symbol of power that helped me free myself from the aliens, which totally came from Buck's experience in Korea. The aliens on motorcycles represented the adventure of the road and the dangers of life's journey, like the biker gang who chased us in Indiana. Finally, the yearning to return home when I see Aunt Evelyn's yellow house on the Salt Flats, but still not being able to reach it.

"Well, my boy," Dr. Freud said when we finished interpreting it. "This tells me just about all I will ever need to know about you..."

Chapter 20

One morning Dr. Spielman called me into his office before breakfast and told me since I wasn't making as much progress as expected he was going to increase my dosage of medication. He had caught me talking to Dr. Freud and John Dillinger on several occasions lately, and I'm sure that's what this was all about.

"I'm very concerned about you, Calvin," he told me. "Instead of improving, your delusions seem to be getting more serious by the day. You've got to make an effort to contribute to your own healing."

So at medication time I received three little white pills instead of two. I swallowed the first two as usual, but I hid the third one under my tongue so Dr. Spielman wouldn't see it when he checked.

There was another surprise at the group therapy session that afternoon: Dr. Spielman announced two new additions to our ward. "Everyone, please welcome the newest members of our group, Kate and Penelope. I am certain that those of you who are long-time Sunnybrook residents will reach out to them and make them feel right at home."

They were almost identical twins. By their physical features, there was no difference at all. Both had round, cherubic faces and long silky hair. Both had large, angelic, hauntingly dark eyes. The only way you could tell them apart was that Kate had raven black hair and Penelope had blonde hair that was so light it was almost snow-white.

They displayed an ethereal, almost supernatural beauty that, when taken together, was both beguiling and at the same time unsettling. Their siren-like allure immediately intoxicated me and reeled me in – against my better judgment. How these celestial beings came to be at a place like Sunnybrook was any-body's guess.

Within a couple of days, I began to see real differences in their personalities emerge. Kate, the dark-haired one, was kind and friendly to everyone. But, for some reason, Penelope ze-roed in on Stuart, and embarked on a campaign to unsettle him every chance she got.

One of the ways she tortured him was with language. It was common knowledge that one of the things that set Stuart off was improper syntax. When Penelope discovered this, she began purposefully jumbling her words up whenever he was within ear-shot, just to make him nervous.

One time during a group discussion about the schedule, Dr. Spielman asked Penelope her thoughts on changing the recre-ation time to *before* dinner instead of after.

"I think before dinner should recreation time be," she said, glancing over at Stuart. Stuart's head twitched slightly, and he slowly started to rock back and forth.

"But that would necessitate having dinner later than we do now," Dr. Spielman pointed out.

"I don't a little later mind having my dinner," Penelope replied. She looked at Stuart again, who was now grimacing and rocking a little faster.

"Well, I'm not certain everyone else feels the same, Pene-lope," Dr, Spielman said. "I think we'll have to put it to a vote."

"Of course, the wisest thing that is," Penelope said.

Stuart was starting to come apart. He was rocking more vio-lently now and covering his ears with his hands.

"It seems Stuart disagrees with changing the schedule," Dr. Spielman observed. "I didn't realize talking about it would upset him so much. Perhaps we should table it for now and come back to it some other time."

But it wasn't changing the schedule that distressed him so much. It was Penelope's jumbled syntax. She sat there with a pleased smirk on her pretty little face while Stuart rocked and moaned and finally Bart had to be called to take him to his room to be sedated.

She seemed to enjoy having that kind of power over another human being.

Structure was very important for people like Stuart. Rituals ruled his life, and any deviation from routine resulted in an ugly meltdown. One of his most important rituals was the *Howdy Doody Show*. Every evening after dinner, like clockwork, Stuart was in front of the TV set waiting for that comforting and familiar theme song to begin: *Hey kids, it's Howdy Doody Time!*

But one night, the TV wouldn't turn on. Bart came in and fiddled with it, but couldn't find the problem. As the show's starting time came and passed, Stuart became more and more agitated. Finally, Bart discovered the problem: someone had cut the power cord clean through. Everyone was gathered around the set, trying to calm Stuart and figure out who would do such a thing.

Everyone but Penelope.

I looked around for her and saw her sneak into the kitchen. I followed her in and saw her return a sharp butcher knife to an open kitchen drawer, then sneak back out. She saw me as she snuck away and I could tell she knew that *I* knew what she'd done.

A while later, after Bart had fixed the cord with some electrician's tape and all the kids were gathered around the TV or playing games, Penelope came and sat down beside me.

We were alone, so I asked, "Why did you do it?"

"Are you going to snitch on me?" she asked.

"I don't know," I admitted. She had a way of getting my emotions all jumbled up and confused. "Why do you like doing that to Stuart so much?"

"It's not my fault he's so nervous," she said defensively.

"It's his condition," I said. "He can't help it."

"Well, it annoys me."

"Then why do you try to make it worse?"

"Because *he* annoys me," she said. "That's all."

Then she tucked her chin in and looked at me with those big, dark eyes. "You're not going to snitch on me."

"How can you be so sure?" I asked.

"Because you and I have a secret now," she said confidently. "Something only *we* share, and no one else knows about."

I was too taken aback to say anything.

"I know you like me," she continued. "Now we have something that's *ours*. Secrets are exciting. Secrets are *intimate*."

I could feel my face burning and I wanted to flee, but I made myself stay.

"Okay, maybe I won't tell." My voice was shaky. I felt embarrassed. I knew I was out of my league – she was smarter than me, she had my number. I mean, here she'd done this terrible thing to Stuart, but I was the one on the hot seat. How did she do it? It was like witchcraft or something.

I didn't snitch on her. I realized she had a power over me I couldn't explain.

And Penelope found more secrets for us to "share." Like how she'd made friends with Minnie, the depressed girl on suicide watch, and convinced her to ditch the orderlies and sneak up on the hospital roof in the middle of the night to smoke cigarettes and talk about what dying must be like.

How did she get the cigarettes? She found out that little Nell's "Nina" personality had been stealing them from the orderlies' office when they weren't around and blackmailed her into handing over half of the loot to her.

Penelope would fake illnesses to get out of school and while in the infirmary she would steal drugs whenever the nurse forgot to lock the medication cabinet.

She had the orderlies wrapped around her sweet little finger. One time she took me to her room and showed me a dresser drawer full of contraband: chewing gum, soda pop, candy, perfume, Moon Pies, cigarettes, fashion magazines, a Zippo lighter, bottles of pills from the infirmary – even a can of beer.

"Where did you get all this stuff?" I asked.

"From the orderlies," she said. "They bring me whatever I ask for. Go ahead, take whatever you want. They'll always bring more."

She picked up the can of beer. "I bribed Raoul to smuggle this in. Cost me five bucks. Let's go up on the roof tonight and split it."

I was horrified. "What if we get caught?"

"What are they gonna do – kick us out of here?" she asked.

A few hours after lights out, we met in the hall and snuck past the orderlies' office where we could hear Raoul snoring. She had the can of beer and a pack of cigarettes. We made it to the roof without being seen and found a nice place to sit.

It was cold out, but the stars were brilliant. We looked up at them in silence for a while, and then she opened the can and took a long sip of beer. "Ah...just the ticket," she said, handing it to me. I had never had beer before. I tried it but it was so fizzy and warm that it went down the wrong pipe and I almost choked.

"Don't spill it!" she said, grabbing it back from me. Then I watched in amazement as she pulled out a smoke and lit it with the Zippo lighter with the dexterity of a sailor on shore leave. *Who was this girl?*

She took a long drag and passed it to me.

"No thanks," I said. "I don't smoke."

"Take it," she ordered. "We're bonding now."

I took it and gingerly took a puff. It was my first cigarette. I didn't like it. It tasted like dirt.

"Inhale," she said. I did, and coughed. "You'll get used to it," she said, and took the cigarette back. "So, what are you in for?"

"I see dead people."

She didn't look impressed at all. "Oh. Is that all?"

"Yep."

"Seen any around this place?"

"Yeah, a couple."

"Well, you seem pretty normal to me," she said.

"Thanks."

She handed me the beer and I took another sip. This time it went down a little smoother.

"What about your parents?" she asked. "What do they say about it?"

"They don't know," I told her. "I was living with my aunt in Cleveland when it started. The school psychologist found out about it and called in a social worker and – well, here I am."

"How long have you been here?"

"About a month."

"You know, I've only been here a week but I already know there are so many ways you could escape from this place," she said. "There's no security, just a couple of orderlies and nurses who don't know what's going on. And that doctor, Spellman –"

"Spielman," I corrected.

"Whatever. He doesn't have a clue. You can tell he's just watching the clock tick down until retirement. You could probably just walk right out of here and no one would even notice for like five hours or something."

"The only place I could go is my aunt's house, and they wouldn't have much trouble finding me there."

"Yeah, but you'd have a little holiday on the outside at least," she said.

"It's not so bad here," I told her. "You'll make more friends."

She laughed. "Making friends is not a problem for me, pal." She sat the can of beer down and laid back on the roof. We were quiet for a few minutes, just looking up at the stars, then she said, "Well, aren't you going to kiss me?"

"I dunno," I replied.

"Don't you want to?"

"Yeah, I guess."

"Have you ever kissed a girl before?"

"Well...no."

"You can kiss me."

"Okay." I lowered myself down to her level and tried to kiss her in the darkness. I ended up kissing her chin.

"That was really atrocious, Calvin," she said. "Come on. I know you can do better than that."

I tried again. This time, miraculously, our lips touched. She tasted like cigarettes and beer, but it was warm and moist and kind of nice in an unexpected way.

"That was better," she said. "But what are you doing with your hands, Calvin? No girl wants to be kissed like that. Look, put one hand under my head like this, and put the other hand on my waist like this." She did it for me. "Now, try it again — and you can open your mouth this time, Calvin."

I tried it again, making sure I followed all of her instructions to a "t." It must have been better this time, because she didn't say anything afterward.

"Well?" I asked.

"Promising," she said. "I might let you kiss me again some-time."

"Okay," I said. Now we had another secret. And that was that.

We finished the beer and then went back down into the building before someone came up and caught us. I laid in bed the rest of the night thinking about kissing Penelope and wondering why she was paying so much attention to me. I mean, why was she "sharing" all these secrets with me?

The more I thought about it, the more I began to feel like I was being set up. Like she was telling me all these things as an insurance policy – the more I knew, the more I'd have to spill, and then explain why I'd waited so long to come clean. By drawing me into her web of crime and illicit love, I became an accomplice. She knew I was in too deep now and would never be able to rat her out without taking the fall myself.

Penelope was an evil genius.

Chapter 21

Kate, on the other hand, was the opposite. If Penelope had a dark side, Kate definitely had a light side. Where Penelope was cruel and unfeeling, Kate was compassionate and caring. And Kate had some kind of sixth sense. Ever since the night on the roof with Penelope, I could tell Kate knew I had become involved with her sister. I chalked it up to spooky twin stuff, but I would soon find out there was much more to it than that.

One day in the exercise yard, Kate pulled me aside when Penelope wasn't around.

"I just wanted to warn you about my sister," she said, smiling kindly. "I know she looks pretty and harmless, but she's damaged goods."

"What do you mean?"

"I mean, she lacks empathy," Kate said bluntly. "My sister plays with people like other girls play with cut out dolls. She doesn't know she's being cruel. To her it's normal, and everyone else is off. I guess what I'm trying to tell you is, my sister's a sociopath."

"Okay," I said.

"Don't get me wrong," Kate said. "I love her to pieces. I'm just telling you to, you know, watch your back. If you plan on staying involved with her."

"Okay," I repeated.

"Look, you seem like a real nice boy," she continued. "And my sister's wake is littered with nice boys like you. Stunned and senseless. Gasping for air like gutted, discarded fish."

"Thank you."

"You have no idea what she's capable of," she said. "Honestly, you don't stand a chance."

"I get it now."

"I'm sorry," she said. "I just don't want to see it happen to another nice boy like you."

"Fairly and duly warned."

We got to talking, and I quickly discovered that Kate liked to talk. A lot.

But she never asked me why I was here. When I told her, she said, "I know."

"Did Penelope tell you?"

"She didn't have to," Kate said. "I just know."

Kate had ESP. She finally admitted as much to me. That's how she already knew things I hadn't told her. She just *knew*. She also had other gifts. Like telepathy and psychoscopy.

"That's knowing things by touching objects or people," she explained about the latter.

"So, if you've got those powers, Penelope must also," I observed.

"Similar, but different," she said. "Penelope can't read someone's mind, but she has telekinesis. That's being able to move things with your mind."

When I asked Kate how long they had these powers, she said, "We've always had them, ever since we were babies. Our parents thought we were weird, and didn't want to have much to do with us. I think they were relieved when the school social worker suggested putting us in this place."

"But you're not crazy, like the others," I said.

"I know. In fact, our IQ's are quite high. I'm 137. Penelope's 140."

"Then why did they put you in here?" I asked.

"I guess they just didn't know what else to do with us."

Kate knew things. She knew things about me I'd never told her. I guess it was on account of the ESP.

"When are you going to let me read your story?" she asked me one day. I thought she meant the one about Dick Contino.

"No, the other one," she said. "The one you're writing about your life." So I gave her some typed pages to read.

"This is really good, Calvin," she said encouragingly. "Who gave you the idea to do this?"

I told her it was Miss Underwood's idea – my English teacher at Calvin Coolidge Junior High School back in Cleveland. Kate wanted to read more, so I gave her more pages. The more she read, the more she wanted to read.

"I feel like I'm getting to know you so much better now," she said admiringly. Kate was sure a nice girl. And she got so involved in the process, she offered to help out.

"I found a few typos," she told me one day. "If you'd like, I could read through your manuscript and fix them, and type up new pages for you – you know, like an editor or secretary would."

"Gee, that'd be swell," I said, grateful for the help. She got to work right away, and was she ever great at finding and fixing typos! She even found some syntax and grammar errors, and fixed those, too.

Now everything was going fine with the writing and all, but there was just one little problem. Over the next few weeks I started to realize there was a triangle forming.

Kate liked me but I liked Penelope, even though I knew I was just her latest toy and would be discarded when my entertainment value faded. Until then, though, we were like three peas in a pod. Kate was the one I connected with intellectually, but with Penelope the attraction was purely physical. She's the one I wanted to kiss.

And we did a lot of kissing, up on that hospital roof under the stars. We drank warm beer and kissed and held hands and laid there side-by-side on our backs and looked up dreamily at the stars. We talked a little, but most of the time we were quiet and I think she felt a little bit lonely sometimes because she held on extra tight to my hand and wouldn't let go.

Then one night she surprised me with a question.

"Who do you like better – Kate or me?"

I knew there was only one right answer. "You."

"Who do you think is smarter?"

"Even Kate said you have a higher IQ."

"Stop evading the question," she said. "What do *you* think?"

"I'd have to agree with Kate," I said diplomatically. It seemed to placate her.

"Who do you like to talk to more? And don't say me, because I know it's Kate."

I knew I was standing in the middle of a minefield, just waiting to get blown up. "Do we have to play this game right now?" I asked.

"It's my game, and I say *yes*," she insisted. "Now, who do you like to talk to more – me or Kate?"

I knew I'd have to be very careful here. "It depends on what we're talking about."

"Don't get cute with me," she said, rising on one elbow and staring right at me. "I know it's Kate. Everybody likes Kate better. She's fun, and smart, and friendly. She knows what to say to people."

"Because she's interested in people," I said. "Don't get mad at me..."

"Why would I get mad at you?" she asked. "You're right. She cares about people, and I don't. People are just nothing to me. People think just because we're twins, we're exactly the same. Well, we're not. I don't even *like* her sometimes."

That's when I realized Penelope was jealous of Kate. "Oh, come on," I said.

"No, really. People just fall all over themselves praising her – how nice she is, how kind she is, how good she makes them feel. It just makes me want to puke."

"She just takes the time to listen, that's all," I said. "That makes people feel appreciated."

"Most people aren't worth listening to," Penelope asserted. "I don't mean you, Calvin. You're smart, like us. I mean the other dolts in this place. They're so dull I could slit my wrists sometimes."

I picked up her hand and kissed her soft white wrist. "Don't do that. *I* like you."

"Only because I let you kiss me up here."

"That's not true," I said.

"You think I'm wicked, for what I do to Stuart and the others."

"I think you could put your brains – which you've got tons of, by the way – to better use, that's all."

"Like what?" she asked disdainfully. "Making people feel good, like Kate?"

"Kate makes people *happy*."

"What's so important about making people happy, anyway?" she asked. Kate was right – Penelope seemed to have absolutely no empathy.

"If I have to explain it to you, you wouldn't understand," I told her.

"I make *you* happy, when I let you kiss me."

She had me there. I looked at her beautiful angelic face and wondered how she'd gotten her hooks so deep into me.

Then her bright eyes darkened in the moonlight. "When we were younger, our parents bought us a puppy. Kate even made that puppy happy. The puppy loved Kate, and wouldn't give me the time of day. No matter how hard I tried, the puppy loved Kate and ignored me. I began to *hate* that puppy. One day, that puppy disappeared. Kate never knew what happened to it. She never had a clue."

"What about her ESP?" I asked.

"Oh, I can block that when I want to," she replied. "It's like twin immunity."

Then she looked at me with ice cold eyes. "I've never told that to anyone else before. Only *you*."

It was another secret – maybe the *ultimate* secret – and I felt the hooks sinking deeper into my innocent young flesh.

"Now I'm going to let you kiss me again," she said, her eyes still icy. "And this time you can touch me *anywhere* above the waist."

I knew I should run as far away from that girl as I could get. But I didn't.

Instead, I kissed her again.

* * *

We went up to the roof every night after lights out. We would start with kissing and light making out, but before things got too out of hand she would stop me and want to talk – mostly about herself.

"How many times do you think about me during the day?" the little narcissist asked.

"All the time," I promised. It was the truth. I couldn't get her out of my mind for even a minute.

"And you dream about me, don't you?"

"Every night."

"What do we do in your dreams?"

"Pretty much the same thing we do up here."

"Just that, or...more?"

"Sometimes more," I admitted. That was true also. In my dreams I let myself go a little bit – you know, gave myself some tether. But in real life, I didn't want to push it too far.

"So, are you going to put me in your book?" she asked, teasingly.

"Of course."

"Even what we do up here?"

"Yep."

"Even your dreams about me?"

"I might keep those just for me."

Her ego was eating it up. She lived off attention the way normal people lived off meat and potatoes.

"How about Kate?"

"What about her?"

"Is she in your book, too?"

Uh-oh, better watch my step here. "You don't want her to be?"

"Oh, no, it's not that," she hedged. I knew what she was driving at. I knew what she wanted to hear.

"Don't worry," I assured her. "You're in it more than she is."

But that wasn't enough. Apparently, it wasn't all about equal time. "Kate *always* comes off better when we're compared."

So that's what this was about.

"How come every time we come up here we end up talking about Kate?" I asked.

"Because that's always what *you* want to talk about."

"That's not true! You're the one who brought her up."

"Well, you're the one making her the heroine of your book instead of me," she accused. "Besides, I can tell you're always thinking about her. It's always Kate this, Kate that – Kate, Kate, KATE! Well, I'm sick of hearing about your infatuation with my sister!"

I tried to stay calm. "I just told you. I think about you all day long. I dream about you every night. I never think about anything else. I never think about Kate."

"And you never dream about her?"

"Never."

"Promise?"

"Promise," I said. "Scout's honor."

"You're not even a scout."

"But I always wanted to be."

She laughed a little, and the tension was kind of broken.

"Why are you so insecure about Kate?" I asked.

"It's *always* been that way," she confessed. "She's always the popular one. She's always the one people like. Sometimes I *hate* her."

"You shouldn't say that. Not about your own sister."

"But it's true. Are you going to put *that* in your stupid book, too?"

"I don't think I'll put *that* in," I said.

"What *are* you going to write about me?" she demanded. I didn't know why she was being extra neurotic tonight.

"Just, you know, what you're like and stuff."

"That I'm cruel?"

"Yeah, that sometimes you are but I'm sure you don't mean to be."

"And you'll write about Kate that she's always nice and kind and cares about people and everyone loves her," she said. "But I'll come off as this cruel, unfeeling, uncaring monster who doesn't like people because she thinks she's better than everyone else."

"Well, that's about accurate, isn't it?" I asked. "What do you want me to do – change your whole character?"

"I just get tired of being the bad girl all the time," she claimed. "Sometimes I want to be the good girl."

I didn't buy it for a second. "But that's Kate, not you," I argued. "Your character in the book has to be like the *real* you, or it won't be true."

"But people won't like me."

"Yes they will," I promised. "You're complicated. You're interesting. Trust me, I'll write it so they *understand* you. That'll be much better than simply liking you for phony reasons."

"It will?"

"You're the most interesting person I know."

"Do you like me?"

"A lot."

"More than Kate?" Even though we'd been over this ground before, I was more than willing to take the march again.

"I like you more than Kate," I said. "Tons more."

That last part got me ten more minutes of neck-time, but that isn't why I said it. I actually believed it, in a way. Anyway, I guess I got carried away and let my hand wander below her waist. She reached down quickly and pulled it back up.

"What's wrong?" I asked.

"I told you, not down there," she said.

"Why not?"

"Because it reminds me of my father."

"What do you mean?"

"Think about it, Calvin."

I did. I thought about it all night. The next morning I asked Kate if her father ever kissed her.

"Of course," she replied.

"No, I mean..."

"Oh, you mean the way you kiss Penelope?"

"Yeah."

"With me, his kisses and touching were always fatherly," she said. "But with Penelope, it was different."

"Different, how?"

"*Different.*"

Holy cow. It was a lot of information for a thirteen-year-old boy to process.

Chapter 22

Convinced I wasn't making enough progress overcoming my "delusions," Dr. Spielman wanted to try to use hypnosis to cure me. He brought me to his office and told me to lie down on his sofa with my head slightly elevated on a cushion. Then he gave me a shot.

"Just a sedative to help you relax," he said. Then he turned on a curious machine that had a spinning spiral picture on it and told me to watch it until I felt nice and relaxed. He spoke to me in soothing, hushed tones during the whole procedure.

I was dimly aware of a third person in the room and saw John Dillinger sitting comfortably in a chair in the corner.

I guess the sedative was kicking in and I felt a little bit light-headed. "What are you doing here?" I asked the outlaw.

"I think you know perfectly well what I'm doing here, Calvin," Dr. Spielman answered.

"I'm curious how this whole hypnosis thing works," Dillinger answered.

"Okay, just stay quiet then and watch," I said to Dillinger.

"You know I can't stay quiet, Calvin," Dr. Spielman said. "We've got to have a conversation. That's how the whole thing works. Now, are you nice and relaxed?"

"Sure," I replied.

"Good," the doctor said. "I understand you've been doing a bit of writing. I think that's excellent therapy, Calvin. Would you mind telling me what you're writing about?"

"It's about me," I said. "My life."

"That's wonderful," Dr. Spielman said.

"I should have you ghost-write *my* life's story, Shakespeare," Dillinger said. "Now *that* would be some book!" He'd taken to calling me 'Shakespeare' after finding out about my book.

"I already did that for Uncle Joe," I told Dillinger. "This one is all about me."

"I think that's fine, Calvin," Dr. Spielman said. "I'm glad that you're putting the Cleveland episode behind you now. That's the only way you'll be able to move on."

"Oh, it's going to be in my book," I told the doctor. "Uncle Joe, Aunt Evelyn, Buck, Miss Underwood – even Mrs. Riley."

"Who gave you the idea for this project, Calvin?"

"Miss Underwood, my English teacher."

"She's a real dish, eh, Shakespeare?" Dillinger said with a wink.

"Splendid," the doctor observed. "Now I'd like to talk about your parents. Will they be in your book?"

"Yes," I said.

"Do you miss them?"

"Yes."

"I don't miss *my* parents," Dillinger interjected. "I never knew my mother. She died when I was a baby. My older sister raised me. My father wasn't around much, but he was a real disciplinarian – you know the type: *spare the rod, spoil the child...*"

"This isn't about you!" I cut him off sharply.

"I understand that, Calvin," Dr. Spielman said, a bit confused. "That's why I would like to focus on your parents now. Can you tell me about them?"

"My Old Man's a gambler and a con artist," I said. "He sprung me from foster care and we drove across the country on Route 66 last summer."

"Did you enjoy the trip?" the doctor asked.

"Parts of it," I confessed. "Parts of it were fun, but parts of it weren't fun."

"What parts weren't fun?"

"The parts where he conned people out of their money," I said.

"What do you mean?" Dillinger asked. "Those should have been the best parts, kid!"

"No, they *weren't* fun," I insisted. "He made me snatch an old lady's purse for seventeen dollars and some change. I hated it."

"That's pretty low," the loquacious bank robber admitted. "I never stole from old ladies."

"So, you harbor animosity towards your father, for making you steal. Is that correct, Calvin?" the doctor soothingly asked.

"I don't hate the Old Man," I said. "I just hated taking people's money. He was doing the best he could to provide for me. He didn't know any better."

"That's very understanding of you," Dr. Spielman said. "But don't you think he could've gotten a job and earned money, like other people do to take care of their children?"

"A *job!*" Dillinger scoffed. "There's a sucker born every minute! I learned the hard way: there *were* no jobs during the Depression. A man had to go out and *take* what he needed to support his family."

"Will you *please* be quiet?" I said to Dillinger.

"Listen, kid," Dillinger continued. "Your Old Man sounds all right to me, except for the stealing from old ladies part. I wouldn't have done that, myself. Not my style. But I won't judge a man unless I've walked a mile in his shoes."

"SHUT UP!" I shouted.

"Calvin, you appear to be carrying on multiple conversations here," Dr. Spielman calmly observed. "Are you hearing voices? Are you seeing dead people again?"

"Yes," I replied, though it would've been smarter to lie.

"Who do you see?"

"John Dillinger," I said. "He's sitting right over there in that chair in the corner."

Dr. Spielman looked at the chair. "Calvin, that chair is empty."

"He's there," I insisted. "And he never stops talking!"

"Where exactly did you start seeing him?" the doctor asked.

"Here," I replied. "At first it was swell meeting him, but all he does is hang around and talk too much and now he's kind of getting on my nerves a little bit."

"Ouch, kid," Dillinger said. "I got feelings too, you know..."

"Of course, you know these apparitions aren't real, Calvin," the doctor said. "You could just tell them to go away."

"It doesn't work like that," I told him.

"But your mind is producing these delusions," Dr. Spielman said. "If you can regain control of your mind, you will be able to banish them forever."

"I find this quack small-minded and provincial," Dillinger commented.

"Calvin, I'm very concerned," Dr. Spielman admitted. "As you know, I believe these delusions you're suffering from are a result of your deep feelings of abandonment by your parents. Parental structure is very important to the developing psyche, and when that structure is torn away so suddenly the mind will begin to invent comforting delusions as its only means of defense. Right now you are trapped in a prison of your own design, and it will continue to get worse unless we can wrestle back control before it's too late. If we don't see an improvement in your condition soon, I'm afraid we'll be forced to move on to more radical forms of treatment."

More radical forms of treatment. I was pretty sure I knew what he was talking about, and it didn't sound pretty.

He snapped his fingers in front of my face to bring me out of hypnosis and end the session. I quickly left his office, with Dillinger following close behind. We walked down the hall toward the recreation room.

"Hey, Shakespeare," he said. "What's it like, anyway?"

"What's what like?"

"You know, hypnosis – being put under like that?"

"Oh, it's a lot like when you're lying in bed at night and you're half awake and half asleep, only you can talk and answer questions and stuff," I told him.

When we got to the rec room I saw Kate and immediately knew something was wrong. She wouldn't make eye contact and I could tell she'd been crying.

"Kate, what's wrong?"

She turned away from me. She walked over to another table and sat down.

"Jeepers, kid. What did you do to that girl?" Dillinger asked.

"Nothing."

"Well, you must've done something," he said. "I know that look all too well, and it's never good."

I went over and sat down across from Kate. The bank robber followed.

"What happened?"

She still wouldn't look at me.

"Kate, tell me what's up," I pleaded.

She burst out crying so suddenly and uncontrollably that it made my heart jump right into my throat. "How could you do it, Calvin? How could you say those things about me?"

"I don't know what you're talking about," I said breathlessly.

"Don't lie to me, Calvin!" she said through tears. "How could you say those things about me – and to my own sister, too!"

I was beginning to get the picture: this was a Kate-Penelope thing. Which meant I was going to get sucked into it like a vortex.

"I didn't say anything to Penelope," I said. "I promise."

"She said you told her you thought I was shallow and phony," she got out between staccato sobs.

"That's – that's not true!"

"And she said you told her you thought I was ugly and boring to talk to," she continued. "You told her she was much prettier and smarter than me. And how could such a beautiful girl like her have such a plain, stupid sister like me?"

"Holy Toledo, did you really say all those things about her, Shakespeare?" Dillinger asked.

"Of course not!" I replied. "Kate, you've got to believe me, I never said those things."

"Get away from me, Calvin," she said. "I thought you were my friend."

"Kate, think: this is coming from *Penelope*. You *know* her character, and you know *mine*."

"You mean you didn't say those things?" she asked.

I knew I had to be very careful here. Penelope had taken a few benign comments made in the throes of passion and turned them into poison darts for her sister. This charming little triangle that I had so cavalierly and naively stepped into was quickly spinning out of control.

"She took a few innocent comments and, and, *exaggerated* them," I said. "Blew them completely out of proportion."

"So, you did say some of them!"

"I...I...not in those *exact* words," I stammered. "She took a few things I said and, and *twisted* them a little bit. Look, you know what she's like."

"I don't believe you." She was really sore. Boy, I should've seen this coming, but I'd been too blinded by love.

"I never said I thought you were ugly or boring or shallow or plain or stupid or phony, or anything like that. *Honest.*"

"What *did* you say, then?"

"Well, she just kept asking me all these questions, you know, about her and you, and what I thought about this and that and we were up on the roof and in the heat of the moment I guess I made it sound like she was just a tad more desirable to me than you were and it made her real happy and then she made me real happy and I guess I never thought she'd remember everything I said and that she'd never tell *you* those things. I guess I just wasn't thinking."

"Oh, you were thinking all right – just not with your *brain.*" Even though she'd stopped crying, I could tell she was still real sore.

"I'm sorry, Kate," I said sincerely. "You're my friend, and I'm sorry I hurt you. I never wanted to do that." I took her hand in mine and held it softly.

That's when Penelope walked in and saw us. *Oh boy, here we go...*

She walked right up to us, as bold as you please.

"So this is the other woman, eh?" Dillinger asked, looking Penelope over. I ignored him.

"What's going on?" Penelope asked coldly, looking at our hands. Kate held on tight, so there was no way I could let go.

"Calvin says he never said those things about me," Kate told her sister. They stared daggers at each other for a few moments.

"Well, maybe not," Penelope finally admitted. "But Calvin said he loves *me*, not you. Isn't that right, darling?" She turned those beautiful cold eyes on me. I looked at Kate, then at Penelope, then back at Kate. She wouldn't let go of my hand.

"You're in a real pickle now, Shakespeare," Dillinger wryly observed. "Can't say I envy you one bit."

Note to self: Never – *ever* – get involved with sisters again.

"Well." I heard a quivering voice but didn't recognize it as mine. "Both of you are just swell, and I really like you both just tons and tons..."

I looked at Penelope to see how things were going. From her icy stare I knew it wasn't enough.

"But, I guess what I'm trying to say is, I like you both, but in a little bit different ways..."

I looked at Penelope, but she still wasn't having it. Her eyes: *Say it...*

"Keep digging, kid," Dillinger suggested. "You're not out of the hole yet."

"But, I have to say that I think I like Penelope in the like kind of way that's more like *love*..."

That did it. Penelope stopped giving me the evil eye and turned a smug, satisfied smirk on her sister. Kate let go of my hand and wiped her still moist eyes.

"Thank you, Calvin," she said curtly. "I understand. I understand what you're saying completely. And I'm sorry that I accused you of saying those things about me. I should have known that even though your feelings for me are merely platonic, you would never have said such things."

"Classy dame," Dillinger said with approval.

"It's okay," I said.

Then Kate looked up at her sister. "Why did you tell me those lies?"

"Because I think you've been spending too much time with Calvin lately," Penelope coolly explained. "I didn't like it."

"I've only been helping him edit his book," Kate said.

"I'm not stupid," Penelope said. "I know how you feel about him. The work is just an excuse. But he's *mine*, not yours. And now, because of your selfishness, you've allowed Calvin to come between us as sisters. I don't think I can ever forgive you for that."

Kate stood up and looked at Penelope. "Why is it *you* always get to have boyfriends, but you never let *me* have one?" Then she walked out of the rec room in a very sad but dignified manner.

I looked up at Penelope. "Is she right?" I asked. "Do you only like me because *she* likes me?"

"Oh, what difference does it make?" my dark angel said impatiently. "We're both getting what we want, aren't we?" Then her face softened, and she smiled sweetly at me. "I'll see *you* later tonight, as usual." She looked around to make sure no one was watching, then kissed me softly on the lips. And Penelope turned and walked out of the room.

"You picked yourself a real winner with that one, Shakespeare," the bank robber said sardonically. "Maybe you should've picked the other one."

"What do *you* know?" I replied impatiently.

"I know a lot about broads," he continued. "I've had my share in my time – good ones, bad ones, all kinds. There's the kind who are just as sweet as your little sister, and the kind you've got to slap right across the face every once in a while. And if you ask me, that's the kind you've got right here."

"Who asked you?"

He completely ignored my impertinence. "It's obvious, kid. The way she treats you she thinks she *owns* you. That never turns out good."

"Will you please stop talking?"

"I'm just trying to help you out, kid. Love's a rough business, almost as rough as robbing banks. I know a little bit about both, believe you me. Maybe you should think about breaking it off with Bonnie Parker here and going after the sweet dark-haired one instead."

"You don't understand."

"Oh, I understand, kid," he said. "They're called *hormones*. You get your kicks with the blonde. She really sends you, I get that. But she doesn't *respect* you. The dark-haired one – what's her name, Kate? – it looks like she really likes you. She'd probably treat you a lot better, too."

"Don't you think I know all of this?" I asked, exasperated.

"Then what are you waiting for?"

"It's not that simple," I said. "There are good things about each one. I like being around Kate and we connect intellectually. But I love the way Penelope looks and how she makes me feel. If I could put them both together into one girl, it would be perfect."

"In a perfect world, Shakespeare," Dillinger lamented. "In a perfect world..."

Some moments just have a way of staying with you forever – and the more absurd they are, the harder they are to shake.

Here I was sitting in a mental hospital in love with a pair of unstable, semi-neurotic twin sisters, receiving relationship counseling from John Dillinger's ghost.

This had to be one of those moments.

* * *

That night I had a new dream.

I'm standing in the middle of Mrs. Riley's backyard with my accordion. The sun is shining and the flowers in her garden are blooming. But she's not there. There's fresh lemonade on the little patio table, but her chaise lounge is empty.

Buck is swimming laps in her pool – back and forth, back and forth. I call out to him, but he doesn't hear me. Two fish-headed alien creatures are peering over the fence from Aunt Evelyn's yard, watching him swim with great interest. I want to warn him, but he doesn't hear me. He just keeps swimming back and forth.

Maybe he will hear the accordion. I start playing, but no sound comes out. Instead, the music I play is coming from the pool house.

Mrs. Riley's pool house.

I want to stop playing but somehow I can't. The crayfish aliens in Aunt Evelyn's yard are controlling my fingers, and they won't let me stop.

Now I am drawn to the pool house. Because of the music. I can't help it. I start walking towards it.

Is she in there? No, I don't want to go in the pool house, but I have no choice, I'm being controlled by the aliens who are playing my accordion through me.

I am pulled to the pool house as if on a tractor beam. Fear grips me when I realize what awaits me inside.

Buck keeps swimming. Maybe they are controlling him, too. At the pool house door I hesitate a second, but then I'm compelled to open it and step inside.

It's darker inside. My eyes adjust. There's a figure near the back wall. It's her. Her back is to me.

"Calvin, I've been waiting..."

I'm frozen in terror. My legs have been immobilized. This time I can't run. My fingers still press buttons and keys, creating a frightening polka sound.

Then Mrs. Riley turns around. And I see that she has Penelope's face.

"Calvin, I've been waiting..."

"No!" I scream, horrified. Now my legs work. I drop the accordion and manage to run from the pool house. Outside, Buck still swims like an automaton. The aliens are no longer at the fence. I see them walking towards Aunt Evelyn's house.

I look up at the attic window expecting to see Uncle Joe there. But it's not him – instead, it's Kate.

She sees me looking up at her. The crayfish aliens are getting closer, closer to the house.

"Kate!" I call up to her, but she can't hear me through the window. "Kate! Get out of the house!"

The aliens are inside the house now. I try to get to Kate, but I can't. "Kate! Get out!"

There's nothing I can do.
Buck swims and swims.

* * *

The next morning, I told Dr. Freud about my dream. He asked me what the pool house represented. I told him what had happened there with Mrs. Riley.

"Initiation into Manhood," he nodded, puffing on his cigar. "Of course it's terrifying. You're just a boy. So the pool house represents a frightening place, a place where something very traumatic nearly happened. Who is this Buck?"

"My older cousin," I replied. "He went over to Mrs. Riley's pool house a lot."

"Yes, he is swimming in her pool, you see – having a *relationship* with her. And what do you think the presence of the two alien creatures signifies?"

"They're watching him swim," I replied. "He's in danger, but he doesn't know it."

"Who is the girl's face you see in the pool house?"

"Penelope," I replied. "A girl here at Sunnybrook."

"And you like this girl?"

"Yes."

"How do you feel when you see her face on Mrs. Riley's body?"

"Scared."

"Why?"

"Because I'm not supposed to be in that pool house."

"Go on."

"She – Mrs. Riley – lured me in there. It was a trap."

"I see," Dr. Freud said. "So Penelope being in the pool house is troubling to you."

"Yes. But it wasn't Penelope – it was Mrs. Riley – *and* Penelope..."

"You sound all mixed up."

"I AM!"

"Are you afraid of Penelope?"

"...No."

"Why the hesitation?"

"I'm not afraid of her," I said. "I'm just kinda stuck between these two sisters..."

"Sisters?"

"Yeah. Penelope and Kate, the girl in the attic window."

"Do you like one more than the other?"

"Yes. No. I don't know. Sometimes I think I do. But I'm not sure."

"Tell me about it."

"I started out liking Penelope," I confided. "But lately I guess I've been thinking more and more about Kate."

"Is that why you were trying to get to Kate in your dream?"

"I guess so," I replied. "It's complicated, because they both have qualities I like. One day I like one of them, but the next day I can't stop thinking about the other one. Sometimes I feel like they're both driving me crazy."

"It's not crazy to be attracted to two people at the same time," Dr. Freud said. "Listen, I loved my wife Martha very much. But when her sister Minna came to live with us in Vienna – well, I must admit that I found myself thinking about *her* just as much as Martha!"

"You, too?" I asked.

"Yes, I admit it," the doctor said. "I was infatuated with my sister-in-law. And the feelings were quite mutual. Listen, narcissism isn't always bad. You are attracted to Penelope's boldness and physicality because you yourself possess those traits. Just as you are attracted to Kate's kindness and intellect because you, too, share those traits."

The way he explained it made so much sense. Talking to him really helped me understand why my feelings were so jumbled up. And finding out that he went through the whole sister thing just like I was really bonded us, too.

"But how do I ever pick one?" I asked.

"You don't have to," he smiled. "Not right now. Penelope excites but terrifies you. Kate comforts and stimulates you intellectually. If I were you I would just relax and enjoy the best of both girls. You're young, you've got all the time in the world. You're only young once, you know!"

"Okay."

"In time, you'll know which one makes you happier."

Talking to Dr. Freud really got me thinking about my feelings for the twins. At first, all there was was Penelope. I told her the truth when I said all I thought about was her, day and night. There seemed to be no room left in my life for Kate. But I found myself thinking more and more about Kate lately, and I didn't know why.

The kerfluffle over what I'd said to Penelope had blown over by now, and Kate was coming around again. Spending time with her was easy and light. We enjoyed each other's company and laughed at the same things and liked the same kinds of books and movies and TV shows. It wasn't like that with Penelope. With her, you were always walking on egg shells not sure if she was pleased enough or entertained enough or getting enough attention at any given moment.

I still went up on the roof almost every night with her. But afterwards I would lie in my own bed and fall asleep thinking about the best parts of both girls, and how they could be put together in various combinations to make my Dream Girl.

Chapter 23

Mistletoe and eggnog. Medication, hypnosis, and chestnuts roasting on an open fire. Throw in a pair of spooky twins with psychic abilities and a kid who screams when he thinks he's on fire, and you've got Christmastime in a mental hospital.

Yes, it was time for Bing Crosby and *White Christmas*. Ringing sleigh bells and strings of popcorn. Placing the star atop the Christmas tree and lots and lots of Thorazine.

In kid world, Christmastime was tops. But with all the depression around the place, it took a lot of medication to put us all in the Christmas spirit.

But with the tree trimmed and all the decorations in place, Sunnybrook never looked so cheerful. The first snow came about a week before Christmas, and Penelope and I went up to the roof and joyfully made snow angels. Then Bart and Raoul got all the kids together and we sang Christmas carols to Dr. Spielman and all the nurses. In the rec room, Christmas music played on the radio and all the kids were writing Christmas cards and letters to their families back home.

I wrote a card to Aunt Evelyn and Buck and told them I was doing just swell, then wrote one for my Old Man but didn't mail it on account of I didn't know where to mail it to anyway.

Every year the kids at Sunnybrook put on a Christmas Pageant. It was the highlight of the season, and even parents and other important people from the community were invited to attend.

But, of course, what should have been a joyous experience got off to a rocky start when Penelope thought it would be cute for me and her to play Joseph and Mary. Orson and some of the others immediately objected.

"Kate should be Mary," Orson declared. "She's more like Mary than Penelope is."

"You don't have to be like a character to play a part," Penelope protested. "Ingrid Bergman isn't like Joan of Arc, and she played *her*. Ingrid Bergman isn't even French – she's Swedish!"

"I think Penelope has a good point," I said after she shot me a loaded look.

"Mary didn't have blonde hair," Nell/Dot pointed out. "Kate has dark hair like Mary did."

"How do you know Mary didn't have blonde hair?" Penelope snapped.

"In all the movies she has dark hair, like Kate," Nell/Dot replied.

"Plus, Kate's nicer," Orson said. "Like Mary."

"Well, if I can't be Mary, then Calvin isn't playing Joseph," Penelope decided.

There followed a discussion about who would play Joseph, with Edmund coming out on top.

"Not Edmund," Orson objected. "He's an atheist. I don't think it would be reverent for an atheist to play the father of Jesus."

"Besides, he might think he's on fire and start screaming in the middle of Jesus's birth," Minnie said.

Someone suggested Orson, but he bowed out.

"I'm playing the Inn-keeper," he said. "I already know how I'm gonna tell Joseph and Mary to get lost when they knock on my door."

"I think Calvin should play Joseph," Kate spoke up. "He's the best one for that part."

Everyone agreed.

Penelope looked at me, then at Kate, then back at me. I could see the wheels turning inside her pretty little head.

"Definitely *not.*"

"But there's no one else who can do it," Orson said.

After a great amount of haggling, Penelope finally relented and allowed me to play Joseph to Kate's Mary – on condition that she got to play the Angel of the Lord and explain to Mary how she got pregnant without Joseph ever even touching her. She seemed strangely placated by the idea of Immaculate Conception – especially the part about Joseph and Mary *not* having relations.

The scripts were all dog-eared and had Hershey's chocolate and Coca-Cola stains on them from years of use. We passed them around and started rehearsing on the creaky old stage in the basement auditorium. Backstage there were trunks full of costumes and props, everything we needed to stage the pageant. There was even a fake donkey with wheels for pregnant Mary to ride on and a rope for Joseph to pull it with. The part of the baby Jesus would be played by a plastic doll.

Orson, of course, had dibs on the Inn-keeper's part. He'd been practicing how to tell Joseph and Mary to get lost all year. Edmund, Bertram, and Trevor would play the Three Wise Men. Stuart would play a shepherd. Nell would get to put her multiple personalities to good use by playing the Inn-keeper's wife, the Roman guard, and the shepherd who announces the Savior's birth. If she could get the timing right, she was supposed to employ Dot as the Roman guard and Sarah, the evangelist, as the shepherd. But which personalities would bob to the surface during the actual performance was anybody's guess.

Penelope got to work right away crossing out lines in her script and re-writing her part. It was clear she intended to do something with the Angel of the Lord that hadn't been seen before. I asked her what she was planning, but she wouldn't tell me.

"It's a surprise," she said with a gleam in her eye.

The rehearsals went really well, until we got to the part where Joseph and Mary had to go to Bethlehem to be counted in the census.

"Why does Mary have to ride on a donkey?" Nell/Dot wanted to know.

"Because the script says it's a very long journey to Bethlehem," Kate replied.

"Then why didn't they just take a Greyhound bus?" Nell/Dot asked.

We hit another snag getting the shepherds outfitted with their costumes. If the costumes weren't exactly the same, Stuart would start his anxiety shtick. We had a devil of a time going through all those costumes to find matching pieces, but finally came up with something that both still looked like shepherds and also calmed Stuart down.

Then when we got to the manger scene, there had to be the same amount of cows and sheep on each side or Stuart would start his routine again. When we finally got the balance of livestock right, there was another problem: the OCD shepherd didn't like the number of wise men.

"There have always been *three* wise men," Orson tried to explain to him. "That's what the script says."

"But three is an odd number," Stuart complained.

I could see Penelope rolling her eyes and prayed she wouldn't do anything to set Stuart off. Fortunately, she kept her mouth shut and just glared at him.

"How about two?" I asked Stuart. "Would two wise men be all right?"

"Two is an *even* number," Stuart said, looking relieved.

"Good," I said. "Bertram, change costumes. You're a shepherd now."

There. Problem solved. Our Christmas Pageant would have two wise men instead of three, and if anyone didn't like it they could ask for a refund.

Overall, I was pleased with the casting arrangement. It allowed Kate and I to spend time together going over our lines, and Penelope couldn't say much about it. I began to realize how much more relaxed I was around Kate than I was around Penelope. Kate never made you feel inadequate or nervous about saying the wrong thing and starting a big fight. She was just easy to talk to and way less intense than her golden-haired sister.

Plus, she was getting easier on the eye all the time. And I could tell by the way Kate looked at me that she felt the same way. It was nice, but I knew I still had a ways to go to get Penelope completely out of my system.

I confided as much to Dr. Freud, who always seemed to be there when I needed to talk. Funny how that works.

I told him I felt something new going on with Kate. Like an awakening. But at the same time I was having a hard time letting go of Penelope. He asked me what I'd been dreaming about lately. *Funny you should ask...*

So I told him about my garden dream.

I'm in Aunt Evelyn's attic all alone. Uncle Joe is not there. I am playing my accordion. It's nice. I feel okay. Not super – just okay. But everything around me, everything in the attic, is gray and dusty. The air is stale and hot. But everything is also very familiar. I feel a sense of never leaving that attic – in fact, the thought of leaving never occurs to me.

I am just there.

Then I see something out the attic window. Instead of Aunt Evelyn's crummy backyard, there is a beautiful, lush garden full of exotic-looking plants and juicy fruits of all types. The garden is colorful and teeming with life: birds sing and squirrels frolic. Running down the center of the garden is a babbling brook of fresh, cool water. I can see a cool breeze stirring the leaves of the plants.

The garden is beckoning me, but I don't move. I don't want to leave the attic. If I go to the garden, I may never get back to the familiarity of the stuffy attic. Someday I may go to the garden, but not today.

Today I stay in the attic.

Then I told him about my island dream.

I'm on an island all by myself. My island is nice, but it only has the bare necessities for survival: coconuts and some fresh water.

There is also a motorboat. It's a very nice motorboat, but I never use it because I do not want to leave my island.

Then one morning I notice in the distance a much nicer island. That island has beautiful shade trees bearing all kinds of delicious-looking fruit. It's a better island than mine. I want to go there, but that would mean leaving the island I know so well and which has sustained me for so long. Something keeps me there on the old island, even though all I do is look at the other island and wonder what it would be like to live there.

Then one day I get in my motorboat. I am going to go to the new island. But there's no key to start it. I look everywhere, but there's no key. I think about trying to row the boat over to the other island, but I'm afraid of getting caught in a current and being swept away from both islands forever.

I sit on the boat and stare sadly at the other island.

"Those are very interesting dreams," Dr. Freud admitted when I finished.

"Will you help me figure them out?" I asked.

"I think you already know what they mean," he smiled. "But let's talk about it. In the first one, when you are in your aunt's attic. What do you think the beautiful garden represents?"

"Something new," I replied. "A change."

"And why don't you leave the attic?"

"I'm afraid," I said. "Afraid of losing something."

"But it's hot and dusty there," Dr. Freud pointed out. "And the air is stale. Why do you stay?"

"Because it's *familiar*," I answered. "The garden looks beautiful, but I'm afraid because it's new and I don't know what it will be like."

"So you stay in the attic where you feel safe," he said. "Which means, there's no risk. Why are you not willing to take a *risk*, Calvin?"

"I don't know."

"Now, in the second one about the islands. Do you see a similar dynamic?"

"Yes," I replied. "I don't want to leave the place I'm used to for something new."

"You are settling for what you know," he said. "Even though it is lifeless and stale."

"I guess so."

"But in this dream, you have a motorboat," Dr. Freud pointed out. "I'm very curious about this motorboat, Calvin."

"I can't find the key to start it."

"Exactly. What do you think that means?"

"The boat is useless," I ventured.

"Go on."

"The boat represents the way I can get to the other island, but it doesn't work without a key."

"And what does the key represent, Calvin?"

I thought a long time. That was a tough one. "I don't know."

"Could it represent your *will*?" he asked. "Without the will to use the boat, it is useless."

"Oh, I get it now."

"And the currents between the islands – they intrigue me as well. What do you think they represent?"

"My fear," I said. "I'm afraid if I try to go to the other island, I'll lose *both* islands..."

"You're getting very good at this, my boy," Dr. Freud said. "Now let's put it all together: What is going on in your life right now? What kind of change is your unconscious wrestling with?"

I knew exactly what it was about.

"The twins," I told him. "Kate is the garden. Kate is the new island. I've got to make a decision. I've got to choose."

"You don't need to choose today, Calvin," he told me. "Take your time. You will know when it's right."

Dr. Freud was right. There was time. I was too torn to make a decision right now, even though I knew which direction I was leaning. I felt like my world had been turned upside down. I had been captivated by these enigmatic twins since day one and I was still unable to extricate myself from their strange powers. They seemed to have gotten under my skin and into my blood, and I didn't understand why.

My agony must have been written all over my face.

"My boy, I have been studying and thinking and pondering and writing about love for most of my life – and *death* – and I'm still not sure what it's all about," Dr. Freud told me. "It does things to your brain that no drug can do. It makes old men feel young and young men feel invincible. Empires have been built and empires have fallen because of it. The ancient Greeks believed it was a kind of madness. The Song of Solomon calls it 'more delightful than wine.' Shakespeare wrote one hundred and fifty sonnets and thirty-six plays about it, and still couldn't exactly pin it down. But even after all the joy and trouble and pain and pleasure and sorrow and misery it causes, I wouldn't want to live in a world without it. Would you?"

To this day, I've never heard a better definition of romantic love.

* * *

That night at dinner a heated discussion broke out about using a real baby for Jesus in the pageant.

"We could use my little cousin Emily," Nell/Dot suggested hopefully. "My aunt and uncle say she cries too much and I heard them tell my mom and dad that they sure wouldn't mind getting rid of her for a few hours."

"Jesus is supposed to be a boy, not a girl," Stuart told her with authority.

"Baby boys and girls are almost exactly the same, stupid," Nell/Dot retorted. "Nobody would know the difference anyway."

"God would," Stuart replied.

"God loves all babies the same," Nell/Dot argued. "With everything going on in the world I'm sure he wouldn't mind my little cousin Emily sitting in for baby Jesus just for our stupid little play."

"I don't think we should use a real baby at all," Minnie said. "Real babies are disgusting. They do disgusting things like pooping and peeing and throwing up at the worst times. It might ruin our play."

"My cousin Emily *never* does those things," Nell/Dot promised.

"Oh yeah?" Orson asked. "She'd be *dead* if she never did those things!"

"I think we should use the doll," Penelope said. "Real babies aren't reliable actors. That's why you never see them in the movies."

"I've seen lots of babies in the movies," Edmund said.

"They're all artificial," Penelope insisted. "Hollywood's got a rule: all artificial babies. They're easier to work with."

"They sure look real to *me*," Edmund said.

"Besides, babies always get cranky when they haven't had their naps," Minnie added.

"Baby Jesus never got cranky," Nell said, now in the voice of Sarah the evangelist. This personality had a slight southern accent.

"How do *you* know?" Minnie asked.

"Because he's God," Nell/Sarah explained. "God never needs to take naps because He never gets tired."

"Baby Jesus wasn't God yet," Minnie responded. "He had to grow up first."

"You're wrong," the little evangelist corrected her. "Jesus was *always* God. Even before He was born."

"How could He be God before He was even born?" asked Edmund.

"He just was," Nell/Sarah insisted. "The Bible says so."

"Is she right?" Kate asked me.

"Yes, it does," I replied.

"Baby Jesus couldn't be God because He didn't heal people," Orson said. "Only God can heal people."

"Who says baby Jesus didn't heal people?" Nell/Sarah asked.

"Whenever Mary or Joseph got a cold or the flu or a headache or something, baby Jesus didn't do anything about it," Orson said.

"How do *you* know?" Nell/Sarah asked. "Were *you* there?"

"No, but I never heard about baby Jesus healing anyone in Sunday school," Orson reasoned.

"Baby Jesus was God," Nell/Sarah declared. "And if He was God, He could heal people."

"But what about Mary and Joseph?" Orson asked.

"He didn't have to heal them because they never got sick," Nell/Sarah explained carefully, as if talking to a small child. "Just being *around* Him kept them from getting sick."

"You're making that up!" Edmund said.

"Am not."

"Where does it say that in the Bible, then?" Edmund challenged. "Come on, show us."

"It doesn't have to be in the Bible to be true," Nell/Sarah said defensively.

"Then how do you know?"

"Because if God lives in your house with you, you just won't get sick."

"I don't get it."

Nell/Sarah took a deep breath. "Look, it's simple: Germs make people sick, right? Do you think God is going to live in a house full of *germs*? Germs can't even survive around God – they just shrivel up and die in His presence. When Moses came down from Mt. Sinai with his face all glowing with glory after talking to God, do you think he still had any germs on him? Huh? Think about it."

That quieted down the doubters.

"Well, I still don't think we should use a real baby in the play," Minnie said.

* * *

On the evening of the pageant, the backstage area was complete bedlam. Kids were running around everywhere, switching costumes and teasing each other and pulling hair and calling each other names in an attempt to release all their pent-up nervous energy. No one was really in charge, but as Joseph, Jesus's father, I felt it was incumbent upon me to step up and try to restore a sense of order.

I wasn't doing very well at all, until Nell/Dot stepped forward in her Roman guard costume and yelled, "SHUT UP, EVERYONE, AND LISTEN TO JOSEPH!" That quieted them down a bit, so I said something about working hard and having a lot of fun but don't forget what the important message of the pageant was all about.

"Yeah, expensive gifts from rich guys from the East," Orson cracked wise.

"It's about the baby Jesus being born, you idiot!" Nell/Dot roared. The Roman guard costume seemed to give her an extra aura of authority. Orson piped down immediately.

I peeked between the curtains to see what the audience was like. There were some parents and relatives there, but only about half of the sixty or so folding chairs were full. I knew Aunt Evelyn wouldn't be there on account of her agoraphobia and all, and I didn't see Buck out there either. Oh well, the show must go on...

The curtains opened on a dark stage, and everyone in the audience found a seat and quieted down. Then the lights came up and we started the first scene: the Angel of the Lord coming to notify Mary about what God was going to do to her.

Mary was supposed to be in an orchard gathering olives or something in a basket when the Angel appears and startles her at first on account of most people have never seen an angel before and it would be kind of a startling thing, even to someone as devout and holy as Mary.

Kate did a good job of looking startled when the spotlight turned on and there was the Angel of the Lord standing on a big fake rock looking down at her in an angelic but creepy kind of way.

Penelope looked beautiful in her white frilly dress and big sparkly angel wings and her golden hair done up with flowers and holly all in it and the light shining on her so bright and all. She kinda took my breath away for a minute there.

"Do not be afraid Mary, for you have found favor with God," Penelope said all mysterious and angel-like. "Behold, you will conceive in your womb and bear a son, and you shall name Him Jesus. He will be great and will be called the Son of the Most High; and the Lord God will give Him the throne of His father David; and He will reign over the house of Jacob forever, and His kingdom will have no end."

"How can this be, since I am a virgin?" Kate asked, all humble and meek.

"The Holy Spirit will come upon you, and the power of the Most High will overshadow you," Penelope explained. "And for that reason the holy Child shall be called the Son of God."

She should have left it at that. But not Penelope.

"I just want to make it perfectly clear: Joseph had *nothing* to do with this," she ad-libbed to the audience. "It was the Holy Spirit, plain and simple. Joseph never laid a hand on her. And if he knows what's good for him, he never will, either!"

Oh, this is going to be a disaster, I thought. But then I heard a couple of parents laugh in the audience and felt like maybe it would be okay after all.

The next scene was where the Angel appears to Joseph in a dream. So there I was lying on my bed in my itchy fake beard pretending to be asleep when the spotlight comes on and Penelope appears in my bedroom. When she started talking I could tell she'd thrown out the script and was ad-libbing the whole scene.

"Look, Joseph, this is supposed to be a dream so don't get up," she said. "Mary's going to have a baby with God. But people around here might start talking so the Boss wants you to marry her so everything looks on the up-and-up. Any questions?"

Next came Nell as the Roman guard. She walked out into the middle of the stage and unrolled a scroll.

"All you people listen up!" she ordered. But something wasn't right. She'd gotten her personalities mixed up and was talking in Nina's voice instead of Dot's, so she sounded a little bit like a gangster. "Caesar says there's gonna be a census so everyone has to go back to the place where they were born, on the double! Anyone who doesn't show up will be taken out and shot!" Then she rolled up her scroll and officiously walked off stage.

After that things went pretty well until it was time for the Angel of the Lord to make her next appearance to the shepherds in the fields keeping watch over their flocks by night. The Angel of the Lord suddenly stood before them, and the glory of the spotlight shone all around them.

"Hey, why are you guys so afraid, anyway?" Penelope demanded in her angel voice. "I'm just an angel. Angels never hurt anyone. And I brought you some news: That baby over there in the manger, wrapped in swaddling clothes? The *Savior.* That's right, the one everybody's been waiting for, right here in Bethlehem. Christ the Lord. The Son of God. Now get up off the ground and start giving Him glory!"

Penelope led the shepherds across the stage to the manger.

"See? I told you so," Penelope told the shepherds. "Here He is right here – Baby Jesus. Hold him up so the shepherds can get a good look, Mary." Kate held the plastic baby doll wrapped in swaddling clothes up for the shepherds to see.

"Well – why aren't you bowing down and adoring?" Penelope asked in a bossy voice. The shepherds bowed and adored. "Now go tell everyone you see about the baby! Go on now – shoo!"

The shepherds got off their knees and left the stage. Then Penelope turned to the audience and broke the fourth wall again.

"See? Mary's treasuring all these things," Penelope assured the audience. "She's pondering them in her heart, right now."

When the wise men appeared, Nell the Roman guard was with them.

"I found these two lurking about outside the manger," Nell said, like a cop. "I don't think they're from around here. You know 'em?"

"Yeah, yeah – just put the gifts over there and start worshipping the baby," Penelope ordered.

Everyone got on their knees in a circle around Mary and her baby and worshipped. Then we finished the pageant by singing "Silent Night" and "O Little Town of Bethlehem" before the curtains closed to less than thunderous applause. The clapping died out to almost nothing, but we opened the curtains again and took a bow anyway.

"Well, that was quite...*unique*," Dr. Spielman told us afterwards. He seemed to be searching for something positive to say about it. "I could really see how much effort you all put into coming up with a fresh approach to telling the story..."

But most of the parents seemed to enjoy it.

"I hadn't expected a comedy," one dad said.

"These pageants can be so stuffy and boring," someone's aunt said. "But this one wasn't boring at all."

After the reception, Santa Claus showed up and passed out gifts to all the kids. When he got to me I noticed he had red-rimmed eyes and rye on his breath. His once-white beard was grey with grime and hung loosely, not even pretending to cling to his stubbly cheeks. His red Santa coat had grease stains and smelled like broiled salmon.

He handed me a small package. "Merry Christmas, kid."

I tore the wrapping paper off. It was a brand-new Hohner harmonica.

"What's the matter, you don't like it?" Santa asked.

"I already play the accordion," I said.

"No law against knowing how to play *two* instruments."

Santa was right. I decided to keep it and give it a try.

Chapter 24

The day after Christmas, Dr. Spielman called me into his office to give me the news.

"Your lack of progress has been troubling," he told me gravely. "We've tried increasing your dosage of medication and even hypnosis, but it doesn't seem to have done any good. Therefore, I've decided to implement a more aggressive form of treatment. Do you know what electroshock therapy is, Calvin?"

"No," I replied. I didn't know what it was, but it sure didn't sound good.

"It's a procedure in which small amounts of electricity – say, a hundred volts or so – are passed through the brain to induce seizures," Dr. Spielman cheerfully explained. "The seizures are only temporary, to reset the brain's functions. The treatment shows positive results in about fifty percent of cases. Most patients start feeling better after the first treatment."

"You mean there's more than one treatment?"

"Oh yes," he said. "You'll be receiving shock treatments two or three times a week for six months or so. It's safe, effective, and almost completely painless."

"How can it be safe, passing electricity through my brain?"

"Well, of course there are some side effects," the doctor admitted. "Disorientation, confusion, slight memory loss, headaches, small changes in personality – but the benefits far outweigh the negative effects."

"I don't want it," I said.

"You don't seem to understand, Calvin," Dr. Spielman smiled an odd little smile. "I'm afraid you don't have a choice. As the physician in charge of your case, I'm prescribing the treatment for you, and that's that. Your first treatment will be tomorrow morning."

"Let's do the hypnosis again," I said. "Please – I'll try harder this time."

"I've already made the decision, Calvin," he said coolly, avoiding eye contact again. "It's for the best, son..."

That night I lay in bed unable to sleep. The thought of what awaited me the next morning was almost unbearable. Unmoored, my mind drifted to thoughts of escape. Buck had escaped from a place like this. Even Penelope had commented on how lax security was here. I'd talk to her tomorrow, see if she was still interested in –

Movement outside my door captured my attention. Orson was loudly snoring away in his bed. Who was out there? I waited quietly, barely breathing. The door slowly opened. In the darkness I could see a white jacket – one of the orderlies. But lights out was hours ago – they never checked on us this late.

"Bart?" I whispered.

"Sshh!" the orderly said, coming inside. When he got to my bed I could see it wasn't Bart or Raoul – it was Buck dressed as an orderly!

"I told you I'd come visit you sometime," he whispered. "Remember?"

"Buck – what are you doing here?"

"I came to get you out of this place, kid. Come on, get up and get dressed, pronto!"

"But, I can't just leave..."

"Who says?" he asked. He was right. I got up and got dressed, careful not to wake Orson. I pulled my suitcase out from under my bed and packed it with my things: underwear, clothes, my Bible, my Dick Contino records, and my bundle of Big Chief tablets. I put my Buffalo nickel and new harmonica in my pocket, and my Lone Ranger cowboy hat on my head. Then I thought about it and took it back off. I carefully hung it by its string on Orson's bedpost – a little parting gift.

We took my suitcase and accordion and started to leave the room. "How did you get in here?" I asked.

"Through a downstairs laundry room window," he said. "The orderly's asleep in his office. We can sneak right past him."

"Wait," I said impulsively. "I'm not going without them."

"Without who?"

"The twins."

"We can't take anyone with us," he said. "It's too risky."

"Then I'm not going," I said. We looked at each other a long time.

"Okay, kid. Where are they?"

We silently padded down the hall to the girls' dorm. I went into their room and gently cupped my hand over Penelope's mouth. Her eyes opened but she didn't scream. I put my finger across my lips and took my other hand off her mouth.

"Calvin, are you crazy?" she asked. "It's too late to go up to the roof!"

"Get dressed and packed," I said. "We're getting out of this place."

"Oh, Calvin – quit joking around and go back to bed!"

"I'm not joking," I said. "My cousin's here to take us."

She looked at me, suddenly wide awake. "I'm in!"

That's my girl! She jumped out of bed and started to get dressed. I went over to Kate's bed and woke her up.

"*Calvin?* What..."

"Get dressed," I said. "We're getting out of here. One suitcase each, we've got to travel light."

I went out into the hall to wait with Buck. A minute later the twins joined us, dressed, hair brushed, and holding suitcases. Buck stared at them uncomprehendingly. I realized he probably expected *boy* twins.

"Why do we have to take *both* of them?" he whispered to me.

"Because I can't decide which one I want," I whispered back.

"That's good enough for me, kid," he said approvingly. "Let's get outta here."

We tiptoed down the hall and snuck past the orderlies' office one at a time. The door was open. Raoul was inside, his feet up on the desk, snoring away. Bart had the night off.

Once we passed Raoul, I knew we would make it out. We descended the flight of stairs to the first floor. There was nobody around. Then I remembered something.

"Wait a minute," I whispered to Buck. "I need to get something."

"Well, hurry up," he said. I went into the front office and found the drawer where I thought Dr. Spielman had put the Lone Ranger and Tonto pocket knife I got for my birthday. I can't help it – things mean a lot to me. I opened the drawer and, sure enough, there was the manila envelope with my name on it. I opened the envelope and took my knife out. I replaced the envelope and closed the drawer, then put the knife in my pocket and rejoined the others. The whole thing took about thirty seconds.

Buck led us downstairs to the laundry room in the basement. There was a broken window, high on the wall. It did not have bars on it. Buck lifted us up and through the window one at a time, then handed our suitcases up to us on the outside. When we were all out, he used a chair to climb out the window himself.

We were out!

We walked down the long gravel driveway toward the road without talking. Buck took off the white jacket and threw it into some bushes. At the big front gate I could see that Buck had cut through the chain to get in, so we were able to walk right out without a hitch. He'd parked his car about a quarter of a mile down the road. We walked quietly to the car and put our suitcases and my accordion in the trunk. Then I put the twins in the backseat and got in the front passenger seat, next to Buck.

And we drove away from Sunnybrook State Institute for Children into the sweet freedom of the dark night.

"Why are you doing this?" I asked Buck.

"I just couldn't leave you in a place like that, kid," he said, lighting a cigarette as he drove. "I know what those places are like, remember?"

"Are we going back to Aunt Evelyn's house?"

"I don't think that would be a good idea," he said. "That's the first place they'd look for you."

"Then where *are* we going?"

"You tell me, kid."

I thought about it. I turned and looked at the twins in the backseat. They were out cold, nestled together like raccoons, Kate's head resting on her golden-haired sister's shoulder. It made a very sweet picture.

"You'll have to tell me the story on those two sometime," Buck said. I was wide awake so I told him all about the twins and going up on the roof with Penelope and Dr. Freud and John Dillinger and Edmund the kid who screamed when he thought he was on fire and little Nell and all her personalities. Then I told him about Dr. Spielman and his plans to give me electroshock therapy in the morning.

"I guess he'll have to find someone else to fry," Buck smiled. "So, where do you wanna go, kid?"

"How much money you got?"

"I got a couple bucks," he said. "Enough to last us a while."

"Then let's go to Florida."

Buck drove all night to get out of Ohio. He knew the State Police would be looking for us in the morning. When the sun came up he turned on the radio to listen to the news. Sure enough, there was a report of three children – two sisters and an unrelated boy – missing from the state hospital. The State Police put out an all-points bulletin. But we were already in a different state, and Buck said it would take a while for the Ohio State Police to coordinate with the surrounding states.

"They'll be looking for you back in Ohio for a while," Buck said confidently. "That'll give us time to stay well ahead of them."

The twins slept peacefully until we stopped at a roadside joint for donuts and hot chocolate. The minute Penelope saw Buck in the light of day, I knew there was going to be a change in our relationship.

"That's your *cousin*?" she whispered to me, eyeing him up and down like a truck driver looking at a steak dinner.

Buck wanted to keep moving, so we took our breakfast to go.

"I'm sitting in the front now," Penelope informed me, sliding into the seat next to Buck.

"Okay by me," I said, getting into the back with Kate. A few minutes after hitting the highway, the little operator had scooted to the center of the seat, right up close to Buck. She flirted with him the whole trip, laughing playfully and touching his bicep when he let her feel his muscle. She was really something else. But I didn't feel jealous. I didn't feel anything – I had Kate all to myself in the back seat.

We talked and held hands, and sometimes just held hands and didn't talk. Whenever Penelope saw us she got mad and shot me a dirty look. She wasn't ready to let go of me quite yet, knowing that when she did, Kate would finally have me. But it was just a matter of time.

We drove hard all day, putting hundreds of miles between us and Sunnybrook. We passed the time by listening to old-timey Western music on the radio. I took out my brand-new harmonica and tried to play along with some of the songs. It wasn't like the accordion; it would take some getting used to. But Kate liked it and told me I did a good job playing along with the bands on the radio.

At the end of the day we were pretty exhausted and a little bit grimy from the road. Buck thought it would be a good idea to stop somewhere for the night and found a nice little mo-tel outside Chattanooga. He got two rooms — one for me and him and one for the twins. But before he let them go into their room, he took out his revolver and searched it for North Kore-ans first.

"All clear girls," he said, coming back out. "Sweet dreams."

In our room, we laid on our twin beds watching TV until we dozed off. It was a variety show from New York City, with lots of different kinds of acts. One act was a dance routine with a group of young ladies. There was a close up shot of one of the girls, and would you believe it, it was Darleen Fontaine! Our Darleen Fontaine, from Route 66! And she was a fabulous dancer, too.

Good old Darleen. I was so happy for her. She'd made it onto television, after all!

The next morning, we had flapjacks and strawberry syrup at a diner before piling into the car for the day's drive. It was good to be on the road again — staying up late watching TV and eat-ing in diners — but I really couldn't wait to get to Florida and find my parents.

"What's your plan?" Buck asked me.

"I don't know," I replied from the back seat.

"You gotta have a plan, kid."

He was right. I took out my harmonica and started playing it while I tried to come up with a plan. Florida was a big place. It must've had about a million people in it. How would I ever find them?

I stopped playing. "How long will it take us to get there?"

"Three or four days, if we take our time," Buck replied.

"I'll think of something by then," I said, but I really wasn't too sure about that.

We drove and drove. Penelope laughed and flirted with Buck in the front. He humored her, but I knew he was well-aware she was just a young girl. Buck was kinda crazy and all, but I knew he wasn't like *that*.

I played my harmonica softly in the backseat while Kate leaned against my shoulder and dozed. She liked to touch me, and I liked it too. And I was getting better on the harmonica. I was starting to be able to pick out a few songs by ear, like "She'll Be Coming 'Round the Mountain When She Comes" and my old favorite, "Deep in the Heart of Texas." Maybe someday, with lots of practice, I could be as good on the harmonica as I was on the accordion.

At lunch, we stopped in a small town for burgers and shakes and while we were eating Kate slipped away for a few minutes and came back with one of those travel typewriters that have a lid and close up just like a little suitcase when you're not using it so you can take it with you on vacations or business trips and whatnot. It was used and she found it at one of those second-hand stores for two dollars and bought it for me with her own money so I could keep up with my writing on the trip.

"Your story is still unfolding," Kate said as she presented it to me.

I didn't know what to say. Kate was turning out to be one of the best things that ever happened to me.

Later that afternoon we stopped at a small-town gas station to fill up. There was no attendant in sight, so Buck got out of the car to take a look around. Presently, a tobacco-chewing hayseed wearing a tattered baseball cap came out and looked Buck over pretty good.

"Fill 'er up, please," Buck smiled. The hayseed obliged, staring in the windows at the rest of us as he pumped the gas. He looked at the twins a long time, then looked back at Buck.

"I noticed you got Ohio plates," he said. "Whereabouts in Ohio you from?"

"Cleveland," Buck replied.

"You a long way from home, ain't ya?" the hick said. "What you doin' all the way down here in Georgia?"

"Just takin' in the sights."

"Family vacation, huh?"

"Something like that," Buck said, looking away.

"Most families take their vacations in the summertime," the hick said. "You ain't really on vacation, are ya?"

"Look, friend, just finish filling the tank and mind your own business, okay?"

"Sorry, didn't mean any offense," he said, replacing the hose and screwing the gas cap back on. "That'll be two dollars and seventy-six cents."

"Here you go." Buck gave him a five-spot.

"Right back with your change," he said, and disappeared into the station. He came back out a moment later carrying a shotgun.

"Here's your change, sir," he said, handing it to Buck. Then he raised the shotgun and pointed it right at him.

"What's this, friend?" Buck asked.

"I'll be takin' them twins now."

"Say again?"

"I'll be takin' them twins now."

"I don't get you, friend."

"TV says there's a reward for them twins," the hick said. "There's no reward for the boy, so you can keep him. But I'm afraid I'll be takin' them twins now."

"No," Buck said.

The hick raised the shotgun higher. "You the one bust them out? Maybe the Sheriff would be interested in meeting you. Now you either hand them twins over right now, or I'll go get the Sheriff. Either way, their parents are offering a nice reward, and I'm gettin' that money."

"Okay, okay – just take it easy, friend," Buck said. "Girls, get out of the car."

"No, Buck," I said.

"Girls – out *now.*"

"What are you *doing*?" I asked.

"Shut up!" Buck said. The twins got out of the car, eyes wide with fear. "This is it, girls," Buck said. "You're going home to your parents now, where you belong."

The twins looked at me in desperation. "Calvin, please..." Kate said.

I looked at Buck. He looked away. Then he got in the car, started it up, and pulled out of the station in a hurry leaving the twins with the hick with the shotgun. I couldn't believe what was happening.

"We can't just leave them here!" I said.

"I know kid, don't worry," Buck said. He pulled off to the side about fifty yards down the road. He reached under the seat and pulled out his revolver.

"You stay here," he said, with a combat gleam in his eye. "I'll be right back..."

I waited in the car with a lump in my throat. My mind was racing. I couldn't bear the thought of never seeing them again – especially Kate. Time seemed to stand still in the eerie, thickly-wooded Georgia countryside. Finally, I saw them in the rear-view mirror, running up the road from the gas station to the car. When they got to the car, I could see Buck had the hick's shotgun. He threw it into the bushes off the side of the road and they all got into the car.

The twins were white as ghosts and breathing heavily. Kate immediately grabbed my hand and held on tight. She wouldn't let go for hours.

Buck stuffed his revolver back under the seat and started the car.

"Did you...?" I asked.

"He'll live," Buck said, pulling the car out onto the highway. Kate held my hand tight. She put her head on my shoulder and didn't say anything. I wanted to get out of Georgia as fast as we could.

Buck and I decided we had to keep the twins out of sight as much as possible. If the old hick saw the news about the reward on TV, other people did, too. When we stopped for gas, they hid under a blanket in the backseat. When we stopped for food, we brought it to the car for them to eat.

That night we drove extra late and stopped at a motel when it was good and dark. We parked well away from the front office, and after Buck had checked us in we smuggled the girls into the room. We would all be staying in one room from now on, to make it look less suspicious. Plus, it would make Buck's money last a lot longer.

Buck told us to keep the curtains closed and lay low while he went out to get us some hamburgers for dinner. He came back twenty minutes later with the food and a pair of scissors and some dark sunglasses.

After dinner, the twins cut each other's long locks off nice and short with the scissors Buck brought. Then he gave them the dark glasses and told them to wear them whenever they were outside. These cheap disguises would have to do for now, until things died down on the TV and radio news.

The twins looked strange at first, with their new haircuts. I was so used to their long, flowing hair. But they looked different and cute this way, and I started to get used to it by bedtime. The twins got the beds and Buck and I slept on the floor with blankets over us. It wasn't too bad – a lot like I imagined cowboys slept out on the lone prairie.

The next day we crossed the Florida state line. It felt like a real milestone. But I still didn't have a plan about finding my parents.

That's about when Buck started hallucinating about being tailed by the North Koreans. Poor Buck – he'd been pushing it pretty hard since springing us from Sunnybrook, and I was a little worried about him cracking up.

"They're in that blue Oldsmobile behind us," he said, squinting into the rear-view mirror. I turned around and looked out the back window. It looked like a typical blue car to me.

"Are you sure?" I asked.

"It's been tailing us since Macon," Buck insisted. He reached under his seat and pulled his revolver out.

"Here, take this," he said, handing it to me in the back seat. "If they get too close, let 'em have it."

I took the gun and held it very gingerly. "Is it loaded?" I asked.

"What good's an empty gun?" Buck responded, keeping his eye on the car behind us. I watched it, too. It did appear to be following us, at a very steady forty-yard length.

It followed us all day as we leisurely wove our way down the Florida coast. Maybe we *were* being tailed. But by *North Koreans*?

As the hours ticked by, Buck grew increasingly nervous. The twins were captivated by the beautiful beaches and seaside scenery sliding by outside the window, and begged Buck to stop so they could dip a toe in the water.

"I don't know, girls," Buck said, peering into the rear-view mirror for the millionth time.

Penelope, especially, wouldn't take "no" for an answer. She finally wore him down just north of Daytona Beach.

"Okay, but just for a few minutes," he said, pulling off the road near a deserted section of beach. Thrilled, the twins tumbled out of the car and ran to the ocean with squeals of delight.

Buck and I watched as the blue car pulled over and parked a few car lengths behind us. Nobody got out.

"Go watch the girls," Buck said, taking the revolver from me. I got out and went down to the beach where the twins were already frolicking in the surf, their capris neatly rolled up to the knees. I took my shoes off and stepped into the water expecting it to be freezing cold, but it was warm like bath water, even in late December.

Buck got out of the car but stayed close to it, eyeing the blue car warily.

"Come on, Calvin," Penelope teased. "Don't be chicken! Come in *deeper*..." Both of them laughed and splashed me with water.

"We'll see about *that*," I said, picking Penelope up in my arms and dunking her in the next wave. She screamed but came up laughing like a little kid. The twins had never been to the ocean before, and were having a blast after being cooped up in the car and motel rooms for so many days.

I was having a blast, too, holding hands with both of them and kicking at the waves lapping against the shore with our bare feet. Then Kate and I sat down on the sand and watched as Penelope continued to splash in the surf and get completely soaked.

"It's so beautiful," Kate marveled, looking out over the endless expanse of jade green water. "Why is it so warm?"

"I think it's on account of the Gulf Stream," I said. "It brings warm water all the way from the Gulf of Mexico."

"How far does it go?" she asked, meaning the ocean.

"All the way to England, I guess."

She looked up at me with those big dark eyes. "You're so smart, Calvin."

We were holding hands again. It was so automatic that we didn't even notice anymore. She always held my hand so tight.

"I always want to be with you, Calvin," she said.

"I want to be with you, too," I told her, and it was true.

"Okay, everyone," I heard Buck call in a tense voice. "Time to hit the road."

Penelope sloshed out of the ocean like the Creature from the Black Lagoon. I'd never seen her enjoy herself so much. Kate and I stood up and we all walked back to the car. Buck got some blankets out of the trunk and Kate and I wrapped ourselves up real tight in one blanket and relaxed in the big cozy backseat.

Penelope was more soaked than we were. She wrapped herself in the other blanket and got in the front with Buck. He took one last look at the blue car then started the engine and drove back onto the highway.

"Are they following us?" Buck asked.

"Yep," I said, looking out the back window.

Buck was extra nervous for the rest of the day. He kept chain smoking and looking in the rear-view mirror every ten seconds. The blue car stuck with us. Yep – we were officially being tailed.

When it got good and dark Buck started looking for a motel. We found one with a pretty pink neon sign that said *Seaside Inn*. It looked like a real charming place so Buck pulled into the parking lot and went into the office to register.

The blue car pulled into the lot and stopped a few spaces away. Again, no one got out. They just sat there, watching us.

Buck came out of the office and unloaded the suitcases from the trunk. We smuggled the twins inside the room as usual, then closed and locked the door. Buck immediately parted the curtains and peered out at the blue car.

Jeepers, Buck was acting *real* jumpy.

Before we settled in, Buck took his revolver out and searched every nook and cranny of the room. He searched in the bathroom and behind the shower curtain. He searched the closet and behind the TV set. He searched under the beds – *twice.*

"Okay, it's all clear," he said without a hint of relief. "Everyone just relax and take it easy."

He reached into his pocket and gave me some cash. "You go get dinner. Go to the joint next door and pick up some hamburgers and shakes. I'll stay here with the girls."

As I was going out the door, he added, "And pick up something special for the girls – you know, a Moon Pie or something." I knew what he was saying – something to take their minds off what was happening.

I went outside and started walking to the burger joint. The blue car sat ominously facing our room. I tried not to look at it, but couldn't help it. Then I saw Buck part the window curtains in our room and peer out at it, a lit cigarette in his mouth.

When I got back with the food, the door was locked. I knocked three times – my special knock. Buck unlocked the door and unfastened the safety chain. He pulled me inside and slammed the door shut. I could tell he was really spooked.

I handed out the food to everyone while Buck peered through the curtains again. "Hey, kid, why don't you find something to watch on TV while we eat?"

I turned the TV on and found an old Western. We sat on the beds and ate our meal to the sounds of ricocheting bullets and cowboys and Indians fighting.

Buck didn't touch his hamburger. He just paced back and forth and smoked cigarettes, parting the curtains to look out the window every thirty seconds.

"Why are you so worried, Buck?" I asked.

"I'm not worried, kid," he said. "Everything's under control."

After dinner, the twins went into the bathroom and took showers while I finished the Western and watched Buck pace and smoke. He looked out the window again.

"Are they still there?" I asked.

"Yeah."

"Why are they following us?"

"I don't know, kid," he exhaled smoke. "I think it might have to do with Buzz-saw Ridge."

"What's that?"

"It was a trap. They nearly wiped out our whole company there."

He still thought it was the North Koreans.

The twins came out of the bathroom in their nightgowns and got into bed. I kissed them both goodnight and said, "Don't worry. Buck was in the Army. He knows how to handle himself."

They didn't look too worried. They drifted right off to sleep and I made my little bed on the floor between them. Buck turned out the lights.

"Good night, Buck," I said.

"Sweet dreams, kid," he replied. But I don't think he ever went to bed that night.

When I woke up the clock said it was two in the morning. The door was wide open and Buck was nowhere to be seen. The twins were still sleeping, so I got up quietly and looked out the door.

Buck was at the blue car, pulling the door open and violently jerking somebody out of the driver's seat. It was a fat guy in his fifties, wearing a crumpled brown suit. Buck dragged him across the parking lot and into our room. The guy didn't seem to be putting up much of a fight, and he didn't look in too good of shape, anyway.

Buck threw him into a chair and before the poor guy knew what happened his hands were tied behind his back with a piece of cord.

"Close the door and lock it," Buck ordered me. I did it.

I looked at the man in the crumpled brown suit. He looked like he'd been living in his car for days. He was sweating and panting and he looked like he was having a heart attack.

"Look what I found sleeping behind the wheel," Buck said triumphantly. He was really pumped up.

"Whatever you're thinking, you got it wrong, mister," the fat guy huffed.

"No, I think I got it right," Buck said. "You've been tailing us since Macon."

"Actually, since Atlanta," the guy wheezed.

Buck looked at me. "Take the girls into the bathroom. I don't want them to see this. Then you come back out here."

I woke the twins up gently and led them to the bathroom. "Buck wants you to stay in here for a while," I said, then closed the door and rejoined Buck and the wheezing man.

Buck grabbed a lamp and shined it right in his face, interrogation-style. "Is this about Buzz-saw Ridge?"

"Buzz-saw *what?*"

"Who are you?" Buck demanded.

"Name's Beiderman," the man huffed.

"Why are you tailing us?"

"I'm a private dick out of Cincinnati," he replied, finally catching his breath. "You – you almost scared me to *death* out there, pal..."

"I'm not your pal," Buck said. "Who hired you?"

"The twins' parents," he replied. "They want 'em back real bad."

"Oh, they want 'em back, do they?" Buck said, laying on the sarcasm. "That why they left them to rot away in that filthy place?"

"Kidnapping's a federal crime."

"No one was kidnapped," Buck pointed out. "They left of their own free will. Right, kid?"

I nodded. "It was my idea, not Buck's. He didn't want them to come at first, but I made him take them."

"All of that's immaterial," the private dick said. "They just want their girls back. Look, they told me to tell you they won't press charges if you let the girls come with me. They're a very prominent family and they just want this whole thing to go away, get me?"

"I don't think so," Buck said.

"Okay, listen: you turn those girls over to me and I bet I can get the parents to send you a nice fat check, just for you. How 'bout it?"

"He hurts Penelope," I blurted out.

"What?" Beiderman asked.

"Her father," I clarified. "He *hurts* her."

"What do you mean he *hurts her*?" he asked.

Buck looked at my face and knew exactly what I was talking about.

"She told me herself," I said. "And Kate verified it."

"Now wait a minute," Beiderman said. "I didn't know anything about that. I promise. I'm just doing my job, I don't pry into my clients' private business..."

"*Private business?*" Buck said. "That's not what *I* would call it."

"Look, you don't have a choice," Beiderman said. "You've got to turn them over, sooner or later."

"We're not sending them back to a pig like that," Buck said firmly.

"Then the deal's off," Beiderman said. "They'll definitely be pressing charges now."

"You're in no position to set the terms here," Buck reminded him. He took his revolver out. "You're off the case, tough-guy.

You're going back to Cincinnati and tell those people I said to stuff it. And if I ever see you again, it won't be a pleasant little tea-time chat like we're having now. Get me?"

Beiderman gulped. "So – so you're letting me go?"

"First thing in the morning," Buck said. "You're spending the night in the bath tub."

I told the girls to come out now and get into bed and pull the covers over their heads.

"What's going on, Calvin?" Penelope demanded.

"Buck just wants you to do it," I said, and they did.

Then Buck took Beiderman into the bathroom, stuffed a washcloth into his mouth, sat him down in the bath tub, turned off the light, and closed the door.

"You kids go back to sleep now," Buck said. "We've got an early start in the morning."

At sunrise, Buck woke us up and told us to get dressed. Then he took Beiderman out to his car and locked him in the trunk.

He came back to the room and wrote a note on motel stationary saying that a man was locked in the trunk of the blue car outside. Then he left the note and Beiderman's car keys on the dresser for the maid to find when she came to clean the room later.

"That ought to give him a good two or three hours of quiet thinking time," Buck said.

Chapter 25

We left the *Seaside Inn* and continued down the coast. We didn't have a particular destination in mind, we just knew we had to keep moving.

Gee, Florida was sure a swell state. We passed by miles and miles of gorgeous beaches and sparkling seascapes and marinas full of big fishing boats and all sizes of sailboats. There were still a lot of Northerners down there for the holidays, and the traffic got pretty heavy sometimes on account of carloads of families and kids headed for one last day at the beach before going back to New York or Boston or Philadelphia.

Buck said that was just swell because we would blend in with them and it would be much harder for the cops to pick us out. But no sooner had he said that then we passed a State Police car parked just off the highway. I don't think Buck was speeding, but he got real nervous anyway.

Sure enough, as soon as we passed him the trooper pulled out behind us.

"What's he *doing*?" Buck asked. "I'm under the speed limit."

Then the red light came on and Buck had to make a choice: stop and try to talk his way out of it, or try to outrun the trooper. He decided to stop.

"Girls, get down on the floor," Buck ordered. They did, and I covered them with a blanket. Then I got in the front seat with Buck. He pulled onto the shoulder and stopped the car.

"What are you going to do, Buck?" I asked.

"I don't know yet, kid," he said.

The trooper was at the window looking in. Buck rolled it down and flashed a smile.

"Afternoon, officer."

"Can I see your license and registration, sir?"

"Sure," Buck said. And to my horror he reached under the seat, pulled out the revolver, and stuck it in the cop's face. "Now put your hands up, nice and easy," he said, as cool as you please.

The trooper looked like he was going to wet himself. He slowly raised his hands as the color drained from his face.

"That's real good," Buck said calmly. "Now, take your gun out of its holster and hand it to me. And don't try anything cute."

The cop did as he was told. I realized I was holding my breath, and finally exhaled. Buck had the trooper's gun now, and he was still holding his revolver on him.

"You – you're not going to kill me, are you?" the trooper asked.

"Now, why would I do a thing like *that*?" Buck asked in a friendly tone. "I mean, you're cooperating, aren't you?"

The trooper nodded enthusiastically. "Yes, sir! I'm cooperating!"

"Good. Now what's your name?"

"Ed."

"Okay Ed, here's what we're going to do to get out of this little jam," Buck told him. "I know how much trouble you fellas get in when you lose your gun, so if you'll just go back to your car now, get your keys, and bring them to me, you'll get your gun back."

"Really?" Ed asked, surprised.

"I promise," Buck assured him. "A gun for a key. Fair trade?"

"Yes, sir."

"Oh, and if I see you touch your radio, the deal's off. Got it?"

"Yes, sir." The trooper went back to his car and got his keys. Then he walked back to the window and handed them to Buck.

"You're doing just great, Ed," Buck told him. Then he took the trooper's gun, opened the cylinder, and emptied all the bullets out onto the seat. He closed the cylinder and gave the empty gun back to the trooper. The trooper looked confused.

"Um, when do I get my keys back?"

"Probably in about an hour or so," Buck told him.

"I don't get it," Ed said.

"I'm going to leave them about a mile up the road, right on the shoulder where you can find them. That way you can get a little exercise and enjoy this fine Florida weather."

"You mean I have to walk there?"

"Unless you want to thumb a ride and explain to a carload of New Yorkers why your keys are a mile up the road," Buck said. "I'm thinking you'll probably be walking. And praying one of your trooper buddies doesn't see you and stop to ask what you're doing."

You could see Ed working it all out in his mind. "Yes, sir."

"Remember, a mile up ahead."

"Got it," Ed nodded. "Do you want me to start walking *now*?"

"Maybe you should count to a hundred first," Buck suggested.

"Okay," Ed said.

Buck put his revolver back under the seat. "Have a nice day, officer." Then he drove off, and, good to his word, left the trooper's keys on the side of the road a mile ahead.

"Well, that buys us an hour or two," Buck said. "But now we've got to ditch this car and get another one."

In the next town, we found a supermarket and pulled into the parking lot. "Stay here, I'll be right back," Buck told us, and got out of the car. He went from car to car looking in the driver's window of each one until he was out of sight.

"What's he doing?" Kate asked.

"I think he's trying to get us another car," I said.

A few minutes later, Buck drove up in a shiny green Buick. "Get the suitcases and put them in the trunk, girls," he said. "Calvin, empty out the glove compartment and get the revolver." We cleaned out the old car and put everything in the Buick. Then Buck drove back out to the highway and headed south.

"It never fails," Buck said. "Somebody always leaves their keys in the car when they're grocery shopping."

"You mean you stole this car?" I asked.

"No, kid. We're just borrowing it for a while."

Florida seemed endless. We drove and drove and drove. We drove for hours and hours, and still nothing but pristine beaches and ocean and motels and boats and diners and tourists, tourists, tourists. We ached to just stop somewhere and stretch our legs on the beach or window shop in a town or something. But Buck said it was too risky, that we needed to keep moving.

"You stop too often, that's when they get ya," he said.

I asked him to find a Western music station on the radio so I could practice playing my harmonica. Western songs seemed best suited for playing harmonica along with. Every Western movie has a cowboy playing harmonica around the campfire at night. Harmonica just didn't sound too good playing along with polka music.

So he found a station and I played along with *Git Along Little Dogie*, *Red River Valley*, *The Yellow Rose of Texas*, *The Old Chisholm Trail*, and *Bury Me Not on the Old Prairie*. It was sounding pretty good, too, until it started grating on Penelope so much that she turned around in her seat and said, "Calvin, will you *please* stop playing that annoying thing?"

So I stopped and wiped the mouthpiece on my shirt and put it away in my pocket and Buck turned the station to one that played the Hit Parade and Penelope seemed to like that a lot better. Penelope was the most easily bored, so we had to keep switching things up for her to keep her from getting in a foul mood and all.

So I leaned over the seat and got real close to her ear and gently whispered, "Pen, how about a game of *I Spy?*" knowing it was one of her favorites.

She said okay so we all played that for a while but she got bored so we switched to counting cars. We each picked a different color and counted cars with our color and the winner would get a Mars bar someone had left in the Buick's glove compartment. So we counted cars and I made sure to keep my count below Penelope's count to give her a better chance of winning and the others must have done the same thing because Penelope won and got the Mars bar.

Then we played a game that I can't remember the name of but one person says a sentence and everyone takes turns adding a sentence until you end up with a whole kooky story that's real funny but doesn't make a lick of sense.

But we were still driving so we played charades for an hour and got tired of that and we were still driving but we ran out of games so Kate and I took our shoes off and played footsies in the back and that eventually evolved into handsies and that's when I found out how ticklish around the waist Kate was and after that I had to tickle her every chance I got and she begged me to stop but I could tell she really wanted me to keep doing it and then Penelope had enough and turned around in her seat again and shouted, "WILL YOU TWO MORONS *PLEASE* KNOCK IT OFF ALREADY?"

"Everybody just quiet down now," Buck ordered. "Or I'll pull over right here and put somebody out of the car!"

We all quieted down and I found that Kate made much less noise when I tickled her if I put my hand over her mouth so I kept tickling her with the new quiet method for a while until I finally got bored with it and stopped. Then I got an idea and started a round of *John Jacob Jingleheimer Schmidt,* and that got everybody singing along for about forty-six choruses before we switched to *The Happy Wanderer* for another thirty-two choruses.

But then I couldn't think of any more songs so I leaned forward and whispered into Penelope's ear again.

"Pen, want to play another game or something?"

She turned around and shouted "No, Calvin. I'm sick to death of games!"

So I dropped the whole thing and sat back down and started thinking about what I was going to type in the next section of my book. I knew I had to catch up on this whole road trip since we left Sunnybrook, and so much had happened since then it was hard to keep it all straight. Things were getting all jumbled up in my mind and the scenery all started to look the same and some of the excitement of getting to Florida had worn off and I *still* didn't have a plan to find my parents and that's not like me because I'm usually *over-prepared* for things and I just didn't know where to begin.

So it seemed like the best thing to do was just put it all out of my mind and tickle Kate some more.

By that time it was finally getting dark and Buck should have been looking for a place to stop for the night, but he just kept driving. I noticed he was getting edgy again and wondered if he thought the North Koreans were tailing us again.

I wasn't far off.

"That black car's been following us all afternoon," he finally announced. So he kept driving until it was good and dark and stopped at a place called the *Sandpiper Lodge.* Its marque advertised "FREE TV and COFFEE. Vibrating Beds!"

Buck was right – the black car followed us into the parking lot. Buck registered in the office and we snuck the twins into the room as usual. Buck did his whole search routine and declared the room safe.

Then he said, "I'll leave like I'm going to pick up dinner, but I'll be watching from around the corner." He handed me the revolver. "If anyone comes into the room, hold this on them until I get back." Then he left and I locked the door behind him.

The twins and I unpacked our things and turned on the TV. We fed nickels into the coin boxes attached to the wall and laid on the vibrating beds listening to how funny our voices sounded.

"*John Jacob Jingleheimer Schmidt!*" I sang in a quivery, high-pitched voice.

"We sound just like the Munchkins from the *Wizard of Oz*!" Kate observed.

Then I heard someone trying to open the door. They were jimmying the lock from the outside. I grabbed the revolver and aimed it at the door and waited for it to open.

It finally opened and a fat man in a crumpled brown suit came into the room. *Beiderman!*

He saw me with the revolver and stopped. "Now, take it easy with that thing, kid."

"Hold it right there, mister," I warned him in my best Western movie voice.

"You don't wanna shoot me, kid," Beiderman said. "I'm just here for the twins. You and the other guy are free to just go on your way."

"You can't have them," I said, pointing the revolver at his chest.

"Come on now, we gotta get this done before your friend gets back. So just give me the gun..." he took a step toward me.

I pulled the hammer back like I'd seen the cowboys do in the movies. "I said, you can't have them, mister..."

Then, like a commando, Buck was there in the doorway behind him. He grabbed Beiderman's arm and twisted it up behind his back. Beiderman howled in pain. Buck searched him and came up with a gun.

"I *thought* you'd be packing this time," he said, tucking the gun into his belt. He took a piece of cord out of his pocket and had Beiderman's hands tied behind his back in no time. Then he sat him down roughly in a chair.

"Good job, kid," Buck said to me. Then to Beiderman: "I told you to go back to Cincinnati, and all you did was rent a different car. Very sloppy, Beiderman."

"Look, I screwed up, okay?" Beiderman said. "If you let me go, I promise I'll go home this time."

Beiderman had to be the worst private detective in the world. Why the twins' parents ever hired him in the first place was beyond me.

"Hold onto that gun, kid," Buck told me. "Don't let *anyone* in this room. I'll be back in a couple of hours."

"Where are you taking me?" Beiderman asked.

"Shut up!" Buck said, stuffing a washcloth into his mouth. Buck left with Beiderman, hands still tied behind his back.

The twins were hungry, but I knew Buck wouldn't want us to leave the room to get food. All we had was a package of salted peanuts, so I divided those up and gave the girls their share. It would have to hold them until Buck got back.

We ran out of nickels for the vibrating beds, so the twins fell asleep watching old movies on TV. They looked so peaceful sleeping – just like angels. I kissed each one good night and they didn't even wake up. I watched them sleep and thought about them and just couldn't imagine life without them. I realized I'd grown quite attached to both of them – even Penelope.

Maybe, if we couldn't find my parents, we could all just go on living like this forever.

I must've dozed off myself because the next thing I remembered was waking up when Buck got back. It had to be the middle of the night or something.

"Did you kill him?" I asked.

"I'm not like that, kid," Buck replied. "I drove him out in the middle of the everglades and left him there. It's a long walk, but someone's bound to find him."

* * *

The next day, Buck thought it would be a good idea to get another car. He said it would keep the cops "good and confused." So we found a supermarket and this time he found a beige Pontiac someone had left the keys in. While he was looking he had me go inside the market and buy a loaf of bread and some bologna and mustard and stuff on account of he was running low on cash and we needed to cut back on expensive diner chow. While I was in there I also got some Moon Pies and a couple of Snickers bars and some hard candy and jaw-breakers for the twins.

After that we drove all day and ended up in the Fort Lauderdale area by evening time. Buck felt sure we weren't being tailed anymore, and we all felt relieved about that. We checked into a motel and had a good night's sleep, and the next morning Buck didn't wake us up too early because he said he was tired and wanted to take a day off from driving.

"You mean, we're staying here another day?" I asked.

"That's right, kid," he replied. "We need a break from the road."

Buck went out to get us some breakfast, so the twins and I stayed in our pajamas and watched TV. We were all very happy to not have to spend another day in the car, and the twins were getting along just swell, for the most part. As much as Penelope resented Kate and was jealous of her, the more I got to be around them the more I got to see how much they really loved and depended on each other.

I thought about how much my relationship with Penelope had changed over the last week. As our romantic feelings for each other faded we seemed to draw even closer, and became more like brother and sister. But with Kate it was just the opposite: I was definitely beginning to see her as something much *more* than just a good friend or sister.

When Buck returned with breakfast, he had a surprise that I never could have guessed in a million years. Miss Underwood was with him.

Miss Underwood. I couldn't believe my eyes.

"Hello, Calvin," she said. I was too dumbstruck to respond.

"I called her yesterday to let her know you were okay," Buck said. "She said she had some news she wanted to tell you in person."

"And these must be the twins I've been reading about in your book," Miss Underwood said. I introduced her to Penelope and Kate.

We had breakfast and Miss Underwood couldn't wait to tell me her news. She said she had been receiving my pages in the mail and had enjoyed reading them so much that she decided to submit them to *The New Yorker* magazine.

"They accepted them and will be publishing your work in monthly installments," she beamed. "They already sent me a check for you. There'll be another check each month. You're a published author now, Calvin!" She handed me a check for fifty dollars. I couldn't believe what was happening.

It was surreal.

"The first installment comes out this week," she told me. "They're very excited about publishing your work – they even want to put you on the cover for the first installment!"

"I don't know what to say," I said.

"All they need is a title before they can go to press," she said. "Have you got a title, Calvin?"

I had been using the working title *My Story*, but I knew that wouldn't do. But another title had been knocking around in my head lately, and I must say I rather liked it.

"*Living in Cleveland with the Ghost of Joseph Stalin,*" I said. "Do you think they'll like it?"

"I think that's a wonderful title, Calvin," Miss Underwood assured me.

Miss Underwood called New York right away to give them the title. "They *love* it!" she said, hanging up the phone and giving me a huge smile. "You've got the cover of the next issue!"

Miss Underwood stayed the rest of the day, getting to know the twins and catching me up on the doings at Calvin Coolidge Junior High School. Mr. Stone, the school psychologist, had been in a tizzy since hearing of my departure from Sunnybrook, but Miss Underwood didn't tell him about keeping in contact with me or her spontaneous trip to Florida. She just told the school she was taking a couple of days off for "personal reasons."

Miss Underwood rented the room next to ours, and invited the twins to spend the night with her. "I think a real old-fashioned girls' night is in order," she said. "That'll give Calvin and Buck a chance for some quiet guy-time on their own." The twins loved the idea, so Buck and I spent a quiet night alone watching TV and snacking on salted peanuts and soda pop.

"You really did it," Buck said, referring to *The New Yorker.* "My little cousin, a real author. I'm proud of you, kid."

Gee, it was swell seeing Miss Underwood like that. Too bad she had to leave first thing the next morning to get back to her class in Cleveland. I promised to stay in touch so she could keep me updated on things and send me future checks from the magazine.

The twins had a wonderful time with her. "We ate popcorn and drank soda pop and watched TV and did each other's nails and hair and talked about boys and *everything,*" Kate gushed. "Gee, it was just the *most!*"

"They're just delightful," Miss Underwood told me when she said goodbye. "Especially the dark-haired one."

I blushed, and Miss Underwood smiled like she knew the secret.

We cashed my check at a supermarket and suddenly felt rich. I wanted to splurge and go to a nice hotel and buy everyone a steak dinner in a fancy sit-down restaurant, but Buck said it would draw too much attention to ourselves so we kept staying in crummy motels and eating hamburgers and French fries instead. But at least we had plenty of money now, and sometimes Buck let us stay in the same motel for two nights in a row like when Miss Underwood came.

Later in the week *The New Yorker* magazine came out and we picked up a few copies from a newsstand. Sure enough, there was my name and the title of my book right there on the front cover, along with the tagline "Imaginative new fiction from a talented young author." Wait a minute: *fiction?* This was my *real* life! *Oh, well,* I thought, *as long as those beautiful checks keep coming.*

I was a famous author now, but our life didn't change very much. It was still just a flurry of highways and gas stations and motel rooms and diners. In a way, nothing had changed.

The next time Buck called Miss Underwood, she told him the FBI had seen *The New Yorker* issue and contacted the editors about me. They told the FBI they had no idea where I was and referred them to Miss Underwood in Cleveland. She said she told them she didn't know where I was either, which was at least half-true, but they bought her story and told her to contact them if I tried to get in touch with her.

Boy, the FBI was sure getting the old run-around but things were sure heating up for me down here in Florida, too. And I'm not talking about the weather, either. The TV and newspapers were starting to put it together that the kid from *The New Yorker* and the missing kid from the state hospital were one and the same – namely, *me.* All of a sudden it was crazy town, and my picture was everywhere. On the news they stopped talking about the twins and focused mostly on *me*. I had to comb my hair different and start wearing dark glasses and all kinds of kooky disguises and stuff all the time to not be recognized, just like a Hollywood star when they don't feel like signing autographs.

And Miss Underwood also told Buck that *Life* magazine had called her and they wanted to do a cover story on me and that the reporter agreed to meet me anywhere and not tell *anybody* where I was – including the FBI and State Police.

So we set it up through Miss Underwood for the *Life* reporter to meet us at a motel called the *Driftwood Inn* in Miami and do the secret interview.

The reporter, Mr. Bannon, arrived at the motel with a photographer, and he was right on time. He wore a neat dark blue suit and tie, and the photographer was well-dressed, too. Buck checked them out carefully just to make sure they were on the up-and-up.

"You're sure you weren't followed?" Buck asked him.

"Positive," Mr. Bannon said. "Nobody knows we're here. Even my editor back in New York doesn't know exactly where we're meeting."

"Glad to hear it," Buck said.

Mr. Bannon had a tape recorder and note pads and ballpoint pens. He and the photographer sat down in some chairs, and Buck and I sat on the beds. The twins were in an adjoining room.

"We'll be snapping some shots of you while we talk," Mr. Bannon said. He also said he wanted to get my side of the story. Then he turned the tape recorder on.

"What happened at Sunnybrook?" Mr. Bannon asked.

"Dr. Spielman told me he was going to give me electroshock therapy, so I left."

"Why was he going to give you electroshock therapy?"

"He told me I wasn't making enough progress."

"Do you agree?"

"I think I was making a lot of progress," I said. "But not because of *him*."

I told him about Dr. Freud and all the talks we had about feelings and dreams and how talking to Dr. Freud made me realize that being crazy wasn't necessarily a bad thing and how I began feeling better about myself because of it.

Mr. Bannon listened carefully, and then said, "When you say Dr. Freud, you mean...Dr. *Sigmund* Freud, correct?"

"That's right."

"But, he's dead, Calvin."

"I know."

"Now this is starting to sound like your fiction in *The New Yorker*," Mr. Bannon said.

"Oh, they got that wrong," I said.

"They got what wrong?"

"The part about my story being fiction," I said. "It isn't fiction at all. It's all true."

Mr. Bannon laughed nervously, then looked confused. "You authors. Always pulling a guy's leg, right?"

"No, it's all true," I insisted. "I was writing about my life."

"Now, just to clarify: we *are* talking about your installments in *The New Yorker* – the ghost of Joseph Stalin, the Rosenbergs, your spiritualist aunt in Cleveland..."

"She's not a spiritualist," I corrected. "She doesn't do séances."

"You mean, you're saying that's all *true?*"

"Yes."

"Well, that's...that's certainly..." he turned the tape recorder off to compose himself. "That's very interesting, Calvin, because, because most people just *assumed* you were writing *fiction*."

"Now we can set them straight," I said.

"All right," Mr. Bannon said, turning the tape recorder back on. "Let's continue where we left off at Sunnybrook. You left because they were going to give you electroshock therapy. Why did you take the twins with you?"

"Because I would miss them too much."

"And they left of their own free will?" he asked.

"Yes."

"Why do you think they agreed to go with you?"

"I think they were tired of Sunnybrook," I said. "They're not crazy. They're probably smarter than you. They never should have been there in the first place."

"Calvin, the FBI believes you and the girls were kidnapped," Mr. Bannon said. "Now you're telling me no one was kidnapped."

"That's right."

"How did you escape?"

"My cousin Buck busted us out," I said, pointing to Buck. "But he didn't force us. We all wanted to go with him."

"Are the twins safe?" Mr. Bannon asked. "Are they here, with you?"

"They're in the other room, watching TV," Buck said.

"Can I talk to them?" the reporter asked.

Buck deferred to me. "What about it, kid?"

"Sure, why not?" I said. Buck went and got them. Mr. Bannon said hello to them. Then he asked them a bunch of questions about being kidnapped and held against their will. They said they hadn't been.

"Why did you leave Sunnybrook?" Mr. Bannon asked.

"Because we didn't want to stay there anymore," Penelope said.

"And we wanted to be with Calvin," Kate added. "We wanted to go wherever *he* went."

The old jealousy started to emerge in Penelope – I could see it in her eyes. "Calvin and I are – *were* – in a very serious relationship at the time," she told Mr. Bannon matter-of-factly. "Of course, if *he* was leaving, I wasn't about to let him leave me behind. My sister liked him, too, but at the time *we* were a couple – not her."

Kate immediately grabbed my hand and squeezed it tight. "But things have changed since then," she said possessively.

"I can see that," Mr. Bannon said, trying to keep up. "And neither of you want to, you know, go home to your parents?"

"No," Penelope said.

"So, if I offered to take you with me right now and take you home to your parents, you wouldn't go?"

The twins looked at Buck. "You can go with Mr. Bannon right now if you like, girls," he said.

"We want to stay here with Calvin and Buck," Kate said.

"I agree with my sister," Penelope chimed in. "Buck has just been a doll this whole time. He takes care of us and protects us from dangerous people. He was in the Army and knows how to handle himself, you know."

"Well, thank you, girls," Mr. Bannon said. "I'd like to ask Calvin a few more questions now." Kate let go of my hand and Buck took the twins back to their room.

Mr. Bannon asked me some more questions while the photographer snapped more pictures of me. He asked me how I came to be in Cleveland and I told him about my road trip on Route 66 with the Old Man and how he left me at Aunt Evelyn's so he could come down to Florida to find my mother.

"But he promised to come back when he found her, so we could be a family again," I said.

"Have you heard from him yet?" he asked.

"No. That's why I asked Buck to take us to Florida, so we could find him."

He asked a few more questions about my writing, and I told him it was all on account of my English teacher Miss Underwood and her encouragement to write about my own life, so that's just what I did.

When we finished, Mr. Bannon turned off the tape recorder and gathered up his notepads and ballpoint pens. "Well, Calvin," he said slowly, "I think what we have here is one heck of a story."

When the article hit the stands, it was titled, "New Yorker Sensation Tells All: Boy Author Sets the Record Straight." Mr. Bannon included almost everything we talked about that day at the *Driftwood Inn.* In the article, Mr. Bannon wrote that after spending twenty minutes interviewing the twins, he didn't believe they'd been kidnapped. He said there was absolutely no indication that anyone was being held against their will. "This reporter even offered to take the twins to their parents himself, but they strenuously declined," he wrote. "They were under no duress that I could detect."

It was that part – the part about it *not* being a kidnapping and what the twins said about being treated well – that was so explosive.

It was crazy town again on TV and radio and in the newspapers. Everyone was shouting over everyone else about whether the FBI should crack down harder to find us or just back off and leave us alone. And poor Dr. Spielman didn't come off too good when people found out he wanted to give a thirteen-year-old boy electroshock therapy.

To tell you the truth, it was kinda creepy and exciting having everybody in America talking about every intimate detail about you and your life. One talk show host on the radio said I was "a positive role model for young boys, a Howdy Doody Don Quixote tilting at the windmills of tired adult conformity and archaic social mores." Another radio host called me "a symbol of the new wave of rebellious youth permeating Hollywood with their sexy bad-boy looks and anti-establishment appeal."

Gee, it was interesting to hear from complete strangers how I was trying to do all of this important cultural stuff, when all I wanted to do was find my Old Man. And it was kinda weird how people who didn't even know me appropriated my image to use it to stand for whatever junk they were trying to push at the moment.

One night when we were watching the *Tonight Show*, Steve Allen mentioned my name and said, "Kid, if you can make it to New York City we'll give you a whole hour. That's an open invitation." Steve Allen always seemed like such a nice, funny man that I thought I might just take him up on it when things calmed down a bit.

Not to be outdone, Ed Sullivan said on the air that he would let me play accordion – with my idol Dick Contino – on his show. It was tempting, even though I knew Rockefeller Center and the CBS studios in New York would be swarming with FBI agents just waiting to nab me after hearing those invitations.

The New York Times ran a story about me on page one. The reporters interviewed just about everyone who ever knew me, and boy they sure had a lot to say. Reverend Welles told them, "He stole my Bible. I'm sure that boy's headed straight for hell!" Miss Underwood was very kind. She said I was her top student and that she thought I was a savant or something. She told the reporters she was sure I wasn't crazy – just "misunderstood." Coach Axelrod said, "He's the most un-athletic, uncoordinated boy I've ever seen."

Mr. Stone said he was very concerned for my sanity. "He's a danger to himself and those around him. He hates his parents and he's got a serious death fixation." Mr. Hayvenhurst, the school principal, said, "He had no friends. Very anti-social young man."

Aunt Evelyn had a lot to say: "I thought he was an okay kid. Even though he spent the whole summer in my attic smoking cigars and holding séances and talking to dead people. Creeped me out a little bit, to tell you the truth. But other than that, I really liked the kid."

Dr. Spielman: "I have never treated a more disturbed child. All the classic signs are there. An unusually robust Oedipal Complex driven by any number of severe psychoses. I believe the boy is crying out for the most radical forms of treatment available to modern science."

They even interviewed that old librarian in Cleveland, who said, "The poor boy would just sit at an empty table talking to himself for hours. It was so sad."

Gee, willikers. How could so many people have so many different opinions about the same person – namely, *me*?

Nearly every day the newspapers ran polls about whether we should turn ourselves in or keep running. On any given day, at least two-thirds of the people wanted us to keep running. Something was happening with the national mood. It was like they were living vicariously through us or something. The radio and TV people were starting to cheer us on.

"I think the cops oughta lighten up on this kid," the DJ of the biggest radio station in Miami said one day. "After all, he's just trying to find his parents." He said his phone bank was lit up with calls of support after saying that. "I've been talking to listeners all day. At least ten to one say lay off the kid and let him find his parents."

The newspaper said Calvin Jefferson Coolidge fan clubs were popping up all over the country, and one of their main goals was to obstruct the FBI and prevent our capture. As a result, phony tips and sightings of us were called in in Wyoming, Idaho, Iowa, Nevada, Oklahoma and many other states, just to confuse the feds and tie down their resources on fake leads.

Because of me, Dick Contino's records were selling like hotcakes all over the country. *The New York Times* said the record company couldn't press them fast enough to keep them in the record shops. Glad I could help out, Dick!

And kids all over the country were putting down their hoola-hoops and learning to play the accordion, and they all wanted to play my signature song, *Deep in the Heart of Texas*.

One morning when Buck was checking us out of a motel, the guy behind the counter winked at him and said, "The cops were here last night looking for you. I told 'em I never seen you." I gave the guy my autograph for his trouble.

Yessiree, it looked like public opinion was swinging our way, all right.

And we were starting to get recognized more – you know, by just everyday people – working stiffs – waitresses filling our take-out orders putting in a couple of extra slices of key lime pie or some extra fries, gas station attendants pumping an extra gallon or two of gas into our tank and throwing in a few bottles of cold pop and some Mars bars when they recognized us.

But wherever we went, people kept it on the QT. They never let a crowd or mob or anything that would draw the attention of the police happen. It was good to find out how much regular folks – strangers, even – cared about us.

Before this, everyone I knew thought I was crazy. I even thought I was a little nuts, too. But now everyone seemed to think I was just swell – even people who didn't even know me. It was kind of touching seeing a whole diverse country like ours putting aside their petty differences and coming together behind a common cause like this.

We started to feel a little like how Bonnie and Clyde must have felt. Only, without the killing of innocent people part.

But we still had to be careful around the cops. I didn't take it personally – I knew they had a job to do. And I'd bet most of them were secretly rooting for us, too. It kinda gave you a warm feeling knowing you weren't all alone, after all.

Chapter 26

But it couldn't last forever. The cops finally caught up with us at the *Sea Breeze Motor Lodge* just south of Miami. It was a relief, to tell you the truth. The bubble had burst. The other shoe had dropped. I was tired of living on the run, a wanted man. We could breathe again.

We woke up to pounding on the door. I got up and looked out the window. There were about seven hundred state troopers surrounding the motel, standing behind their cars, guns drawn.

"It's all over," I said to Buck. I kissed the twins good morning and told them to get dressed and wash their faces and brush their hair. I knew there would be lots and lots of press there with lots and lots of cameras, and I wanted them to look good.

The cops told us to come out one at a time. Buck left his revolver on the dresser and walked outside with his hands up. Two troopers grabbed him and cuffed his hands behind his back.

Next, Penelope walked out. Still inside the room, Kate took my hand and squeezed it tight. We would be walking out together. I kissed her for the first time like I used to kiss Penelope, and saw fireworks. And every time I kissed her after that it was the 4th of July all over again.

Then we walked outside still holding hands. Pandemonium instantly broke out and I'm not sure about everything that happened next. I think the cops couldn't hold the press back any longer and we were immediately surrounded by a throng of jostling reporters and photographers and state troopers. Kate and I were snatched apart and thrown into the back of separate patrol cars. I didn't see what happened to Buck and Penelope.

Reporters were gawking at me and photographers were snapping pictures through the windows all around the car. Then we started driving slowly through the crowd and got on the main highway.

They took me to a police precinct in Miami and smuggled me in through the back way on account of the precinct was also surrounded by reporters and photographers and all sorts of civilian looky-loos. When we got inside the precinct it wasn't like I expected at all. It didn't even seem like we were in trouble anymore. Kate and Penelope were already there, and all the cops were smiling and trying to get their snapshots taken with them. When I got there, a bunch of cops swarmed around me asking for my autograph. I didn't see Buck around anywhere.

After a while some guys in black suits came in and cleared all the cops away. They took us into separate interrogation rooms and started asking us all kinds of questions about what happened since we left Sunnybrook and all.

"Hello, Calvin," the suit in my interrogation room said. "I'm Special Agent Calloway, with the FBI. I'm going to need to ask you some questions now, son."

"Okay."

"First of all, how are you? Are you all right? Do you need some water? Would you like to see a doctor?"

"I'm fine," I replied. "But a glass of water would be nice."

Agent Calloway opened the door and ordered a cop to get me a glass of water.

"Now Calvin, I need you to take me through this whole thing, step by step, from the very beginning."

So I did. I told him the truth about everything, just like I had with the reporter from *Life* magazine, Mr. Bannon. When I was finished, he asked me to think real hard and try to remember if I'd left anything out – even the teeny-tiniest detail. I thought real hard and told him I didn't think I'd left anything out.

By that time it was about noon and Agent Calloway said we'd take a break for lunch. They brought in a grilled cheese sandwich and French fries and a bottle of pop for me and I ate it all because I was very hungry on account of missing breakfast and all. Then they let me use the restroom and relax a little bit. I asked if I could see the twins but they said that wouldn't be possible right now, but that I didn't have to worry because they were both safe and sound.

"What's going to happen to us?" I asked.

"We don't know yet, Calvin," Agent Calloway said. Then another man in a suit entered the interrogation room and looked me over pretty good. He was older than Agent Calloway and had gray hair.

"This is Mr. Deacon, Calvin," Agent Calloway said. "He's a U.S. Attorney. He's here to listen to your story and decide if a crime has been committed or not."

And Agent Calloway had me go through the whole thing all over again in front of Mr. Deacon, which took up most of the afternoon. When I was finished, Mr. Deacon had some questions.

"Did you know your cousin was coming to take you away from Sunnybrook?" he asked.

"No," I replied. "All I remember him saying when I left Aunt Evelyn's house was 'I'll come visit you, kid.'"

"Did he force you to leave Sunnybrook with him?"

"No."

"So, if you had chosen to stay at Sunnybrook, he would have left you there?"

"Yes."

"How can you be sure?"

"Because I told him I wasn't leaving without the twins," I said.

"And the twins – Buck didn't force them to leave?"

"No. They *wanted* to come with us."

"Why did they want to leave Sunnybrook?" Mr. Deacon asked.

"They didn't like it there," I replied. "Penelope had talked about escaping before. She said it would be real easy to do. That's how I knew they would go with us."

Mr. Deacon looked at me a long time. "All right, Calvin. Thank you for talking to me today." Then he and Agent Calloway huddled together in a corner of the room. They were talking real low but I could still pick up bits of their conversation.

"What do you think?" Agent Calloway asked.

"I don't know," Mr. Deacon said. "All their stories match to a 't'. We could probably get him for transporting minors across state lines, but everything I'm hearing says this was *not* a kidnapping. And with all this media pressure to go easy on him, I'm thinking we might have to settle for something less than kidnapping."

Mr. Deacon left the room, and Agent Calloway turned to me. "What do you say we stretch our legs a little, Calvin?" He took me outside into the hallway and we started walking.

"What's going to happen to Buck?" I asked.

"Your cousin made some really poor choices in this situation, starting with taking you out of Sunnybrook," Agent Calloway said. "When an adult does that, even though he might mean well, there have to be consequences. Mr. Deacon and I are going to try and figure out what's appropriate in this case."

We walked past a break room. Several cops were gathered around a TV set drinking coffee. President Eisenhower was talking on the TV.

"I don't think these young people should have to live the rest of their lives with this incident hanging over their heads," the President said. "Now that we know they're safe and being well taken care of, I think we should enter a time of national healing and put this troubling episode behind us as a nation."

Then Edward R. Murrow came on the screen and started talking. "In a new CBS News poll, seventy-six percent of Americans show solidarity with the three children taken from the Ohio hospital, as well as a surprising amount of sympathy for the Korean War veteran who spirited them away."

The broadcast switched to a woman being interviewed in a supermarket parking lot.

"I don't think that fellow meant to harm those children at all," the woman told the reporter. "I read the *Life* magazine piece and it said he took real good care of them. It even said the twins refused to leave him and go back home to their parents. That doesn't sound like a dangerous man to me."

Then another man in the same parking lot told the reporter, "I heard he was in Korea. A lotta guys came back with their heads all messed up. Maybe he just wasn't thinking straight. But I don't think they oughta throw the book at him."

Agent Calloway was listening to those people very carefully. Then a cop looked over and saw me. He came over and asked me to autograph his copy of *The New Yorker*.

Agent Calloway kept us at the precinct all night while they decided what to do with us. They didn't put us in jail cells, though. I had a nice room with a bed in it that some of the cops used on overnight shifts. They brought me in more food for dinner, then took me on a tour of the precinct so I could see what real-life police work was like. All the cops were super nice and all of a sudden I didn't feel like I was in trouble anymore.

But I sure missed the twins. Agent Calloway said we couldn't see each other until everything got straightened out, though. So I slept really well in that little room in the police station and got a real surprise the next morning: breakfast in the station house break room with Vice President Nixon. He'd come all the way down from Washington to meet me and relay President Eisenhower's best wishes.

We ate flapjacks with maple syrup and I asked the cops if they had any fresh strawberries and whipped cream and they sent a car right out to the supermarket to pick some up for us. Vice President Nixon said he liked fresh strawberries and whipped cream ever since he was a boy growing up in Yorba Linda, California, which was a farming community back in those days and there were always plenty of fresh strawberries around.

He told me all about how when he was my age his folks ran a little gas station and café in Yorba Linda and how he and his brothers and sisters used to love helping out around the place. Then he told me how he played football in college and all about his adventures in the Navy during World War II. He wasn't a big general like his boss President Eisenhower had been, but he did rise to the rank of Commander and saw some action against the Japanese Navy.

Mr. Nixon was a very nice man with a soothing deep voice. He told his Secret Service guys to sit down and have some flapjacks with us, and they did. He seemed very interested in my writing. He said he'd read my stories in *The New Yorker* and had really enjoyed them. He asked me if I intended on making a career out of writing and I told him that I liked writing very much but I hadn't really thought about it much. I told him I might want to become a teacher someday, and told him all about Miss Underwood.

"You might want to consider a career in politics, young man," he told me. "I just might need a good running mate in a few years."

At the end of our chat he reached out and shook my hand. "Well, I just think you're a fine fellow, Calvin," he said. "It was charming having breakfast with you, and if you ever need anything you be sure and let Pat and me know." Pat was his wife back in Washington.

I spent the rest of the morning meeting more dignitaries, like the Mayor of Miami and the police chief and the Dade County Sheriff and a bunch of city aldermen and muckety-mucks like that. It was exhausting, but part of every celebrity's job so I tried to keep a smile on my face through the whole ordeal.

Then Agent Calloway told me I could spend some time with the twins if we promised not to talk about the case. He showed me to an interrogation room and there they were, as beautiful as ever.

"Oh, Calvin – it's so good to see you!" Kate said. I sat between them holding both their hands and talking about everything except the case. They told me they'd met Vice President Nixon briefly, but didn't get to have breakfast with him like I did. Then we talked about how famous we were now and how good it felt to know so many people cared about us and were pulling for us. They said the cops had treated them like little princesses – like their very own daughters – and had gone out of their way to get them whatever they wanted.

When we ran out of things to say, we just sat holding hands and drinking each other in with our eyes. I'd never felt closer to *anyone* in my life then these two enigmatic sisters.

"Oh, Calvin, after this is all over, I want to be together forever," Kate told me.

"We will," I promised.

Then it was time to go to my room for dinner, so Agent Calloway led me out. On the way to my room he told me that the twins' mother was on her way from Ohio to see them, but that their father had died of a massive heart attack due to all the stress of the situation. The twins didn't know yet; he was going to let their mother tell them when she got there. I had mixed emotions, of course. I was sorry the man was dead, but at least he wouldn't be touching Penelope like that anymore.

Over dinner, Agent Calloway filled me in on what he and Mr. Deacon, the U.S. Attorney, had decided to do about Buck. To my relief, he said they weren't going to charge him with kidnapping. It would be too difficult to prove and public opinion was almost unanimously against it. So they decided to charge him with one count of breaking and entering at Sunnybrook, two counts of grand theft auto, and one count of threatening the safety of a law enforcement officer. That was when Buck pulled his revolver on the state trooper and took his gun away.

Agent Calloway said it sounded like a lot, but if Buck agreed to plead guilty on all counts he may be able to avoid prison time and just serve probation and community service instead, given that nobody got hurt and none of his actions were violent.

I slept easier that night believing Buck was probably going to be all right. The next morning, I had another surprise visitor: Miss Underwood. It was so good to see her again, and she brought more good news. She said she'd landed me a publishing deal with Random House in New York City. She said they wanted to put all the parts together into one book, and sent me a five-hundred-dollar advance. Miss Underwood had the check. They said it would be a huge best-seller – preorders were already going through the roof. And they said with all the press I'd been getting on my own, they wouldn't have to put a single dime into publicity.

"Mr. Pryce, your new editor, says you're one of the most talented young writers he's ever seen," Miss Underwood said. "He said they're honored to publish your book."

Good old Miss Underwood. My former English teacher and freelance literary agent. She was the one who made this whole thing happen. I would never forget what she'd done for me.

"What's left for you to do now, Calvin?"

"Mr. Sullivan invited me to play the accordion on his TV show," I told her. "And he said I could do a duet with Dick Contino."

Miss Underwood said she'd be glad to make the call and set it up for me. As I sat talking with Miss Underwood, Agent Calloway appeared at my door. "You're free to go now, Calvin," he said.

"Go where?"

"Follow me." Miss Underwood and I followed the FBI agent to the precinct's front desk area. There was all my stuff – my suitcase, my accordion, and my portable travel typewriter – sitting on the floor waiting for me.

And there *he* was – the Old Man himself – standing there looking at me like a latent apparition from my past. "Hey, Sport," he said in that familiar long-ago voice.

"You're free to go with your father now, Calvin," Agent Calloway said.

But I didn't move. "You said you'd come back for me."

"Aw, come on, Sport – don't be sore at me now."

"Where's mom?"

He just shook his head. He hadn't even found her yet. *What had he been doing all this time?*

"But I've got a few leads," he said hopefully. "I want you to come help me find her."

I just stood there looking at him. There were a lot of jumbled-up feelings to process.

"Look, Sport, I know I'm a loser," he admitted. "I screwed up with your mother, and I screwed up when I left you in Cleveland. But you gotta give me another chance."

It was sad seeing him grovel like this, but I wasn't ready to let him off the hook just yet.

"I won't leave you again," he said. "I promise."

"You gotta go straight," I said.

"You got it."

"And we still gotta find a preacher and get you dunked."

"Aw, come on, Sport..."

"I promised the sheriff."

"All right," he said. "I'll get dunked."

I picked up my suitcase and accordion, and Miss Underwood picked up my portable typewriter.

"Miss Underwood's coming with us," I said.

"Just for a few days," Miss Underwood said.

"Sure, Sport – whatever you want," the Old Man said.

"Goodbye, Agent Calloway," I said.

"Goodbye, Calvin," he said. "It was a pleasure meeting you."

We left the precinct and walked to the Old Man's car parked in front. Cops smiled and waved goodbye to me. We put my stuff in the trunk and piled into the car.

"We need to find a place to cash this," I said, handing the Old Man my advance check.

He looked at it and his eyes nearly popped out of his head. "Whoa – that's quite a nut, Sport."

"It should be enough to do what we need to do," I said.

We drove to seven banks before we found one that would cash the check. After that, the Old Man wanted to check out one of his leads. We drove to a diner in Miami and sat down in a booth for lunch. When the waitress came to pour coffee and take our orders, she stopped cold.

"Hey, aren't you that kid who..."

"Yes, I'm Calvin."

"Well, isn't that something," she gushed, almost spilling her pot of coffee. "You sitting right here in the diner...and at *my* table, too!"

I noticed other diners starting to stare at me and whispering to each other. I guess it's just something I would have to get used to from now on.

The Old Man took a snapshot of my mother out of his jacket pocket and showed it to the waitress. "Does this woman work here?"

The waitress studied the picture and handed it back. "Not anymore. She quit two weeks ago."

"Do you know where she is now?" the Old Man asked.

"Before she left, she said something about getting a job singing at a night club in Tallahassee," the waitress replied.

"Did she tell you the name of the place?"

"Yeah, Dick's Place, or Dave – Dave's Jazz Cave, or something like that."

"Dave's Jazz Cave?" the Old Man asked.

"Yeah. I think that was it," the waitress replied.

"Thanks a lot," the Old Man said, putting the picture back in his pocket.

"Say, are you gonna order anything, or what?" she asked.

We ordered, and while we waited for the food Miss Underwood went to a payphone by the restrooms and called the Ed Sullivan Show in New York City.

"Hey, that reminds me," I said to the Old Man. "I saw Darleen Fontaine dancing on a TV show the other night."

"No kidding?" he responded. "That's great, Sport. Was she any good?"

"Yeah, she's a natural," I said.

The food finally came so we tucked in. A few minutes later, Miss Underwood was back.

"It's all set up," she smiled. "February twenty-first. You've got to be in New York the day before for rehearsals."

"Say, that gives us just enough time to swing through Tallahassee first and check out this night club lead," the Old Man said. "Then we can drive up to New York for the show."

"Yeah, and maybe we can look good old Darleen up while we're in town," I suggested.

I had to laugh. A few days ago, I was a wanted desperado on the run. Now here I was, sitting with the Old Man and Miss Underwood, free as a bird, my pockets stuffed with cash, a couple of weeks away from meeting my musical idol and playing the accordion on the Ed Sullivan Show.

Gee whiz – life sure has a funny way of working things out.

About the Author

Marc Sercomb was born in Salinas, California. He grew up in Southern California and attended California State University, Northridge, where he studied Journalism and English Literature. He currently resides in the foothills of Los Angeles with his wife, Robin. His hobbies include reading, music, and motorcycles. He has been a teacher for 23 years.

He is also the author of the novel *Picasso's Motorcycle*.

www.ingramcontent.com/pod-product-compliance
Lightning Source LLC
Chambersburg PA
CBHW070059120726
47909CB00002B/436